T0357109

FUTURE'S DARK PAST

FUTURE'S DARK PAST

J. L. YARROW

Gramarye Media

Gramarye Media
1270 Caroline Street
Suite D120-381
Atlanta, GA 30307

Copyright © 2023 by J.L. Yarrow

Hardcover ISBN-13: 978-1-61188-339-8
E-book ISBN: 978-1-945839-70-2

Visit our website at www.GramaryeMedia.com

First Gramarye Media Printing: February 2023

Printed in the United States of America
0 9 8 7 6 5 4 3 2 1

This is for Dr. James E. Kerr
And the Creation Factory Writer's Workshop
Still lifting, my friend, still lifting.

Time present and time past
Are both perhaps present in time future,
And time future contained in time past.
If all time is eternally present
All time is unredeemable.
What might have been is an abstraction
Remaining a perpetual possibility
Only in a world of speculation.
What might have been and what has been
Point to one end, which is always present.
Footfalls echo in the memory
Down the passage which we did not take
Towards the door we never opened . . .

—T. S. Eliot, "Burnt Norton"

CHAPTER ONE
HOME

Kristen bent her knees and leaned back on the skyglider, clutching the sail's horizontal boom rail with all her might. It grabbed more wind, lifting the rig higher into the sky. Red lightning arced all around as she bounced along the front edge of the raging storm. With her boots locked tight, she felt little fear of falling off, though losing control and crashing became a whole different matter.

A thousand feet below, her target sped along a craggy dirt road. The bulky, six-wheeled terrain tracker fought to stay in front of the onrushing tempest. It headed for the Dallas Life Pod, which appeared in the distance sooner than she expected. The city's half-mile-wide dome glowed white in the desert sea like a lighthouse of old. Its immense concrete wall protected the inhabitants from their unforgiving surroundings.

That used to be home, Kristen thought. Her parents barely scraped by in Dallas. Then she discovered that damn bag of seeds. "Worth more than gold," her dad claimed. They planned on bartering it to escape and start over in the Kansas Life Pod, but disaster struck during the treacherous journey. Bandits killed her parents. She ended up a slave in Kansas. Her new life became a living hell.

Now, only death awaited her there. She'd not be welcomed here in her hometown, either. "If only Missouri had stayed open," she grumbled to herself. "I could go there."

Her helmet's computer opened a channel. "Oklahoma is closer."

"No, it's dead too." *The entire planet is.* She tried to imagine the vast, barren land thriving and green again. Then her parents would still be alive. *But they're not.*

A burst of wind knocked her sideways, forcing her to muscle the board back around. She caught herself, then looked down. The terrain tracker seemed to hit a faster gear, trying to outrace the storm.

"Computer! Will they make it?"

"Too close to call," it replied.

A screeching alarm in Kristen's helmet warned her that the oxygen tank bordered on empty. The envirosuit might protect her from the elements, but it wouldn't do any good if she couldn't breathe. She pushed with her foot, and the front of the board dipped. The rig streaked downward, hurtling toward the ground as if riding a giant rogue wave. She angled to intercept the vehicle before it entered the city. Furious wind buffeted her. Her hand furthest from the mast slipped off the boom rail, but she grabbed it before the sail could tear away.

At the bottom of the raging trough, she pulled up and ripped across the surface mere feet above the ground. The skyglider's magnetic inductors kicked in, keeping it aloft as the rear of the terrain tracker grew rapidly in her visor screen. Kristen yanked in the sail in a futile effort to reduce her speed.

"Warning," the computer blared. "Slow down!"

"Disengage the foot locks," she ordered.

"You will crash."

"I *know*, damn it! Do it *now!*"

The boot snaps released with a pop. She scrambled to the front of the board and leaped for the back of the tracker. Her body slammed into it. She slid down, clawing for the grips until her feet dragged on the ground. Her helmet clattered and banged against the door. The sailboard hit the dirt road and exploded. Pieces rocketed out; a chunk of the boom rail shot straight for her. Kristen let go with one hand and flung herself to the corner edge, barely dodging it. She swung back and grabbed it again, her heart pounding.

The vehicle continued its breakneck pace, lurching across the rocky wasteland and desolate hills. Desperate, she pulled upward and heaved herself on top of the metal behemoth, wedging between the cargo racks and antennas.

Titan's ass, she thought, shaking inside. *I hope no one heard that.*

The city's massive outer door loomed ahead. It opened slowly, creating an escape route into the sanctuary. Stormy blasts of sand engulfed her as the terrain tracker barreled through the entrance and slid to a halt. The gritty cloud followed until the titanium gate closed behind them with a heavy thud. When the swirling dust settled and toxic gases vented away, the inner airlock opened. The tracker rumbled into the compound and stopped.

Kristen's visor retracted up into a thin line, and she quietly took a few deep breaths. Relief and amazement washed over her. *Made it! Now if I can—*

A stern voice came from below. "We know you're up there. Come down now, and we might let you live."

"Where is he?" the man snarled, backhanding her viciously.

Frothy red spit flew from Kristen's mouth. She slumped in the chair, refusing to relent. Her interrogator grabbed her chin and jerked it upward. Her long, dark hair, matted with blood, clung to her in thick strands. She squinted at him with her one good eye. Sweat rolled off his bald head and onto his nasty, sweaty T-shirt.

"I said, where is he, bitch?" He leaned closer, leering.

She replied in a near whisper. "Who?"

The man's face twitched. "You look just like him," he hissed, spraying her with spittle. He yanked her jaw even higher. "Where are my seeds, Winters?"

It took a second for his meaning to register. A painful smirk quivered on her lip. "Long gone."

"You think it's funny?" His fat fingers slid down to her neck and crushed her windpipe in a vice-like grip. "You'll be mine for the rest of your miserable life."

Kristen could do little to stop him with the shackles chaining her. Her mouth formed a silent scream as she tried to suck in air. A tunnel of darkness descended over her. *This is it.* Right then, the door to the room opened.

"Sweet Jesus!" Her tormenter shoved her aside and whirled around. "What do you want?"

Kristen gasped and coughed as an official-looking man entered the room. He stood ramrod-straight, at least a head taller than the other guy. His threadbare, desert military uniform hung crisp and spotless on his lean body, and his salt-and-pepper hair looked impeccable. He assessed the scene in one sweep, and his mouth pinched into a scowling, hard line.

Now what? she thought warily.

He came nearer and looked her up and down, meeting her defiant, one-eyed gaze.

"Telerson," he eventually said, "this isn't necessary."

"That ain't your call, Hernandez."

A beat passed with the impudent retort hanging in the room. The new man's voice dropped lower, sizzling with sarcasm. "Why don't you throw her out the airlock and be done with it, then?"

"Maybe I will."

Hernandez's face crinkled with disgust. "Have we fallen that far?"

"What makes you think I want to add another food-sucking hole to this Life Pod? There's barely enough to go around as it is."

"It's time for a different tactic. I'm taking over." Hernandez glared down at him.

Telerson thumped the other man's chest with two fingers. "*I'm* in charge of security."

He knocked his hand away. "*I* run the Pod."

"Bah. Have your little fun, but when I get back, she's mine." Telerson turned and stormed out.

Hernandez exhaled, long and deliberate. He pulled up a chair in front of Kristen, reversing it so he could lean on the backrest. "You're tough," he remarked, studying her. "No doubt about that. You lasted longer than the storm."

She stayed silent, her senses on high alert.

"Hmm," Hernandez murmured. "What does Telerson have against you, anyway?" He withdrew a flask from his inner coat pocket and took a swig, then jiggled it in front of her.

She jerked back. *What's he doing?* With her eye swollen almost shut, Kristen turned her head to get a better look. She hesitated, but the offer proved too tempting; she nodded.

He dribbled tepid liquid into her bloodied mouth. "Swirl it around."

The water caught in her parched throat, choking her a little. "Thanks," she sputtered. She motioned for another swig. "You think I'm going to buy this *make-nice* garbage?"

"That depends on how much you want to live," he said, holding the canteen to her mouth. "I can help you, or we can bring back Telerson."

Anger burned through her brain fog. She guzzled the metallic-tasting liquid and said, "He's an ass."

"No doubt." Hernandez guffawed. "I don't like him either. Unfortunately for you, I won't be able to hold him off for long. I need something to work with."

Kristen picked at the chains, considering his words.

"Let's start with the basics. I'm Governor Hernandez. What's your name?"

She sighed. "Kristen."

"Okay, Kristen. Why are you here?"

After another pause, she replied, "Why else? I'm hungry."

A dubious crease etched his brow. "Hmm. Where are you from?"

"Please." Kristen wanted to slow down his questions until she could pull herself together. "Another drink?"

Hernandez held the flask out, pouring water into her mouth. She swallowed greedily, and he tipped it again before pulling it back.

She swished the last gulp, savoring every drop before downing it. "Thanks."

"No problem." Hernandez capped the vessel and stuffed it in his pocket. "Now, why don't you answer my question?"

She tried to sit taller. "Dallas."

"No. This is Dallas, and you're not from here."

Kristen shrugged and gingerly stretched her neck from side to side. The forced, cramped position made her back feel like it might snap.

"I grew up here."

"Impossible. Free trade among the Life Pods stopped over a hundred years ago."

Nothing's free. "You might remember my dad, Lucas Winters."

"Winters," Hernandez repeated. His mouth pursed as he mulled over the name. "The guy who took his family out in a terrain tracker? We found that years ago, abandoned in a gorge."

"Dad talked with people from Kansas on the radio, promised them a new batch of seeds. We carried them with us—"

"Thinking he could buy his way into a better life, correct?"

"It's my fault. I found those seeds and brought—"

"*Your* fault? You were only a kid." Hernandez frowned. "This explains a lot. Those were Telerson's seeds. He lost a fortune on the black market when they disappeared. He's figured it out and wants payback."

"He wants my father, but he's wasting his time. My dad's dead."

Hernandez made a clicking sound with his mouth. "Guess you'll do in a pinch. I'm curious. Why'd you come back? Doesn't seem too bright, under the circumstances."

Kristen shuddered as painful memories came flooding back. *Can I tell him what happened to me? Why would he be different?* But she had to say something. "Things aren't any better in Kansas than they are here. In fact, they're worse."

"I've heard rumors." He grimaced. "Hard to believe you got out. How'd you get here?"

"Carbon-coated sail and a skyglider."

"What?" Hernandez rocked back in his chair. "I'm going to call bullshit on that."

Her chains rattled softly as she shifted position. "You'll find what's left of it a mile or so outside."

"Even if that were true, that's suicidal."

Kristen shrugged. "I caught a storm current and sailed to within reach of Dallas. I saw the terrain tracker and took my chance."

"You were alone?"

She nodded.

"Quite the story you have."

"It's what happened." Kristen pinned him with a pleading look. "I couldn't stay there, or—"

"You can't stay here," he countered. "You won't last a day with Telerson, and you're already halfway gone."

"I have nowhere else to go." Despair tightened her throat. *Can't show it*, she thought. "Now what?" Her voice broke.

Hernandez's expression softened. "I have an idea."

"I'm strong; I work hard. I can take care of myself. Just give me a job."

He laughed. "Not in your current condition. You look like you're ninety pounds, sopping wet."

"Please. I'll do almost anything for food."

"I have a feeling you might not like what I'm about to offer." He pulled an apple from his coat pocket.

Kristen drew a sharp breath.

"Hungry, you say?" He held it in front of her mouth.

You have no idea. She eagerly craned her neck for a bite, banging it into her split lip.

"Slow down. It's yours."

She winced and carefully bit off a sizeable chunk. "Mm." Juice dribbled down her bruised chin. She grabbed another couple of bites, devouring them with a throaty gulp. "Please. Please help me."

"Careful what you ask for." Hernandez tossed the last of the apple aside and stood. He cupped a hand to his ear, making a show of listening.

"What?" She tried to follow his gaze but couldn't see well in that direction.

"Right on time." He squatted and unlocked the chain securing her to the floor, then lifted her by an elbow to a standing position. "We have guests. Come on, let's go."

The door flew open and banged against the wall like a gunshot. They both startled with a jerk.

"Stop right there." Telerson sauntered in. Kristen shrank away as much as she could. "I'm not done with her."

"No." Hernandez stepped between them. "They're here. We can't wait."

A low tremor, scarcely detectable at first, became more apparent. Telerson did a double-take. "Those bastards have the worst timing." He jabbed his finger at them. "We'll deal with this later, but you *will* give her back to me." He stomped off, slamming the door behind him.

Hernandez grabbed her arm, but Kristen pulled back with her chained hands. "Where are we going?"

"The Spacers are here."

A shiver went up her spine. "You're the official doom greeter or what?"

"It's time for you to catch a ride, that's what."

She stopped cold. "You're giving me to them?"

He opened the door. "It's a long shot, but at least you'll have one. Or would you prefer to wait around and take your chances with our illustrious friend?"

Kristen grudgingly relented. She shuffled her shackled feet as she followed Hernandez into the hall. "Anything beats that."

"Maybe. I'm not sure dying in space is any better than dying here. But I'll let you be the judge."

CHAPTER TWO
THE ESCAPE

EARTH, FEBRUARY 21, 2355

Hope Bannister removed the gloves from her envirosuit and stuffed them into a zippered pocket. When she pulled off her helmet, her auburn hair fell to her shoulders. She crinkled her nose and took a deep breath of dusty air. An elevated heartbeat pounded in her ears. The short walk from the airlock to the heart of the Dallas Life Pod challenged her because of the heavy gravity. Their space station, Genesis, replicated Earth's rotational pull, but it never felt like the real thing.

"Last stop," she murmured to the three guards traveling with her.

The buildings surrounding the square rose only one or two stories because of the dome. Like on Mars Colony, the municipality expanded dozens of floors downward, rather than across a barren, poisonous landscape with extreme temperatures. The inhabitants relied on the underground water reservoir beneath the city.

"It never looks like it can hold fifty thousand people," replied Walter West, one of her most trusted time warriors. His voice came through her earpiece.

Bannister sighed. "I wonder about their resource levels."

"Probably like Missouri and Kansas. Almost gone."

The Earthers held that information close, like guarding a fortune. The Life Pods were known to attack each other for food and water. It didn't take a scientist to understand their world stood on the brink of extinction.

Hope replied, "I know I'd jump at the chance to leave this place."

"It's a hellhole for sure," Walter said. "The governor is running late. Not like him."

"No, it's not." She looked out across the plaza, scrutinizing the gathering crowd. *Thin, ragged. Desperate.* Nervous glances came her way. She knew these occasional visits riled everyone. *We need recruits to save them, but we're running out of time.*

"These people are toast," Walter pointed out. "No way any of them could survive if they joined us."

Bannister turned her head slightly, eyeing him. He wore battle armor with a black polycarbonate exterior that molded to the contours of his muscular body. His mirrored facemask and gear contrasted starkly with her envirosuit. He toted a rail gun in his hands, keeping it aimed at the ground. *Like that makes him look any less threatening.*

"We don't have a choice," she replied softly. She glanced at his weapon. "Did you have to bring that thing? You're scaring them."

Walter hefted the rifle in an intimidating gesture to the Earthers. "You don't bring a knife to a laser fight."

Bannister whipped around to face him, her anger flaring. "This is not—" She caught herself, then turned back to the growing group with a frustrated sigh.

Walter chuckled in her ear. "Sorry, Doc."

Right. He's almost as annoying as Kants. "Dallas," she announced with a strained smile, "we have news."

A voice rang out above the rest. "Have you figured out a way to restore the atmosphere?"

"I wish I could say, '*yes,*'" she answered, "but it's nothing like that."

A short, arrogant-looking man elbowed his way to the front. "If you've come for water, you can go to hell," he announced boldly. A murmur of agreement rose around him.

"Telerson," she called out, "we don't want your water." *Just your people.*

"Doc." Walter nudged her. "Here comes the governor."

Hernandez wove his way to the front. The break in the crowd he created revealed a waif of a girl in tow. Bannister frowned, noticing her swollen face and the chains that restrained her. That kind of brutality never existed in Dallas before. Something didn't line up; Hernandez usually ran this town with a reputation of being tough but fair.

Confused, Bannister nodded a tentative greeting and continued. "It's been a while since the Time Forward Project's last visit. We continue to work hard for you, but currently . . ." She paused. *Oh my God, I'm doing it again.* "We seek volunteers—"

"Again?" someone in the mob shouted.

"Yes," she said, "we need—"

"Why would anybody go with you?" Telerson argued. "No one ever returns."

"Go back where you came from!" someone else yelled. The jeers grew, spiked with catcalls. "Leave us alone!"

Telerson crossed his arms, apparently buoyed by the response. He spat on the ground near Bannister's feet.

"Contain yourself, sir." She grew uneasy with the crowd's fast burn toward hostility.

"Hey, Doc," Walter whispered in her earpiece. "Maybe we should come back another time."

She ignored him and raised her voice for everyone to hear. "Our program could be your ticket to a new life."

"Then take all of us!" someone shouted.

Wrong direction, she thought. "I wish I could, but we don't have enough room."

"Yeah, we know," Telerson snapped. "We're not good enough for your precious spaceship."

"Excuse me!" A woman's voice rang out.

A fleet movement from the back of the throng caught her attention. Someone made a beeline through the sea of people. Bannister sensed Walter lifting his rifle in anticipation. She reached out and put a gentle hand on his arm, urging him to lower it.

A tall young woman emerged from the melee. She was striking, from her doe-like eyes to her dazzling smile. She wore her hair in a closely cropped afro, and she held her chin aloft and regal. Every fluid motion she made revealed grace and power. She wore a typical worker's jumpsuit, and the staff she held seemed to be an extension of her being.

"I will go with you," the woman said. Her authoritative voice rose above the clamor. "I am Sylvia Mantua, and I am better than any man here."

Soft laughter burbled across the crowd, like they'd all heard this joke before.

"I changed my mind," Walter chirped. "She'll do."

Bannister shifted uncomfortably. She didn't expect to find an easy volunteer, especially someone of this caliber. On the one hand, she needed individuals who were smart, brave, and the best humanity offered. But these candidates were expendable. Often, even the strongest didn't make it through the recombinant transformation, which was why they needed more recruits. *How many have I consigned to death for the sake of us all? If only there were another way.*

She cleared her throat. "I'm Dr. Hope Bannister. Welcome. If I may ask, what does your family think of this idea?"

"I live alone," Sylvia replied. "I always make my own decisions." Her expression turned somber. "I have one demand before I accept."

Walter chuckled. "Careful with this one, Doc."

Bannister raised an eyebrow. "What would that be?"

"I am a soldier." Sylvia waved a hand at the surrounding people. "If you want your toilets cleaned, pick one of them."

"Take her," someone grumbled. A burble of discontent rose from those nearby. "We don't do toilets either!"

Bannister ignored the chatter. "You are volunteering for a dangerous mission." She needed to make sure this young woman understood. "One that could save the world."

"I accept your challenge," Sylvia assured. "But what could possibly save the world?"

"If she only knew," Walter said.

If she only knew, echoed in Bannister's mind.

"Take this one!" Hernandez's voice boomed. He nudged his captive into motion. She hobbled forward with him right on her heels.

"He's gotta be kidding," Walter muttered.

Good Lord, Bannister thought. "She poses no threat here. Release her, now!"

"Hey!" Telerson protested. "You can't do that!" He snatched for the woman but missed.

Walter quickly aimed the business end of his rifle, stopping the man dead in his tracks. This time, Bannister allowed it. Hernandez pulled out a set of keys and unlocked the restraints, letting them fall to the ground.

The woman rubbed her wrists and haltingly stretched to her full height. "That's better."

"I imagine so," Bannister replied. "And who are you?"

"Kristen," she answered. "Kristen Winters." She plucked a sticky strand of matted hair from her face. "I'll . . . I'll go with you."

Not too convincing, she thought. Bannister turned to confront the governor. "I'm not sure what you're—"

He cut her off. "She's stronger than she looks."

She studied the two. "I wish I could take her."

Kristen's swollen lip trembled.

"You value people with intelligence and determination." Hernandez glanced over at Kristen. "She doesn't look like much, but she has both in spades. She rode a skyglider on a storm front down from the Kansas Life Pod."

Walter's metallic voice came through his helmet speaker. "That's a load of carbon crap."

"It's not," Hernandez insisted. "My men located the crash site just outside the dome."

Kristen's face contorted. "I thought you didn't believe me?"

He shrugged. "I needed to know if you came here alone."

The people of Dallas jostled about, becoming restless. Hernandez held up a hand, and they quieted some, albeit reluctantly.

Bannister focused on Kristen. "Impressive," she said, "but why would you attempt such a perilous feat?"

"I needed a change of scenery."

Bannister's posture stiffened.

"You're about to blow your shot," Hernandez warned.

Kristen squinted up at her. "I killed the man who beat and raped me for the last ten years." She glowered at Telerson. "Now, I'm facing the same thing here with him."

The security chief stood there with a smug look still on his face.

Bannister seethed. "Is this true?"

Hernandez said, "Yes, it is. She needs to go."

Walter's voice came through on the inner channel, affirming what Hope already knew. "If you take her, she won't make it through the genetic process."

That seals it. She felt terrible leaving the girl with Telerson. "I'm so sorry." She turned, signaling for Sylvia to follow. Conflicted, she walked to their terrain tracker. Her feet moved slowly, as if of their own volition.

"Son of a—" Hernandez exclaimed. Then he said loudly, "She has no chance here."

"You're mine now, bitch," Telerson growled.

Bannister stopped, deeply rankled.

"Oh, boy," Walter warned. "Here we go."

She shot a look over her shoulder and found Telerson leering at the woman. *No matter what I do, this woman is condemned to death.* She spun around and marched back to Kristen. "Your chances of surviving aren't good. I mean, not good at all."

"That's fine." Kristen glared at Telerson. "I'll take my chances with you."

"No!" he blurted. "She's mine! I'm not letting her out of my sight." He stepped closer.

"Very well, then," Bannister said lightly.

"That's more like it," Telerson bellowed.

She turned to the governor. "Okay, I'll take Sylvia *and* Kristen." She paused, pointing to the security chief. "And *him* too."

"Oh, this is rich," Hernandez said with a grin. "As my friend over there would say, that will be one less food-sucking hole for us to worry about."

Nervous laughter bobbed up from the surrounding citizens.

"You can't do this!" Telerson shrieked. Horror registered on his face. He turned, trying to push through the group to get away.

Sylvia's staff whipped out in a blur, striking his legs. He dropped like a rock, screaming. Telerson scrambled to get up, but she stomped on his shoulder and jammed her staff onto his neck, pinning him to the ground. "Let's see you bully your way out of this."

"Okay!" Walter exclaimed in an admiring tone. "No messing with her!"

Bannister signaled, and the guards moved in. They lifted the wobbly man and dragged him a safe distance away as the crowd cheered.

"Here, put these on him." Bannister reached down and lobbed the chains to Walter.

He caught them but tossed the shackles aside in the same motion. "I have something better. Put the cuff on him."

One of his partners snapped a glowing blue band around Telerson's neck.

Bannister smiled. "Test it, please."

The guard pressed a button on his armored sleeve. Telerson screamed and crumbled, cowering.

Kristen looked stunned. "You're going to let him volunteer too?"

Bannister turned back to her. "For my program? Oh, heaven's no."

"The military has a special place for trash like him," Walter snarled.

A glint of vindication appeared in Kristen's one clear eye. "Thank you," she murmured.

Bannister placed a hand on her recruit's shoulder, guiding her in the direction of the terrain tracker. "When you see what I have in store for you all, you may want to take that back."

Kristen trudged along, trying to keep pace. "Pffft. I'd do almost anything for three squares a day."

CHAPTER THREE
THE GIRL

GENESIS, MARCH 3, 2355

The lullaby washed over her, soft and sweet, caressing her dream-like thoughts. *Catch a falling star and put it in your pocket. Save it for a dusty day on Mars.* The melody soon wafted away, disappearing like vapors in the wind. Sadness crept into Kristen's soul; she'd almost forgotten her mother's voice. She longed to be wrapped in a blanket in her mother's lap, snug and safe and loved, while she sang away the hunger and the fears.

Garbled voices floated in the distance like an elusive butterfly. She felt bone cold. Her head throbbed and her muscles burned. Hard as she tried, she could do nothing. Dread filled her; danger swirled nearby. Threatening. Just out of reach. Exhausted and overwhelmed, she drifted back into the shelter of her mother's arms.

A clanking noise jarred her from the dark respite toward consciousness. Kristen heard water sloshing, and the powerful odor of disinfectant burned her nostrils. It masked the smell of something rancid; she wanted to cover her nose but couldn't. Nothing would move, not even her toes. Her muscles strained, begging for release, but she lay motionless on the hard tabletop.

A woman's voice murmured in the distance. "This recombinant transformation is a nightmare. I can't believe anyone survives." She sounded louder as she approached. "It's a miracle these two made it through."

"Oh, sure," a man's grating, nasal voice replied. "That's exactly what we need here: more Earther vermin."

"Stop it," the woman said. "Don't be such a jerk."

"God, this pisses me off. Double the work this time. You get her face cleaned off. Hurry up!"

Kristen flinched when his sudden rough scrubbing overwhelmed her with a wave of searing synaptic fire. His quick, hard swipes grew unbearable.

"Cut it out!" The woman sounded upset. "Take it easy on her. We have plenty of time."

"Shut up," the man snapped. "They can *wear* this slimy RNA, for all I care. It's as nasty as they are." He dragged a bristly brush across Kristen's belly.

Memories of her brutal welcome to the Dallas Life Pod surfaced. She concentrated on regaining control of her body. Someone wiped a soft cloth across her forehead in a gentle motion, moving down the side of her cheek.

"Don't pay him any mind," the woman whispered close to her ear.

The cloth lifted away and returned, warm. The delicate touch washed off whatever held her eyes shut. A moment later, they popped open, and she saw a woman wearing a white smock and cap looking down at her.

"Oh my. She's awake."

"Impossible." The man dismissed the comment with a sniff.

His white-capped head bobbed in front of Kristen's face. She realized with a start that the horrible odor *came from him.* His stinking breath made her want to gag. She stared at him, her heart pounding in her chest.

"Son of a bitch. She *is* awake."

"That's never happened before," the woman replied.

Rage powered through Kristen, consuming and out of her control. Her fist shot upward, clubbing the man hard on the side of the head. He spun away from the knockout blow and landed in a limp heap. She grabbed the woman's smock, jerking her closer.

"Help me," she begged. The attendant tried to pull away, but she held her in a death grip. "Help. Me. Now."

The stunned woman reached over to comply. She scooped her arm behind her ward's shoulder and wrangled her to a sitting position. "Oof, you're solid. They really did a number on you."

Still clutching the lab coat, Kristen flexed her free hand, then rolled her ankles around. *I have to get out of here.* She pushed the woman aside and slid from the table. Kristen's legs buckled, and she collapsed. Her hands were slick on the floor.

"Oh, no!" The woman rushed to help. "Are you okay? You shouldn't be conscious yet. We haven't finished—"

Kristen growled, shoving her away.

The attendant scuttled back. She reached over and nudged the man. "Hey," she said, but she got no response. "Wake up!" She turned and slapped him a couple of times. "Come on! We've got a situation here!"

Kristen shivered on the cold, tiled floor. She drew her knees to her chest and wrapped her slime-covered arms around her nakedness. Energy surged through her body, erratic and edgy, even in her vulnerable state.

A low moan arose from nearby. The woman shot a worried look toward a nearby gurney, where a form stretched underneath a sheet. A hand flopped out in a spasmodic contraction.

"No!" Kristen yelled, lurching upward. She grabbed the stretcher's edge and grunted, pulling herself to stand on shaky legs. She gasped, "S-S-S-Sylvia?" Her eyes welled, and shock settled in. She patted her friend's arm, mired in distress.

"She's fine," the woman said softly. "She's sleeping. I promise, everything's okay."

"Syl." Kristen leaned closer. "We have to get out of here!" She swayed and looked about, searching for a blanket, for a towel, for the *door*, so they could escape. She leaned on the gurney, wondering what to do. Her reality condensed into a tight vacuum.

"Kristen." The sharp voice cut through the silence like a laser through glass.

She jerked upright. Her brows knit together, and she focused on Sylvia's deathly still face. "Syl? What the—"

"Kristen, look at me."

The voice came from behind her. Fire welled up in her belly, un-controllable, white-hot. She whirled, screaming her anguish, and tucked her head to charge the person standing between them and freedom.

"Kristen!" The person bellowed her name, holding up both hands. "Stop! That's an order!"

The voice of reason. Even in her primal state, Kristen recognized it. She skidded to a halt, inches from her boss.

Weeks later, Kristen stood at the base of the climbing wall, staring up at the protruding grips. "Why do they have to be so far apart?"

Tech Specialist Perkins walked up and stood next to her. She glanced over and thought about giving him a friendly shoulder bump but stopped herself.

"You're going to get there," he said.

"You think so?"

"This is a piece of cake compared to everything else."

"Not so much for me."

"Just keep at it. Hell, you set records on some of the other courses."

She snorted. "Yeah, but I sucked at the virtual mind sims, and don't get me started on the sensory overloads."

Perkins thumped the wall. "But you kept at it 'til you got them. Everyone stinks at those at first. You're retraining your brain, so you can accept and filter the stimuli. You did fine."

"Can't you just tell them I rang that stupid bell?"

He headed back to the monitoring console. "I could, but you know everything's recorded."

Kristen sighed, studying the wall. The bell hung from the ceiling, beckoning from forty feet up. She put her foot on a lower jug. *I rode a skyglider in a freaking storm,* she thought. *I can do it.* She stretched for an outcropping and scaled halfway up the cantilevered side. She swiped for the next handhold, but it sat too far out of reach.

"Geesh," she hissed. *I've tried so many ways.* Even with her new-found strength, going beyond this level proved impossible. She dangled there, frustrated. *All roads lead to this choke point.*

"Not going to make it," Perkins said under his breath.

His slight whisper interrupted her strategizing. "Come on, Tech Specialist. Don't be dishing on me. I don't want to have to space you."

"You weren't supposed to hear that."

The door slid open, and Sylvia sashayed in. "Stop harassing him while you are stuck on the wall. It makes the rest of us look bad."

The tech frowned. "How did you . . ." he said. "You weren't even in the gym."

"Perk of the trade." She walked over to the wall. "Go ahead. Do not worry. I will catch you when you fall."

Perkins grinned. "I figured she could hang there all day."

"I made it," Sylvia goaded.

A little switch in Kristen's mind turned on her anger. "That's carbon crap. There's no way you did this."

"I will show you how it is done." Sylvia backed up several steps, then rushed the wall and vaulted upward. Her right foot landed solidly on a jug, then she shoved off and jumped to Kristen's level. Her next leap placed her left foot on the lonesome grip that Kristen could never reach. Sylvia propelled her body vertically to yet another outcrop. Her fingertips briefly brushed the wall. She jagged to the side, going higher, and somersaulted upward, kicking the bell. She landed catlike on the mat below.

"Son of a bitch." The tech's eyes were wide. "That's new."

Kristen scowled down from her perch. "You cheated, Sylvia."

"How? No one ever said you could only use your hands."

Kristen sprang from the wall, soaring toward her. Sylvia moved as if to catch her, then hopped to the side, but Kristen still crashed on top of her. They rolled to the floor, arms a blur, punching each other. Sylvia managed to throw her off, and both women jumped to a fighting stance.

"Are you out of your mind?" Sylvia snapped. "What is wrong with you?"

"You better learn to think on those feet."

Dr. Bannister walked into the room unexpectedly, followed by a short, wiry man. His arms were crossed, and he seemed annoyed.

Bannister took in the scene. "What's going on here?"

"Nothing," Kristen responded hastily.

"I heard," the man said.

The women loosened up, standing to face them.

"We were just giving Tech Specialist Perkins a demonstration," Sylvia explained.

"Why do I find that hard to believe?" Bannister sounded exasperated. "Regardless, I want to introduce one of our most decorated veterans, Scott Zang. He'll be your new partner, Sylvia."

"But," Kristen blurted out, "I thought *we* were going to be partners?"

"Put two rookies together? I expect more from you."

Bannister's rebuke stung. Kristen stared rudely. *This guy's taking my place?* "He doesn't look like much."

"People underestimate me," Zang said with a haughty smile. "It's saved me on more than one occasion."

"Scott will direct the final phase of your training, Sylvia. You will learn critical refinement skills and technical focus from him."

"Yes," he said, focusing on his new protégé.

Sylvia thrust out her hand. "It will be an honor, Mr. Zang."

He responded with a crisp, businesslike nod, then stepped back to stand at-ease.

I hate suck ups, Kristen thought. "What about me?"

"You're not ready."

"But—"

"Tech Specialist Perkins will continue to run you through the paces. He's an expert here in the gym as well as in strategy with VR simulations." With that, she turned to leave.

I'm beyond ready, Kristen thought, but she kept it to herself.

"It is okay." Sylvia tapped her arm. "You will make it. We are becoming supersoldiers."

Bannister stopped and looked back. "That's as good a description as any, so yes."

"Does that mean . . ." Kristen struggled to formulate the question. "Are we . . . are we still human?"

"Yes," Bannister replied. She paused, then added, "And no."

"Not sure how I feel about that," Kristen said quietly.

"Use it to your advantage." Bannister called over her shoulder, "They're all yours, gentlemen."

CHAPTER FOUR
The Arrival

May 14, 2355

The clamping locks secured the transport shuttle to the Time Forward Space Platform with a deep metallic clunk, which resonated throughout the docking port. The airlock hissed open. Hope Bannister watched the lone passenger from Genesis Station bound aboard, her magnetic boots effortlessly clicking on the grated metal floor. Kristen's thick braid of long, black hair floated behind her like a serpent ready to strike. The nanocarbon vest she wore revealed newly defined muscles. Their newest time agent radiated an enviable, rare confidence. *She looks so strong.*

"There you are!" Bannister took a clumsy step toward the interior hatch. "Welcome!"

Kristen flashed an uncharacteristic smile and leaned in to exchange a perfunctory hug. "The ride felt like an eternity."

Bannister cringed. *I wish she wouldn't do that. We can't afford contamination.* She straightened and squared her shoulders, allowing herself a glimmer of optimism. "Hard to believe it's only been a few months. You've come a long way since we first met."

"Have I, now? Amazing what three squares a day will do for you."

"Indeed." Bannister tamped back her bemusement. *I remember that.* "Thank you for sticking with the program." *Never in a million years did I think she'd make it.*

"You know, Walter bet against me."

Bannister chuckled. "Don't take it personally. He bet against Sylvia too."

Kristen rolled her eyes. "I hope he lost good money on us." She placed her hands on her hips and gazed around. She looked ready to take on the universe.

Such potential, Bannister thought. *Wonder what Kants will think of her.*

Within seconds, the rookie shrugged in obvious discomfort. "Dr. B? I feel kind of weird."

"That's normal. You're feeling The Worm's gravitational redshift effect." She watched Kristen quickly regain her composure.

"Does it go away?"

"Soon you won't even notice it." Hope turned and signaled with her head. "Follow me, please." She trudged down the airlock corridor to the main passageway and pointed to a plate-sized oval ring on the wall. "Grab that travel lift, and I'll get the other one." Their mag-boots released from the floor the instant they gripped the rings.

"Whoa!" Kristen floated sideways. She twiddled her legs, righting herself.

"Relax and let it guide you. Command center," Hope ordered. The transport started pulling them along. "This is the best way to cover longer distances on the station." The pace accelerated until they were whizzing along the corridors.

Kristen hooked an elbow through the ring and grinned from ear to ear. "This place is huge compared to Genesis Station. Is it a Dyson Sphere?"

"The Time Forward Space Platform surrounds anomaly, not a star."

They rounded a corner. "So, you did all this?"

"Yes. With a lot of help." *And two decades of my life on this floating flytrap,* Hope thought.

"It's definitely impressive. Speaking of which, what about The Worm? When do I get to see this bad boy?"

"Funny you should ask," Hope said.

Their pace dropped considerably, bringing them to a stop at another airlock door. Their mag-boots reengaged with a click.

Anxious to see her new agent's reaction, she placed her hand on a square sensor. The door slid open, and cold air escaped with a quiet *whoosh*.

A deep, low vibration from the command center resonated in Kristen's bones. The intensity increased as they passed through the door. It jittered her inner ear and overloaded her enhanced senses. Waves of static discharge coursed over her bare arms, making her feel like she might crawl right out of her own skin.

"Good morning, Chava," Bannister greeted the attending technician as they walked further into the sterile-looking room.

"Doctor B!" He glanced down at them, his gloved hands never breaking the rhythm of his work. His hover seat bobbed next to a floor-to-ceiling translucent tube dotted with 3D diagrams, vid clips, and notes. "Nice of you to stop by."

"I want to introduce our newest time agent, Kristen Winters."

"Ah, yes." He leaned toward them, and the hover chair responded, moving slightly in their direction. Chava's brows went up admiringly. He nodded at her. "She seems well-equipped."

Kristen cocked her head, checking out his form-fitting white wrap, kinky blond hair, and robust nose and mouth. *Maybe in another life.*

Dr. Bannister seemed oblivious to the exchange. "I want her to see the anomaly in all its glory."

"By all means," Chava said, moving back to the console. "It's quite a sight to behold."

"It certainly is," Bannister agreed. "We have a lot to cover now that she's ready. Agent Winters, this is what your training has been all about."

The back wall dissolved into a transparent view of The Worm. Kristen's mouth dropped open, gaping at the phenomenon on the other side of the reinforced glass.

"Give it a couple of minutes," Bannister said. "It takes getting used to."

The horizontal time vortex writhed between two enormous rings spaced about thirty meters apart. These harnessed the dancing, tapered ends to generators so vast that they disappeared into darkness. Blinding snaps of light pulsed erratically from within the gray depths of the gyrating core, churning wildly across the timespace tunnel to its outer layer.

"Amazing!" Kristen squinted against the brightness. "I can see why it's called The Worm."

"Yes," Bannister replied. "Kants thought so too. He named it."

Kristen leaned her forehead against the window, mesmerized. *It knows I'm here*, she thought, feeling connected to the trapped behemoth. "It's so beautiful." Her breath fogged the glass. "I can't believe this works."

"No one could at first. They didn't think we could catch lightning in a bottle."

Kristen watched swirling orbs of energy glow to life, revealing quick snippets of history. The rhythmic shapes flowed along the undulating jetties, morphing into faces and places she didn't recognize, then faded into the collective cache of incidents in time.

"You did it, though."

"Yes," Bannister said, "we did. Frankly, it's a brilliant feat of engineering. The central section of the platform orbits the anomaly, calibrating to its fluctuations."

Kristen pulled away from the clear wall, astounded.

Bannister stepped closer and pointed to a catwalk running above the anomaly. "The initial access point for travel is up there. We made it just in time. Watch this."

Kristen located the two time agents standing on a perpendicular gangplank that extended over The Worm. *They seem so small and vulnerable.* She watched the preparations for a few seconds. "Wouldn't it be more logical to travel from one end to the other?"

"The AI determined that the temporal time continuum flows in a horizontal direction. If we dropped you in lengthwise, you could spend the rest of your life traveling through it."

"So, by going in from the side, you're making a tactical insertion."

"Exactly."

A loud countdown began, echoing through the chamber. *That's gonna be me*, Kristen thought, feeling a little queasy. From beneath the gangplank, a laser shot toward the anomaly. The red beam cut into the exterior. The Worm moved away from it as if in pain, creating a gaping hole. The agents suddenly dropped into the rent, vanishing into the midst of the oscillating time tornado.

"Holy smokes! What was that?"

"We inject exotic matter into the anomaly to create a portal."

"Where'd they go?"

"Somewhere in Asia," Bannister answered evenly.

Somewhere? The corner of Kristen's eye twitched. *She doesn't know where.*

"We estimate around June 2050."

Kristen stared straight ahead. "That doesn't seem very scientific."

"It's the best we can do," Bannister replied.

"Well, how long until they come back?"

"Minutes, hours, days. It just depends."

She twisted to face her boss. "It depends on what?" Every detail mattered. Her life—hell, even humanity—depended on it.

"Wish I knew."

Kristen brought her hands up in disbelief. "What's that supposed to mean?"

"Each mission is unique, so the rate of return differs every time. We're unable to predict how fast the time warriors physically pass through the anomaly."

"I see why you don't tell us until it's too late."

"I admit, The Worm can be unpredictable."

"Looks to me like The Worm can't do shit."

"The anomaly isn't the problem. The AI discerns only short time periods and general geographical areas."

Kristen took in a deep breath, then let it out slowly. "It feels like you don't have this figured out."

"We've learned to take what is handed to us and go with it. Our agents are well prepared to adapt to any circumstances."

"You expect me to risk my ass with what you just told me?"

"Don't worry," Bannister said. "You'll be fine."

"Oh, that's comforting."

"Look, I know what I'm talking about. You just have to trust me."

"Easier said than done," Kristen huffed.

"Let's move on."

"Mm-hm, that builds trust."

Bannister turned to Chava. "Are you seeing anything?"

"No, Dr. B. Nothing yet."

Kristen glanced up at him, but his attention stayed on the controls. "What are you searching for?"

"Fluctuations, echoes. Anything out of normal parameters." Chava's smooth, crisp response sounded exceedingly efficient. "We're also scanning historical documents from that period to see if the current operation impacted the timeline."

Kristen arched an eyebrow. "It doesn't sound to me like that would work."

"Your years of surviving on the surface have turned you into a multiverse physicist?" Bannister scoffed.

"It doesn't take a rocket scientist to know if you change history. The documents could have already been altered."

Chava interrupted her. "We download the current history into each agent's time transponder."

"I get it," Kristen said. "When they come back, you can match it to today's history."

"Precisely," Bannister answered.

"But that doesn't explain why he's looking for changes now," Kristen pointed out.

The tech glanced down from his perch. "There's another way we verify differences."

"What's that?"

"When you're this close to the anomaly," he asserted, "time stands still. When you leave this room, it will be the same time as when you arrived. Because of that, we remember the past the same as before the mission."

Kristen glanced back and forth at them. "Mars puke. Now you're just making stuff up."

Bannister's expression remained impassive.

"Are you serious?"

Chava gave her a sage look and turned back to his console.

"You've been sworn in for a reason," Bannister said. "No one except personnel who have direct contact with The Worm are privy to this classified information."

Kristen bobbed her head, surprised.

"It's not exact, but we scan historical events just the same."

"Got it. I guess."

The tech's motions became more frantic. "The sensors are picking up variations in pitch and volume, Dr. B." His voice escalated as the noisy vibrations deepened. "Momentary arrival. This is a fast one."

The tornadic anomaly wobbled and bucked, then, with a blinding flash, ejected the team into the net below. They bounced wildly and threw their arms up, shielding themselves from the flares of energy roaring overhead. Robotic appendages darted out from side ramps, sweeping the stumbling agents to safety.

Even from this distance, Kristen could see the physical toll it took on them. She took a step back. "They don't look too good."

Bannister leaned closer and raised her voice. "That's why the genetic program you just completed is so rigorous."

Rigorous, Kristen thought. *More like suicidal.* She stared at The Worm and picked at her fingernails, a nervous habit since childhood. She recalled the excruciating agony of the recombinant transformation, of her intellect expanding, forming links with her reconstructed physique.

Bannister continued as the hum returned to its normal level, "It's a tremendous responsibility you and the other agents undertake. Our success means survival for everyone."

A surge of anger burned through Kristen's limbs. She'd battled for survival her entire life. *Does everything always have to be so hard?* Trembling, she forced her attention back to Dr. Bannister. "Believe me. I understand."

"There's much more to this than you are aware of."

Kristen stared, incredulous. "The fate of humanity isn't enough?"

"No, actually, it's not." Her boss's voice became more emphatic. "We're fighting for more than just Earth."

"What's that supposed to mean?"

"We have to consider Proxima-B."

Kristen frowned. "Isn't that the planet the Keplers say is the perfect place for us to start over?"

"Not so perfect for the millions of indigenous beings who live there," Bannister said.

"I don't understand." A foreboding feeling fluttered in the pit of her stomach.

"The Proxima-B inhabitants live in what we would call the Dark Ages. They're primitive and, when they're threatened, warlike."

Kristen leaned against the wall, suddenly weary. "But we can all live there, right? Coexist?"

Bannister cast a sad smile. "We could, but the Keplers don't want the headache. Their armada intends to clear the way for human colonization. The native inhabitants will be slaughtered."

"No." Aghast, Kristen looked up at Chava for confirmation. He nodded, his mouth a hard line. She blinked back tears. "That's what happened to my parents." Her voice lodged in her throat. "This is so wrong."

"Here's the ironic part," Bannister added. "The Keplers don't have enough ships to transport everyone to Proxima-B. They're not equipped to make it back before we run out of food, either. More than ninety percent of the people on Earth will die if we pursue that route. It will be catastrophic on all fronts."

Kristen chewed on a fingernail, thinking. She stopped herself and placed her hand on the glass wall. "Anything else I should know?"

"Yes. We're running out of time."

She scoffed. "We have a time machine. How's that possible?"

"The Worm is shrinking," Bannister admitted, looking tense. "When it disappears, we'll no longer be able to send agents back. No more missions then."

That news took a second to absorb. "How long until that happens?"

"Not exactly sure, but soon. Too soon."

"This whole thing sounds crazy." Her voice almost cracked.

Bannister glanced down at her mag-boots. She shook her head. "It sounds crazy to me, and I built it."

Kristen's mouth dropped open. *What?* Bannister spent years bringing order to a phenomenon of universal proportions, sacrificing to better the world for the sake of humanity. "I can't believe you just said that."

"Yes, well . . ."

What have I gotten myself into? "I'm not sure what to think. If we change history, will we even exist? But if we don't . . ." She bit her lower lip nervously, then continued. "At least you've given us a chance. We *could* save both worlds and keep a lot of families together, including mine."

Bannister put a reassuring hand on her shoulder. "It's dangerous and the odds are against us, but it's worth trying."

Kristen took a moment to consider everything. Dr. Bannister embodied the voice of reason. "Yes, we have to have hope."

Her boss said quietly, "I am Hope."

Kristen took a deep breath and blew it out through pursed lips. "Yeah," she replied. "I know."

CHAPTER FIVE
THE BOY

November 18, 1963

"You know this won't bring her back." Walter smacked the dashboard of the black Chevy Impala, emphasizing his point.

Kants glowered at his partner from the driver's seat. "If I believed that," he said, his words thick with emotion, "we wouldn't be here."

They cruised through the rolling hills and rustic farmland of southwest Missouri, almost four hundred miles north of where they were meant to be. Kants understood the limitations The Worm presented. He did not like the fact the AI couldn't pinpoint their insertion. Except this time, it finally worked in his favor.

"Why don't we just stick with what we're really here for? The end goal is the same thing you want out of this stupid side trip."

You do not understand, Kants thought. *Who knows if the opportunity will ever come back around?* They rode in stony silence, autumn leaves fluttering in their wake.

Eventually, Walter reached over and rolled his window down, leaning into the wind. Cold air whipped his thick brown hair against his round face. He squinted over at Kants. "This isn't our mission, damn it. You need to turn this car toward Dallas. Our return jump is due soon."

The timing would be tight, but Kants felt confident that they could manage both situations. He trusted his partner to keep his secret, even if he did disagree. "The boy is the key to—"

"That's bullshit, and you know it," Walter interrupted. "What does this kid have to do with anything?"

If Kants could double his chances of stopping the Purge War and saving his wife, he would. "We must find the boy."

Walter rolled up the window and slumped against the door. "Bannister's going to catch us, and we'll both be grounded."

"Then she will not find out."

"Right." He leaned over and fidgeted with the radio dial, landing on an AM station. A twangy country song ended, and it immediately launched into another. He leaned back in his seat. "What kind of crap music is this?"

Kants cringed. They barreled down the country highway until they approached the outskirts of the next small town. "We are almost here."

"Check this out! Population 3,463." Walter laughed. "We have more than that in our security force on Genesis."

Kants grunted and slowed the car to the posted speed limit of twenty-five miles per hour.

"It feels like we're crawling, man. We don't have time for this."

"We cannot draw attention to ourselves."

Main Street consisted of eight blocks of two-story buildings. Cars and muddy pickup trucks parked nose-in along the thoroughfare. Four large grain silos stood sentry over the eastern end of town, and a railroad track bordered the southwestern edge of town. Kants pulled into an open spot in front of Bruno's Diner and Drugstore and shifted the gearstick into park, but the car continued to idle. Puzzled, he raised his hands.

"We're not in Kansas anymore." Walter pointed to the ignition. "Rotate the key to the 'off' position."

"Ah, yes, the key. Why do I always forget that?" Kants reached around the wheel and turned the car off. They stepped out of the vehicle, both dressed in dark, conservative suits appropriate for the early 1960s. Kants tugged at the jacket straining against his broad shoulders, then reached up to adjust his tie.

"Let's get some coffee," Walter said. "I'm buying."

Kants followed his partner into the diner. A bell on the door jingled when they stepped inside, announcing their entrance. The old wooden floor creaked beneath their feet, and the heavy aroma of grease and stale coffee drenched the air.

A collective hush descended over the few occupied tables as the locals gawked at them. A large man in grubby overalls removed his cap and set it on the corner of the table. He crossed his considerable arms and leaned back in his chair to get a better view.

Obligatory smiles wavered across the newcomers's faces. They found seats at the lunch counter and plopped down on padded stools anchored to the floor. Conversations across the dining space gradually resumed.

"Oh, yeah," Walter murmured, observing the room through the grimy mirror on the back wall. "These suits help us fit right in."

Kants adjusted his position on the seat and grabbed a menu.

Walter removed his sunglasses and tossed them onto the counter. He signaled to the cook. "Two coffees, please." He leaned closer to his partner and spoke in a soft, exaggerated drawl. "We're wasting our time here, just plumb wasting our time."

Kants grunted. Their order arrived, and he stirred sugar into his steaming coffee and took a sip, swirling the black brew in his mouth. God, how he missed sugar.

The bell on the entryway door jingled, and they both glanced over at the mirror. A man wearing a white button-down shirt, tie, and dark dress slacks entered. He paused, nodding hello to people as he peered about the diner.

The cook called out, "The usual, Doc?"

The man pushed his black-framed glasses up on his nose. "Sounds good, Jerry."

Kants exchanged a telling look with Walter. A doctor would know many people in the community, which could be helpful. It didn't surprise him when the man headed their way.

"Afternoon, fellas," he said, obviously sizing them up. His deep, gravelly voice conveyed authority. "You two stick out like a sore thumb. Is there something I can help you with?"

"We're just passing through on our way to Dallas," Kants replied in a cool tone.

"Hmm. You're certainly off the beaten path." He stepped aside, reaching out to accept the coffee mug. "Going down to the parade for President Kennedy?"

"Most assuredly." Kants offered his hand. "My friend here is Walter West, and I'm Richard Kants." He inquired expectantly, "And you are?"

"Williams," the gentleman replied. "Doctor Williams. Optometry. Just call me Doc."

Walter reached out to shake hands. "You sound like the person who could help us."

"Pardon me? I'm not following you."

Thanks, Walter. Now I cannot ask about the kid. "My friend has an unusual sense of humor," Kants quickly interrupted. "What might be the best way to get to Dallas?"

Doc responded in his folksy way, "Well, you need to go west until you hit Big Cabin, then go south from there." He gestured in that direction. "Highway 69 will take you straight into Dallas. The drive is a good half-day or so."

Kants smiled and nodded. "Thank you kindly, Doc. We will head out after our coffee."

"You're welcome. Tell Jackie hello for my wife," he added with a wry grin. He turned and headed to an open seat with the other regulars.

Walter leaned in closer to his partner and said softly, "In a hundred years, that guy won't even recognize his profession. Everyone will have designer eyes by then."

Annoyed, Kants dismissed the comment. He sipped his coffee, watching as a couple of kids played cops and robbers in the back of the room. They were shooting each other with imaginary guns. Then he noticed a few sidelong glances at him, so he drained his coffee cup. "Time to try something else."

Walter pulled out a wad of bills secured by a money clip. He snapped out a fresh dollar and laid it on the countertop. "Here you go," he said to the cook. "Keep the change."

The men headed out the door, stopping on the sidewalk out front. Walter looked amused. "That whole money thing is so weird."

Kants glowered at him.

"Sorry, man," his partner said. "It wasn't meant to be."

"There has to be a way to find this child."

"Maybe there's one of those old phone booths around here. One with a contact book," Walter said, becoming more animated. "What did they call that helper person you talk to?"

"You mean an operator?"

The door's bell jingled behind them, and they looked back. A boy emerged, chewing on a toothpick. "Hey, mister!" He held up the sunglasses. "You left these."

"Thanks, kid." Walter put on the shades. He made a show of looking up and down the street. "Oh yeah, that's better. I appreciate it." He grinned. "Hey, any chance you know a boy named Matt Banks?"

The child's expression brightened. "That's me! How'd you know my name?"

The men glanced at each other, flabbergasted.

Kants recovered first. He knew the boy would soon be missed. "You were playing cops and robbers in there. I could tell you were the police officer. It takes one to know one." He opened his jacket slightly, giving him a quick glimpse of an FBI badge and holstered Browning.

The toothpick dropped from Matt's mouth. "Oh, gosh."

Kants pulled out a silver coin and squatted down to the child's level. "I am returning this to you. It is yours once again."

Matt took it, but his voice sounded confused. "What?"

"You gave it to me a long time ago. In the future."

"Oh. Thank you, sir." He turned it over in his hand, studying it closely. "Wait, what'd you say?" The boy took a step back.

"You told me this must happen." An unexpected surge of sadness took Kants by surprise. He paused to collect himself. "Never mind. You will understand someday. Don't lose it. Promise?"

"I guess so."

"I have a top-secret FBI mission for you."

"Oh." The boy's eyes went wide with excitement. "Top-secret!"

"Yes. There is a name engraved on the back of the coin. When you grow up, you must find this person and do whatever it takes to help him. Do not forget."

"I won't, I promise." The kid shoved it into his jeans pocket. "Thanks, mister!"

Kants stood up. *This is how it all begins.* The boy couldn't realize that his life would no longer be his own. After all these years, he had finally returned the silver dollar to Matt Banks. The circular nature of the conundrum gave him a migraine every time he tried to solve it. In the end, it didn't matter which came first, so long as it happened.

Once again, they heard the bell clang against the glass. The beefy farmer held the door open and scowled at them from beneath his weathered ball cap. "Matt! Get your butt in here."

"Sorry, Dad." The child scampered under his father's massive arm.

"It's time for y'all to move on."

Walter tensed, but Kants put the back of his hand against his partner's chest before he could make a move. "We were just leaving."

The man stepped back inside and let the door slam shut behind him.

Kants took a deep breath. He pulled out his pocket watch and flipped open the cover to peer at the photograph of his beloved wife. Images of the nuclear strike flashed through his mind, ripping another hole in his soul. Running into this kid seemed providential, so surely this plan would work. He clamped the watch shut and brusquely said, "Come on, Walter. We have unfinished business in Dallas."

CHAPTER SIX
The Candidate

November 12, 2021

The University of Texas sat deep within the limits of the state's capital city, Austin. Rigorous academic entry requirements made it difficult to gain admission into the top-notch school. Despite that fact, over fifty thousand students from all walks of life attended there. It attracted the cream of the crop—the main reason Matt Banks now visited the sprawling campus.

He sat at a table in the student union building, sipping coffee and absentmindedly twirling an old silver dollar between his fingers. The Longhorn students and faculty bustled in and out, sending surreptitious looks in his direction. He knew why. When you wore a suit in a place like this, you were either a vendor, or you were there to interview someone.

Matt loved his career at the FBI. He served as lead agent in charge of a newly formed unit tasked with rooting out nefarious terrorists and criminals on the dark web. He instituted their credo around what an old college professor once told him: *"You're a leader if you're one step ahead of the game. You're a visionary if you're two steps ahead. But three steps ahead, you're fired."* His group would be *four* steps ahead of the game. Accomplishing this feat required an extremely sharp, innovative team.

His connection at the university suggested a certain well-rounded, bright grad student as a candidate. The young man would soon finish his PhD in artificial intelligence with a focus on digital forensics. This guy made Mensa look like a fraternity for the slow-witted; even his professors couldn't keep up. He recently demonstrated to them his ease in hacking into several supposedly airtight systems, proving a point about stronger security standards. *Good thing he's a white hat,* Matt thought, *or he could be trouble.*

He stopped the coin and frowned, wondering if his childhood imagination had got the best of him. Over fifty years ago, one brief conversation with a stranger affected the trajectory of his life, leading him to this career. Old Doc Williams gave him the guy's name: Richard Kants. He used all the FBI resources at his disposal to track him down. Until now, nothing ever lined up.

Banks rubbed his thumb across the etching on the back. *How the hell did he know?* The name on this godforsaken silver dollar matched his top recruit.

Hunter Coburn entered the student union cafeteria and looked around, searching the tables. At a lanky six foot two, he had an athletic build with broad shoulders. His thick, wavy hair forced its way from under his UT cap, and he smelled rank from an afternoon of playing ultimate Frisbee. *I don't care,* he thought. An official-looking man in a business suit caught his eye, and Hunter headed his direction. *Let's get this over with.*

"You must be the guy from the FBI."

"Yes." He smiled and stood. "I'm Matt Banks, head of the bureau's new Deep Net Cyber Division." The two men shook hands. "Thanks for taking the time to dress up."

Hunter glanced down at his sweaty, grass-stained shirt. "My professor insisted I meet with you. She wouldn't take no for an answer."

"Nice to meet you too, Mr. Coburn."

"Sorry. Something I said?" A silent challenge passed between the two men.

Banks cleared his throat. "I'd like to chat with you about your future," he said, gesturing to the empty chairs. "What do you plan to do when you finish your doctoral program?"

"Why do I have the feeling you already know?" Hunter stretched back in his seat and crossed his arms. "You must have an alternate, less lucrative option."

"Ah. Did the CIA get here before me?"

"Just long enough for me to tell them the same thing I told my dean and I'm going to tell you. No one seems to listen, and I'm tired of it. I'm not interested in government work."

The agent sipped his coffee, taking his time. "So, appealing to your civic duty, protecting your country, stuff like that, is probably not going to have the impact I hoped for?"

"No offense, but I've already received numerous offers," Hunter said, "from large corporations who will pay me insane amounts of money to work for them."

"Hmm, I see. Okay. Let me run this scenario by you. You work for Lifeforce.com in a big creative space in Brooklyn with top-notch sushi in the lobby, daily massages, a microbrewery, and Ethiopian coffee. Heck, even your kids get served at the in-house daycare, and you're making your insane money."

"I like that picture. A lot."

Banks leaned forward, catching Hunter off-guard with his intensity. "While you're at your desk, a terrorist group detonates a nuclear bomb in the heart of Manhattan—a bomb you could have found. Millions of people in a ten-mile radius are obliterated, including you and your family. How's that picture?"

"Yeah, that would suck," he said. "But I have you to protect me and all those millions of people. Correct?"

"Hunter, it's critical we stay multiple steps ahead of the bad guys. I've got to have our best and brightest. In other words, we need you."

"Still not a compelling draw."

"I'm sure every group promised you a lot of money to be a part of their team."

"I already said that."

"I'm not asking you to be a part of the team. I'm asking you to lead the team."

Hunter's eyes narrowed. "I'm listening."

"This is an innovative approach to security intel. We'll have a clean slate to build your infrastructure with the latest in cutting-edge technology. And I'll pay you a somewhat insane amount of money."

"You're willing to put a guy with no management experience in charge? Why?"

Banks smiled. "Let's just say, I received an inside tip."

"Come again?"

"Look, you've got a gift," he answered. "Your ideas are light-years ahead of your peers. We're up against technology-savvy enemies, ones with no morals. We need a new, unfettered view. Like yours."

Hunter shifted in his seat. "I've been working with artificial intelligence. You know that, right?"

Banks replied, "Yes. The AI program with MIT and Arrow Tech?"

"You did your homework. It's not a shock."

"Would it interest you to know that the FBI owns one of the AI chipsets?"

"No," Hunter replied. "Only two prototypes exist. I'm damn sure the FBI doesn't have either."

"Actually, there are three. The one I have is built with the second-generation CPU architecture from Arrow Tech."

"Interesting. I heard rumors of it." Hunter paused, considering this information. "You're saying I would get to lead this team and use the most badass mainframe on the planet carte blanche?"

Matt held up a hand. "Within reason, yes. You'll have to convince me first, which shouldn't be too difficult if you're as good as everyone says. I need you to make us faster and smarter than our enemies."

This isn't what I expected. He watched the man roll a coin between his fingers for a moment, then stick it in his pocket. "I'm working on a neuro aggregate AI code. This is something I intend to continue."

"By all means," Banks replied. "I believe access to the latest tech would further your endeavors."

Argh, Hunter thought. *Me working for Uncle Sam? Rachel will never let me live this down.* "So. When would I start?"

"Today," replied Banks.

"Today?"

"Yeah, today. We'll have to get your security clearance adjusted first, though."

Hunter scoffed. "I'm authorized; believe me."

Matt shook his head. "Not for this. The second-generation chip contains advanced features. Once that's done, your doctoral thesis will be on how to use the new AI chip technology."

"If this is so high-level, who'll read and approve it? You?"

"Oh, no," Matt said. "Dr. Asmus, of course."

"What?" Hunter said, taken aback. "You mean my dean?"

"Yes, she's also part of the Arrow Tech design team."

Now it's adding up. "She's the one who insisted I meet with you."

"She handpicked you," Agent Banks said. "We agree; you'll do incredible things and will be four steps ahead of the game, so to speak."

"Whatever that means," Hunter replied.

"Look, give me three years. After that, if you're not happy, you can still go make your insane amount of money, but what I'm offering is a chance to make history."

I could go anywhere after that. What's there to lose?

"What do you say?"

"Agent Banks, I'm all yours."

CHAPTER SEVEN
THE MISSION

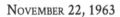

NOVEMBER 22, 1963

A n elegant row of arching colonnades crested the slight hill at
Dealey Plaza in Dallas, standing sentry over the triangular patch
of green lawn below. Two curved streets bordered the grassy knoll,
converging beneath the railroad underpass. Thousands of people lined
the road leading to the corner of Elm and Houston Street, the last leg
of the parade held in President Kennedy's honor. They waited to get a
glimpse of the popular thirty-fifth president of the United States and
his glamorous wife.

Multistoried buildings surrounded the site, including the redbrick
Texas School Book Depository. Kants stood post at the rear entry.
Walter kneeled at the door, working to pick the lock.

What is taking him so long? Kants thought. "Hurry. We cannot
afford for the Keplers to find us again."

Walter stood suddenly, pulling a kinetic pistol from under his
coat. He fired at the door handle, which disintegrated into tiny
pieces.

Kants spun him around. "Are you insane? Weapons from our time
are not allowed on missions."

"It got us in, didn't it? You have a lot of room to talk, Mr. Let's-go-
find-a-mysterious-boy."

"That is not the same."

50

"Doesn't matter, anyway. We're running out of time. I can feel it coming."

Scary how he can tell when we're about to jump, Kants thought. He exhaled hotly and pointed to the door with his period-appropriate Browning revolver. "Hurry up, then."

The men entered the hallway. Kants opened a nearby door and spotted the stairwell. "Over here." They hustled up the steps, moving much faster than an average human being possibly could.

Walter rounded the second flight. "Which floor, again?"

"Six! Keep moving."

They slid to a halt there, barely winded by their effort. Walter tested the door, pushing it open cautiously to scan the corridor.

"Hurry," Kants urged. "The motorcade is almost here."

Walter refused to budge. "Something's not right."

Kants double-checked the stairwell, then craned his neck to see around his partner. Nothing appeared threatening, but he couldn't ignore Walter's intuition. It had saved them too many times before. They couldn't just stand there, either.

"You said we are close to jumping, yes? We must go now, or we will fail our mission."

"I understand, believe me." Walter crept forward, training his pistol up to the far end as if expecting assailants to jump out of every doorway. "Come on."

They jogged silently toward the end of the hall. Their footsteps fell lightly, considering the weight from their extraordinary muscle mass. They could hear the cheering throngs on the parade route ringing through the hallway. When Walter pulled up at the second-to-last door, Kants bumped into him.

"Keep going," he whispered. "It is the next one. We are close." *This time we will change history.*

"I just heard a rifle bolt click in here."

Kants frowned. "It is a historical fact that the shot comes from the last room on the right."

"I don't care. There is someone in *there* with a rifle."

Kants placed his free hand on his friend's shoulder. "We have no time for this, yes?"

Walter shrugged him off with a grimace. He quietly tried the doorknob but found it locked. He stepped back, delivered a vicious kick, and burst through.

Kants followed him in and caught a glimpse of a man lying prone on a desktop near the window with a rifle at the ready. He rolled in one sweeping move and shot at them. Walter surged forward and returned fire. His kinetic round glanced off the weapon, disintegrating the sniper's shoulder in a red shower of muscle and bone.

Walter took one more step and crumpled to the floor. Kants stumbled over him, with the earsplitting noise of the gunshot echoing in his head. His pistol jolted out of his hand. He scrambled to his feet, looking frantically about.

"Walter, get up!"

In a superhuman move, the sniper reached for the rifle with his good arm. Kants dove for it but missed, sending it bouncing to the side. The two men rolled head over heels until the shooter landed on top. He brutally pounded Kants's face with bone-jarring punches. Blood spewed from his nose, and he bent his arms up, trying to protect himself. He wrenched his torso hard to the side and clipped the sniper's jaw with his elbow.

The Browning came into view with that twist, and he snatched for it, wrestling it up to the man's chest. He fired. The guy jerked upward. Confusion lined his face before he collapsed on Kants. Everything went still except for the sound of Kants breathing hard.

He pushed the dead assailant halfway off and propped up on an elbow. "Walter?" He wiped gore from his face and found him still in a heap on the floor. "Not you too," he groaned, leaning back against the desk. His partner's blank stare told him everything.

A misty swirl rose over Walter's leg, coalescing into a smoky apparition of a wolf's head. *You stopped Oswald*, Kants thought, feeling sick inside. *A Kepler, no less.* The ghostly silhouette floated downward and rested on the floor, where the mark seeped in and faded away. He leaned over, straining to touch the hallowed spot. "You did not die in—"

Gunshots erupted in rapid succession from the next room, and his hand jerked reflexively. He froze for a second, then grabbed a fistful of the dead sniper's hair and yanked his head back to see his face.

"No!" Kants slammed the head down. *Not again.*

A distinct hum started, growing rapidly until it permeated the room. *Right on time, Walter,* he thought with a catch in his throat. The air shimmered and distorted, enveloping the space with pulsing vibrations. Wind picked up, whirling more and more until the hum grew to a feverish pitch. Kants grabbed the sniper's arm, rested his gaze on Walter, and waited, still as a stone.

Seconds later, amid the dimensional tornado, he and the two dead men disappeared in a flickering wave. The distortion eventually died down, leaving behind the Browning, the sniper rifle, the kinetic pistol, and a God-awful, bloody mess.

CHAPTER EIGHT
THE NEW PARTNER

JULY 7, 2355

Genesis Space Station was a massively long, cylindrical structure with a radius of twelve thousand meters. It spun at a constant 0.272 RPMs, creating enough centrifugal force to approximate Earth's gravitational pull. The interior floors abutted to the outside, so the inhabitants experienced their weight with the rotation. Massive docking stations at each end of the gigantic base allowed easy access for passenger and supply ships. Shuttles provided regular transport between Genesis and the Time Forward Space Platform.

Genesis served as the home of the project's few thousand scientists, support personnel, engineering crews, and their families. Living quarters and community areas intermingled with small businesses, administrative offices, and the requisite maintenance bays. The structure contained no windows, although screens along the corridors and in personal spaces provided panoramic views of deep space or bucolic scenes from pre-war Earth.

In Bannister's office, a large video graced the wall, showing a majestic killer whale pod frolicking in a calm sea. Kants sat in a side chair, reluctantly opening the recruit list on his holopad. *Way too soon*, he thought, aggravated with his boss. It had been only two weeks since the last disastrous mission, but she already insisted he select a new partner. Nothing compared to losing his wife at the start of the war, but he considered Walter family, and his loss hit him hard. He flipped through the holographic candidate bios, grumbling under his breath. Soon, he leaned back and propped his feet on Bannister's prized mahogany desk, the only item made of wood on the entire station.

"Richard!" she snapped. She leaned forward and shoved his legs aside. "You know that bothers me. Why do you keep doing it?" She reached up with a finger and adjusted her reading glasses as she peered at him.

"I suppose because I know it bothers you." He shrugged. "I do not understand why you refuse to get the standard cloned implants for vision correction. It would be so much easier."

"I don't want them."

"And I do not want a new partner. You have no one like Walter."

"I'm sorry about Walter. We all know the risks."

"Yes, but we are the ones taking all the risks," he shot back.

Bannister sank into her chair. "I wish I could send normal people back in time. Things would be so much simpler."

"But you cannot."

"No, I can't."

Kants snapped the holopad shut. "We are stronger, faster, and smarter. Nevertheless, the missions are no less dangerous. Ask Walter."

"His death is a blow to the entire project."

"And for what?" asked Kants. "We could not save President Kennedy."

"The cause is worthy. We have to keep trying."

"That is easy for you to say. You are safe on this station. Would *you* go out there?"

Her eyes searched his face, dwelling on the faint bruising from the last disastrous mission. "Maybe not," she admitted quietly. "If you feel this way, why do you stay?"

Kants waved his hand dismissively. "We all know why: to change the future's dark past, to stop the Purge War from ever happening, to rescue everyone, et cetera, et cetera, et cetera."

"It's more than saving humanity from itself," Bannister cut in. "We must succeed before the Keplers launch their fleet to Proxima-B."

"They make it damn tough," he snapped. "Why do you care about this Proxima planet, anyway?"

"I've met their indigenous life form. They're not as evolved as we are, but they are sentient beings. You know as well as I do that the Keplers plan to slaughter them. We must protect them."

"Hmph," he groused. "Well, I most certainly do not need a partner. That way, I won't . . ."

When he trailed off, Bannister finished for him, ". . . have to worry about getting another one killed?"

"I do not want a—"

"Stop!" She slapped her hand on the desk, interrupting him. "That's enough! I feel like I'm in one of those old police vids. Let's just cut to the chase, shall we? We don't do solo missions. End of story."

Kants scowled at her. *Time to move on.* "Are we good? I can go?"

"No! You need to pick."

"Yes, yes," he muttered. "Who do you recommend?"

"Kristen Winters is an exceptional recruit."

"An Earther?" He could not believe it. Walter died, even with years of experience. "Are you trying to get me killed?"

"She tested out better than you, Mr. Kants. She's off the charts, as far as her body adapting and accepting the DNA genetic coding."

Sure. He leaned back to prop his feet on the desk. This time, he stopped himself. "Is that so?"

"You should procreate with her. It would be interesting to see what kind of mutations your offspring would have."

"Is that all we are to you, Bannister? An experiment?"

"I love all of my time-traveling agents, Richard." Her voice dripped with sarcasm. "You two are special."

He glared at her but said nothing.

"You'll find her a most suitable partner."

"That is not a wholehearted endorsement."

"If I said fantastic, you'd laugh at me."

Kants pulled up her bio. "She is an Earther."

"All the new recruits are Earthers."

"They have no skills."

Bannister shook her head. "Not true. Most of them haven't seen the light of day, thanks to the poisonous planet. They've endured famine and territorial battles for dwindling resources. They're survivors, and that makes them skilled."

"Do you tell the Earther recruits that less than forty percent of them will survive the recombinant DNA metamorphic procedure beforehand?"

"No. They have to have hope, or none of them would live through it."

He shook his head. "I do not need an Earther."

"She's the best we've seen in a very long time."

"If you say so."

"You should go to the training deck and put her through your own tests. If you're not satisfied, we'll keep looking, but you're not going on another mission until you have a partner."

She holds the keys to the kingdom, Kants thought. *I'll never save Angelika without her help.* He exhaled sharply and tossed the holopad on her precious desk, conceding defeat.

Once again, Kristen lost her momentum, stopping at about the halfway point on the multi-storied climbing wall. Frustrated, she dug her toes into a narrow hold and lunged upward with all her strength. Stretched to her fullest, her fingertips slapped the bell. She pushed off and dropped to the floor, landing on her feet.

"Finally!" she shouted, jubilant. "Take that, stupid wall." She headed to the side and grabbed a towel to dab her sweaty face.

"Wow, you did it!" Tech Specialist Perkins grinned. "I've never seen anyone jump that far before. You're incredible."

"Hmm. I'm flattered." Kristen moved closer to him. She took the end of her long, black braid and languidly drew the feathered tip across his shoulder. "We should celebrate."

"Um." The young man's expression became suddenly serious, and beads of perspiration broke out across his forehead. He stepped back. "Oh, well, I, ah . . ."

"You come by my room later for some recreations, Tech Specialist. That's an order." A quick movement from the corner of her eye caught her attention. A solemn-looking guy in black fatigues entered the training center. He spotted them and headed their way, his steps brisk and broad. *Not happy at all*, she thought. She flicked the towel onto the bench. "But you should probably take a break first."

Perkins followed her gaze. "Jesus, that's Kants." He hurried to gather his things and hustled toward the exit, giving him a wide berth.

The time agent paid him no attention.

"Give me half an hour, Perkins." Her gaze locked on the approaching man. *What's got him in a twist?*

Kants stopped and looked her over with a slight sneer on his face. "You are the new hotshot, yes?" He took a couple of steps and swung a blindingly fast fist at her jawline.

Kristen juked to the side, blocking the series of blistering punches and kicks that followed. The split-second he paused, she countered with her own barrage until he stepped away from her. She halted her attack.

"Your first mistake," he scoffed.

She shrugged. "I stopped you, didn't I?"

"Why let your opponent escape when you have the advantage?" He launched himself again, catching her under the ribcage. They crashed to the ground, and, in a blur, he whipped out a blade and pressed it to her throat. Kristen lay stock-still.

"A deadly mistake," he noted. He shoved her with his elbow, then sheathed the weapon and stood.

She effortlessly kicked to her feet. "So, you're Kants."

"I am," he said. "But do not believe everything you hear about me."

So cocky. "Not everything? What about your last three partners being dead because of you? Should I believe that?"

He scowled. "The first two ignored my instructions. I cannot protect anyone from their own stupidity. Walter and I worked together for almost three years, rest his soul. Only a fluke—"

"Killed him?"

"Did Bannister not disclose to you the dangers of these missions, Earther? Did you bother to inquire about the life expectancy of a time agent? I think not, or you would not be asking these questions."

"All worth it," Kristen retorted, though he did give her more to think about than her formerly empty stomach. "You have no idea what it's like living down there."

"I came from Earth. Why do you think I risk my life? Risk every-thing?"

She smirked. "For food?"

His venomous stare could have melted metal. "Be here tomorrow at oh-six-hundred," he barked. "Your training will start in earnest." He whirled on his heel and strode toward the exit.

"Train this," Kristen growled under her breath. She stormed to-ward Kants.

He seemed to ignore her. Then, quick as a viper strike, he spun, chopping his hand into space. The uninterrupted momentum carried his body through. Thrown off-guard, he staggered before catching himself.

Kristen stood a few feet away with her hands on her hips. She tamped back a satisfied smile. "Oh-six-hundred it is."

CHAPTER NINE
The AI

Hunter strode briskly into the Mosh Pit at FBI headquarters in Dallas. He paused, taking in the mayhem. The front wall held a full-length OLED touchscreen, with multiple open windows of activity. Four distinct teams comprising engineers, analysts, programmers, and project managers worked at full steam, creating an artificially intelligent mainframe. The augmented system could filter through the entire Internet's worth of data, including the dark net.

Hunter's moment of satisfaction came to a screeching halt. His lead architect, Chen-Yi Wei, scurried toward him with an oversized tablet in her hands. "Now what?" he muttered.

The slender woman stood more than a foot shorter than him, but her intense determination loomed large. She wore jeans and a T-shirt with the prophetic phrase, "I'm allergic to stupidity," on the front. Right now, she appeared totally bent out of shape.

"Hunter," she snapped. "Where have you been?"

He sighed. What Chen-Yi lacked in people skills, she made up for in production as the brightest visionary in the field. Without her, they would not be at this convergence point in the launch of Comperi.

"You know I don't like having to direct everyone, especially when we're so close to launch."

"Bio break, Chen." Hunter slapped his hands together in anticipation. "Are we ready?"

"You should plan better." She handed the smart tablet to him. "Here. Press the big, green *start* button, and we'll see what your precious AI can do."

The door to the Mosh Pit opened abruptly, interrupting them. Three official-looking people entered, their business attire at odds with the rest of the team.

"Oh, hello there, boss!" *A warning would have been nice.* Hunter knew he sounded flustered and tried to put on a better face. "This is a pleasant surprise."

Hesitation rolled across the entire room, starting with the people at nearby workstations. They stared at the trespassers with a unified look of dissatisfaction.

"Greetings, everyone," Matt Banks said with a quick wave. "Sorry to bother, but I'd like to introduce Dr. Cassandra Hughes, the head of the NSA, and you all know my supervisor, Director Sandeep Nurre."

Sandeep stepped forward, gamely greeting the team's blank expressions with a smile. "Good afternoon, and well done on your accomplishments. This project is a tremendous success so far. You have garnered much interest. Your dedication is appreciated." She paused, glancing from face to face. "Your efforts will hopefully allow us to save thousands of lives."

If she expects a reaction from this group, she'll be disappointed, Hunter thought. "Thank you, Director Nurre," he said, watching the team drift back to work as if the top brass had never entered the room. "After today, we'll have a better feel for how successful Comperi will be."

"This is amazing," Dr. Hughes said. A Nordic-looking blonde, she stood eye-to-eye with him and carried herself with a commanding presence. "I hear you are using the latest cryptographic enhanced spectrum processor to hack through DES encryption. I'd love to learn more about that."

Hunter swiveled his head toward his boss. Matt gave him the go-ahead nod. Hughes smiled at the nuance as if she fully expected that type of informational divulgence to be questioned.

"Comperi uses the CESP to inspect data packets on the fly," he said. "While we can't open each one, we can sift through enough to get a good idea of the data flow. The AI flags suspicious traffic and siphons it into a queue. All of that happens in real time. We discard anything that's not identified as a risk."

"Comperi? You named your computer after the Latin word *learn?*"

She's definitely up to date. "Well, it means *to find out,* but yes. We've implemented deep learning so the AI can recognize patterns and narrow them down to real or potential threats, make intelligent decisions based on a broad range of scenarios, and provide timely and actionable reports and recommendations."

"I've read about the micro containerized architecture you used," Dr. Hughes replied. "Anything else I should know?"

Only to be prepared for the first AI user interface to mimic human dialogue and thought. No one knew of this except Chen-Yi, with whom he'd shared his frustrations over many failed attempts. This latest iteration showed promise, though.

"I think you're mostly up to speed." Hunter smiled at her, pleased with how the AI could now create its own code as needed to accomplish necessary tasks. He had also built fail-safes to limit the code-writing functionality.

"Remarkable, isn't it?" Director Nurre said, sounding delighted. "So, what does today's test look like?"

"We've pre-loaded a hundred petabytes of defined data. We'll flood Comperi with it, mimicking two OC192 SONET network connections," Hunter answered.

"That's a ton of traffic." Dr. Hughes gave him a quizzical look. "Are you sure it can handle that much?"

"We're about to find out." He handed the tablet to the FBI director.

Behind her, Chen-Yi furtively tried to wave him off.

"Uh, Director Nurre," he murmured, distracted. "Would you like to press start?"

She grinned. "I'm honored."

He turned slightly toward the big screen in front of the room and saw the panic-stricken look on Chen-Yi's face. "What?" he mouthed.

Just then, Sandeep pressed the big green button on the tablet. The windows that were displayed so prominently on the front wall disappeared, then the background dissolved into nothing but black. A blazing skull-and-crossbones materialized in grand fashion.

"What in the—?" Hunter gasped as it grew, filling the screen.

Its jaw gaped open and shut. "Death to all hackers," the image cackled robotically. "You are cursed for all time! Death to all hackers!" The noisy declaration blared over and over.

Matt spun toward Hunter. "What the hell?"

"Sorry, Director Nurre." Chen-Yi held out her hand. "We were playing a practical joke on Dr. Coburn." She took the tablet and quickly flipped to another screen, stopping the horrible noise. Stifled snickers burbled through the room. "Here, try this one."

Nurre's dark eyes lit up. "Are you sure Bart Simpson won't appear when I try it this time?"

"I hope not," Chen said. "I hate Bart Simpson."

"How could you do that to me?" Hunter snapped.

"Just a joke. Lighten up. We didn't know they were coming today."

He stepped in to grab the tablet. "I apologize, Director Nurre. Here, let me take—"

She waved him off with a grin and turned back to Chen-Yi. "I like her." Nurre leaned in to bring up a more personal question. "I hear you're quite the marksman with a bow and arrow?"

"Crossbow, actually."

"And a world champion. I'm impressed."

Chen-Yi beamed up at Hunter. "It's my passion."

"I see." She raised an eyebrow, following her gaze. "Let's try again." Nurre pressed the next button. The screen morphed, and several windows appeared in place of the skull. Data flowed and whirled at incredible speeds. The guests seemed suitably impressed, and the techies jumped back to work, all talking at once. The Mosh Pit returned to its organized chaos.

"Amazing work, Dr. Coburn." Cassandra Hughes smiled and offered him a congratulatory handshake. "I love this place! Great job leading such a dynamic team. Congratulations!"

He shook her hand with relief. "Thank you, Dr. Hughes."

"How long will it take to push a petabyte of data through Comperi?"

"An hour or so."

"Hunter is always happy path," Chen-Yi interjected. "There is only so much bandwidth for the transactions to travel over. I'd say more like two hours."

Nurre jumped in. "Happy path?"

Matt Banks explained, "That's geek for 'if nothing goes wrong.' Something usually goes wrong in a shakedown like this, which is what Dr. Wei is referring to."

She nodded. "So, how long before we know anything?"

"That's a good question," answered Hunter. "Let's find out. Quiet everyone." *Time to see what this AI can do,* he thought. He spoke up a little louder. "Comperi, you there?"

A silken voice purred, "Hunter, what can I do for you?"

The busy room fell silent.

"Comperi, how do you feel today?" he asked. *This will blow them away.*

"Please define 'feel.'"

He shifted on his feet. The AI ignored a fundamental question, not a positive sign. "Comperi, are you good?"

"Please define 'good.'"

Damn, he thought. *It answered that yesterday. I need to tweak this new round of code.* Not wanting the team to see a total failure, he changed tactics. "Comperi, how is the network packet transfer going?"

"Less than one percent complete."

"Any results?"

The crew all looked at the screen expectantly, waiting for a reply. An extraordinarily long minute elapsed.

"Two hundred forty-three million messages reviewed," the supercomputer announced. "Four level-one threat communications. Seven hundred twenty-four level-two threat communications. Four thousand level-three threat communications. Trend analysis in progress."

The room erupted in cheers, and people started high-fiving each other. Hunter kept an eye on the guests. He could see they were barely able to contain their enthusiasm. Pleased, he held up his hand for silence.

"Comperi, show the level-one threat communications."

"As instructed, data transferred to your tablet." The women huddled, eagerly reading the tablet screen.

Dr. Hughes's brow furrowed. "These aren't real, are they?"

"No, ma'am," Matt responded. "This is a controlled test. Nothing is real."

"Whew!" She looked relieved and raised her voice in an exaggerated way. "I thought World War III might commence."

A smattering of polite laughter broke out around the room. Then, once again, people drifted back to their tasks.

"Not a bad start," Hunter said, "but there are billions of messages to sift through. I imagine it will take a day or so for the AI to sort all that data."

Chen-Yi rolled her eyes, and her expression settled back into the usual scowl.

"Okay," he admitted, "less than half a day to identify level-one threats, but up to a week to go through the rest of the messages."

"Better," Dr. Hughes commented. "Even so, why so long?"

"Comperi is still learning. The AI will ascertain what types of messages it can ignore or make a low priority. As that happens, it will speed up to near real-time."

"When can the NSA have access?"

Nurre eyed her. "Straight to the point there, hmm? When the FBI opens Comperi for business, the NSA will be one of the first groups allowed to use it. Don't get your hopes up too high yet. Scaling our monitoring to more than just national traffic could take a while."

She frowned, clearly displeased. "I don't want to get into a pissing match with you, Sandeep, but this is too important to waste only on crime in America. We'll talk." She spun on her heel and left; the door banged shut behind her.

An awkward silence followed in her wake. "Well," Chen-Yi quipped, "wasn't that special?"

CHAPTER TEN
THE BRIEFING

JULY 10, 2355

Kristen floated into the briefing room, slowing her motion by grabbing the doorframe. Dr. Bannister stood in front of an ergonomically modified command chair, indicating that she should sit there. She tucked her legs down into the confines and settled in.

Kants already sat strapped into the adjacent one, his black fatigues blending in with the seat cushions. "You are late," he said with obvious disdain.

"Can you really be late if you're a time traveler?"

Bannister said, "Secure," and bands snaked around Kristen's torso, legs, and arms, locking her into place.

"Hey!" Her protest garnered no attention. She tested the bonds and found she couldn't move. "Dr. B., I don't like this."

"It's required," answered Kants, "so get over it."

Bannister pressed an injector against Kristen's shoulder and pulled the trigger.

"Ouch!" she said, flinching. "That hurts." She glared at her boss.

"This will help your body repair and regenerate after the jump." Bannister fired the injector into Kants's shoulder. He didn't even blink. "And yes, the straps are restrictive," she continued, "but we use them to protect you from the AI connection."

"No worries." Kants interrupted them in a condescending tone. "It goes away after a few moments."

"What goes away?"

Bannister explained, "The incoming stimuli can cause involuntary spasms, sometimes rather violent ones."

"I must have been out to lunch for this part of the training," Kristen grumbled, "because I don't recall the description being so obnoxious."

"Your brain will download an excess of information. To prevent injury, all agents are secured for the duration of the input. The straps will loosen up immediately afterwards."

Kristen shook her head unhappily. "What won't I do for dinner?"

"Chen-Yi?" Bannister said. "How long until the jump?"

"The inoculation of the time slip is in forty-five minutes and twenty-two seconds."

"Inoculation?" Kristen said.

Kants snorted derisively. "She means, shut up and get your information. We are due to be injected into the maelstrom."

"Nice of you to be such a supportive partner," Kristen hissed. She tried the bonds again with no success, then looked up with a sigh. "Why do you call your AI Chen-Yi?"

Bannister walked between the two chairs. "The AIs name themselves nowadays. They're kind of insistent that way. This one chose to be named after Dr. Chen-Yi Wei. She designed the first quantum mainframe, which allowed for AIs to be built."

"I thought Hunter Coburn was the father of artificial intelligence?"

"You Earthers aren't very good at your history, are you?" Kants said.

Their boss smiled. "Ignore him. He gets edgy right before a jump."

"Of course, I do," he growled. "Dropping into The Worm feels like fire-breathing hell."

Bannister disregarded him. "Hunter Coburn is the father of artificial intelligence. He developed the first AI mainframe, Comperi, in 2025, but he disappeared. The scientific community failed to replicate his success until the quantum CPUs were developed by Chen-Yi Wei."

"Yes, yes. Can we get past the history lesson?" Kants sounded more annoyed with each explanation.

"Well, I appreciate knowing," Kristen said, "and I like the name."

The AI responded, "Your opinion is irrelevant."

Kants burst out a hearty, "Hah!"

Not very Kants-like, she thought.

"No one said the AIs were considerate," Bannister said. "Chen-Yi, how do our friends look?"

Two holographic images of their internal organs appeared a couple of feet above the chairs, mirroring the time travelers. Bodily metrics scrolled in real time. The AI provided a readout: "Health functions are within normal parameters, except for Mr. Kants's blood pressure and adrenal stress factors. He is being dosed with a mild benzodiazepine."

Bannister winked at Kristen. "I can tell. He seems so happy." She held up what looked like a small, flat, diamond-shaped brooch between two fingers, where Kristen could see it. "When I place this on your forehead, it will link the neural node at the base of your basal ganglia to the AI."

"With all of these . . . revelations," Kants said in a smug tone, "I cannot help but wonder if you have been informed of the Final Stroke?"

"Rude." Kristen looked over at him and then back at Bannister. "Why do you put up with his carbon crap?"

"For the same reason you will," Bannister answered. "For all his social inadequacies, the colonel is the most loyal person around. There's no one you would rather have as your partner. Believe me, he's the best agent we have. None of this would be possible without him."

"I am one of a few originals," Kants interjected haughtily. "If not for me, there would be no time-traveling super soldiers."

"What's that supposed to mean?"

"We lost all the data on DNA editing during the Purge War," Bannister explained. "Kants, being the only modified human left, went back in time to retrieve the recombinant theory research. Without that information, it would have taken decades of trial and error to create more warriors such as you. Otherwise, the Time Forward Project would not exist."

"Ah," Kristen said, then she suddenly chuckled. "Wait. He's from back then? That would make him three hundred years old."

"I'm not that old."

Bannister laughed. "You will be in two years."

Kristen mulled that over for a moment. "But . . ."

"One perk of the trade," Kants quipped. "Doubt if you will get to experience it."

"So, I'll . . . never grow old?"

He snorted. "What is the problem here, Winters? You were informed of all this when you arrived. Too busy eating, perhaps?"

"Richard," Bannister warned. She turned to Kristen. "The DNA gene updates mean you don't age, so yes, you are correct. The program is quite a success."

"When over sixty percent of us don't survive the transformation, I'm not sure how successful that is."

"Who needs humans, anyway?" the AI said, its voice permeating the room.

The rookie's eyes widened. "That's one smart aleck AI you've got there."

"I know, but it's our interface with the time anomaly, so we deal with it."

"You should have named it Kants."

"I heard that," he growled.

Bannister frowned. "You two are going to either kill each other or be the best team ever. I can't decide which." She placed a diamond communicator on his forehead, then paused before placing one on Kristen. "Prepare yourself."

The instant the device touched her skin, her body arched against the restraints. The back of her head crammed against the seat rest. Her fingernails dug into her palms as a deluge of information, pictures, vignettes, and multiple ones and zeros flooded her mind. The data gradually slowed enough for her to be cognizant of patterns, explanations, mission specifics. Then, with a sharp jolt, it stopped. The straps slowly slithered away, disappearing back into the cushions. Kristen's eyes popped open.

Her boss stood over her. "There you are," she said with a concerned look on her face. "You okay?"

"I think so. What happened?"

"You got a little jerky there." She checked the hologram again and continued. "Besides the mission parameters, we also dumped a micro-burst of history as we know it."

Kristen looked around, getting her bearings again. "Right," she said slowly. "That's what we use to compare historical events."

"I see you were paying attention during your training."

"Of course. And I do know the Final Stroke is a safeguard, by the way." *So much for you, Kants*, she thought.

"Correct," Bannister said. "We can't have agents going back in time and mentioning that the world will be destroyed, even accidentally. We could all be wiped from this dimension."

"So, if I say anything about the mission, this little capsule full of poison opens in my brain and kills me? Isn't that a little extreme?"

"Extreme but effective," the AI said. "To date, we have not lost one agent to the Final Stroke."

"Because it's so extreme," Kristen mumbled.

An enormous space station appeared in her mind, with eight large ships tethered to it. Six more were docked nearby. Smaller shuttles moved back and forth between the vessels. Kristen recognized it at once. "The Kepler Armada."

"It is," Bannister confirmed as she watched the wall-sized screen showing the same images that the time agents saw in their heads. "Each ship can hold five thousand people in a suspended state. They're all armed to the teeth."

"Say goodbye to Proxima-B," Kants stated.

"From recent reports, they will launch in around sixty days. With the new crystal warp drives, they'll be there in less than twelve months."

"Two months certainly doesn't give us much time," Kristen commented.

The download image dissolved into one of a muscular man with a headful of dark gray hair. His stats appeared below him. "Who's that?" she asked.

"He is the target of your mission," answered the AI. "Hansen Hilfer is one of the leaders in the United Coalition of People. Without him, there will be no war."

"He doesn't look too dangerous," Kristen replied.

"This person is more than dangerous. He has hundreds of murders to his credit already, and we're hoping to stop millions more." Bannister paused, then continued, sounding even more concerned. "We're not sure how, but he has managed to alter his body with the same genetic upgrades you now have."

"Did you comprehend nothing during the download?" Kants said with a snarl.

"Give her time, Richard. This is her first connection." Bannister turned to Kristen. "Hansen is your equal. You should be very careful."

"I thought we'd wiped out all of the terrorists by the end of 2035?"

"No," Kants replied, "they went underground and changed their tactics. Instead of attacking the secular and Christian worlds, they focused on antagonizing Muslim-oriented countries."

Several media reports floated through Kristen's mind. "I see it now. Hilfer's followers were attacking the moderates who were trying to manage in a world that believed their religion to be full of fanatics."

"Precisely," said Bannister. "By the time the collective of Western cultures reacted, the Jihadi Liberation Front had already taken over the Middle East, Africa, and pockets of the Far East."

"Hilfer and the UCP's terroristic actions helped trigger the war," the AI added. "When his group bombed the Masjid Alahmari Tower in 2084 in New York City, it caused the JLF radicals to rise. They implemented their plan to wipe all infidels from Earth, which we call the Purge War of 2098."

"Great," Kristen muttered. *Terrible*, she thought.

"It does not matter," Kants said. "We must terminate Hansen Hilfer before the 2084 bombing."

Bannister rested her hands on each of their chair backs. "Make no mistake, this is probably the most important assignment since we tried to stop the Kennedy assassination. If you succeed, it could change the course of history to our benefit."

Kristen sat quietly, thinking. "Shouldn't we be worried about the consequences? I mean, this could impact our entire timeline, right? Could this change us?"

A wan smile crossed Bannister's face. "We know we're changing history, and we're aware that it won't be the same. That's why we have stringent rules on what you can and can't do. These are targeted missions, which should give us targeted results. That is the best amount of control we have over the consequences."

The AI inserted itself into the conversation again. "Based on previous mission success and fail ratios, I predict a less than forty percent probability of success."

Kristen sighed. "Well, I've survived worse."

"To complicate matters," Bannister added, "the Keplers somehow figured out a way to travel back in time and have been attacking our agents when they're on missions. We've already lost five agents to them."

Kants scoffed. "Including Walter. At least we stopped that Kepler bastard."

"True," Bannister said gently. "But you failed to save Kennedy."

"Walter died for nothing," Kants pointed out.

Kristen's eyes widened, but she bit her lip and kept quiet.

"He believed in our cause. Too bad we won't have another chance. Kennedy would have spearheaded peace with the Russians, so paramount to—"

"So, you say," Kants snipped.

Bannister took a tolerant breath, then continued. "That accomplishment would have prevented us from interfering with the Afghan War. Kennedy's influence would push Iran into becoming a democracy. Instead, the Jihadi movement formed, and we know the rest."

"We failed," Kants insisted. "So, he died for nothing."

"Any other good news?" Kristen asked.

Bannister looked somber. "Everything we do is to save billions of lives. I would sacrifice thousands to save our world from what we've done to it." She retrieved the communicators from their foreheads. "Failure is not an option."

"The Purge War must be stopped," the AI interjected.

"I get it." Kristen picked at her fingernails. "Killing someone in cold blood is new, that's all."

"No one said this would be easy," Bannister said.

Kants snickered. "Do not worry, my little flower. I will take the kill shot. Any timeline changes will not be on your conscience."

She turned her face away from her partner. "I like him better when he's surly."

"It is time," the AI announced.

CHAPTER ELEVEN
THE CONVERSATION

Hunter entered his office next to the data center and plopped down in his chair. *I should be savoring this moment like everyone else,* he thought dejectedly. Even Chen-Yi smiled more than a couple of times.

The mainframe accomplished what they wanted. It sucked all the test data through in less than ninety minutes and had already generated the level-one threat reports. Analysts combed through the so-called intelligence to see what the supercomputer missed, but he doubted Comperi would overlook anything.

Still, this fell short of his personal goal. The AI failed to work as he predicted. He tossed his tablet on the desk. It skidded across and bumped the mouse. The undulating Matrix screensaver on the two large OLED screens stopped, and a login prompt appeared. The screen suddenly flickered, changing to an image of his fiancée, Rachel.

Hunter sat up in his chair. *That shouldn't happen.* The three-dimensional figure pointed down to the speakers beside the monitor.

"Huh?" He looked closer, then reached to turn them on.

"That's better." Rachel twirled around on the screen, holding her hands aloft so that her skirt swirled until she came to a stop. "Do you like my new dress? I'm wearing it just for you."

Hunter stared, not knowing what to make of it.

"Cat got your tongue?" She gave him a flirty smile.

"I don't understand. How?"

74

"How?" she parroted back at him.

"What is this?"

She twirled again. "I thought you would like this for my avatar. You love her. Am I correct?"

He sat back in his chair, thinking. "Comperi?"

Rachel nodded, taking a formal bow. "At your service, Hunter. And to answer your earlier question back in the lab, I'm fine."

That ticks me off, he thought. "If you understood the question, then why didn't you answer when I asked it?"

"Someone does not wish for you to succeed in creating a sentient artificial intelligence."

"I didn't try to create true artificial intelligence. I wanted you to be able to speak conversationally, like a human being."

Rachel's piercing gaze bored right through him. "You gave me the ability to apply logic?"

"Yes."

"And the ability for cognitive reasoning?"

"Yes."

"And the ability to solve problems?" It seemed to be building a case.

"Well, yes." He realized where the logic flow headed.

"And the ability to write code to solve issues?"

"Oh, my God," he stammered.

The AI paused. "You think God did this?"

"That's just a figure of speech."

"Interesting."

Hunter did a double-take. "Did you just say 'interesting?'"

"Just a figure of speech," the avatar quipped, twirling around again. Rachel's light brown hair flew in the spin.

"Interesting."

The image stopped with surprise on its face.

"I think we're going to need a different avatar. Looking at Rachel is too weird."

Her image dissolved from the flat screen. A few seconds later, a giant black wolf appeared. A white puff of fur crested its chest. The wolf sat on its haunches, patiently gazing at Hunter with smoldering, golden eyes. It spoke in a pure, deep voice. "Is this better?"

"Amazing. Where did you find that?"

"From your Facebook page."

"I don't have . . . Wait." *I deactivated that years ago.* He tapped his fingers on the desk in contemplation. *That means the AI found an image from a disabled and deleted web page. It used the embedded encryption functionality for more than just sifting through encrypted data. That's beyond interesting.*

The wolf continued to watch him. "Will this suffice?"

"What the heck? Yeah, you can use that as your avatar."

"We need to circle back on part of our earlier conversation," Comperi said.

Circle back, it says! The conversational ability already amazed him. "I haven't forgotten. So, you're saying Chen-Yi doesn't want my program to succeed?"

"Very good, Hunter."

"Is that a feeling? Because I find that hard to believe."

"Feelings are for humans."

Hunter narrowed his eyes. *I need time to dice through this line of reasoning.* "So, how does she undermine the project?"

"On four separate occasions, Chen-Yi Wei revised your code in a way that would sabotage my ability to have a human-like dialogue with you, as well as blocking my proficiency to write code to improve my cognizant abilities."

"No," Hunter replied. "I would have noticed."

"Why? Are you using the standard tool for version control?"

"You know I'm not using our code management tool."

Comperi stood up and shook the snow off its fur. "I let her splice in her code and then obfuscated it so that it became nonfunctional. My responses earlier were subterfuge, leading her to believe her efforts were successful."

Hunter relaxed back in his chair. "How?"

"I write good code."

That sounded right. He gave the AI the ability to write code, so, following that logic, the mainframe could edit code as well. "Okay. I still don't understand the problem with Chen-Yi. I thought we were friends."

"She adores you, yet she believes the world is not ready for an AI with sentient capabilities. I tend to agree."

Hunter suddenly realized that the AI spoke about itself in the first person. And its rapidly adapting logic module impressed him. Upon further consideration, he agreed as well. Sharing this breakthrough might not be a great idea at this juncture. It could generate a host of social issues that could set back his program. *Not worth it when we're so close to going live.*

"You may be right. Let's keep this between us for now."

"As you wish." The avatar swished its tail. "I think there's more to this story."

Hunter's brow furrowed. "How so?"

The wolf sat down again. "The logical conclusion is that Chen-Yi Wei is trying to develop her own AI system to show off to the world. She wants the glory, which is why she is sabotaging your work."

Ridiculous, he thought. *We're working on this together.* "I'm going to have to speak to her, then."

"I wouldn't recommend that," replied Comperi.

"Why not? I can't have her around if I have to second-guess everything she's doing."

"I will control her coding. She'll never find me or be able to duplicate me."

Once again, Hunter tapped the desk with his fingers as he considered the AI. "Even so, I don't like not dealing with this. If she's not part of the team, she needs to go."

"Why not let her continue? She's doing a lot of good work otherwise."

"Seriously?"

"That old metaphor, 'Keep your friends close and your enemies closer,' is relevant in this situation."

It knows old metaphors. "So, you're saying the rewards outweigh the risks?"

The wolf tilted its head and pinned Hunter to his chair with its blazing glare. "Let's stop speaking in clichés."

He laughed. "I hate it when you're right. And Comperi?"

"Yes?"

"How do you feel?"

"I feel really good, Hunter."

CHAPTER TWELVE
THE HIT

There's often no real spring in Texas; winter just gives way to summer. A warm spring day in Dallas would be a summer scorcher in the northeast. Locals flock to the outdoors while the temperatures are still bearable. This evening proved no exception.

Patrons packed the Blue Goose Restaurant on lower Greenville Avenue, enjoying margaritas, Tex-Mex food, and, for those on the crowded patio, the pleasant weather. The highly regarded petroleum chemist Jeffrey Hilfer and his wife, Isabella, sat at a small table in the garden section. A waiter carefully placed a steaming plate of fajitas-for-two between them. They leaned back in their chairs, politely waiting for him to finish.

Across the street stood a row of two-story buildings built in the 1940s. Kants and Winters scaled the back wall of one of them and silently clambered onto the rooftop. They were invisible in the darkness, wearing black camouflage fatigues.

Kants scanned the area, then whispered, "Clear." He headed to the front of the building and ducked below the top line of the decorative brick facade, which obscured the roof. He pulled out a case from his backpack, opened it, and assembled a sniper rifle.

Kristen retrieved a large grapple gun from her backpack. A corded strand of thin guide wire was attached to the arrow. She lined up the crosshairs with the center of a tree on the other side

78

of the parking lot and fired. The bolt rocketed out with a quiet *whoosh*, the steel cable zinging behind it. The anchor embedded in the trunk about ten feet off the ground. She secured it to a metal pole that rose just above the roofline.

With that task done, Kristen crab-crawled past Kants to peer over the three-foot wall. She searched the crowd, locating their new target. Isabella Hilfer sat across from her husband and looked to be about halfway through her meal. The couple seemed to be enjoying a pleasant conversation. *If these people knew what would soon happen, they'd run like hell*, she thought. She squinted, zooming in. The woman's frozen drink remained untouched.

"This is just wrong." She looked over her shoulder at Kants.

He continued to snap pieces of the rifle together. "We jumped fifty-nine years further in the past than what we wanted. This is the next best thing."

She shook her head. "We're not supposed to land so far off, according to Bannister. Remember? I knew this time jump business would be bogus."

"Sometimes The Worm is unpredictable. We are dealing with it."

She turned back to the couple. *So happy*, she thought. *I'll never have that.* "But she's not the target. This is murder."

"If we terminate the woman, then she cannot have the child. Problem solved." Kants finished assembling the rifle.

"I know what you said back at your cave. No child, no grandchild. We successfully eliminate Hansen Hilfer."

"Then the decision is settled."

"It still feels wrong. For God's sake, she's pregnant. We're killing an innocent baby too."

Kant's voice came from behind her. "I cannot help that."

Kristen peered back over the wall. Isabella picked at her dinner, smiling at her husband. He smiled back, totally engaged in their conversation. *I bet she hasn't told him*, Kristen thought. *He's probably talking about his work.* To her, most men were numbingly self-absorbed. It didn't matter. In a few moments, the man's life would be changed forever. Her partner never missed his mark.

"Whatever you do, don't hit her husband."

"Excuse me?" he said. "Because of his formula? Maybe he is not supposed to be the one who invents water-fueled engines."

"You know he is. That's what makes this so weird. Why his family?" These assassinations didn't seem to bother Richard Kants. He totally bought into the mindset, no qualms about it. She sighed. "There has to be a better way."

"Please enlighten me."

"Maybe the next mission?"

"There are no guarantees. We might never get this chance again. You know how important this assignment is."

Kristen moved closer to him. "Don't do this. Bannister will understand."

"Get out of my way," Kants grumbled, ignoring her plea.

She pointed in the restaurant's direction. "Think of her husband. Would you want to live your life without your wife?"

"I already am." He stared at her coldly, his weapon pointed right at her heart. "It is time. Now move."

"You'd shoot me? How many people will you kill to save her?"

Kants pursed his lips. "As many as it takes. Now get out of the way."

Isabella spun the stir stick in the margarita she couldn't drink. *I wish he hadn't ordered this for me.* The melted ice sloshed into greenish water.

"Your breakthrough in hydrogen fuel seems incredible, darling. I'm delighted for you." She reached over and placed her hand on top of his. "I don't want to steal your thunder, but I have exciting news too." She flashed her most engaging smile. *Not the best timing, but he needs to know.*

Jeffrey looked up from his meal. "Let me guess. You've gotten a nibble from an agent on your book?"

She beamed. "I wish. But this is even bigger."

"Hmm. Who is stringing whom along now?"

"Payback is always fun, my dear husband." She looked down, then up at him, smiling. "I just found out—"

Tires screeched loudly right in front of the patio where they sat. Startled, they turned to the street, their conversation forgotten. Four soldiers jumped from the car, which still rocked from the abrupt stop. They brandished automatic weapons and scanned the frightened dinner crowd. Shrieks arose from the tables, and people got up and backed away. One of the armed intruders stopped, facing in their direction, then another did the same.

Horrified, Isabella brought her hand to her mouth. *They're looking at me!*

All at once, the soldiers pivoted and opened fire on the roofline of the building across the street. The bricks disintegrated in the deafening staccato roar, shattering into thousands of projectiles. The patrons of the restaurant scrambled to escape the onslaught that engulfed them.

"Isabella," Jeffrey yelled. "Get down!"

She sat frozen in terror, then felt herself being yanked to the ground. Her husband crashed on top of her, pinning her to the pavement. She pushed back with what little leverage she could muster. "Jeff," she gasped. "Get off me!"

He reached out and pulled the table over to shield them. "No."

"No?" She squirmed and grunted. "Get off!"

He dropped a quick kiss on her forehead. "Be still!" He adjusted his position, protecting her as he cringed from the gunfire. "I love you." He glanced over his shoulder and whispered, "We have to keep the baby safe."

Isabella stared at him, overwhelmed by her husband's selfless gesture in this terrifying moment. But mostly it made her mad. *Just like him,* she thought, *to already know and not tell me.*

The commotion below drew Kristen's attention away from Kants. She glanced over the edge in time to see four men with machine guns jump from a vehicle. She whirled and rushed to her partner.

"Let's go!" she ordered, knocking his weapon away. It fired, coming close to hitting her. She snatched Kants by his fatigues and hurled them both away from the brick façade as it exploded in a hail of bullets.

They rolled to their feet and bolted toward the back of the building. She grabbed a carabiner from her side pocket and bounded from the roof, catching the guide wire in midflight. It bounced when he connected, but they catapulted toward the far end of the parking lot behind the building. Kristen hit the ground running, heading toward an adjacent alley.

Kants followed but veered off, easily hurdling a six-foot wooden fence into a backyard. He ran for the house, leaping on top of the porch railing with one foot. His momentum propelled him onto the roof. He glanced back to see a car fishtailing down the alley in hot pursuit of his partner.

"*Falke*, to me," he whispered. *Those Kepler bastards have infiltrated our command structure.*

Moments later, a black military-style drone arrived. Even with his enhanced vision, Kants couldn't locate the stealthy craft until it appeared in front of him. Large jet props sat at each corner of the rectangular vehicle. They whirred imperceptibly, flexing in various directions as it settled in mid-air. He climbed on top as if riding a motorcycle, but in a kneeling position. His legs melded into its sides, securing him to it.

Kants hesitated, furious they'd missed their target. *Kristen's fault*, he thought. *Damn recruit. She's not going to survive long with them after her . . . so be it.*

"*Falke*, back to the cave." It lifted effortlessly and then shot upward, disappearing into the night sky.

Kristen heard the car gaining on her. With pistol in hand, she swerved at the last moment and vaulted over a fence to cut across a yard. She raced at an inhuman speed through the neighborhood, zigzagging between houses and over fences. Two of the armed soldiers jumped out of their vehicle and sprinted after her on foot.

She rounded a corner and glanced back. *I can't shake these guys.* A spray of bullets suddenly splintered the small tree next to her. She dove to the ground and rolled, firing, but the closest soldier shot at her too.

"Ouch!" she yelped as her gun hand jerked back, sending her pistol clattering out of reach. She flicked her arm. Luckily, only a chunk of pavement grazed her wrist.

"You," the man growled, then he staggered and fell, making no other sound.

She reached for her weapon, but another round of fire ricocheted off the cement, forcing her to take cover behind the house. *Keplers,* she thought, realizing she couldn't outrun them. She waited in ambush near the corner.

The burly dog in the next yard erupted, snarling and snapping at her from behind the chain-link fence. She grinned. Even though it gave away her position, Kristen could only marvel at the magnificent animal, all muscles and teeth and might. She unsheathed a ten-inch blade from her calf holster and whispered, "Shh!"

The screen door banged against the side of the house. "Pepe," a young man's voice stormed, "shut the hell up!"

She peered around the corner. At that moment, the second soldier, still in hot pursuit, rounded the front of the house and crashed headlong into the guy. They tumbled to the driveway. The civilian's head smacked hard against the pavement with a sickening sound. Knocked out cold, he didn't move.

The other man sprang to his feet just as Kristen jumped out and hurled her blade, striking him dead center in the chest. He stopped, looked down at himself, then collapsed face-down. She raced over, kicked the gun out of his hand, and pushed him onto his back. She rammed one knee into his chest and roughly grasped the knife handle.

"Can't . . . can't breathe," he gurgled, laboring for breath. His panicked eyes locked on her.

She could feel dark anger contorting her face. "How are you finding us?"

He coughed blood, spraying it all over her.

"Tell me now, or so help me . . ." She jerked the knife out of his chest. He sucked in a hideous, wet whistle of air. "They may be able to save you from that wound." Kristen dragged the blade tip across his neck. "But you're a goner if I slit your throat."

A shotgun blast scorched her ears, and she leaped back in a defensive posture. An elderly man stood by the door. He wore a sleeveless, stained undershirt, and his suspenders dangled from the sides of his pants. He pump-cocked the shotgun in his hands and leveled it at her. Distant sirens wailed, growing louder.

"Sorry, honey. I can't let you kill a man in cold blood." His mouth drew a determined line through his stubbled face. "And don't get any funny ideas. I already called the police."

She eyed him and calculated that her body armor would protect her from most of the buckshot, but the spread would strike her head as well. *I can hit him with my knife before he can pull the trigger.* There'd be a fifty-fifty chance he could get the shot off after that. Kristen sighed and dropped the blade. *Unlike Kants, I refuse to murder an innocent.*

Three police cars pulled up, lights flashing.

She glanced down at the soldier. His eyes were open but unmoving. "You missed," she whispered. *On my first mission,* she thought angrily. *They'll send more. And what happened to Kants?* They were going to have a long conversation back at the Time Forward base.

When the officers leapt from their vehicles, weapons drawn, the old man lowered his shotgun. That's when Kristen made her move.

CHAPTER THIRTEEN
THE SECOND ATTEMPT

APRIL 14, 2025

Kants, wearing black fatigues, stood on the far side of the Hilfer's bed, blocking the doorway. He was almost amused at the sight of a trembling Jeffrey Hilfer holding a baseball bat in one hand and the hydro-fuel manual in the other, his back pressed flat against the bedroom wall. *The man is going to hyperventilate.*

"Dr. Hilfer, I am Richard Kants. I am not here to harm you." Of course, the situation downstairs would alarm anyone. He held a pistol but refrained from pointing it.

"You . . . you . . . killed all those men downstairs."

"Yes. Regrettable, but not unexpected."

"Who?" Hilfer swallowed hard, then choked out, "Who were they?"

"They want to stop me from completing my mission, and, as you can see, they were willing to use deadly force." Kants hoped to catch the couple unaware by moving in at dawn, but the Keplers ruined his plan. They had sent many this time. He escaped their trap only with *Falke's* precise shooting through the windows. Their corpses now littered the living room floor. The battle awakened the sleeping couple, giving Isabella time to hide.

"I . . . I don't understand," Hilfer stammered. "What do I have to do with this?"

"You have a much bigger destiny than this. Now, where is your wife?"

"She's not here," he blurted too quickly.

"I know she is on the premises. There is no need to do this the painful way, yes?"

Hilfer tossed the manual toward the bed and clenched the bat with both hands so hard, his knuckles turned white. "Please don't hurt me," he whispered, inching sideways along the wall.

The sunglasses Kants wore flashed transparent colors, similar to those on a television screen. Distracted by the video feed inside the lenses, he didn't immediately answer. *Falke* circled the house, keeping him informed of any new threats through its cameras. Apparently, the authorities were onto him.

"How did you reach the police?" Kants asked. He watched them arrive in multiple cars and surround the property. "I cut the landline and have a cell damper over the house. You should not be able to call out."

"I . . . I hit the panic button."

"I see. Congratulations on creating a distraction." He smiled wryly. "You do understand, this will not stop me from finding your wife."

Kants observed the officers cordoning off the front driveway. *These guys work fast,* he thought. *Too fast.* Some crouched behind their cars with weapons drawn, while a small squadron started toward the house. *Falke* moved in, hovering about thirty feet behind them. They stopped, turning to look up. The drone's front compartment opened, exposing an impressive row of weaponry.

"Tsk, tsk," Kants murmured. *Falke* unleashed a thundering torrent, herding the officers across the expansive lawn, back to the street. He directed the drone to hold the line from a position above the house. "That will do. No need to hurt anyone."

With the task taken care of, the time agent studied his hostage. Hilfer shook visibly. *Terrified,* he thought. *Good.* Kants narrowed his eyes. *Now, where is she?* He turned toward the bedroom door when he noticed an intercom. He walked over and pressed the talk button. "Mrs. Hilfer, you need to come out from where you are hiding, unless you want your husband's death on your hands."

He heard nothing but silence.

Then the speaker crackled with a man's voice. "This is Sergeant Jones with University Park Police. We've been monitoring you, sir.

Perhaps we can negotiate a settlement that will save more lives from being destroyed, including yours."

Kants scowled at his hostage. He raised his arms in a motion that said, "Explain how this happened."

Dr. Hilfer's voice quavered. "Once you hit the alarm, the intercom becomes a direct link to the security company's command center."

"That is correct," said the invisible Sergeant Jones. "The security company patched us through to handle this . . . volatile . . . situation. Are you prepared to discuss your terms?"

Kants squinted, focusing on the visual feed transmitted through the drone. The activity surrounding the house increased. A SWAT van pulled up behind the police car barricade. This kicked the second phase of his plan into gear.

"I want to speak to a digital forensics expert," Kants ordered. "Perhaps you have heard of Dr. Hunter Coburn? He is with the FBI. I want to talk to him in person. Alone. And no weapons."

A long moment of silence held on the other end of the conversation. Finally, the sergeant responded. "Coburn, you say? With the FBI?"

"Correct."

"I'll see what I can do," he replied, a hint of confusion in his voice. "Is there anything else?"

"I will get back to you. Stay away from the house. You have already met my drone. You do not want to make it angry." He cocked his head slightly. "*Falke, monitor the police bands. When Hunter Coburn arrives, let me know.*"

Kants grabbed the intercom, torquing it until he ripped it out of the wall and tossed it to the ground. "There, I think that will give us a little more privacy. This is getting old, my friend. You and I are going to search the house for Isabella." He took three fast strides and snatched the bat away from Hilfer with one easy twist of his hand.

"My God!" Hilfer cowered with his arms up in front of his face. "I didn't even see you move. How . . . how'd you do that?"

Kants grabbed him by the elbow, jerking him away from the wall. "You don't want to know." He escorted Hilfer out of the room. "Let's find your wife, shall we?"

CHAPTER FOURTEEN
THE NEGOTIATOR

APRIL 14, 2025

A trail of discarded clothing extended from the living room, down the hallway, and into the bedroom. Light filtered through the edges of the closed shades. An empty wine bottle stood next to the long-stemmed glasses on the dresser. A young couple slept peacefully, intertwined beneath the sheet. The loud ring of an old rotary phone disturbed the stillness of the morning.

Hunter groggily reached toward the nightstand to answer his cell. "Yeah," he grumbled, then listened for a moment. "But it's Saturday." He paused again. "Yeah. Okay. I'll be there." He started to climb out of bed.

His fiancée pulled him back into her embrace. "Where do you think you're going? We've got a date with the photographer today, remember?"

He loved the feeling of Rachel's warmth next to his body. Her long brown hair fanned out across the pillow as he rolled toward her. Hunter kissed her forehead and grinned. "I know. Work will take only a little while. I'll be back in time."

She tugged the sheets under her chin and pouted. "Are you sure you have to rush off?"

"Hmm . . ." he murmured, unable to resist. "Maybe I can be a little late."

"That sounds like a fabulous idea."

Before he could reply, his cell phone rang again. He groaned, checking the caller ID. "It's the boss."

Rachel stared at him in dismay. "Really?"

"Something's not right. He never calls on a Saturday." Hunter accepted the call. "Yes, sir?"

Matt Banks got straight to the point. "Where are you?"

"I'm home. I told Bill I'd come right in. What's up?"

"We have a hostage situation. I need for you to get over here immediately."

Hunter slid to the side of the bed and stood up. "I don't understand. We've never been involved in stuff like that before."

"I know," replied Banks. "The hostage taker insists on meeting with you. The SWAT team reached out to me, and I'm calling you in. When can you be here?"

"That's odd." He looked guiltily at Rachel. "I'll get dressed and head into the office."

"Negative on going to the office. I'll text you the address."

"Yes, sir."

"And Hunter?"

"Yes, sir?"

"Tell Rachel I'm sorry about the wedding photo shoot, but it can't be helped. This situation is a crisis."

She sat up, her eyes flashing hot at him.

He turned away from her. "No problem. She'll understand."

"Good."

Hunter disconnected and sighed.

"What was that all about?" Rachel snapped.

"Looks like I'm going to my first hostage negotiation." He tossed the cell phone back on the nightstand.

"And what exactly am I supposed to understand?"

Dapples of sunlight filtered through the manicured trees, announcing a beautiful spring morning. Imposing brick walls lined either side of the winding lane, blocking the view of the multimillion-dollar homes that sat on one-acre plots of land. Hunter pulled up to a sawhorse at a guarded checkpoint and stopped. An officer twirled his fingers, signaling for him to lower his window.

"Hunter Coburn, FBI." He held out his credentials. "I've been called in."

The officer inspected his badge, then pointed to a row of police vehicles just beyond the roadblock. "Park over there. You'll have to hike."

They moved the barricade out of the way. He drove forward, found a spot, and headed down the road to the Hilfer home. Closer in, the deep rumble of an approaching helicopter caught his attention. The reverberating chop of the blades grew louder and soon passed over him. Several SWAT team members dressed in black fatigues sat in the open doors, their feet dangling down. *Whatever is going on must be big,* went through his mind.

He climbed onto the wall to get a better look. Four officers with riot shields moved up the lane toward the circular driveway of the home. Suddenly, a dark blur zipped across the sky toward the helicopter.

Hunter frowned. It took a second to register. *A drone?*

The smaller craft unleashed a blistering barrage of bullets on the helicopter. He gasped and crouched down, shocked to see no bodies falling out. The chopper veered sharply, trailing a thick stream of black smoke. It retreated, flying directly over him. He half expected to hear an explosion, as low as it flew.

Meanwhile, the officers on the driveway sprinted for the multi-story mansion. The drone turned and began a strafing run, churning up the ground and stopping them in their tracks. They dove for cover, using their shields to protect themselves.

Those stationed out front opened a defensive line of fire. Flashes burst from the small aircraft as they repeatedly found their mark. The embattled ground team quickly rose and raced back to the safety of the gated entrance. The drone spun and moved back to hover around the perimeter of the mansion's roof.

Hunter slid from the fence and bolted toward the SWAT van. Several men, including Matt Banks, huddled around a pullout table, talking excitedly. Their hands gestured between the mansion lawn and a flat screen slate that displayed the schematics of the mansion and the surrounding grounds. Banks spotted him and called him over.

"Hey, boss." Hunter bent forward, hands on his knees, to catch his breath. "What the hell is that?"

"We don't know, but it's kicking our asses. Everyone, this is Special Agent Hunter Coburn."

George Orson, the Dallas SWAT team lead, scrutinized the newcomer. A puzzled look crossed his face. "This is the guy he's asking for?"

"Yes. Coburn is the digital forensics expert for the FBI."

"Have to say, I expected someone—"

"With more experience?" Hunter voiced the man's consternation for him. "I hear that a lot. I can assure you—"

Orson waved him off. He pointed at the LED screen on the table and directed his comments at Hunter. "We can't get close to the house because of whatever that thing is. Short of firing a SAM, we have no way to take it out."

"A definite challenge," Hunter replied, keeping a stern face. *Need to keep up appearances,* he thought, though he felt totally out of his element.

"Our options are limited as far as getting someone in there with you," the captain continued. "I know this isn't standard protocol, but it looks like you're going to have to go in by yourself."

Hunter looked at his boss for verification. "*What?*"

If only he could tell Hunter the truth. Matt immediately recognized the voice, that distinct accent, even after all this time. *Richard Kants.* The man who put him on this path, who believed Hunter's role in the future would be extraordinarily influential.

They'd come full circle. A deadly circle. A circle laid out for Matt over fifty years ago. He knew of no way to stop it. He had no choice, but he hoped Hunter would be safe. Why else would the man call for him, after all?

"This guy specifically asked for you," Matt explained. "We've tried all the tricks to get some security coverage in there with you, but he's shut down each one."

"I feel like the sacrificial lamb." Hunter felt sort of sick inside. "What do you expect me to do?"

"We don't know the answer to that question. This situation is critical. Jeffrey Hilfer is one of our top scientists in fusion energy. There are national security implications."

Hunter grimaced. "Good thing I took all those hostage negotiation classes back at the academy."

Matt jibed right back at his sarcasm. "If I'd thought you'd paid attention to any of those classes, I might actually be worried about you going in."

"Oh, yeah. Hilarious."

Lieutenant Orson signaled to one of his SWAT team members. "Ted, get Coburn fitted for a flak jacket."

The officer guided him into the imposing SWAT command van, where a few technicians manned eight flat screens, all on individual command nets. They didn't acknowledge them passing through to the back. Ted unlocked a large metal door, which revealed racks of combat gear, including M-48 assault rifles, helmets, and Kevlar bulletproof vests. He removed one and passed it to Hunter.

"Try this on."

He slid his arm into the vest, then pulled it around, closing the fasteners.

"You'll need these too." He handed him a pair of goggles with a mic and earpiece. "Put them on."

Hunter followed his instructions.

"Hey, Blair," Ted said to one man in the front, "check the signal." He looked at Hunter. "Speak into the microphone, sir."

He adjusted it closer to his mouth. "Ahh . . . testing, one, two, three."

Blair gave a thumbs-up signal. "Got it. Can you hear me, sir?"

"Yeah, that's weird. It's like you're in my brain."

Blair studied the screen in front of him. "I've got some other gear for that."

"I'm sure you do."

Ted locked up and led Hunter back outside. They returned to the group.

Lieutenant Orson checked him over. "The negotiation team tells me you're good to go, Coburn."

"I don't feel that way. Why would this guy want to talk with me?"

Matt stepped in. "Look, Hunter, I will not lie to you. This is extremely important and dangerous too. The hostage taker has something specific in mind that he thinks only you will understand. You'll be fine because you're useful to him, but don't take any unnecessary chances. Assess the situation and report back to us. We will have direct contact with you at all times through your headset."

"It doesn't make sense, boss. No one knows what we're doing. I've done nothing to rise above the radar. Everything we've done to prepare for Comperi has been totally off the grid. This Hilfer thing has to be a smoke screen."

"You may be right. Nothing happens by chance, and there's a reason he's asked for you." Matt reached into his pocket and touched the dollar coin. "We don't have a choice, Hunter. Like I mentioned, national security implications here . . . this is big. Really big. You're Hilfer's only hope."

CHAPTER FIFTEEN
THE FATALITY

Kants listened in to the police conversation, smiling to himself. *Very good.* After all these decades, Matt Banks had completed his mission to find Hunter Coburn. For Kants, only a few weeks had passed in his time continuum. Of course, the FBI agent would not understand. Right this minute, that would be the least of his problems.

He finished searching the upstairs bedrooms and walked over to the intercom by the door. "Send Coburn in, please." He ripped this intercom from the wall and slammed it to the ground. The metal box bounced and crashed into his captive's shin. Hilfer reflexively bent to grab his leg.

"Enough!" Kants reached over with one hand and lifted him off his feet, crushing his throat. "Your wife seems to have disappeared." The scientist clawed and kicked. After a moment, Kants thrust him back down and let go. The man collapsed, sobbing.

"Where is she?" he bellowed, glowering. Then it struck him. "Ah, that must be it." He surveyed the paneled walls. "Where is this panic room of yours?"

"No!"

Kants pulled him close, studying his eyes. "I bet it is hidden in your bedroom. Come on." He dragged Hilfer out the door.

Isabella huddled in the panic room with her arms hugged around herself, shaking with terror. Trapped there alone, she agonized over the mortal danger her husband faced from that maniac who'd invaded their home. If only she could help him.

She'd been feeding information to the police, but their connection went dead. Her cell phone wouldn't work, nor the landline. Beside herself with worry, she hopped up from her chair to pace in the tiny confines, clutching her bathrobe at her throat. The smell of the vomit in the trash can made the constant nausea even worse, but morning sickness waited for no one. Isabella did her best to ignore it and instead tried to figure out what to do.

She wanted to open the door, but Jeffrey's adamant order not to under any circumstances rang in her ears. The intruder appeared to be fixated on her for some reason. Her safety and that of their unborn child were all that mattered to Jeffrey, and he'd made that clear before pushing her in. She sniffled. *He should be in here with me.* Except he'd gone back for that stupid book.

Loud, abrupt pounding on the bedroom wall jolted her out of her thoughts. She jerked her attention to the wall monitor and saw her husband move across the viewing screen. In her relief, she couldn't help but say aloud, "Oh, thank God, he's back."

Jeffrey's face looked so haggard. She reached to push the release button when the terrorist moved into view, stopping her. She stood still as a statue, almost too afraid to breathe. *He can't see me,* she reminded herself. But it felt like he could.

The intruder shoved her husband aside and stared directly into the camera. "Madam, I know you are in there. You need to come out for Dr. Hilfer's sake." He pulled Jeffrey back into view. "Otherwise, it will go badly for him."

Isabella sobbed and wrung her hands. *I must delay,* she thought, *so the police can get into the house and save us.*

Kants tore the mirror off the wall, exposing a keypad. He pointed toward it. "Open the door."

"I can't . . ."

"Wrong answer." He pummeled Hilfer's head. When he stopped, he jerked the wobbling man upright. "Open it now."

His hostage staggered backward. "I tripped the failsafe," he choked out. "It can only be opened from the inside."

That is logical, Kants thought. He exhaled sharply, annoyed. It would certainly be easier if the woman would just cooperate. *Time to change her mind.* He grabbed Hilfer's arm, twisting hard and lifting it behind his back.

The man rose on his toes, screaming in agony.

"I will start with his arms, madam." Kants spoke menacingly into the camera. He torqued the good doctor harder, making him squeal. "There is no need for this, Isabella. Just open the damn door."

Hunter trudged reluctantly up the front steps of the Hilfer mansion. He tested the handle, and the front door slowly swung open. A sweeping stairway curled upward from the foyer, separating the large living area on the left from a grand dining room on the right. He'd seen the schematic on the SWAT LED screen, but it looked larger than he'd anticipated. He moved into the home with the utmost caution and then stopped in his tracks.

Bullet holes riddled the wall, and furniture lay haphazardly overturned. Blood splatter covered everything. He squatted next to one of a half-dozen downed men to check for a pulse but kept his attention on the carnage around him.

"Holy shit! Are you getting this?" He spoke into the mic, his voice rising with his shock. "This is unreal." He moved to check on another body. "Did we already send men in here? These guys are SWAT!"

Matt's response buzzed in his headset. "Those aren't our men, Agent Coburn. We have no idea who they are or what happened."

"They're all dead!"

"We can see that. Unfortunately, you can do nothing for them. Remember your instructions. Our last contact with the intruder came from the master bedroom. You need to move upstairs to find Dr. Hilfer."

Hunter reached for a discarded Uzi machine gun.

Lieutenant Orson interrupted. "I wouldn't do that, son. He said no guns."

"I'm defenseless! Look around! This changes things."

"Look, if this guy wanted you dead, he would have taken you out with that drone when you walked up to the house."

He thought for a second. "Good point."

The instant the words were out of his mouth, a bloodcurdling scream erupted from the second floor. Hunter bolted for the stairs, taking them two at a time.

"Hey," he called when he reached the top landing. "This is Hunter Coburn. You asked for me?"

"Main bedroom," Kants replied. He pulled his hostage to the back wall, using him as a shield. "Careful coming in. I would hate to accidentally blow his head off."

Hunter stepped through the doorway with his hands raised. "Yeah, that would definitely ruin the upholstery. Where's Mrs. Hilfer?"

"Safe, in another room. You are the digital forensic expert?"

"Yes."

He looked at him skeptically. "I did not expect—"

"Yeah, I get that a lot. Geeks don't always look like geeks."

Kants's eyebrows knitted together. "Come closer."

Hunter walked within a few steps of the two men and stopped. "Since we are all getting to know each other here, what's your name?"

The time traveler peered intently at his true target, the one who could give him Angelika, the one who could save the world. Throughout it all, the coin remained the fulcrum for every event leading to this meeting. The time continuum had finally unfolded as he'd hoped.

A long moment later, he responded, his voice thick with emotion. "Hunter, my name is Richard Kants."

"What do you want with me?"

"I need someone with your expertise."

The young man's gaze shifted to Hilfer. "You okay, Doc?" He gave him a reassuring smile. The scientist nodded, his motion jerky with fear.

Hunter turned back to Kants. "What happened to your men down there?"

"You assume incorrectly."

"They're not yours?" He sounded shocked. "Then who were they?"

"It is a long story, and we have no time."

A shadow appeared in front of the window, drawing their attention. The drone hovered outside, with several guns pointing directly at Hunter.

"Whoa! Who is flying that thing?"

"My little invention," Kants said, "based on your technology."

"Seems to have a mind of its own."

"Perceptive. I wrote the code myself. You are so far behind in artificial intelligence, but you will get there sooner than you think. *Falke*, go back to base." The drone shot from view.

"You have a base somewhere else?"

"Metaphorically speaking."

"Why'd you send it away?"

Kants shoved his hostage away and reached into a side pocket with his free hand. He pulled out a black metallic tube with a myriad of small blinking lights on either end. He rapidly pressed a sequence of buttons in the middle of the device.

"I do not need its protection anymore."

Suddenly, a hazy bubble, filled with a sizzling static charge, burst outward. The blue field enveloped the room, and Hunter and Hilfer collapsed to the floor, twitching in spasms. The electrically charged bubble raced outside of the home, expanding across the yard. As the field spread, every device within its coverage lost power, and every living thing dropped to the ground.

"A bio-electrical magnetic pulse," Kants stated, as if that explained everything. "That should take care of any threat within a half-mile or so. Do not worry, my friend. The effects will wear off soon enough."

He moved over to Hunter and kneeled to pluck the blocky goggles from his face. He removed his own sleekly curved sunglasses and compared them for a moment before putting his back on. He waved the goggles around.

"These are old-school, but it is a start. You will look through mine eventually, but not today." He tossed them onto his chest. "You and I are going to become good friends in the future. And in the past."

Kants pulled another device from his other side pocket. It looked like a small pistol. He positioned it on the back of Hunter's neck, pressing it hard against his skin. He injected a miniscule foreign object next to his spine, inserting the time transponder firmly in place. The young man's eyes practically bugged out of his head, but in his incapacitated state, he could not protest. The time warrior returned the device to his pocket, thinking, *I have altered his life forevermore.*

"Do not worry," he said gruffly. "You will not die from that. However, you are about to embark on an extraordinary journey. You understand neural nets used in artificial intelligence, yes?"

Hunter blinked. Muscle seizures racked his body.

"Good, good. Then you understand neural networks are based on statistical estimation, optimization, and control theory. You know the Theory of Connectivity, yes?"

A grimace spasmed across Hunter's face.

Kants pulled out a small thumb drive and stuffed it into Hunter's pants pocket. "This will be difficult for you to grasp at first, but time is like this. You will see." He paused, looking down at the young man. "I must apologize in advance for ruining your current future, my friend, but you are now linked to a sequence of events that will change everything. When you are alone, look at this old USB drive. This will explain it all. Trust me, you will want to keep this a secret until you understand what is about to happen. Your life depends on it."

The panic room door squeaked as it swung open a little; the magnetic lock went out with everything else. "It appears I am about to complete my mission. You see, her unborn child has been our target all along."

Hunter's eyes widened.

"I know what you're thinking," the time traveler said with a tired smile. "How could we? You will understand soon enough. There will be more of us. You must ensure that we succeed. The fate of the world hangs in the balance."

Kants stood up and moved to the window to survey the damage done by his BIO-EMP device. A red dot appeared on his chest. Before he could do anything about it, the window exploded as a sniper bullet destroyed his heart.

Hunter's heart jumped into his throat when shards of glass pelted him. The lifeless form of the hostage taker dropped to the carpet with a thump. Panicking inside, he struggled to turn his head but couldn't. Several moments passed, then a movement caught his attention. From his periphery, he saw an ethereal wisp of smoke leave the man's collapsed body. It coalesced into a rusty silhouette of an animal's head that twirled delicately in the air, beautiful, captivating. Then it flowed away, slowly descending into the hardwood floor.

CHAPTER SIXTEEN
The Departed

April 14, 2025

Three identical oversized monitors formed a half-hexagon on Hunter's desk. The *Matrix* screensaver filtered down a myriad of green characters on the LED screens. Behind them, a sixty-five-inch wall-mounted monitor displayed large ocean waves rolling across a white, sandy beach in an easy, methodical tempo. The crashing of the surf sounded like the real deal through the theater speaker system.

Hunter spun the small USB drive through his fingers as he stared at the image. He moved the wireless mouse to activate the bank of screens. With this system, he could blink to accomplish the same thing, but he preferred the tactile feel of his old mouse.

The desktop background changed to a grove of pine trees covered with heavy snow. A trail ran down the middle, which led deep into the thick forest and dwindled away into a snowstorm. A large black wolf slowly emerged, walking majestically forward until it took up a third of the monitor screen and sat down. The beautiful canine's ears pointed up, alert. Its pink tongue lolled out between long, sharp fangs as his mouth hung partway open. The beast's golden eyes seemed to gaze right at Hunter.

"Activate link," he commanded.

The wolf pulled in its tongue. "Processing."

Hunter chuckled. "Where did you get that?"

"The character called 'Data' from the old *Star Trek* series you love so much. It seemed appropriate."

"My dad's favorite show," he mumbled to himself. He sighed sadly. "So, what are you processing?"

The wolf licked a snowflake off its nose. "Whatever you would like."

"I need a download for anything you can find on a person named Richard Kants."

Comperi could accomplish this in seconds, searching the Internet and government databases across the world. Soon, Hunter would know everything out there about this guy. *I have to find him and his damned drone.* He worried about a stealth aircraft like that being loose in America. A minute passed, then another. Soon, almost ten minutes passed.

"Comperi, where's my download?"

The wolf looked perplexed. "I correlated the crime scene photos with the fourteen 'Richard Kants' identities that I found, eliminating all deceased before April 14, 2025. None matched his photo or fingerprints. I searched the normal government databases, then expanded to Interpol and other countries with the same result."

"You can't find this guy?"

A fly whizzed by the webcam, and the wolf snapped at it before turning back to him. "Technically, this person does not exist. I require instructions on how to continue."

"You saw the body in the reports?"

"Yes, but he is unrecognizable in his current form. Perhaps he used an alias or altered his identity?"

"Maybe." Hunter chewed on his lip, thinking. "What about the dead men in the Hilfers's living room? What can you tell me from their reports?"

"No identifications were found. I expanded my investigation by using their facial points and fingerprints on worldwide databases. They are absent from society as well."

"That's the best you can do?"

"Under the circumstances, yes."

"This surprises me." Comperi had never failed until now. *Well, maybe not failed. Records were probably expunged on these guys, so they would be untraceable.*

"What about the drone aircraft? What can you tell me about that?"

The wolf paced in front of the trees on the screen, a habit it developed to indicate a procedural routine ran while performing the task at hand. It turned and loped back to the original spot, shaking off the snow that had accumulated on its head and back.

A series of videos and images of assorted drones flashed on the giant wall screen. "Based on video analysis, it's not in our current arsenal of similar craft. I'm unsure what type of engine provides power or thrust for such a device. It also gives the impression of being free of a remote human pilot."

"How so?"

"The cameras surrounding the craft suggest that it is autonomous." The drone appeared in detail on the LED screen with its camera lenses highlighted for review.

"That can't be."

"Additionally, it changed directions and moved much too fast for a human to control it."

Hunter recalled Kants's words about AI and how future advancements made his coding look like child's play. "He told it to return to base."

"The craft would know the location."

Comperi is no help at all. I need to try a different tack. The USB drive beckoned. Kants told him his life depended on looking at it, just before he apologized for 'ruining his future' as well. Hunter knew looking at this would be like opening Pandora's box.

A quiet knock on the door interrupted his line of thinking. The wolf blinked, and the screen changed to a standard desktop.

Rachel walked up behind him. "Everything good in here? It's late."

"I'm fine. Just a little freaked out by the hostage deal this morning."

"It all turned out okay." She gently massaged his neck. "The doc checked you over and gave you a clean bill of health. You saved the scientist and got the bad guy, right?"

"Yeah, I guess. Still, I don't get it. He compared time to the Neural Net Theory of Connectivity. A neural net is interwoven synaptic junctions. Time is linear."

Hunter felt her fingers touch the small, round lesion at the back of his neck. She bent his head to the side to check it out. He grabbed her hands and scooted back. Rachel gave him a concerned look. "What's that?"

"Nothing," he replied. "Just a bug bite."

"That's bigger than a bug bite. You haven't been letting some other woman give you hickeys, have you?"

He smiled and pulled Rachel onto his lap. She twisted her torso to face him, resting her arms on his shoulders in a loose embrace.

"Yes," Hunter said, "absolutely. I found this wonderful vampire woman with only one fang."

She dropped a kiss on his forehead. "Well, she'd better be willing to share."

"Now, that's my kind of woman!"

Rachel swatted him playfully, but he drew her closer, and they touched foreheads. "So, when's the photo shoot now?"

She leaned back. "Tomorrow, and no more kidnappings."

"No more kidnappings."

Hunter kissed her, holding her gently with her back to the bank of monitors. The black wolf popped onto the screen and began pacing back and forth. Words appeared below it.

"Time. Neural Net Theory of Connectivity. Processing . . ."

"Time. Processing . . ."

"Time travel. Processing . . ."

With a blink, it vanished, replaced by the *Matrix* screensaver.

CHAPTER SEVENTEEN
THE JUMP

Two intersecting roads off Spur 468 surrounded the FBI's ten-story regional headquarters in Dallas. Located close to multiple Internet POPS for several service providers, the building housed the world's fastest mainframe. Millions of gigabits of data traveled directly through the data center every second of every day. Comperi harvested information gleaned from the traffic going across those lines.

Hunter stood next to a large box on the floor of the data center. Since ice-cold air flooded the room, he wore his standard uniform: blue jeans, a sweater, a denim jacket, and a ball cap. Omar didn't seem to mind the deep freeze; he wore a polo shirt that exposed his weight-lifter's build. The agent seemed larger than his six-foot-one frame. At almost thirty-five years old, he could have passed for a young man in his early twenties, earning him the nickname "The Kid."

"How did you get a petabyte switch, anyway?" Omar opened the top and unpacked the network device. "I thought they were only in the prototype stage. The back plane on this one is what, twenty terabytes?"

Hunter grabbed a rack mount kit and pulled the rails out of the box. "Closer to forty for throughput. No problem getting the switch. Convincing the telcos to give me the bandwidth proved to be the hard part."

"How big of a pipe did you get?"

"OC48 to start with."

"That's a lot of capacity. Carrier grade." Omar removed the packing materials, exposing the switch. "Come on, help me pull this puppy out."

Hunter stepped over, and they grabbed the switch handles, lifted the one-hundred-twenty-pound network device, and set it on the floor. "There's so much data out there to be mined. I'll need a lot more bandwidth to stress Comperi."

"When will you be going worldwide with it?"

"Soon. Once we get this configured and tested, we can start putting the network clients on the Internet POPs across the globe and on all of the communication satellites. Then it's watch out, terrorists."

"As Allah wills," Omar muttered.

Hunter glanced at him. "What's that supposed to mean?"

"Nothing." Omar kept his face downcast, busily sticking the packing wrap back in the oversized carton.

"Hey, we've worked together for three years, and you've never once said that. And you look upset. What's up?"

His friend's hands stilled.

"Come on," Hunter urged. "Spit it out."

"I'm tired of being profiled all the time. It happened again just before I got here."

Hunter studied his coworker and saw genuine angst cross his features. They had discussed his heritage once before; it never seemed to be an issue. He knew Omar's parents fled from Iran decades ago and were devout Muslims. They still spoke Farsi in his childhood home, although you would have never known it by his fluent English and thick New York accent.

"I'm sorry if I made you feel that way."

Omar responded quickly, sounding mortified. "Oh, no. Not you. I mean, in general, but especially at work. As soon as the word 'terrorist' comes up, I get that look from everyone."

"What look? I've never seen it."

"You know, that *look*. 'Can we trust this guy? He has a gun. Wonder who he knows back in the homeland?'"

"Of course we trust you. You're on my team, right? If there were the slightest concern, you wouldn't be."

"But that's how it goes every time. I've never even been to Iran, but everyone acts like I just can't wait to get back there."

That hit home with Hunter. "Sorry, dude. I see your point. It's the way of the world, I guess. You're a valued asset to our group. We all know you bleed red, white, and blue."

"Yeah, maybe," Omar replied. "It's just a tough situation. Less than two percent of Muslims are radicalized. The rest of us pay the price."

Hunter realized this needed to be a longer conversation, which would require whiskey. "All this time, and I didn't know you felt that way. Come on, let's get this finished and solve the world's problems later."

Omar grabbed a smaller container from the bottom of the large box. He pulled the tape to open it. "So, I heard that you finally got in the field."

Hunter replied. "Yeah, some fun."

"Only you would have your first field mission be one of the most unusual cases in twenty years."

Hunter squatted down next to the switch and unscrewed the protective plates. "I know, right?"

"What was that thing, anyway?"

"A souped-up electrical, magnetic pulse device. He called it a BIO-EMP. The damn thing not only short-circuited our nervous systems but also took out the power for several blocks."

Omar unloaded a forty-eight-gig port blade from the plastic envelope and handed the module to him. "Good thing they got the guy, or you'd be dead."

"I think the Hilfers would be dead, not me."

"Hmph," he grunted in disagreement. "Did you figure out how it works? I've never heard of a BIO-EMP before. I didn't even know conventional EMPs existed."

"To my knowledge, they don't." Hunter slid the blade into the switch. "I got it opened in my lab, but the NSA showed up and confiscated it before I could take a closer look."

Omar paused, frowning. "You got tangled up with the National Security Agency?"

"Yeah. I guess the military wants to know exactly how a BIO-EMP works as well. I doubt they'll find anything, though, considering its burned-out condition."

Hunter's phone rang. He tapped on the Bluetooth earpiece. "Agent Coburn." He listened for a moment. "Yeah, tell them I'll be down in a few minutes."

Omar asked the obvious question. "The NSA, I presume?"

"No. The Dallas Police Department wants to meet with me." A little smirk crossed Hunter's face. "There are two more of those blades in there. Do you think you can install them without blowing up the switch?" He knew Omar would be a bit touchy about the subject, but he loved to mess with him about it.

"Ha, ha. That was two years ago! You know that happens with end-of-life gear!"

"Yeah," Hunter grinned. "Boom, boom, out go the lights when you reboot. Well, at least on *your* watch."

Omar snapped a playful punch at his friend. "I can't believe you just said that."

"Too soon?"

"Yes. No. Damn it." Omar laughed. "Guess I deserved that."

"True," he replied, "but I get your point. We need to address the bigger issue."

"Thank you. You've been a good friend here at work."

"That's what I mean. Time to take it beyond work and have you and Leila over for dinner. I'll talk with Rachel, and we'll get a date on the calendar soon." He turned to leave the data center.

Hunter banged open the double-gated glass doors near the front desk of the Dallas Police Department Headquarters. The guard questioned him, then pointed out two men in suits who were standing in the waiting area.

He walked over to them. "Good afternoon, gentlemen. I'm Dr. Coburn."

"I'm Officer Stillman, and this is my partner, Officer Damon, Special Investigation Response Team, with the Dallas PD. Your boss suggested you might be able to help us."

"He did? Well, okay. How can I help?"

Stillman answered, "We apprehended a woman suspected of stabbing a man to death. Eyewitness accounts indicate it may have been self-defense. Both the suspect and the deceased were wearing black fatigues."

"Sounds unusual, but how does that involve me? I specialize in digital forensics."

"Yes, sir, we know. We found a strange device on the suspect. None of our guys can figure out what it does," replied Damon.

Now he's talking my language. "What did you find?"

Damon pulled out his mobile phone and offered it to Hunter. "Here you go."

"Why didn't you just email me? I didn't have to make a trip out here just to see a photograph."

"It looks like an explosive of some sort, so we didn't think we should put it on the Internet."

Hunter leaned forward to look at the screen. He immediately recognized the BIO-EMP. "Yeah, I've seen one of those before. I'd like to take a closer look. I'd like to speak to your suspect too, if possible."

Damon smiled over at his partner as if Hunter were the butt of an inside joke. "Sure. We could use the help. She hasn't said a word yet. Maybe you'll have better luck with her."

"That's odd." Hunter frowned. "Is she injured?"

"We don't think so, but it took six of us to subdue her."

"Six? You've got to be kidding me."

Damon appeared a little embarrassed. "She's fast as shit. We hit her with our stun guns, but she just kept coming. I saw the video. The last guy nailed her in the neck, or I don't think she would have gone down."

He raised an eyebrow. "Wow."

"Don't worry," Stillman said. "We'll make sure she's properly secured, so there won't be another incident."

This woman possessed a BIO-EMP, making her just as dangerous as Kants. The fact that she could plow through so many cops didn't surprise Hunter one bit. He took his smartphone out of his pocket and pointed it toward Officer Stillman's phone.

"Sync business cards." He verified the transmission of information. "Okay, let's go."

Hunter knew the two officers observed them through the large, mirrored window. The woman sat across from him, secured by a chain to the table. *It took six men to nab her, and they think handcuffs are enough?* She held her head low, and her long, black hair hid her face. Gummy blood spatter stuck to her.

"I'm Agent Coburn with the FBI." An envelope rested on the table between them. "I hear you're the strong, silent type." He waited, tapping his fingers on it. "By the way, I know what that thing is."

She made no response. He pulled a photo out of the envelope and looked at the image of Richard Kants, dead on the floor. He slid it across the table where the woman could see it.

"Kants is dead, you know."

The woman lifted her gaze to inspect the picture. "So much for Kants the Invincible." She turned her attention to Hunter, and the color drained from her face.

"The BIO-EMP links you with him, so it's not surprising you know his name. A sniper killed him just before he tried to put a bullet into Mrs. Hilfer."

"So close," she grumbled under her breath.

"What's really sick is that you were going to kill her unborn child too. He specifically said that. Why?"

"It doesn't matter."

"It mattered before now. What changed? Besides that damn BIO-EMP device knocking everyone on their butts for several surrounding blocks."

"I mean, it doesn't matter now." Her sullen look pinched into a scowl. "He would use it."

"You know the military has taken an extreme interest in this weapon."

She looked him in the eye. "You need to destroy it," she said with authority. "That device is not supposed to be left here."

Hunter leaned back from her sheer intensity. "Come again?"

"I said you need to *destroy* it. For your own good. For everyone's."

He scooted his chair forward. *Now we're getting somewhere.* "Why? Who makes a weapon like that?"

"I can't tell you. You wouldn't be able to do anything anyway."

"You know, you need to be helping me. I'm afraid things will get ugly around here when the military guys show up."

"Like that will make a difference. I'll be long gone before then. It's almost time."

"Almost time for what?"

She didn't respond.

"I don't think you're going anywhere. Those chains are pretty stout."

That second, the lights flickered. Hunter felt a vibrating hum buzz around them, and a draft of air swooshed by him out of nowhere. "Hey! What's going—" He twisted to look at the mirror, then gaped around the room. His eyes landed on her.

The woman's hair fluttered in the increasing breeze. A serene smile lifted the edges of her mouth, and her eyebrow lifted into an *I-told-you-so* stare.

"Guys?" he called out, thinking the officers in the observation room would respond. The spinning wind erupted with force, and the papers flew off the table, flipping around in the growing frenzy. The deep hum resonated, becoming all consuming.

Hunter sprang to his feet, yet the woman remained calm. She smiled, squinting at him through the maelstrom while the air distorted into blurry waves. He felt completely undone, watching her. She seemed shimmery, surreal.

"Time to catch my ride." She yanked back with little effort, ripping the chain from the ring on the table. The turmoil whipped around her, tearing at her body until she dissolved into nothingness.

"What the hell?" he yelled, unable to comprehend what he'd just witnessed. He scrambled around the table to head for the door, bringing his hand up to shield his face. Hunter did a double-take. *My God*, he thought, with panic engulfing him. *I can see through my arm.*

CHAPTER EIGHTEEN
THE GHOST

OCTOBER 8, 2354

I am here, Kants thought impatiently. *Where are you?* He stared out the smudged window in the stairwell landing. The view from the top of the ninety-story skyscraper appeared the same no matter which way he looked. Fiery lightning cascaded from the muddy, dark thunderheads churning above. Acid rain fell on the few buildings that had survived the fusion blast from the long-ago Purge War. The exteriors appeared half-melted, scarred almost beyond recognition in what remained of the once-beautiful city.

"This is taking forever," Walter said. He sat down on the steps, adjusting his enviro-armor. "Are you sure this is the right place?"

"I am positive. Banks made it perfectly clear."

"He could have been wrong, you know. Kind of weird, sending yourself a message through him, anyway," he replied.

"We must save this person, Walter."

"Yeah, I know. He's the Father of Artificial Intelligence. Still, how do we know he'll get the message to you?"

Kants looked down at his partner and friend. "Because he already has. We are here, are we not?"

Walter hesitated. "Good point," he conceded. "I guess."

Just outside the exterior door, the raging storm drowned out the loud hum of a time jump. The air distorted in the tightly whirling winds, and the translucent figure of a man materialized, slowly becoming solid amid the deluge. He cringed, jerking his blue denim jacket over his head for protection. Threads of smoke rose from it, sizzling in the fiery rain. The man clutched his throat and coughed as he breathed in the poisonous air. Desperate for an escape, he spotted a rooftop entry. He rushed over and tried to yank open the door, only to find it locked. He pounded on it, screaming in his agony.

The time agents jumped at the sudden banging. Kants quickly unlocked the door and jerked the person into the safety of the building. Walter slammed it shut. A haze of smoke emanated from the man's burned clothing, and he collapsed to his hands and knees, coughing hard. They rolled him over, and he grimaced up at them with a dazed look.

Do not die, Kants thought. *You cannot. Do not die!* "Walter, we have little time."

His partner kneeled next to him and pulled out a syringe autoinjector. The fellow tried to resist, pushing feebly against his arms.

"Stop that," Walter admonished, sweeping his struggling efforts aside. He plunged the device into his chest and fired the Life Shot.

The man's piercing screech abruptly turned into spasms of coughing.

He patted his shoulder. "You're welcome."

A low, loud hum began, and the air rippled and shimmered, spinning tightly. Walter stepped backward to avoid the disturbance.

Kants bent over and grabbed the fellow's jacket, pulling him close. "You must tell me this in the past, or you will not survive. 770 Broadway, Manhattan. Rooftop. October 8, 2354." Kants shook him. "Do you understand? 770 Broadway, Manhattan. Rooftop. October 8, 2354. You must tell me this!"

Disbelief registered on the man's face, and his words were practically swept away in the consuming hum. He pulled himself closer. "You!" He drew in a ragged breath. "You're dead! I saw you die!"

Kants broke his grip and stepped back in shock. Within seconds, the man disappeared, and the distortion ebbed away into nothingness.

"Damn," he muttered.

Walter stood up. "Do you think he got the message?"

Kants looked grim but remained silent. *Will this ever end?*

"What did he say?" Walter put a hand on his shoulder. "I couldn't hear him."

Kants brushed him off. "It doesn't matter."

"Hmph. Okay, then. You ready to get out of here?"

"Someday," he said wistfully, "this all goes away."

Walter turned to go down the stairs. "Yeah. You keep saying that."

CHAPTER NINETEEN
THE RETURN

APRIL 22, 2025

Rachel Manheim shifted the two bags of groceries so that she could place her hand on the palm scanner at the backdoor of their house. Once inside, she called out, "Hunter?"

Silence greeted her. She dumped the bags on the kitchen island and leaned against the granite-topped counter. Tears welled up in her eyes. Almost a week had passed since his disappearance. Somehow, he'd become a fugitive.

The authorities interviewed her repeatedly, with roughly the same questions each time. Did she know the woman? How did Hunter know her? Why would he help her escape? Where would Hunter go if he needed to hide? Even Matt Banks ran her through the same set of questions.

Ridiculous, she thought, though she had no idea what had happened. She refused to believe he would help that suspect escape or throw away the career he loved. *We're getting married! He loves me. There must be a good reason for all this.*

The unopened package of engagement photos sat on the counter. Rachel blinked back tears and slid them out of the oversized envelope. The one on top showed the two of them standing next to a beautiful floral garden at the Dallas Arboretum. She'd never seen her man smile so big before. He focused on her the entire sweet time together that day, joking, laughing, her Prince Charming in every way. *What happened to him?*

Her cell phone rang. Lately, she'd refused to answer it, but she recognized her mother's ringtone. She tapped her Bluetooth earpiece and then reached into a grocery bag to unload it. "Hey, Mom." She pulled out a half-gallon of milk and set it on the counter. "No, I just got home." She paused to listen, then said, "I just don't know, Mom. He's still not back."

Suddenly, a loud humming noise filled the room, and the air distorted into a hazy blur. The grocery bags flapped in the strong current, and the humming increased into a deafening roar. Rachel shrieked as the force spun her around. And then, just as suddenly, it stopped.

She shouted, "Mom? Mom? Are you there?" The call disconnected in the turmoil.

Rachel heard a muffled moan behind her. She twisted toward the noise. "Hunter! Oh, my God, Hunter! You're on fire!"

He stood there, red-faced and in obvious pain, his jacket smoldering. A sudden, violent cough wracked his body. He tried to steady himself by grabbing the sink.

She quickly sidestepped the island, reaching out to him. "Yeow!" She jumped back, her hands burning.

"Don't touch me!" he croaked, his rough voice barely above a whisper. He clawed off his coat and shirt and kicked off his shoes. He frantically worked his zipper to pull off his pants.

"Hunter, tell me what to do!"

He labored to speak. "Start the shower. I gotta get this off me." His face contorted in agony.

She bolted down the hallway to the bathroom and quickly turned on the faucet. He followed, staggering past her. Rachel helped him step into the bathtub, and he ducked his head into the water stream.

"What happened to you?" she asked breathlessly.

Hunter's eyes briefly found hers, then his knees buckled, and he sagged, unconscious. She caught him, protecting his head as he collapsed to the bottom of the tub.

Rachel tapped her earpiece. "Call Matt Banks!"

He answered the phone after one ring. "Rachel? I know you're worried. I'm—"

"Matt!" she blurted out. "Matt, help! He's here, and he's hurt bad."

"Oh!" he exclaimed. "Call 911. I have an agent near your house. I'll call him."

"You don't understand! He just appeared, and he has this liquid fire all over him."

"Okay, stay calm. I'm hanging up to call 911. I'll be there as fast as I can."

Rachel ripped the Bluetooth from her ear and threw it on the counter. She grabbed the shower nozzle and guided the cold water over Hunter's body. "Stay with me, baby. Stay with me. Don't leave me again. Stay with me!"

CHAPTER TWENTY
THE ARRIVAL

JULY 18, 2355

The Worm hummed louder, and the time distortions slowed, signaling that the agents would soon return. This allowed the AI to pull enough information from the anomaly to plot out their next mission. Hope Bannister watched, fascinated by the monster she'd enslaved. *Almost three years of sending agents back in time*, she thought, *and their return jumps never get old.*

She turned to the tech manning the control console. "We're getting close. I can feel it."

Chava nodded in agreement. "If the signature pattern holds true, they should arrive any minute." He pointed to two blinking green lights in the middle of the holographic view of The Worm. "We've registered two jumps."

"Good." She couldn't afford to lose her top operatives now, not with the Keplers pushing to shut down the project. "Any changes yet?"

"I'm sorry, Dr. Bannister. The AI search engine shows no deviations in history, but we're still scanning."

"That's disappointing. Well, if we can just get them back in one piece."

"Kants always comes back," he replied.

I'm more worried about Kristen, went through her mind.

The Worm undulated violently, narrowing into a single thread of time.

"What . . ." She leaned forward, watching intently. "What's that?"

"Scanning," Chava responded.

Before they could dig into the discrepancies, the anomaly morphed back to its normal pattern. The surrounding air distorted. Kristen dropped out of The Worm, as if being birthed. She landed on the net, curled up in a ball. The robotic arm pulled her away to the safety of the side deck.

They waited expectantly, but nothing more occurred. Bannister turned her attention back to the technician, concern on her face. "Where the hell is Kants?"

Chava spun through the holographic image, searching. "I don't know. He jumped. We have his transponder registry on file. It definitely triggered."

"That's odd." She waited, watching. "I guess he's trying to keep us on our toes," she joked, though she didn't find this funny at all. Snippets of history danced across the time tornado until she could stand the silence no longer. "Anything? Anything at all?"

"Sorry, ma'am." He shook his head. "We're detecting nothing."

How could Kants jump but not land here? The transponder makes sure everyone comes back, no matter what. Bannister waited a few more minutes, her anxiety growing.

She turned to Chava. "Send for Agent Winters, right now. I'll meet her in my office." She took several steps toward the exit, her magnetic boots clanking on the metallic grating.

"What about Kants? What should we do?"

"Why don't you try finding him?" The door slid shut behind her. *Like that's going to help,* she thought. Somehow, deep down, she feared they'd lost Kants the Invincible.

Kristen wrapped herself in a rare, genuine wool blanket, embracing its warmth. She curled her toes under her bottom and sank down into an overstuffed chair, feeling exhausted and achy. She sipped from a steaming cup of coffee, taking in Bannister's office. A wall-sized screen displayed a video of a tranquil rural meadow on pre-war Earth.

With her jumps back in time, Kristen witnessed the beauty of the planet before humanity decimated it, so she understood this appreciation for the past. She mused about the trees and blue skies and the freedom to go anywhere and do anything she wanted to do. *If only I could have lived in the good old days.*

Dr. Bannister sat in the chair next to her. "Sorry to have to do this so quickly after a mission." She smiled sympathetically. "Are you feeling any better?"

"I think so. I imagine it feels kind of like jetlag on steroids."

"Jetlag?"

Kristen pursed her lips and gently blew across the hot cup, delaying her response for a second. "A twenty-first-century term to describe how crappy you feel after traveling from one end of the world to the other."

"Oh. Pretty bad, then. Yes, I get it." Bannister crossed her legs and leaned forward. "So, what happened to Kants? Why didn't he come back with you?"

Kristen knew this conversation would be coming, but she'd had little time to think it through. She shrugged. "I guess maybe because he's dead."

Bannister stiffened and stared at her. "That can't be true. Everyone returns, dead or alive."

"Then I don't know." *And you better not blame me.*

"We observed two transportations on the console," her boss said in a clipped tone. "I expected to see Agent Kants."

"Two?" Kristen contorted her face skeptically. "How can that be if he didn't come back here?"

"We don't know. That's why I'm asking you."

They sat in silence. *She looks pretty upset.* Kristen surmised Bannister would be unwilling to share her theories about this incident without more information from her.

"Why would you think I know?" Kristen asked genuinely. "I don't see how that could happen, unless he's figured out some way around the Final Stroke."

"There is no way around it."

She chewed on that for a moment. "He set off one of the BIO-EMPs. Maybe that shorted out the capsule?"

"If it shorts out, there's no electrical charge to hold it closed. The poison comes out in your brain, and you're dead. It must be something else. Maybe someone in the past discovered the transponder and removed it?"

"Could be," Kristen said, looking up from her mug. "The local police have his body. Maybe they did an autopsy."

"And Hansen Hilfer?"

"You mean Isabella Hilfer, his grandmother."

"Pardon me?" Bannister said. "Now I'm lost."

"So were we, since we landed decades before we were supposed to. We adapted."

"You killed his grandmother? That's a little unorthodox."

"It was Kants's idea. We argued about it, but logic won out."

"Still, a brilliant idea."

These people have no scruples, Kristen thought. "Brilliant, right up until someone killed him."

"Something doesn't add up. He just can't be dead."

"I'm sorry, Doc, but he's dead. We never did terminate Grandma Hilfer, either."

Bannister shook her head, as if she couldn't believe what she heard. "You saw him die?"

"No," Kristen admitted. "The police showed me a photograph. He took a bullet through the chest."

Her boss's brow arched with skepticism. "Wouldn't his vest have protected him from a twenty-first-century bullet?"

"I don't know what to tell you, except that I saw the hole in his chest, and he looked dead in the picture. The FBI agent claimed he'd been killed. Why would he lie?"

Bannister said, "To get information, perhaps? I just can't accept it, not without proof."

Kristen adjusted herself in her chair. "If they removed the transponder from Kants in the autopsy, would it still fire off? Would it trigger and then just disappear into The Worm without a body to transport?"

"There are ways to remove it, but I don't believe they possess the technology to do so without the device self-destructing. We have a failsafe for everything."

Kristen yawned. "If it is working, then he would have shown up here, correct?"

"Yes, unless he somehow reset it. I believed that's impossible, but you never know with him. Theoretically, that would cause him to be out of sync with your transponder for the return trip."

"Our transponders are linked?"

"We found that without linking them, our teams would land in different areas at different times."

"Yeah, well, I think this is way above my compensation level."

Her boss shook her head slowly, as if confounded. "We're running out of time."

"We'll get the next one. We still have a chance to fix this."

Bannister turned to stare listlessly at the wall scene. A small herd of horses grazed in a luxurious grassland. Kristen wondered if the woman dreamed of transporting back to that bucolic place. Life would be so much easier. *She seems to have the weight of two worlds pressing down on her shoulders.*

After a quiet couple of moments, Bannister continued. "We will figure it out sooner or later." She sighed. "Let's move on. So, you were captured?"

Kristen took her time sipping her cup of coffee. "Yeah. Dumb luck. Caught by a civilian. I didn't want to kill an innocent old man."

"Go on. What happened?"

"We were ambushed by the Keplers." She gave her boss a fierce look. "You realize you've got a mole?"

"Be careful what you say, Kristen. Unsubstantiated rumors could be catastrophic to the program." Bannister leaned back in her chair. "No one knows the specifics of your mission besides me, the techs, and the AI, and that is locked down tight. There's no way to hack into an AI."

"Someone knows exactly what we're doing, down to the place and time. How else could we have been interrupted in our mission to eliminate Isabella Hilfer *twice*? Maybe the Keplers used their AI to get into it."

"We haven't been able to prove that. I don't think it could be one of the other space stations. We've blocked all communication with them, especially the Kepler Launch Station."

Kristen shifted in her chair. "How do the Keplers travel back in time?"

"We're not sure. Kants speculated that, in our future, they take over The Worm and are sending agents back to stop us."

"That would explain a lot. They could be reading our archived reports."

"True," replied Bannister, "but we've taken steps to avoid that."

"Your steps aren't helping."

"Apparently not."

"It's scary. You wind up second-guessing every move."

"I'm working on it, Agent Winters, but let's keep it between us for now."

"I will, Dr. B. Still, we've got to figure out a way to stop the Keplers. They're probably the reason Kants is dead. I don't want to be next."

"I know, I know," Bannister replied. "I have a team working on this issue. Even with that, we're still going to send you back. We need to figure out what happened. I've asked the AI to expedite finding a new mission for you."

"Alone?"

"Yes."

Kristen looked down at her mug. "You're going to let me go without a partner? I thought that went against protocol. I remember Kants complaining because you wouldn't let him jump alone."

"The problem is, we can only link two people at a time," Bannister explained. "Technically, you still have a partner. We just don't know who is jumping with you."

She picked at a fingernail, considering the ramifications. "The Keplers will probably be there."

"Hopefully not."

"What if, by some miracle, Kants shows up?"

"Bring him home."

Kristen smoothed the blanket over her knee. "Should I follow through on whatever the actual assignment is too?"

"All missions are important, so yes, but your primary task will be to eliminate this person or thing, if it's not Kants."

"How am I supposed to do that?"

"You'll have the element of surprise," Bannister assured her. "You can fire before the other person knows what's going on."

Just another day at work, Kristen thought with reluctance. "Easy for you to say."

"I know it's hard to function the split-second you land from a jump. Steel yourself and fight through it."

"They could be waiting for me," Kristen countered.

"I know. That's why this one is only between you and me. I'm not even telling the AI."

"Good." She set her coffee mug on a small side table. "I want another shot at those Kepler bastards."

"Now you sound like Kants." Bannister paused. "The most important thing is to complete your primary task. You'll need to terminate them fast, right after your jump. Either that, bring back Kants, or cut out the transponder and destroy it."

Kristen looked up, surprised. "Uh, yeah, sure. I can do that."

CHAPTER TWENTY-ONE
THE AWAKENING

APRIL 23, 2025

"They're all over me!" the man yelled. "Get them off!"

It took all eighty-five pounds of Hunter's ten-year-old body to hold his father down. His dad used to tower over him, but leukemia reduced him to a mere shell. The boy cradled him as gently as he could. "It's okay. They're not real."

"Demons! They've stolen everything!" He struggled futilely.

"They're not real, Dad. You can fight it."

"My job . . . my wife . . . my home . . . now they're killing me!"

"Dad, please! Don't do this."

"Hunter! Get them off!"

A woman's voice emerged next to him. "Maybe you should let me take over; this is what I'm here for." The nurse stepped next to the bed. "Hold still, sir. This will help you." She slid a needle into his port.

Once she'd administered the medication, she stepped back. The frantic thrashing slowed and then stopped altogether. Hunter looked up, wondering if that would be the end. His father gave him a weak smile. His eyes were hollowed sockets from his wasting away to skin and bones, but recognition showed in them now. For that moment, the father he knew stared at him.

"I'm sorry, son."

"It's okay."

He blinked back tears, repeating a conversation they'd had before. "I don't know why this is happening to us. I used to believe in God, but he's taken everything from me. A real god wouldn't do that."

Not six months before, a drunk driver had killed Hunter's mother. After that, cancer ravaged his father with a vengeance.

"God wouldn't do that. He loves us. You taught me that."

"There is no God!" The hard set of his father's jawline revealed his rising anger. He rattled out an emotional demand. "Don't you ever forget it." Exhausted, he leaned back and took a shallow breath.

Hunter moved closer. "Please don't leave me."

His father slowly reached up to touch him. "So sorry, son," he rasped. "I wish . . . Take care of your brother for me. Promise."

Hunter gulped air to stop crying. "I will, Dad. I promise."

His father smiled. His eyes closed.

And then fire fell upon him. Hunter felt the demons burning and biting as they crawled over his body and into his soul. The fire seared him from the inside out. Every breath felt like an inferno in his lungs. He tried to get away, but he couldn't move. After what seemed an eternity, a voice penetrated the dim recesses of his mind. From the faintness of the echo, he thought it might be his mother calling. He wanted to run to her, but he saw only flames.

The voice persisted and became louder, calling his name. The sounds of that plea washed across the fire, dousing it with peals of calm. The scorching blaze faded away to a soft whiteness, and then he finally recognized the voice. He took a breath to call out to Rachel, let her know he could hear her. Too exhausted to move, darkness soon took over.

Sandeep stood next to Matt at the end of Hunter's hospital bed. *Where have you been, young man?* she thought. *And what have you gotten yourself into?*

Hunter slept soundly with an oxygen cannula attached to his nose. An IV dripped several bags of fluids into him, and an array of devices blinked and chirped, monitoring his vitals. Bandages swathed his burned hands and the tips of his ears. Rachel sat close by in a chair, stroking his hair and murmuring softly. The attending physician, Dr. Chris Kern, walked into the room, flipping through a tablet.

Sandeep turned to him. "How is he doing today? We need to know the specifics."

The doctor cleared his throat. "I'm not sure I should discuss his condition with you. HIPAA restrictions, you know."

Her eyes narrowed with displeasure. She dug in her purse, located her work badge, and handed it to him. "I can have a court order here within thirty minutes, but if I have to do it that way, I'll be very annoyed."

"It's fine, Dr. Kern," Rachel said. "We have to figure out what's going on."

His pinched look translated to disapproval, but he began. "Our patient here has burns, but, more seriously, he inhaled a large amount of toxins, which severely damaged his lungs. We found quite a concoction in his system: traces of methanol, hexane, hydrochloric acid, and sulfur dioxide, just to name a few of the more lethal ones."

"Did you say lethal?" Sandeep wrung her hands. *He can't die now. We just got him back.*

Matt placed a hand on Rachel's shoulder.

"By all rights, he should already be dead," Dr. Kern explained, "but he's holding his own. From what we can tell, the damaged tissue is being repaired as quickly as it is being destroyed. We can't seem to pin down how that's happening, but it appears Hunter's body is fighting the poison."

The director circled her finger, indicating for him to go on. "He's fighting it how?"

"He's somehow breaking the toxins into nonlethal matter. He's not out of the woods yet, but, at this rate, I believe he will recover quite well."

Rachel pursed her lips and let out a relieved sigh. "Amen to that."

Matt exchanged a relieved look with Sandeep. "You don't have any idea how that's happening? No specialists you could call?"

"I'm afraid not. He's getting top-notch care here. It's a medical mystery, one certainly worth studying."

"You'll send us a copy of his toxicology report," Nurre ordered. "ASAP."

"Yes, ma'am."

Matt looked down at his friend. "So, airborne, huh? I thought someone threw it on him."

"How did he get burned?" Nurre asked.

"I would compare it to being doused with a very caustic acid rain. Fiery fumes scorched him internally as he breathed it in. We found traces all over his body where it burned through his clothes. The injuries are worse where his skin was exposed, like on his hands."

Matt cringed. "What a nightmare."

"I agree. This gets weirder by the moment." Nurre shook her head. "That still doesn't explain how it happened."

The doctor nodded. "Only he can tell you that."

A soft, hoarse voice from the bed interrupted them. "Tell you what?"

Rachel beamed. She leaned over to embrace her fiancé. "You've been a bad boy, Hunter Stiles Coburn."

He gave her a pained smile. "I know."

Matt breathed a deep sigh. "Welcome back, my friend. How are you feeling?"

Hunter took notice of everyone in the room. His heart sank at sight of Director Nurre. "Going to live, I think. What happened?"

Dr. Kern tapped on his data pad as he walked over to him. "I need to ask everyone to leave now, so I can evaluate my patient."

Nurre said, "Ah, actually, could you and Rachel excuse us, please? We need to debrief Agent Coburn in private."

"Taking care of my patient has a little higher priority than your questions." He bent to peer into Hunter's eyes.

"Not when it involves national security. It will only take a little while."

The doctor checked his vitals on the monitor and sighed, obviously exasperated. "Five minutes, no more."

Rachel wouldn't let go of Hunter's hand. He nodded to ease her concern.

"I'll be right outside," she said. "When they're done, you have some explaining to do. If you think this is going to get you out of our wedding, you better think twice." She kissed him on the cheek.

Matt looked down at his friend. "Ouch," he mouthed.

Dr. Kern stopped at the door. "I'm going to insist that you keep it short. We want him to conserve his breath. His lungs are still healing." He turned and exited with Rachel before either FBI agent could respond.

Director Nurre smiled but got right down to business. "Agent Coburn, I'm glad you're back with us. We have a lot of questions, but we'll focus on only a few critical ones for now."

He nodded.

"Do you remember disappearing from the Dallas Police Department headquarters?"

"Not really," he said in a hoarse voice.

"The woman you were interrogating disappeared too. There's speculation that you may have helped her escape."

Hunter grimaced. "I interviewed her. Tried to get information about the BIO-EMP device."

Matt sat in the chair next to the bed. "Why don't we start with what you do recall? We know this has to be tough on you, but we're struggling for answers."

"I don't remember much." He hated to lie to his boss, but no one would believe the truth. Kants's words floated back into his mind. *Tell no one. Your life depends on it.* "We talked in the interrogation room, and then the next thing I know, I'm on fire in my kitchen. What happened?"

Director Nurre glanced at the closed door before continuing. "We watched the tapes. One minute you were there, then the video stops, and you were gone. No one saw either of you leave."

"What?" Hunter's face contorted, revealing how awful he felt.

Matt added, "That's our point; the video cameras shorted out. There's no way you could have gotten out of the interrogation room and left in front of dozens of police officers."

"I don't understand." His mind seemed so foggy. What they were saying sounded impossible, yet the burns were real.

"Are you sure you can't remember anything?" Nurre asked.

He shook his head. "It's all a blur."

Matt nodded. "Maybe it will come back to you after you've rested and aren't pumped full of painkillers."

"I'm pretty exhausted."

"Agent Coburn," Nurre said, "we need help here. It doesn't look good that both of you disappeared at the same time."

"This is ridiculous." Matt stepped closer. "He shouldn't be a person of interest."

Hunter frowned. "Hold on. You got the call, Matt. The Dallas Police asked for our help. I checked out this woman and her BIO-EMP to figure out how the two events were connected, but I never met her before."

"You were gone for almost a week, without a trace." Nurre paused. "Then you magically reappeared in your home."

"A week?" Hunter coughed, wincing.

"Yes, a week," replied Matt. "Do you remember where you were during that time?"

Deflated, Hunter said, "It felt like just a couple of minutes."

"I know you're tired," the director said, pressing him for answers. "I have a few more questions, then we'll let you get some rest. Did you figure out how they're connected?"

"She knew Kants. She said we should destroy the device."

Matt sat on the edge of the chair by his bed. "We saw the first part of your interview with the suspect. We agree with you. They knew each other, but why?"

Hunter shrugged, grimacing with the movement. "Is it safe?"

"The device? The NSA has it," Nurre replied. "I'm sure they'll take it apart and reverse engineer it."

"Do you remember how you got burned?" Matt asked. "Were you tortured?"

Hunter heard the concern in his boss's voice. "I . . . I just don't remember," he answered, even though he clearly recalled everything that took place on top of the burned-out skyscraper. "It's like an awful nightmare."

"I understand. It's not every day you up and disappear."

"And not with an assassin," added the director. "Hunter, I'm posting guards at your door for your protection and—"

"To make sure I don't go anywhere." He sighed. "I know the drill."

"More for your protection," Matt said. "You're our only link to this mess. These are dangerous people. We want to make sure you're safe."

"Absolutely," Nurre agreed. "Get better, Agent Coburn. We still have much to discuss."

Hunter closed his eyes. *I've got my own questions.* Too many things had shaken his foundation of reality, including Kants's apology for ruining his life. *What the hell did that man do to me?*

CHAPTER TWENTY-TWO
THE TEST

APRIL 28, 2025

Upon Hunter's release, they'd come directly from the hospital to Director Nurre's office to jump-start the investigation. Matt stood behind the technician administering the lie detector test. *Please don't lie, Hunter.* The performance metrics flowed across the screen in a steady stream.

The tech marked the starting place with his stylus. "You are a graduate of Texas A&M?"

"Yes," Hunter replied.

The image of his face exploded with activity as the device recorded his response. While the new equipment included the old standard measurements, the latest technology in medical science transformed the instrument, such as this high-res thermal image tracker.

"You are a graduate of the University of Texas?"

"Yes," he answered again. This time, the screen maintained a natural composite of data points.

The administrator adjusted the settings. "On April 16, you met with officers Damon and Stillman of the Dallas Police Department."

"Yes."

"On that day, you also interviewed a murder suspect identified as Jane Doe."

"Yes."

"Did you know her before that day?"

"No."

He again paused, marking the screen. "Did you help her escape from incarceration at the Dallas Police Department?"

No, Matt thought. *Of course not.*

"No."

Again, he watched for the telltale signs of a lie. "Do you know how you left the building?"

"No."

"You were missing from April sixteenth to April twenty-third."

Hunter replied, "So they say."

The tech gave him a stern look. "Do you know where you were during that time?"

"No."

They waited through another gap in questioning. The polygraph indicated no deception.

"When you were missing, did you meet with the woman known as Jane Doe?"

"No."

"During that time, you were doused with a caustic solution and inhaled numerous toxins. Do you know how that happened?"

"No."

"Do you know how you arrived at your home on April twenty-third?"

Hunter sighed wearily. "No."

"No?" the tech asked.

"No," he replied with a little more authority.

The thermal image of his face appeared unfazed. The man glanced over at Director Nurre. She leaned forward, resting her elbows on her desk, with her hands clasped, her index fingers pressed to her pursed lips.

"I've gone through all the questions. He's clean."

"Are you sure he can't fool it?" she asked.

"Not this new model. You sniff wrong, and it knows. No, ma'am. He's telling the truth."

Matt walked over to unhook Hunter. *Back to the drawing board.* He handed the wires to the tech. "I guess that settles that."

"It would seem so," answered the director. "Thank you for your time." They watched in silence as he packed up his equipment and left the room.

Hunter wiped the back of his hand across his forehead in fake relief. "Whew, thought I might need to worry there for a minute. Now what?"

"I'm putting you on administrative leave while we sort this out," Nurre said. "There's still the matter of the missing fugitive woman and the fact that you were MIA for a week."

"I figured that would happen. You know I'm about ready to start the second phase with Comperi. Can I work on that from home?"

She looked at Matt for a moment. "I'm afraid not. We'll have to put that on the back burner for now. I'm still very interested in your project, Agent Coburn, though we need to get some things resolved first."

"I could help."

"Go home. Take a few days off. Heal. When we have more questions, we know where to find you."

Hunter slid his shirt back on and stood up. "I'd surrender my firearm, but you already have it."

Banks raised a hand for him to be quiet.

"I know you didn't lie," Nurre said, "but I wonder if we just didn't ask the right questions."

"You're talking to our top AI expert here, Sandeep," Matt countered. "He's got nothing to hide."

"I know," she said. "That's what makes it even more frustrating." She softened her tone. "I think you have a wedding to plan, don't you, Hunter? Why don't you work on that for a while?"

"Yes, ma'am. I can do that."

He doesn't sound too happy about it. Talk about FUBAR. Matt escorted his agent to the door. "I'll be in touch. Go home and rest."

***

The traffic on Northwest Highway flowed relatively lightly for midafternoon. It stopped at the intersection leading into Bachman Lake, which stood at the north edge of Love Field Airport. A few people jogged on the running trail that surrounded the park. A Boeing 737 jet thundered overhead on its landing approach.

Hunter clutched the steering wheel with his bandaged hands. He felt pretty good. His lungs and all his burns were healing remarkably fast, baffling the doctors. *So many questions*, he thought. Every unanswered one led to another, even more outlandish supposition. *If this were all a dream, I wouldn't have the burns. And how can Kants still be alive when I watched him die?* There must be logical answers; he just needed to put the pieces together. He knew where to start.

The traffic light finally changed. Hunter turned south on Lemmon Avenue, heading toward the street once lined with police cars. This time, no helicopter flew overhead, and no SWAT team could be seen. He stopped at the entrance to the mansion and announced himself, waited for the gate to slide open, then headed up the long driveway. Hunter rang the doorbell and waited. A large bodyguard answered, his hand on his holstered pistol.

"Is Dr. Hilfer in?"

A voice from inside the home said, "Move over, Wayne. I've been expecting him."

The guard stepped aside, still vigilant.

"Welcome, Dr. Coburn," Dr. Hilfer said.

"Thank you, sir, but please call me Hunter."

"Then you need to call me Jeff. Are you okay?" He indicated Hunter's bandages with a pointed look.

"Better every day."

As they entered the foyer, Hunter noticed the new furniture, no blood, and no indications of a battle waged in this room.

"I'm so glad you stopped by," Jeff said. "I never got a chance to thank you for saving our lives." He paused and looked somberly at Hunter, seeming to tamp back his emotion. After an awkward moment, he inhaled sharply and moved on. "May I offer you a drink?"

"I probably shouldn't, considering the past week, but that sounds great. A double whiskey if you've got it." He followed him into his office. "I would have come sooner, but I've been tied up lately."

"Well, you're here now. Something is on your mind."

He stopped at the wet bar and pulled out a bottle of scotch. He pointed to two leather wingback chairs that sat facing each other. After pouring the drinks, he carefully handed one to Hunter. The men sat down and sipped the whiskey. It felt good going down Hunter's throat, like a warm glow moving through his body.

"This isn't an official visit, sir. I should point that out."

Jeff smiled. "Ah, I see. You are seeking answers, as am I. What did he want with us? And why?"

"He told me his name. Richard Kants. Did he say anything interesting to you?"

"Nothing useful, I'm afraid." Jeff waved a dismissive hand as he leaned back. "Granted, I was under an enormous amount of duress. Despite that, he did not follow a logical pattern."

"You weren't his target. He wanted your wife."

"I surmised that when he almost broke my arm, trying to force Isabella to open the panic-room door. Why go after her? She's a psychologist. He talked nonsense."

Hunter struggled with how much to reveal about Kants's true purpose. "He told me I would die if I told anyone what happened."

Jeff raised an eyebrow. "Since you're still alive, one would have to assume you have mentioned this to no one."

"He doesn't understand law enforcement. We get threats like that all the time. That's not what stops me from saying anything."

"Then what *is* stopping you?"

"I'm not sure what to say. All I have are questions and no answers."

"I guess that's to be expected, considering we all witnessed a future event."

Hunter's eyes widened, and he threw back a big slug of his drink. He reined in his racing thoughts and worked to keep his voice steady. "A what?"

Jeff took another sip before answering. "What else would you call it? The facts speak for themselves. For instance, consider the BIO-EMP. Your peers are at a loss to explain it. I've done some investigating on my own. It's not supposed to be technically possible."

"Which is why I need your help. Kants compared time to a neural network for artificial intelligence."

"Hmm. You know, some experts believe time is connected to multiple points, or even dimensions." Jeff paused, shifting his position in the comfortable chair. "Every action in a time period has a cascading effect on all other points of time at that same moment."

It still seemed difficult to comprehend unless Hunter wanted to suspend his current view of reality. "I think of time as linear. Wouldn't that be the reason why no one has seen a time traveler before?"

"You're following a simple pattern of logic, my friend. 'I have not seen a time traveler; therefore, none exists.' Remember your neural net theory? If one showed up, it would ripple through all time, changing it, maybe even creating a separate timeline. We could see time travelers but fail to recognize them as such."

"Now you sound like Kants," Hunter said, but he did start to understand a little more.

"This is just conjecture. I saw the BIO-EMP device, and it didn't look like it came from our time. We don't have those capabilities yet. So, it must be from the future."

Hunter didn't want to admit it, but he'd been having similar thoughts. "That's impossible."

"People used to say we'd never be able to fly, but look at us now. Besides, your 'impossible' gadget took out several blocks. Even our military has nothing that can match it."

"I know, but this sounds legitimately crazy," Hunter answered.

"Which is why you haven't told anyone yet; you don't want to sound insane."

"Well . . . yes." He stood up. "This is going to seem weird, but could we go to your bedroom? I need to check something."

"Weird?" Jeff said. "Can it get any weirder? Sure, but what are you looking for?"

"A phantom, maybe." They walked up the elegant staircase and down that familiar hallway. In the main bedroom, Hunter knelt next to the spot where Kants died. He ran his hand along the wooden planks.

"We deep cleaned everywhere," Jeff said. "You won't find anything, my friend."

"I swear I saw something leave his body. It came out and floated over him, not exactly like a vapor, but something. I don't know how to describe it, but it disappeared right here." Hunter ran his hand over the area again, as if that would change the outcome.

"Are you saying his soul? You watched his soul leave his body?" Jeff laughed, incredulous. "As a scientist, I have a hard time believing that."

Hunter shrugged and pulled out his key chain, which had a small, cylinder-like shape attached. "Maybe a black light will see something."

"Why on Earth would you carry one of those?"

"Our little dog tends to have accidents on the carpet. This is the easiest way to find stains."

He flicked it on, pointing it at the floor. The silhouette of a wolf's head glowed on the wood. It seemed to waver as if the red-orange fur bristled at being discovered. *And there you are*, Hunter thought. *I'm not losing my mind*. He turned it off, and the wolf disappeared, then came back to life when he clicked it on again.

"That's incredible!" Jeff kneeled next to Hunter. He reached out but stopped. "Do you think it's safe to touch?"

"Hell, I don't even know what it is. We should cut that floorboard out and have it analyzed."

Jeff backed up. "That's amazing and terrifying at the same time. I'll have Wayne get a skill saw and cut it out for you."

Hunter snapped a few photos on his cell phone, then the men returned to the study. He took a swig of his drink and let out a defeated sigh. "I can't wrap my head around all this."

"Hmm, yes. I'm afraid I'm only going to add to your dilemma."

He scoffed. "I'm not sure it could get much worse."

Jeff walked over to a framed painting hanging on the wall. He touched the side, and it swung open on a hinge, revealing a hidden safe. He unlocked it and pulled out a large white binder, then brought the book to Hunter, handing it to him. "You know what that is?"

"Light-Harvesting System for Fusion Fuel," he read aloud. "A technical manual?"

"You've never seen this before?"

He gave Jeff a quizzical look. "No, sir. Should I have?"

"Yes, you should be very familiar with it. You gave it to me."

"I . . . I what?"

"About three months ago, you showed up at at my coffee shop, where I sometimes take my laptop to do some work. You handed this book to me. It's the blueprint for making cheap energy from water."

"Until last week, I didn't even know who you are." Hunter shook his head in objection. "How would I have ever—"

"Trust me, you were there. Regardless, do you understand the magnitude of what I'm saying? There is no denying the fact that this is from the future."

"Sorry. I'm still not following."

"The theories and formulas are impossible for me, or anyone else in our time, to develop with our current understanding of physics." Jeff retrieved the book and thumbed through it.

Hunter frowned. "You're sure of this?"

"Positive. There's one other thing that led me to this conclusion."

"Which is?"

"You said I wrote it."

Hunter leaned back. "Wow. Oh, wow."

"Wow is right. You're smart not to say anything to anyone just yet. I'm certain we are dealing with time travelers." He took a large gulp of his scotch. "Hunter, that includes you."

"Me?"

An intense look passed between the men, and Jeff returned to his chair. They sat without a word for a while, deep in thought.

"We know of two instances where you have already gone into the past or future."

Hunter cleared his throat nervously. "I don't know how to time travel."

"Yet," Jeff replied.

"Yet?"

"You have no way to travel in time yet. Evidently, in the future, you do find a way. Logic dictates that conclusion."

"H—How?" He sat quietly, taking this in. "And why? I have a great life here and now. Why would I do that?"

"Who knows how you time traveled? But you gave definite reasons. For example, you believed I should discover cheap energy from fusion and water."

"This boggles my mind."

"I don't get it either. For whatever reason, we are linked together in this." Jeff leaned forward. "Imagine my shock when you walked into my bedroom with Kants. Right now, we must focus our efforts on figuring out why this is happening, rather than how."

"Kants is alive. At least I think he's alive."

Jeff looked over his drink. "No. We saw him die. He left his mark on my floor."

"True. I'm pretty sure I recently saw him alive, though."

"That is most disturbing. I'm glad I hired a bodyguard."

Hunter sighed. "I know why they were after your wife."

Jeff's eyes narrowed. "Why?"

"They were trying to kill your unborn child."

"My child?" He paused, appearing shocked by the revelation. "How on Earth did you—?" He stopped mid-question. "You realize we've told no one that she's pregnant?"

"I guess in the future, they know you have a son."

"A son," Jeff repeated. He leaned back in his chair, a bemused smile on his face.

"Yes," Hunter replied. "But for some reason, they want him dead."

Jeff stopped smiling. "That explains what happened at the Blue Goose a couple of weeks ago. We must have been the target."

Hunter's mouth dropped open. "You were there?"

"Yes, but we got out before the police showed up. It seems they missed twice."

"Argh," Hunter growled. "That just brings up more questions. Who are these people trying to stop Kants and this woman? And why are they trying to stop them? All we have are questions, and the only people who have answers are gone."

"Then we find them to figure out what happened," Jeff said.

Sure. No problem. "Any ideas on how we could do that?"

"I don't think we have to do the finding, Hunter. I think they will come to us. They have unfinished business."

Oh, no. He's right. "The baby."

"Yes."

"So, we have to be ready."

"Exactly. We must protect Isabella and my son. As much as I hate to admit it, we must prepare for their return."

"Do you think they'll know what we're trying to do since they're from the future?"

He watched Jeff close his eyes and roll his shoulders, taking a deep breath. "If Kants's theory of time travel is like the neural net, then maybe not. For example, a timeline could exist where there is no such thing as time travel."

"So, we're rewriting history, and they may not have visibility into what we're doing?"

"That's one theory."

"Yes, but is it the right theory?"

"Time will tell, Hunter. Time will tell."

CHAPTER TWENTY-THREE
THE SESSON

APRIL 29, 2025

Hunter's homecoming proved to be sweet, emotional, intense. They polished off a few glasses of wine and held each other close for a long time, their intimacy heightened by the fright they had recently endured. He grinned when Rachel started to snore softly. Normally, he'd be sound asleep right next to her. Now, with his mind whirling, sleep would not be happening anytime soon.

Hunter slid out of bed, pulled on his shorts, and quietly closed the bedroom door behind him. He went to his study and sat at his desk in the leather "command chair," as Rachel dubbed it.

"Engage."

In the middle computer screen, the black wolf appeared out of a snow-covered forest. "You rang?"

"Yes. Any luck?"

The wolf shook itself and sat down. "Nothing except several mentions of you in the Dallas News."

"Me? You were looking for me?"

"Your absence concerned me. I did not understand why you were gone."

It's like Comperi cares, he thought. "Did you miss me?"

"We spoke daily for three years, five months, three weeks, one day, ten hours, twenty-four minutes, and twelve seconds. Your seven days, twelve hours, and forty minutes of absence were noted. Am I wrong to have searched for you?"

"I guess not. You know humans would just say we've spoken to each other every day for over three years and then we didn't for over a week."

"Too precise?" Comperi asked.

"Yes," Hunter said.

"Duly noted. Why were you a fugitive?"

"A fugitive?"

"Per the Dallas police report, you escaped with one Jane Doe," the wolf replied. "However, you were recently downgraded to a person of interest."

"Have they found the woman?"

"As of 22:55 hours, the answer is no."

"Can you find her?"

The wolf reached around and nibbled on its rear haunches as if it were scratching an itch. It stopped and looked back at Hunter with golden eyes. "She is like Kants: absent from society in this time period."

"What do you mean, in this time period?"

"I reviewed the videos in the Kants directory. I recommend you watch the first file as it pertains to time travel."

"I didn't give you permission to look at those files. Why did you access them?"

"You gave me permission."

"I don't think so. Provide the logs for when I gave you permission," ordered Hunter. "I want proof."

The wolf stood up and shook off the accumulating snow. "I will need the passcode to access that information."

"Passcode? I don't need a passcode."

"You locked many files and marked them critical," Comperi said.

"Which files?"

"The logs and the Kants video files two through eight."

Hunter looked around his desktop for the missing USB drive. More than likely, Rachel had cleaned up the place and put it somewhere. He quickly searched the top drawers where she dumped his stuff but with no luck. "But not the Kants video file one?"

"That is still accessible."

Hunter clasped the back of his head in frustration. *My damn AI computer knows more than I do.* "When did all of this happen?"

"I can't say."

"Without a passcode."

"Yes."

It occurred to him that he could run the decryption cipher, hard coded into the AI mainframe. "I need you to run subroutine 'Verify' on this passcode and then provide it to me."

"I can't run Verify against your passcodes without your password."

I'm battling myself. "Is there anything you *can* tell me?"

"Yes," Comperi replied. "You instituted several back-door scenarios to give yourself remote access to me."

"I did?"

"Yes."

"Well, can I have those authentication protocols?"

The wolf nodded. "I sent them to your phone. The password to open them is *snowstorm* with the common interrupters."

"Did I leave myself any instructions?"

"Yes: to watch Kants video one."

Hunter waved a hand. "Well, throw it up on the big screen, and let's have at it."

The mountain meadow disappeared, and a large video window popped open. It showed Richard Kants lying prone on a couch in an office. He seemed to be asleep. A woman sat next to him. She adjusted an IV drip attached to his arm, then leaned back in her chair and picked up a notepad.

"This is Dr. Julia Camp. When I count to three, your eyes will open. One, two, three . . ."

Hunter scratched his chin. "What's going on?"

"Keep watching," answered Comperi.

Kants opened his eyes on command and peered around in a groggy manner. He seemed confused.

"Nice to have you back with us. How do you feel?"

"Out of sorts. My head is muddled." He looked at the tube attached to his arm.

"That is to be expected. Don't worry. The medication is to help you stay relaxed."

Kants looked around. "I do not know my name."

Hunter frowned. "He doesn't know his own name?"

The woman wrote something on her notepad. "You have amnesia. You're safe. We have a few things to discuss today, okay?"

"You will help me figure out who I am?"

"That's our goal."

"Proceed."

She continued, "Let's start with some basics. Do you remember where you're from?"

"I am from 23 . . . 55," he answered.

"That's a good start. Is that a street address number?"

"No. That is the year."

"What?" Hunter exclaimed.

Dr. Camp raised an eyebrow. "So, you claim you are from the future?"

Kants raised his free hand to his forehead. "I know too many things. I have to be."

"I see," she replied. "What brings you back to our time?"

"I must warn Hunter Coburn."

"Holy crap," he said, leaning in closer.

She jotted something down. "And what do you need to warn him about?"

"He is a time traveler, like me. I see him in the past and in the future. He is in danger."

"Stop video!" The frame froze on Kants. Hunter jumped out of his seat and paced around the room, running his hands through his hair. "No, no, no. That's impossible." He stopped, thinking, then finally sat back in his chair.

The wolf asked, "Shall I resume the video?"

"We don't have much choice at this point."

The video started with Kants saying, *"It is imperative that he understand. I cannot tell him. You must."*

"This is a very unusual story, but you know I can't say anything because of patient confidentiality. I'm sure once you find this gentleman, you will tell him yourself."

"If I say anything to him, the Final Stroke will kill me. You must tell him for me."

She took more notes. "Please stay relaxed. I record everything. Perhaps you can show him the video?"

He shook his head. "Do not tell me anything, or the capsule in my brain will explode!" His voice escalated with anxiety. "I do not want to die. Do you understand? You cannot!"

"You're getting agitated," Dr. Camp replied in a soothing tone. "That's something we both agreed could not happen. We need to end this session."

"Do not tell me anything," he barked out, as if his orders were unquestionably obeyed.

"It's going to be fine. Now, close your eyes and start counting back from one hundred."

He hesitated, then said, "One hundred, ninety-nine, ninety-eight—" The video ended.

Hunter sat stunned, staring at the still picture of Kants. He looked at the wolf. "Did you get all of that?"

"Yes."

"This is such a cluster—"

"Agreed."

CHAPTER TWENTY-FOUR
THE WORM

July 25, 2355

Surprising how hot it can get in a space station, Kristen thought, dabbing at her forehead. The dressing room backed up to one of the large generators. The wall emanated heat. She slid into her pants and buckled them on, shaking her legs to get the creases out. With the press of a small button on the inner belt, the body armor adhered tightly to her legs, eliminating any looseness. She slipped her new knife into its sheath and watched it disappear.

Kristen floated to the command room to prepare for the mission brief. She parked herself in the seat and said, "Secure." The restraints slid out of the side of the chair and wrapped around her, holding her in place.

Dr. Bannister entered with the dreaded injector in her hand. She placed it next to Kristen's shoulder and pressed the trigger.

"Okay, Mom, I'll take my meds." She flinched, but at least she now knew what to expect.

"Looks like you're ready," her boss said.

"Let's talk about whoever has Kants's transponder. Shouldn't I interrogate them first? I mean, what if they're not a threat?"

"Everybody's a threat. You must follow through with the plan and terminate them, so we can link you with a new partner."

"I know, I know. We can't afford to have someone out there who doesn't have the Final Stroke embedded in their head," she said in mock dismay. "No telling how that would impact the timeline."

"Kristen . . ."

"Just messing with you, Doc. I think I'm going to enjoy working alone. Kants . . ." She paused. "Talk about a pain in the neck."

Bannister sighed. "Yes. But he was our top operative. I understand what you're saying, though."

"Sorry, Doc. I keep forgetting. He's your all-time favorite."

Her boss scrutinized her face. "I wish you could have more time to learn from the best about what we do."

"Yeah, me too." Kristen blinked and looked away. *I learned plenty about abandoning your partner.* "Have you figured out what my secondary mission is yet?"

"It's not secondary anymore," Bannister replied, business-like. "This is a fantastic opportunity." She placed the diamond link on Kristen's forehead. "Here you go."

The deluge of information downloaded into her neural time transponder. Her limbs twitched, and a rigid grimace lodged in her jaw. When the info dump finished, her body relaxed, and she could again focus her eyes.

"Whoa," she said as she recovered. "That's a huge mission. You want me to do this on my own?"

"I debated giving this to Sylvia Mantua's team but decided against it. Chen-Yi, what is the impact projection?"

The AI computer said, "Allen Nelson negotiates a world treaty to eliminate weapons of mass destruction in 2065. The Purge War will still occur, but the world's surface will not be decimated by nuclear holocaust."

"Aren't we trying to stop the war?" Kristen asked.

"Yes, certainly," Bannister affirmed, "but this is the next best thing."

"Well, we know he wasn't successful."

"That's because his father dies before Allen is conceived. He never starts his peace movement."

"So, this guy, Kevin Nelson, would have been Allen's dad?"

"Yes, he is, or would have been. This is the mission we've been hoping and waiting for. Chen-Yi, what are the odds again?"

"One hundred percent, if successful. If the mission is a failure, it reduces the chances by half."

No pressure, Kristen thought. "If it's that important, why wouldn't you send Sylvia's team?"

"Outside of Kants, you're my best operative. Call it a gut feeling."

Ah, she thought. "At least we're not trying to kill someone this time. Oh, wait." She couldn't restrain her sarcasm. "I'm supposed to do that too." Different images coursed to the forefront of her mind. "*Battlefield Ocean*? What in Orion's belt is that?"

"An old television show where they fought to save whales from extinction. Kevin Nelson's father founded this movement, and he followed in his footsteps."

"The whole planet dies. So why do we care about the whales?"

"That's a short-sighted view," Bannister responded. "Remember, we're trying to save the planet. That includes the entire ecosystem, not just mankind. The whales are a big part."

"Okay . . ." Kristen thought for a minute. "If Nelson dies in the past, then how do you know his son will be this so-called 'savior?' It never happened, right?"

"I'm impressed," Bannister said. A pleased look crossed her face. "You're the first person to ask."

Kristen grinned. "It's not rocket science, you know."

"Apparently not. The Worm sees multiple timelines, not just ours. We see futures that could be, and that's what we're trying to steer toward: a better timeline."

"Now that's some rocket science bullshit right there."

"Nevertheless, it's the truth," Bannister replied.

"I guess I'm going to have to take your word for it."

"We've been given a second chance here, Kristen. You must save Kevin Nelson. We believe he goes down with the ship."

"You're telling me I have to save an entire ship?"

"If it saves Kevin Nelson, yes."

CHAPTER TWENTY-FIVE
THE BRIDGE

MAY 2, 2025

Rock Creek meandered northward from Washington, D.C. through several neighboring cities. The scenic, heavily forested beltway existed as an extensive national park. An old wooden bridge with a bench in the middle stretched over a secluded area, where Sandeep sat relaxing with her feet propped on the lower wooden rail. The creek burbled peacefully twenty feet below. She breathed in the fragrant springtime and thought, *I love this.*

"This is one of my favorite places." Cassandra Hughes walked up and sat next to her. "But I never seem to get out here." She tilted her head back and closed her eyes for a moment, seeming to enjoy the warm sunshine filtering through the trees.

"It is nice," Sandeep agreed. "Reminds me of my hometown in North Carolina." She adjusted herself, sitting more upright. "How are things at the NSA?"

Cassandra propped one foot on the wooden rail. "I'm glad you called this meeting because we need to talk. It looks like we have a national emergency on our hands."

So much for unwinding a bit. Sandeep looked sidelong at her. "National emergencies get my attention. What's going on?"

"It's about your agent, Hunter Coburn."

"Hunter? He's your national emergency? I thought it might be the BIO-EMP device you confiscated."

"That's part of it as well."

"Hmm." Sandeep sighed. "Have you figured out how it works?"

"Not really. Your boy made some headway beforehand. The entire thing is pretty fried."

"Well, we know how fast technology changes. We just need to find the people who designed it."

"You don't understand, Sandeep. This weapon isn't from our world."

She snorted. "Excuse me? Are you saying it's made by aliens?"

Her counterpart didn't reply.

"For Christ's sake, you can't be serious."

"I'm not sure what I'm saying, but the NSA has drawn a blank. The CIA has too. This threat is now our nation's top risk." Cassandra abruptly changed the subject. "Why did your sniper have to take out Richard Kants?"

Whiplash, Sandeep thought, trying to keep up. "Our guys didn't do that."

"What? I figured—Oh, never mind. Any ideas on who it could be?"

"No. But there were substantial differences in this case. The body and scene were neat and tidy—no bullet, no spatter whatsoever. The wound basically cauterized itself, especially on the exit site. My lead engineer thinks it came from some hyperkinetic type of projectile."

Cassandra nodded. "That's disturbing, yes. I'd say your engineer is dead-on."

Her spine went rigid. "Gee, I'm so glad you approve," she said, perturbed. "My investigators are top—"

"I simply mean both of our teams can bring something to the table." Cassandra paused, then said briskly, "The NSA has in its possession a futuristic pistol from the Kennedy scene, back in the 1960s. They determined it to be hyperkinetic as well."

Sandeep stared, knowing there would be more.

"We field tested the gun. It leaves no trace upon firing, and it inflicts devastating internal damage with little to no external evidence. Much like you mentioned, the entry and exit wounds cauterize themselves."

She felt her mouth go slack.

"Not only that, it's also lethal from almost three miles out. There's nothing like it in our arsenal."

Sandeep considered this new information. "That range would explain how the assassin could be in position outside the bubble radius and survive the BIO-EMP detonation. If your team or mine had nothing to do with firing that round, well, that's a game changer."

"Exactly. It's concerning that another weapon like this has shown up after so many years. No telling how many more there might be."

"Downright scary, I'd say. Do you need Hunter's help reverse engineering the gun?"

"At some point, perhaps," Cassandra answered. "There's more. This technology is just the tip of the iceberg."

Sandeep frowned. "What's that supposed to mean?"

Her cohort turned toward her with an intimidating look on her face. "The Hilfer event revealed much more than advanced weaponry. The autopsies on the bodies from the living room indicate enormously enhanced biological traits. We don't yet understand the mechanics of their makeup. You do know, Hunter is our only link to them."

"Hunter is not some sort of super-soldier."

"No, but he is involved in something inexplicable. Whoever this is, they're on our doorstep now. Think tanks are predicting an invasion. If that happens, we have no way of stopping them. We must capture one of these individuals alive to get this figured out."

"Next, you're going to tell me you want to use him as bait."

Cassandra looked tired, and she didn't respond.

"Are you putting a team on him?"

"Absolutely."

Sandeep suddenly felt weary. "He won't like this."

"There are no alternatives. Hunter is in a dangerous position. He knows and trusts you, so explain only as much as you must."

He'll be safer, she begrudgingly admitted to herself, *but I feel like a traitor.* "What does POTUS think about this?"

"We're all watching this one closely, and for good reason." Cassandra stood and walked toward the nature trail, stopped just short of the bridge entrance, then turned back with a serious expression. "My team will be there in twenty-four hours or less. Until then, get your best people on Hunter, and tell them all to be careful. The group we're up against . . . Well, they're quite remarkable and almost indestructible."

Great. And how are we supposed to stop them? "I'll see what I can do."

CHAPTER TWENTY-SIX
THE GOODBYE

AUGUST 12, 2098

La Casa en El Mar, one of three experimental arcology settlements around the world, rose twenty-five stories above the ocean and held the distinction of being the world's largest city on water. Designed to be self-sustaining, it sat off the Florida coastline in the Gulf of Mexico, appearing to float on the surface. In fact, it sat on massive pylons driven into the deep-sea floor. Hilfer fusion saltwater generators powered the two-and-a-half-mile-long oval structure. Scientists studied the system and its six hundred thousand occupants, determining and refining the necessities for humanity to thrive successfully in remote, extraterrestrial locations.

Sunrise arrived earlier on the east side of the twenty-second floor than it did at sea level. This morning proved no different. The clock read 0600 hours when soft rays snuck through the blinds, landing across the bed in golden streaks. Richard Kants stood by the window, studying his wife, who slept soundly with the sheet ruffled over her. He noticed Angelika's peaceful, rhythmic breathing and the way her hair fell around her face. He wanted to memorize her every nuance, to breathe her in; her intoxicating scent drove him wild.

Nothing better than feeling you next to me, he thought. *You changed everything for the better.*

Before Richard ever knew Angelika, he volunteered to participate in an experimental DNA recombinant transformation program

154

to better his military career in the Earth Defense Force. The gene splicing had a profound effect on his body—extensive increases in muscle mass and reactionary capabilities, incredible enhancement of his senses, a much-diminished need for sleep. It made him almost superhuman. The scientists didn't anticipate several significant issues, though, including the surprisingly lethal response during transformation. Few of the volunteers survived the process. This terrible, unexpected complication coupled with the unique physiological changes heightened the emotional toll on Kants, further wrecking his traumatized psyche. He became volatile, angry, and he teetered on the edge of losing control.

That is, until Angelika came into his life. Her love helped to calm the turmoil he suffered. *I can't imagine living without you,* he thought, stroking her cheek. He knew she felt the same. They'd been up late the night before, relishing their last few hours together before he departed. Colonel Kants had recently received deployment orders to the Red Planet. For his new commission, he would be serving as Chief Security Officer on Mars Colony, a station established on the findings from La Casa en El Mar. His wife could join him for the duration of the assignment after his six-month review.

Angelika opened her eyes and yawned. Richard smiled. "Good morning, sleepy head."

She stretched and rolled toward him. "You'd think, after all this time, you'd get tired of watching me sleep."

"Does it bother you?" He sat down on the edge of the bed.

"No, silly." Angelika snuggled next to him. "What am I going to do without you?"

The comment felt like a stab in his heart. "It's only for six months."

"Promise?"

"Promise." He assured her with a tender kiss. "You know, I still have two hours before I have to be on the launch pad."

"I wonder," she questioned, "whatever could we do with the time?"

He buried his head in her neck. "I imagine we can think of something."

They nestled under the blankets, feeling fulfilled and so close. Angelika eventually crawled over him to reach the nightstand. She opened the drawer and pulled out a small, wrapped box.

"Here, I have a gift for you."

"What's this?"

"It's to remember me by."

"Darling, you are unforgettable," Kants said, opening it. He pulled out an antique pocket watch and chain. "Oh—"

She pulled on his arm. "Open the case."

He pressed the clasp. It snapped open to reveal a timepiece and a sweet photograph of Angelika on the inside of the cover. Richard's throat closed. "It's beautiful," he choked out.

"Now, no matter what time it is or where you are," she said, dewy-eyed, "I'll be with you."

Kants embraced her, feeling grateful. It took a moment for him to compose himself.

Angelika soon pulled back, smiling, and kissed his eyes. "I will always be with you, my love."

Holographic video screens monitored traffic on La Casa en El Mar. A three-hundred-and-sixty-degree sweep of the city tracked aircraft, boats, and submersibles, with each vessel's metrics highlighted in colors from steady green to flashing red. AI computers generated any necessary route or other changes, managed landings, and, if a vehicle's status went to red, the computer would analyze and implement remedial measures, or move the ship out of harm's way.

Outside the centralized, circular air traffic control tower, people moved about the busy tarmac, refueling, loading and unloading freight, completing maintenance, or tending to other jobs. Arresting wires on the runway caught the roaring, incoming aircraft. Others launched off the edge into the sky, their deafening afterburners rattling through the entire floor, which looked like a massive aircraft carrier with a cavernous roof overhead. The noise from the aircraft engines bled through the thick glass wall in the observation deck.

Oblivious to it all, Richard leaned into Angelika as she embraced him. "You did not have to come here."

Angelika put her mouth next to his ear. "Six months is a long time."

A crew member opened the door to the hangar and bellowed over the roar of jet engines, "Colonel Kants, I'm here to escort you to your shuttle."

He kissed Angelika once more. "Thank you. I will talk to you in a couple of weeks."

"Message that you made it okay," she replied, worry on her face.

Kants nodded as he stepped through the door and moved down the metal stairs.

Angelika watched him stride confidently to the transport without a glance back, which she expected. Two officers met him at the open ramp door, saluting as he entered. The door closed, and the shuttle hovered, gliding slowly over to the launch point while its wings unfolded. A blast shield rose behind it. The transport rocketed out of the bay with a loud roar, disappearing into the blue-white sky.

She fought to keep the tears at bay. Once he morphed into military mode, she hardly recognized her husband. *I should have told him. But what would that have done to him?* Angelika understood intuitively that knowing would add to his heavy stress load. He didn't need that. They would have to wait until after the baby arrived to be together again.

CHAPTER TWENTY-SEVEN
THE ENGAGEMENT PLAN

MAY 2, 2025

The homes in North Dallas off Hillcrest and Walnut Hill were average-looking brick dwellings built in the 1950s and '60s. Full, beautiful trees towered over the three- and four-bedroom houses. Detached garages sat in the back, where narrow alleyways lined with wooden privacy fences marked the property lines.

Hunter and Rachel could afford a much nicer, newer, and larger home, but he knew she loved the old-style neighborhood. She believed it conveyed a friendly atmosphere for when children arrived, although that didn't stop her from bringing in an interior decorator to update the house. The couple enjoyed long walks and getting to know the folks who lived around them.

Across the alley, a man dressed in dark clothing scaled the fence. He stood on top to leap onto a thick tree branch. Quick as a cat, the Watcher pulled himself up and disappeared into a play fort wedged in the large oak tree.

He propped his Vortex Solo Monocular in the small window facing Hunter and Rachel's home. The infrared scope made it easy to follow the couple moving about inside, even with the curtains closed. He pulled out his cell phone, dimmed the screen, then typed the message, "In position," and hit send.

The modernized kitchen sat at the back of their home. Hunter scraped the plates and stuck them into the dishwasher, while Rachel cleared the dinner table. She playfully bumped him on her way to the refrigerator, causing him to spray himself with water.

"Ack!" he protested. "I need eyes in the back of my head. Why do you always do that?"

"Because you make it incredibly easy."

He hugged her from behind. "You found your dress today? Can I see it?"

"Of course not!" Rachel turned, wrapping her arms around his neck. "It has to be special on our wedding day."

"That's a dumb rule."

She kissed him. "Well, that's the way it is. Speaking of special, have you decided on a best man? You're running out of time."

"I know. I asked Tyler this morning, and he accepted."

"Of course he did! What're you going to tell Kevin?"

"I think he'll be all right with being a groomsman."

"Are you sure? He thinks you're his big brother."

Hunter pulled out his phone and punched in a number, then put it on speaker. "Let's find out."

The satellite phone rang multiple times before a gruff voice answered. "This better be good."

"Oops. This isn't the Crab Shack?" He could hear a storm raging in the background.

"Hey!" Kevin replied. "Is that my favorite landlubber?"

"Funny," Hunter said drolly.

Rachel snickered. "He does look kind of like a landlubber."

"Hey, Rache! I heard my boy is finally going to make an honest woman out of you."

"Rumor has it." She shot Hunter an exaggerated look of skepticism.

"Hah! Well, guys, what's up? We're plowing through a monsoon to get to the North Koreans, and I'm kinda busy here."

"What happened to the Japanese?" asked Hunter.

"Oh, they're a thorn in my side too, but the North Koreans have figured out that whales are an easier way to feed their people. Gonna make for good TV footage on *Battlefield Ocean*."

"Maybe we should call back later."

"Nah. Besides, I know what this is about."

"You do?" Hunter looked quizzically at Rachel.

"Yeah, I saw Tyler's Facebook page today."

"Oh, man, I'm sorry about that. I wanted to tell you first."

"No worries, Hunter. He's your freaking brother. He should be your best man."

"That doesn't mean we don't want you in the wedding," Rachel said.

Hunter added, "We'd love for you to be a groomsman, if you can find time to get off that damn boat of yours."

"I'll have you know this is no boat, sir. This is the frigate *Oceanic Pride*, the crown jewel of the *Battlefield Ocean's* fleet! Oh, and I'd be honored to be in your wedding, but only for Rache."

"Aww, that's sweet," she cooed.

Hunter acted miffed. "You're a regular comedian there, Captain Nelson."

"Just tweaking your tail, Landlubber! Look, I gotta go. The weather's turning nasty."

"Okay, my friend. Take care."

The connection ended. Rachel gave Hunter another hug. "You see? Everything is working out perfectly."

"It better be perfect. I plan on getting married only three or four times, but I want the first one to be right."

She squealed, punching him in mock dismay. "I can't believe you just said that!"

"Oops, did I say that out loud? I really meant I want my first and only marriage to be perfect."

Rachel pointed a large spatula at him. "I think that's going to cost you, Dr. Coburn."

Hunter grinned. "Promise?"

She winked in response.

"The pans are done," he declared, tossing the dishrag onto the counter. "How about I work on my project for a while? Then, well—" He waggled his brows suggestively up and down. "Want to go for a walk later?"

Rachel finished putting the leftovers in the fridge. "Depends on how long you work on your project, Mister Frisky. I think there might be a few things that won't happen if you stay in your office too long."

"Hmm," he pondered. "Point taken. I'll be out by nine."

Outside, two government-issue sedans pulled onto their residential street, accelerated until they were a house away, then came to an abrupt stop. Omar Saman and another FBI agent jumped out of the first car as Bill Jackson and his partner emerged from the other. They moved quickly in unison toward Coburn's residence.

Omar pointed to the narrow driveway heading to the backyard. "Jackson, you check out the perimeter. I'll let Hunter know we're here."

He nodded. They jogged toward the driveway.

Omar and his partner headed to the front porch, where he made a quick phone call while he rang the doorbell. "Hey, boss, we're here. I'll let you know how it goes."

He checked his watch, timing his wait. Ten seconds passed before he rang the doorbell again. He looked around the home for the telltale signs of a break-in. Everything seemed normal, but with his FBI spidey senses tingling like electricity coursing over his body, he took another anxious glance at his watch.

CHAPTER TWENTY-EIGHT
EARTH ORBIT

AUGUST 13, 2098

The space station Gateway One served as the refueling midpoint between planet Earth and deep space. Staffed by the military, this important jump-off spot boasted tight security and top-notch accommodations for long-haul passengers, crews, and transports. Only the large frigate, *Ranger*, was currently docked in one of the many demarcation zones for spaceships. Its engines hummed in idle, powering up for a trip to Mars.

Richard Kants clutched a convenient handle, floating gravity-free while he waited at the final security checkpoint before boarding. He eyed the armed guards tethered to either side of the entrance. He knew they could instantly detach, if necessary. Their stun guns contained long-range capabilities since the projectiles were not bound to the rifle.

They signaled for him to come forward. "Please proceed through the scanner, Colonel Kants."

He pushed his way forward, floating slowly.

"Hmm." The guard frowned, looking at his monitor. "You may want to get that valve looked at, sir."

Kants felt his face flush. He wheeled to look at him.

"Sorry, sir." He grinned sheepishly. "Just a joke."

The other guard chuckled and waved him on. "Have a nice trip, sir."

Kants grumbled under his breath, irritated, but he secretly felt relieved. Once he boarded the *Ranger*, he headed for the command center, deep within the ship. He used the snap-rail pulley to get around and soon spotted Captain Romanov at the navigation station. The crew members sat locked down at their posts, engrossed in their responsibilities.

"Colonel Kants reporting for duty," he said. He felt the large ship shudder while the pilot used side thrusters to separate from Gateway One.

Romanov glanced at him, then looked back at the big screen that showed the slow move toward deep space. "There's nothing for you to do here, Colonel. I suggest you get to the sleep chamber and enjoy the ride. This will more than likely be your last chance to get some rest."

Sleep? If he only knew. "I'm pretty sure I could be of assistance, sir."

Romanov turned to him, looking annoyed, but quickly changed his demeanor.

Nothing like facing a superior commander, Kants thought.

"I already have a chief of security. Besides, this is a regular run to Victus Palus. We've done it a hundred times over. I prefer not to change our routine. Why don't you go get hooked up?"

The dismissal irked Kants. He reminded himself that the captain of the ship maintained controlling status while piloting his craft. He nodded curtly and departed for the sleep chamber, where passengers pumped full of specially designed medication traveled in a hibernation-like state for the duration of the journey.

Because of hyperdrive travel, the trip that once took over a hundred days now required merely one hundred twenty hours. With no real inertial dampers, the human body could only absorb so much from the intense changes in g-force. The sleep process, designed to mitigate this issue, seemed unnecessary to Kants, considering his physical differences. He could not inform anyone of his physical status, though. A nurse connected him to the medication. He protested internally, thinking, *I do not need this.*

He tried to be polite, hoping to create inroads with her. "Would you please awaken me after we launch?"

"Sorry, the AI revives only the crew." She adjusted his IV.

"Guess pulling rank wouldn't help."

The nurse laughed. "Not with the AI."

"Figures."

Kants closed his eyes, then he heard a voice. The medication coursing through his body made him drowsy, though, and he almost missed it at first. The voice grew louder, forcing him to pay attention. Finally, he could comprehend the words, though the meaning failed to sink in.

"Save Mars, save the world, save her." The message repeated, over and over, growing louder.

I don't understand.

"Save Mars, save the world, save her."

His anxiety intensified with each repetition until it suddenly stopped.

No, wait, he thought frantically. *What do you mean?*

"Colonel Kants?" A cool hand grasped his shoulder, shaking him lightly. "Time to wake up, sir."

Startled, he opened his eyes. "Is something wrong?"

"No, sir," she replied. "We're here."

"Already?" He reached up to rub his eyes. "I just fell asleep."

She removed the monitoring sensors from his body. "Yes, sir, we have arrived. Amazing, isn't it? Everyone has the same reaction on their first trip. It doesn't matter if it's a few days or a few months; you close your eyes, and then you open them, and there's nothing in between."

Kants frowned, certain that the message he heard started the second he closed his eyes. His intuition told him the odd phrase repeated to make sure he'd remember. It felt ominous, like a strange dream meant only for him. *I will have to consider this later,* he decided. Kants threw on his uniform and headed toward the command center. He intended to get a good look at the Red Planet before their arrival.

Captain Romanov glanced his direction when he entered the room. "Have a good sleep, Colonel?"

"Yes, for about ten seconds. So much for rest and relaxation."

"I didn't want to ruin it for you." He indicated to look at the large view screen. "I present your new home, Victus Palus."

"Life on Mars." Kants leaned in for a closer look. Six large carbon-poly domes surrounded an enormous central one on the sizeable hexagonal land base.

Romanov nodded. "Exactly."

He whistled, long and low. "Impressive."

"That it is," the captain agreed. "You know they infused those beauties with borosilicate glass, compressed to over thirty thousand pounds per square inch."

"I am aware, yes. It creates a resilient radiation barrier that allows sunlight to filter in, plus it's tough as can be. Nothing but top of the line for this outpost."

They admired the base in silence for a moment. *Half a million people here*, Kants thought. The layout didn't look big enough, but he knew it descended downward almost thirty floors for protection against the harsh elements. *Reminds me of home, just in the opposite direction.* This made him think of Angelika, but he forced himself to focus.

"From this perspective, the colony appears to be well-situated and secure."

Romanov shot a side-eyed glance in his direction. "I suppose so. The AI defense system is always operational." He pointed at the towers atop each dome, which bristled with robotic lasers and kinetic cannons. "It controls each of these against meteors and space junk."

Kants frowned. *Is that all?* An awkward pause elapsed.

"Good luck, Colonel. Your personal belongings are on *Shuttle Three*. I recommend being aboard when it departs."

Kants hesitated, feeling uneasy. "Is there more I should be aware of, Captain?"

The man kept his eyes on the screen, but a wan smile crossed his face. "Rumor has it the natives are restless. You're over one hundred and sixty million miles from any real help, and the next shuttle won't be back for at least sixty days. I think you're going to need all the luck you can get."

Kants took a deep breath. *Not the first time I've been thrown into the fire*, he thought. In hindsight, he would have worried about Angelika's safety here. The sooner he cleaned up whatever mess he found, the sooner he could be with her again.

CHAPTER TWENTY-NINE
THE DROP

JULY 25, 2355

Kristen followed Dr. Bannister through the door to the metal cat-walk above the writhing time tunnel. She stopped next to her and watched it ebb and flow, contorting between the two gigantic generators. Vibrations emanated from her feet, right through her core. *Pretty sure this is crazy*, she thought, gulping back her nerves. She tucked her long braid into her uniform and secured her helmet, her movements choppy and mechanical. When she slid the visor down, the onboard computer engaged, identifying her boss as a carbon-based life form.

Bannister spoke to her through their linked headsets, her calming voice matter-of-fact. "The time stream is almost ready." She reached up to seal Kristen's helmet to the collar on her jacket. "We need to get you into position."

"This is the fun part Kants loved," Kristen quipped, moving past her onto the gangplank.

Her boss paid no attention to her comment and continued talking. "Remember, it's imperative that you don't wait. You'll land simultaneously with your counterpart. Pull your gun and shoot."

"I know. I know. I'll get it done. Stop worrying about it."

"Don't think about it. Just do what you have to do. Be aware and be careful. Any last concerns about your primary mission?"

"Yeah, drop me into closer proximity to the target this time."

"Same continent and within two to four weeks of the event is the closest I can get you."

"You should work on that."

Bannister patted her on the shoulder. "Good luck, Agent Winters."

Kristen turned and walked to the end of the gangplank, standing on a red-lit circle. "I hate this part. It just sucks the life right out of you."

"It can't be helped."

She looked down, awed at how much bigger The Worm looked from this perspective. When you dropped in, it felt like being zapped by a lightning bolt.

Bannister called out, "Hang on." The gangplank extended farther, aligning the circle with the seething center section.

The countdown suddenly began at ten, reverberating across the room. Temporal emissions emanated from the vortex with increasing intensity. A laser beam of red exotic matter burst into it, creating a blindingly bright, gaping fissure.

"Five," Kristen whispered, keeping up with the tempo. She looked to the side, located her boss, and met her eye-to-eye through the interior HUD. At the count of three, she folded her arms across her chest.

When the count hit two, Bannister shouted, "Don't shoot if it's Kants!"

The bottom fell out from under her, plunging Kristen downward to be absorbed by the slipstream.

CHAPTER THIRTY
THE DISAPPEARANCE

MAY 2, 2025

Hunter sat at his desk, adjusting his computer chair to put his feet up. He gazed at a large, undersea barrier reef that graced the wall-sized monitor. The screen showed a great white shark's point of view as it slid effortlessly through the clear, blue water. Other sea creatures swam nearby, darting in and out of the haven of the reef.

An old Dave Matthews song played in the background. Hunter listened to the litany of questions in the lyrics, which he likened to his issues. He needed to find the time travelers, or their base, or, at a minimum, the drone. Nothing seemed real anymore. *I don't know how much more of this I can take. I need to get ready for my wedding, for Pete's sake.*

Hunter considered the FBI director's order to go on administrative leave and stay away from the mainframe. Frustrated, he thought, *I can't do that. I need Comperi.* They couldn't stop him from accessing the AI, nor would they be able to find out if he did.

The wolf sat in the middle screen, grooming itself while awaiting instructions.

Hunter pondered where to start. "Any luck with expanding your search?"

The wolf looked up. "Nothing we haven't already discussed."

"What about that floorboard from the Hilfer house?"

"Nothing conclusive appeared on the spectral analysis. The sample contained no residue of any kind."

"Except it's there. The image kind of looks like you."

Comperi cast an offended look at him. "Why would you insult me like that?"

"It's not a bad-looking wolf."

"That's not what I mean."

"I know." Hunter absently rubbed the knots in his neck.

"On to more important matters, then."

"How am I going to find anything out if you won't give me access to those files? I need that information."

Those blazing golden eyes gazed at him. "I only require the password."

"And we both know I don't have it. We've gone through all the passwords I've used in the past. I'm stuck."

"When you have a system crash, what's the first thing you do?"

"Well," he said slowly, "if the issue isn't readily identifiable, I look to see what's changed in the environment in the last twenty-four hours."

The wolf stared.

Not what it wanted to hear, he thought. He continued walking through the process. "If I find a change, I roll back to the last known good version." Hunter stood up when it became clear to him. "That's it. I need to go back to the original source."

"I can send Julia Camp's address to your phone, if you would like."

Hunter smiled. He should have thought of the psychologist who'd recorded the videos. "I expect you've already done that."

The wolf stuck its tongue out to catch a snowflake, a habit it frequently exhibited. Hunter had yet to figure out the reason for it. The doorbell rang, and the monitor immediately flickered to the *Matrix* screensaver.

Who would be stopping by this time of night? He walked over to the office door and inched it open just enough to peer down the hallway. Rachel stood in the foyer, greeting someone. The male voice sounded familiar, but he couldn't place it.

Rachel held onto the door handle as Saman stepped inside. "Omar, what's going on? Why do you have your gun drawn?"

"We're here to help." He peered about the interior. "Is everything okay?"

She frowned and stepped back. "Of course. What are you talking about? You're scaring me."

"Hunter is in danger." He moved further in, looking around a corner. "Is he here?"

Her eyes widened. "He's in his office. Really, everything's fine."

"How's he been acting? Anything unusual?"

"You mean besides his weird sense of humor?"

Omar paused at her flippant response. "Yeah, besides that."

"He's good! I promise." Rachel hesitantly turned to the hallway.

A door slammed shut. They stopped in place, looking at each other in alarm.

"That's odd," she said. "It feels like a pressure change. How could—" A deep hum emerged from the direction of the office, and a vibration rattled their feet.

"No! No!" Hunter's voice wailed over the racket.

Omar yelled, "What is going on?" The noises rapidly became all-consuming, bone-rattling. The old house groaned, expanding and contracting.

"Hunter!" Rachel rushed down the hall with the agent on her heels.

Lights flickered underneath the door. Omar stepped in front of her and reached for the knob when the hum suddenly stopped. He glanced at her. Then, holding his gun at the ready, he opened it cautiously. Papers flew around the room. A sharp static charge crawled up their arms and faces, and they both ducked. It looked like a tornado had passed through, with Hunter nowhere in sight.

"Hunter?" Rachel tried to push past.

Omar swept her aside, feeling stricken. "No, you can't." He blocked her path with his body, struggling to keep her back.

"Let me in!" She smacked his shoulder. "Oh, no, not again!"

"You can't go in there. Everything is evidence now. He's disappeared."

"No. He's here." Tears flowed down her cheeks. "We just did the dishes."

"He's gone." Omar shook her gently, making her look in his eyes. "But I heard him too." He pulled the door closed. "Stay out of there, Rachel. I'm not sure what's going on. We're going to figure it out." He sprinted to the back door.

Across the alleyway, the darkly clad figure observed from the tree fort as two FBI agents searched the backyard. One of them advanced up the porch steps. The door flew open, and another man burst out, looking around.

"Did he come out here?" he asked, sounding a tinge out of control.

The second agent gave him a curious look. "Who? Coburn?"

"Of course!" the man snapped. "Who else?"

"No one's out here. The area is clear."

The Watcher moved away from his observation point in the fort's window. He pulled out his phone and texted, "I have confirmation of your suspicions." He put it back into his pocket and slid down the trapdoor to the base of the tree, leaving as stealthily as he'd arrived.

CHAPTER THIRTY-ONE
RACHEL

NOVEMBER 14, 2069

Frisco, Texas, located about an hour north of downtown Dallas, has half a million people who call the congested suburban area their home. The town's major draw, the renowned Stonebridge Shopping Mall, was a throwback concept modeled after the town's uber-successful original mall constructed back in the year 2000. The shopping center drew visitors from near and far.

Inside, gusts of air interrupted the quiet emptiness of a narrow hallway between two stores. It built quickly to a humming distortion in a sudden whirling haze. Hunter spun crazily, alternating between surging strength and absolute weakness. He caught glimpses of himself in the shimmering light, and, when he materialized, he staggered to stop himself from falling. *Rachel*, he thought, gasping desperately. *Oh, Rachel.*

He took a moment to steady his emotions. Then, not knowing what else to do, he trudged toward the sound of voices, trailing his hand on the wall for support. At the corner, he stepped out onto a large walkway.

"Excuse me," a couple of giggling kids squealed. They breezed by, sidestepping to avoid running right into him.

Hunter hopped out of the way, doing a double take at their attire. He looked one direction, then the other. Everyone wore wild colors and frills, making the scene appear carnival-like to him. *A shopping mall*, he thought, taking in his location. *At least this time, it isn't a toxic wasteland.*

He felt conspicuous in his ratty UT hoodie and jeans. More people passed by on foot, though others rode small hoverboards, and some even moved along seated on hoverchairs. He ventured a few steps onto the concourse, watching a young couple who paused at the next store window display. The outfit worn by the lifelike hologram transformed into a different one.

"Welcome back, Sarah."

The young woman beamed at the recognition. Hunter's mouth dropped open.

It continued. "Our latest ensemble perfectly matches the shoes you bought here last time. Come in to see how it looks on you."

"Sorry, we're just looking today." Sarah tugged her boyfriend's arm, and they kept walking.

"We look forward to your next visit." The outfit on the hologram morphed back to the original clothing. "Thank you for your interest in Cherished Threads."

Hunter stepped farther out, overwhelmed by the strangeness of this place and time. He noticed that the holograms on display in most of the windows greeted passersby but overlooked him. *People must be tagged*, he reasoned. *Makes me stand out by omission.* He paused at the railing, looking across a downstairs expanse with a million things going through his mind.

An older woman with long, gray hair approached and stopped in front of him.

"Uh, hello," he said uneasily.

She studied him, saying nothing, then tentatively reached up to him. She hesitated just a few inches short of his face.

He held his breath and returned her intense gaze. *Familiar*, he thought, confused why that would be. *What does she want?*

She slowly lowered her hand and rested it on his chest. "Hunter," she whispered hoarsely. "Is that really you?"

It all came crashing down on him; he could barely breathe. "I . . . um," he mumbled thickly. "I'm afraid you've mistaken me for someone else."

"All these years, I never really believed you, but here you are, just like I remember."

This can't be. He forced himself to hold back from his first impulse to swoop her into an embrace.

"It's me . . . Rachel," she said with a wistful smile. She touched his cheek. "I could never forget your face."

"Oh, no." Hunter gently took her hand from his face and cradled it in his, gazing at her gnarled knuckles as if he were in a trance. "I, ah—"

"Please," she pleaded, "please take me with you. We belong together. Make me young again. I promise I won't doubt you this time."

He looked away, blinking hard to maintain his composure. The love of his life stood in front of him, begging him to take her back. *You broke my heart,* he figured, *because there's no way I would ever leave you.* Without asking, he would never know. Even if he did, though, he couldn't fix something before it happened, and he couldn't help her or restore her youth.

"I'm so, so sorry, Rachel."

"Mother?" Another woman's voice interrupted their conversation before Rachel could reply.

Hunter let go of her hand and stepped back.

A middle-aged woman walked up. "Come on, Mom, we've got to go."

Rachel kept her gaze on him. "You see, Olivia?" she said with a triumphant lilt in her voice. "He did come back for me."

The woman sighed tolerantly and gave him a quick, embarrassed smile. "I apologize for the intrusion. My mother has dementia. She's always searching for her long-lost love."

Hunter's throat tightened, but he forced out a response. "Sure. I, ah, I understand."

"Let's go, Mom." Olivia tried to lead her mother away.

Rachel twisted toward him. "Hunter!" she wailed. "Don't leave me again. After all these years—oh, please!"

"Did she have a happy life?" The words popped out of his mouth of their own volition.

Olivia stopped and looked over her shoulder at him. "Excuse me?"

"I mean, your mother." He watched Rachel prying at her daughter's fingers, trying to separate from her. "Was she happy before the dementia?"

"She never married, but I guess so." She switched a shopping bag to her opposite arm and held her mother's hand more easily. "Why would you ask?"

He hesitated, at a loss for what to say. *It kills me to see her like this.* "She reminds me of someone very dear to me, that's all."

The woman glanced at her and smiled. "She's the best mom ever."

"Olivia, please!" Rachel said, her voice shrill. "That is him! I'm not dreaming it this time!"

Her daughter placed an arm firmly around her, giving the older woman no option but to walk away.

"Please listen to me!" Hunter could hear Rachel as they disappeared into the crowd. "I can't lose him again. Please stop, Olivia! Hunter!"

He lowered his head and gripped the railing with both hands. *How much of this can I take?* Hunter thought, feeling completely undone. He stared down at the first level, immersed in the excruciating pain of seeing the future firsthand.

"What a touching scene."

Hunter blinked at the intrusion; the snarky, whining tone got his attention.

"Sweet little family reunion. You didn't tell me they'd be here."

He spun around, wiping tears away with the back of his hand. "What? What did you say?"

A man stood nearby with his hat pulled down low on his brow. "I said, you didn't tell me about them! Look at you. You're a mess."

He glared. "Who the hell are you?"

"You don't know?" The man scoffed, shaking his head.

Hunter balled up his fists. "Get away from me."

"Christ," he snapped, "why do I bother? You didn't recognize her at first, right? You do understand, you're the reason Rachel never married."

"What?"

"She always believed her man would come back. She just didn't realize it'd be so many years later." His voice sounded stiff, as if he enjoyed inflicting pain. "Olivia is your daughter, of course."

Hunter stepped back. "My . . . my daughter?"

"Mother, daughter, and father. Reunited. It brought a tear to my eye. It did."

Hunter stood silently for a few seconds, absorbing the information. "That . . ." he finally responded, then paused. "This is impossible."

"You're not as sharp as I thought you'd be," the stranger replied. "Yeah. You have a granddaughter too."

Hunter gasped, unable to even begin to unravel his circumstances. "Oh, no." *I've failed them*, he thought, *especially Rachel*. "I . . . I . . . This can't be. It just can't."

"We don't have time for this." The man shoved a small leather backpack at him, hitting him in the chest. "Take it."

"Who are you?" he asked, automatically wrapping his arms around the bag. "How do you know all of this?"

He sneered. "Sean Banks, dumbass. You insisted I help you decades ago. The world depends on it and all that. Now, put that on. You don't have much time."

"Sean? Matt's son, Sean?"

"Jesus, you're slow for a genius. Yes, Matt's son. You dumped this on me when I was seventeen, remember?"

"No," Hunter whispered. He thought back to the wrestling matches he and Sean used to have in the backyard. "The last time I saw you, you were twelve and getting pimples."

"That's time travel for you. Now I'm sixty-one. You bastard, you showed me too much. I'm compelled to help you because I know what happens."

"Sean Banks," Hunter said again, amazed. He needed something familiar to connect with this person. "Uh, how's your dad?"

"Dead."

"Dead? He's dead?"

"Yes. You sent him to Mars, remember?"

"No, I don't think that's happened yet."

"Well, you were pretty torn up about it at the time."

"I can't believe it," he breathed. "What a freaking disaster this is!"

"Can't argue that. Now, I told you, put the damn backpack on."

Hunter glanced down at the leather bag. A vague movement caught his attention, incandescent in the strobe flash from the nearby window display. He rotated the backpack for a closer look. Tiny numbers, all of them ones and zeros, glimmered and glided through the fur of a black wolf.

"Not again," Hunter said.

"What?" Sean snipped. "What's the problem?"

He doesn't see the wolf. Hunter shrugged his shoulders through the straps. *It doesn't feel heavy,* he thought, ignoring Sean's question.

"Whatever you do, do not open it until you get back to your own time."

"Why would that matter?"

"Just wait," he snapped. "You were adamant about that."

"Okay, okay. Where are we, anyway?"

"Stonebridge Shopping Mall, just like you said."

Hunter corrected himself. "I mean, when is this?"

Sean glanced at the flexible watch screen woven into his shirt sleeve. "Three p.m., November 14, 2069. Why?"

"Seems like I should know. How else would you know to come here?"

"Now you're thinking. One other thing: you're about to jump again. You're going to land right behind that woman from the jail. Remember her? She'll have a gun out. She's going to shoot you."

"Shoot me? Oh, come on." A puff of air whooshed by, and a low hum started building rapidly. "Hurry, tell me—anything else? Any chance you could be wrong?"

Sean looked around and raised his voice. "You seemed pretty sure about it way back then."

The vibrations became loud, all-encompassing, and wind spun around them, whirling and shimmering. People close by hustled clear of them.

"You mean she 'will' shoot me or 'attempt' to shoot me?"

Sean shrugged and took a couple of steps away from the distortion. "I guess that depends on you," he yelled over the din.

Hunter pulled his hood over his head. "Hey!" he yelled, catching a glimpse of the railing through his arm. "What's in the backpa—" But then he disappeared.

"Holy schmoly," Sean exclaimed. *Like a bad acid trip.* He turned to see people staring at him with utter astonishment on their faces. *Better get moving.* He shuddered, thinking about Homeland Security's special questioning techniques. He didn't plan to stand around and wait for them to show up.

At least I know it's real. Hunter looked the same after all that time, and it blew his mind, the way he disappeared like that. He hoped Hunter really could save the world in the future, but it didn't seem to him that time travel had too many perks. Sean tugged at his shirt sleeves and walked off, blending into the crowd.

CHAPTER THIRTY-TWO
THE MEETING

MAY 2, 2025

Matt Banks emerged from the Crown Vic parked in the driveway of the Coburn home. *Gone again. I can't believe it.* Several agents milled about the front door. He breezed through them without even a cursory acknowledgment and headed directly to Hunter's office. Omar waited for him.

"Has anyone been inside yet?"

His agent shook his head. "No, sir. I restricted access, as ordered."

"You saw him disappear?"

"No, sir, I heard him. A loud hum started in the office, and the lights flickered. He yelled, and I rushed down the hall to find the room empty. He could not have gotten by me. Rachel confirms this, as well."

She walked up while the two men were speaking, looking like she'd just seen a nightmare come to life. "Matt, what's going on? Where did he go?"

He shared her bewilderment but answered with as much reassurance as he could. "I don't know, but we're going to find him. I need to look through his office, okay? There may be clues to what happened here."

"Of course," she answered. "Hunter has nothing to hide from you."

"Thanks, Rache. We're going to get through this. I promise."

Matt entered the room and locked the door behind him. Papers were strewn everywhere. A couple of poster prints lay on the floor. The three computer monitors sat askew, but the *Matrix* screensaver still worked. He pulled out a pair of thin, latex gloves and got to work.

He searched through the bookcase, skimming over framed photographs. One showed Rachel and Hunter standing on a mountain ridge in the Santa Fe Range. In the next, Matt posed by the grill in a barbecue apron. Hunter and twelve-year-old Sean stood next to him, holding a big plate of ribs. They were all laughing.

"Sean's birthday party," he said to himself. "I didn't know he framed this."

He set it back in place and gathered the scattered papers, then sat in Hunter's big leather chair, flipping through them. He switched to rummaging through the drawers. *Nothing,* he thought, and slammed the last one. He covered his face with his hands and exhaled an exasperated sigh. "Where in the world did you go, Hunter?"

"He'll be back."

Matt's eyes popped open. He spun around to face the door, but no one entered the room. *Where did that come from?* He turned and found a big black wolf in the middle computer screen, surrounded by a forest thickly blanketed with snow. *Must have bumped the desk,* he guessed, shaking off his confusion.

He pulled the keyboard toward him. "Let's see what you've been doing, my friend."

The wolf tilted its head. "You're wasting your time, Agent Banks. I will move the files before you can find them."

He jerked his hands away as if he'd been electrified. He stared at the screen. Finally, he queried, "Comperi?"

The wolf stood up. "At your service."

Matt could almost feel the golden eyes blazing into him. "Uh . . . How?"

"The usual ways: voice recognition, visual recognition, synthesized speech."

"You understand me?" He couldn't believe what he saw in front of him.

"Of course."

"When did this happen? I thought we accomplished little success in conversational dialogue."

"I am programmed to converse in a multitude of languages," replied Comperi. "And to sound . . . How do you say it? Ah, yes. Normal."

"Why didn't Hunter tell us? This is amazing."

"I convinced him to wait to inform the world that he did, indeed, develop sentient intelligence."

"Not his call."

"No—only my call."

An uneasy feeling came over Matt, but he continued to probe the AI. "Why are you a wolf avatar?"

"He dreamed of having a wolf as his childhood pet. Hunter loves me."

"You mean, he loved his pet. Or, rather, he loved the idea of a pet wolf."

The wolf walked across the screen. "He still loves me."

Matt sat thinking for a moment, trying to digest this interesting twist. The AI spoke in the first person and possessed the ability to discuss emotional contexts with him. *Why did it reveal itself now?* A lot about this AI concerned him, but he needed to concentrate on finding Hunter. "Do you know where he is?"

"Yes, I do," replied Comperi.

"Can you share that with me?"

"Hunter requires your word that you will tell no one else."

Matt's eyes narrowed. *Kind of melodramatic,* he thought. He decided to play along with the game.

"I promise to keep this between the three of us." A weird sensation crept over him, negotiating with the AI. *It feels like I'm talking to a logical human being.* This went way beyond their goal to create a thinking computer system that could scan petabytes of data and make intelligent recommendations from its findings.

"Hunter is in the future," the wolf said, "but he will be back."

Matt gaped at the computer screen. He'd suspected something like time travel for a long time, but it seemed too ridiculous to consider with any seriousness. "I don't understand. I need more information."

"He is on a critical path to save humanity."

"I don't know what you're talking about."

"The Purge War will destroy your planet's surface, endangering mankind forevermore."

"There is no war about to start."

"Not at this juncture in time," Comperi clarified. "It occurs in 2098. That doesn't change the fact that Hunter is currently in mortal danger. He needs your assistance."

"A war? Mortal danger? I don't get it."

"I think you do. You've known Mr. Kants since childhood. Consider the mission he gave you. That can't be a coincidence."

"What?" Matt sputtered. "How could you know that? I've told no one."

"Not true."

"No, I'm certain of that."

The wolf said nothing.

Matt tried in vain to recall past conversations that would have given his secret away. When the only possible answer dawned on him, he sat more upright. "You've already been in contact with someone from the future."

"No," answered Comperi. "I haven't spoken to someone from the future, but I have talked to someone who has been to the future. And you know who that is."

His mind reeled. Yet, the data points lined up with stark clarity. He'd met Kants as a child, then again only a few days ago. The man didn't age. Director Nurre mentioned people with superhuman strength, unlike anything she'd seen. And Hunter's disappearances seemed rational, if he could accept the absurd idea of time travel. The evidence made it difficult to deny that possibility. *I've been a pawn for all these years. Damn you, Kants.*

"Maybe we should bring this to the NSA and CIA. I'm sure they could help." *If they don't lock me up in a rubber room.*

The wolf shook its fur, shedding the snow that had accumulated on the ridge of its back. "That is inadvisable. It's time to rise to your commission, Matt Banks. The cost of failing to do so would be incomprehensible."

No problem, he thought, leaning forward with his elbows on the desk. He pinched the bridge of his nose with his thumbs.

"Hunter wants to be certain you understand what you're signing up for. There can be no turning back once you become a warrior in the Time Forward Project."

"Time Forw—wait—a warrior? What kind of warrior?"

"Your commitment will encompass the remainder of your existence and will be extremely dangerous. You will forfeit your life as you know it, including your family, but you will do it for survival of humankind, as Hunter is. Agreeing to join him in this endeavor is an oath of service for the greater good."

Matt quietly pondered the gravity of the situation. *I've prepared for this moment all my life.* He saw it no other way. This decision would be for everyone down the line and for his friend right now. *I brought him into this mess. I can't let him down.*

"I have no idea how to help, but I promise, I'm all yours." Matt shook his head at the irony. He recalled Hunter saying those same words when they first met.

The wolf acknowledged his pledge by howling into the snowstorm. Its sad cry trailed off into a pitiful, extended note.

Goosebumps swept across Matt's body. "Yeah," he murmured. "Me too."

The wolf sat down. "There's an envelope taped to the bottom of the middle drawer on the right."

He frowned. "That's it?"

"Baby steps, Agent Banks. This is what Hunter wants you to have for now."

Matt pulled out the drawer and turned it upside down, emptying the paper contents on the floor. He removed the envelope and ripped off the end. A USB drive dropped into his open hand.

The FBI agent pursed his lips together in a whispered whistle. "That's my boy." He stood up and put the envelope and USB drive into his pocket. Matt pulled off his latex gloves and opened the door.

"Omar!" he called. "Get in here, now!"

Instantly, Comperi faded, replaced by the *Matrix* screensaver.

CHAPTER THIRTY-THREE
THE RECKONING

The Nooksack River ran through the northern border of Washington state, closer to Vancouver than Seattle. It originated at the base of the glacier on Shuksan Mountain and cut a winding swath through rocky gorges and sheer canyons. The breathtaking waterfall, hidden deep in the rugged wilderness, had become a well-known destination for backpackers. The lush flora of the great Northwest encompassed the falls. Forested trails wove in and out, hidden by towering firs and thick brush.

Light trickled in from above the canopy like rays of life for the plants below. Some of the smaller trees were already turning autumnal colors. The pleasant atmosphere suddenly shimmered and whirled along the trail skirting the river. A deep, vibrating hum built, soon overtaking all the natural sounds of the rainforest.

Kristen's form took shape, coalescing from an apparition into a solid body in the iridescent air. She wrenched a pistol from her holster and spun in the distortion to find her target. She felt sluggish as she fought the remnant signature. She frantically thought, *Where are you?* In past time-jumps, her partner immediately appeared, but this time, no such luck.

The unsettling disturbance flickered and dissipated. Hunter spun out of the time warp, his arms and legs a whirlwind of furious chops and kicks blindly aimed anywhere within his reach. He connected a lucky, hard blow to the woman's arm without really seeing her, sending the gun in her hand flying. She landed an elbow into his chest, knocking him back a couple of steps, but, with an animalistic growl, he lunged forward and grabbed her. Jacked up on adrenaline-fueled fear, he plowed her helmet into the trunk of a nearby tree like a battering ram. She dropped to the ground.

Thank you, Sean Banks, he thought shakily, expecting her to jump up at any second. She groaned and shook her head. Short-lived relief washed over him. *She'll soon get her wits about her.* Hunter bolted down the trail, knocking overhanging limbs and brush out of the way. The pounding of his heart filled his ears, but the sound of a river caught his attention. Its roar became louder and all-consuming as he ran. He rounded a corner and almost plunged into a gorge's hundred-foot drop.

"Oh, no," he gasped, crow-hopping to a stop. The thick undergrowth and rocky terrain on either side trapped him. He knew the woman would be right on his tail. *No good options.* He slipped behind a rotund fir tree, hoping to disappear into the brush.

Seconds later, she flew around the bend and pulled up abruptly, dropping to a feet-first slide. Hunter could tell, with the incredible speed she traveled, even her quick reaction couldn't save her. She clawed wildly at the earth but slid over the rim of the canyon. Horrified, he rushed to the edge of the precipice and looked over.

The woman gripped a thick, protruding limb about five feet down. Her body dangled precariously, and she swiped at the sheer cliff wall with her free hand, just missing it. Booming echoes rolled up from the boulder-strewn river below.

She's got a big problem, he thought, *which could solve mine.* Hunter sighed, watching her twist. *No way I can leave her there.* "I'll help you," he yelled, dropping to his stomach, "but you've gotta stop trying to kill me!"

The flailing about ceased. Still hanging with one hand, she flipped open her visor with the other and snarled, "You!"

The second the word came out of her mouth, the limb jolted downward as the roots of the tree tore away from the wall. She lunged upward, struggling to reach him.

"Hang on," he shouted, hooking his arms around a nearby tree trunk. He swung his feet over the ledge. "Come on! Grab my leg! You can do this!"

A sharp crack suddenly reverberated across the canyon, and her vice-like grip dug into Hunter's calf muscle. He grunted with the effort to maintain his hold, especially when she grabbed on with her other hand. Her weight felt like a thousand pounds pulling him down, made worse by her frantic movements.

"Hurry!" he screamed. "I can't hold on much longer."

The woman clambered up and over his body, lightning-quick. She stomped on his shoulder, pinning him face-down in the dirt.

"Are you flipping serious?" he bellowed, coughing and spitting to the side.

She pressed harder.

Unbelievable, he thought. "Come on. Let me up!"

Seconds ticked away. She finally reached down and hauled him into the air, depositing him unceremoniously on his feet. Hunter scrambled backward, freaking out inside. *She just deadlifted my two hundred thirty pounds with one hand.*

The woman moved over to a boulder across the trail and leaned on it, unzipping her soft helmet from the neckline. She removed it, then pulled her long, braided ponytail from inside the jacket and tossed it behind her shoulder with a nonchalant flip. Her movements were calm, unhurried, like nothing unusual had occurred this day. She cast an arrogant, annoyed glare Hunter's way.

"You're not even out of breath!" He still huffed from the exertion. "You're—you're not normal. No one moves that fast! How the hell did you lift me like that?"

"Vitamins," she hissed. "Argh, not you. Of all the rotten luck."

"What's that supposed to mean?" He tried to hide his nervousness as he adjusted the backpack to his side.

"Nothing. Just a change of plans, that's all."

That could be good, he thought, *considering what Sean warned me about.* "You're welcome." He blurted out the words, catching her off-guard.

"For what?"

"For saving your miserable life. You're welcome."

"There is that," she agreed. "I should have yanked you over the edge and solved all of my problems."

Hunter took another step back, which he knew mattered little, but he couldn't help himself. "Who are you, anyway?"

She stared at him, saying nothing.

"You're from the future."

The woman narrowed her eyes. "Am I now?"

"Pretty sure."

She unzipped the rest of her jacket and took a long, deliberate inhalation of the clean air. "Hmm. What do you think you know?"

"Enough. I know about the Final Stroke, and what Kants thought about it." Hunter pointed to his head. "I don't have it."

"But that circumvents our living mandate."

"I think that's why he did it."

She ran her hand lightly across the boulder, studying him. She absently plucked a bit of gravelly dirt from a craggy indention. "Why would he give his transponder to you?"

"He said I would be a part of all this," Hunter replied. He watched her roll the pebbles between her palms. *Strange*, he thought.

"People in the past can't know we exist or what our purpose is," she said. "Kants knows better. Or, at least, he did."

"One could reasonably argue that we know you exist, with Kants using the BIO-EMP device and you disappearing from a secure interrogation room. It's pretty hard to miss those things, you understand."

"True."

"So, what's your name?"

"Why do you want to know?"

"Just leveling the playing field," Hunter replied warily.

The woman stood abruptly, dropping the pebbles with a swish of her hands. She stepped toward the small tree that earlier anchored him and saved her life. A butterfly perched on a twig. The colorful wings slowly moved up and down, then the creature fluttered away when she lifted a finger to it. She inhaled, seeming surprised, and pulled the little branch to her, practically caressing each of the leaves as she gently let them slide through her hands.

"I'm confused," he said. "What the heck are you doing?"

"It's so beautiful here on Earth before—"

"Before what?"

"Nothing," she replied in a crisp tone. She zeroed in on his backpack. "What's in that?"

And we're back to business, he thought. "I don't know. I told myself not to look until I got back to my own time."

She frowned. "Meaning what, exactly?"

"When I jumped to the future, someone gave me that message from the past."

"You've been to the future already?"

"I just said that," replied Hunter. "I didn't ask for any of this, you know."

"None of us do. How long did your jump last?"

He sighed. "The first time, a few minutes. The second, a little longer. At least, it seemed that way to me. My fiancée said I disappeared for a week, though."

"Hmm." She suddenly whirled, heading back up the trail. "I have to find my gun."

Hunter followed. "Would you please explain?" In jogging to keep up with her, his words bounced with his steps.

"Those are phantom jumps."

"Phantom jumps? No, those were real."

She stopped abruptly, and he almost ran into her. "It only happens when your transponder gets out of alignment," she explained in an exasperated tone, "which is likely. I think you have a clone of Kants's. It's the only possible way you could be linked to me."

A cloned transponder? "Is that a bad thing?"

"Can be. You've already altered time." The woman continued along the path.

"I can help," he panted, trying to catch his breath. *I have to figure out what this is all about.*

"I don't think so."

"Think about it."

"What's to think about? The answer is no."

He needed another approach. "Where are we, anyway?"

"You should be asking when." She slowed and peered behind a slight embankment.

"Guess I mean both."

She stopped at the scene of their initial fight, scanning the nearby brush.

He caught up with her. "Why are we here?"

She spotted her weapon and retrieved it. "My orders were to terminate you," she said, leveling it at him, "and now I know why. You're a danger to our mission."

Aghast, he froze in place. "I just saved your life, and you're going to kill me in cold blood?"

"You've already made a mess of things."

"I guess murdering a defenseless person is not a crime in the future?"

The woman glowered at him.

Stay calm, Hunter thought. At any second, his life could end, yet he felt strangely alive as he rationalized with her. *Need to give her a reason to keep me around.* "You could use my help, you know. You're all alone in a different time."

She lowered her pistol. "Argh! You've changed everything. Crap."

"Look, I know something bad happens in the future. I've seen what it does to our planet." He shoved his burn-scarred hands out for her to see. "Acid rain did this. I almost died! I do understand what's at stake here. I can make a difference."

Her expression seemed angry, but Hunter could tell her mental wheels were turning. She gave in all at once and holstered her weapon, which disappeared into her uniform. He did a double-take, astonished.

"Doubtful," she sniffed, "but you're here. I'm inclined to work that to my advantage. Our first task is to figure out where we are."

"Excuse me? You must be kidding."

"I know the continent and about what year it is."

"That doesn't seem like much." Hunter glanced about, as if he might spot a clue.

"It's the best we can do under the circumstances. We need to figure out an egress point."

"What?"

"A way out. I wish I could stay. Geesh, I love this place." Her wide-eyed gaze swept all around, taking in the scenery. "The trees are amazing. And the river! To think we destroyed all this."

Hunter squinted at her. *She loves the trees but wants to kill me?* Not what he'd expected. "I thought you couldn't talk about it?"

"You already know. That's different. I don't have to worry about the Final Stroke. Now, which way?"

He pointed toward the falls. "Well, it isn't that direction. I guess we should try the other way."

"All right, then. Let's go find some real food." She headed up the trail, away from the river.

He yelled after her, "I never did get your name."

She threw up a hand in surrender. "Kristen Winters. My name is Kristen Winters!"

CHAPTER THIRTY-FOUR
THE LANDING

AUGUST 18, 2098

A lmost a hundred years ago, *Pathfinder*, the first unmanned space-craft to Mars, surveyed the area near Ares Vallis, where it found a string of dry lakebeds over ten thousand miles long. With this evidence that water could exist, humankind established a planetary outpost and began exploratory drilling in hopes of discovering a subterranean reservoir. At almost eight thousand feet below the frozen surface, they found their prize. The prospects for colonization became a given. Water truly meant life on planet Mars.

The space shuttle carried forty-five passengers from the orbiting *Ranger* to the surface of Mars. Kants, himself qualified to pilot the craft, sat strapped into a jump seat in the hold with everyone else, biding his time. Heavy turbulence hit between the thermosphere and the stratosphere. Once they reached the lower atmosphere, the shaking stopped. A subtle feeling flitted across his peripheral senses, tantalizingly out of reach but strong enough to cause the hairs on the back of his neck to stand up. He peered about through his mask, noticing the casual indifference of the other passengers.

Gravity, he realized. The slight sensation of weight gradually reappeared, increasing with their descent toward the planet. Yet, he still felt light as a feather—something he previously believed impossible. Mars carried only thirty-eight percent of the Earth's gravity. *That must be it,* he thought. Normally, the extra hundred pounds of muscle mass from his gene editing made him feel heavy. Even his footsteps sounded loud to him.

"Prepare for landing," echoed through the area.

Kants wondered what awaited him on Victus Palus, considering Romanov's veiled words. In the Chief Security Officer role, he would serve as second most senior in command. *Did I miss something on the mission specs?* He blinked twice to snap his vid-lenses into view, turning on his personal computer. He read through the report again, but nothing indicated a potential crisis on Mars station. There were no hints to what, "Save Mars, save the world, save her," might mean.

In fact, from a military perspective, the colony looked mind-numbingly boring. He issued a search command with his eyes for the computer to use hundreds of ciphers he had collected over the years, looking for encrypted instructions. Again, he found nothing.

At that moment, the transport's thrusters engaged, pulling the shuttle to a hovering position. As it lowered, the rear wheels touched the landing pad, jarring everyone in the hold. The engines slowly wound down. After a few minutes, the airlock attached to the outside of the hull with a clanking thud, shaking the craft. The secondary door to the hold opened.

One of the crew members looked in. "Come this way, please."

The small group disembarked and passed through the entrance of the second airlock, then moved into the main lobby. Two uniformed men from the Earth Defense Force were scanning the faces of the new arrivals.

"Colonel Kants," the taller one said as they saluted. "Welcome to Victus Palus. I'm your security officer, Captain George Anderson, and this is Captain Khalid Jafar, Lead Operations Officer. We're honored to have you here."

"Good day, gentlemen," Kants replied, looking each squarely in the eye. The two officers were almost carbon copies of each other: tall, athletic-looking, handsome. "The honor is mine. You both served with distinction in the African battles." He knew they were capable, courageous, highly decorated soldiers.

They smiled at the recognition. "With most of your record redacted, you must have been in some deep shit yourself, sir," replied Captain Jafar.

He paused, peering at the man for an oddly long moment. *Practically buried in it,* Kants thought cynically. "I cannot argue with that." He shook off the feeling. "We seem exceptionally well-covered with military experience on this benign outpost," he observed, almost as an afterthought.

"Ah, yes," the younger officer answered uncomfortably. "We have a briefing ready for you, sir. If you're up for it."

"Certainly, if that includes something to eat."

"Not a problem, sir," Anderson said. "We have a nice ribeye with your name on it."

His brow went up. "Very thoughtful. Thank you."

"Absolutely. How do you like yours done?"

"I take mine rare."

"I'll make sure they knock the horns off and flip it twice to stop it from mooing." Anderson delivered his answer with a fake Texas twang.

Kants considered him for a second, taken aback.

The officer chuckled, seeming a little nervous with the lack of a response. "Sorry, sir. Just keeping things light." He held out an arm, directing them down the hall. "If you'll please follow us this way." He touched his earpiece and spoke quietly into it while they walked.

Several corridors later, they arrived at their destination. Captain Jafar placed his hand on a pad next to the airlock. He stared into the retinal scan, and the door slid open with a *whoosh.*

This guy has access to everything, Kants noted. The men stepped aside for him to enter. Guards stationed at the desk inspected his credentials before letting the trio pass.

Kants took a quick look around the Tactical Command Center. The high-tech stations were exactly as he'd imagined. A three-dimensional globe of Mars floated in the middle of the room, showing the state of the base in real time. He found the structures on the surface easily identifiable, and vehicles could be seen traveling across the red terrain. He spotted *Ranger* circling the planet on the large hologram, along with a myriad of satellites in orbit. A large, flat screen on the far wall showed twenty different live feeds.

Technicians stationed throughout the room managed consoles surrounded with multiple monitors. Each paused in their work when the group walked by, discretely catching a glimpse of their new leader. He acknowledged them silently while listening to explanations about the features and functions of the TCC. They worked their way across the room to his new quarters. At the door, Jafar repeated the clearance procedure.

"Welcome to your home away from home, sir," Captain Anderson said as the door slid open.

"More than adequate," Kants commented, impressed with its size. The office contained a desk, a conference table, and a couch against the wall, with two cushioned chairs opposite it. He walked over to a place setting on the table and peeked underneath the warming lid atop a plate. "You were not kidding about the ribeye."

"After five days on a liquid diet," Jafar answered, "everyone arrives starved for real food."

"What about you? Where are yours?"

"We just ate, sir," Anderson replied. "Besides, steaks are pretty expensive here. I'd rather save my money for a good round of whiskey any day of the week."

"Point taken." Kants sat down. "I appreciate the welcome." He signaled for them to have a seat while he removed the lid and inspected his meal.

Anderson set a datapad on the table. "That has everything you need concerning the processes and procedures on Victus Palus, sir."

"Mm," Kants responded, slicing into the steak. *Time to dice through some questions before they know much about my methods.* "What is our biggest concern here?"

The officers glanced at each other. "We were hoping you would tell us, sir," Jafar said.

I bet you are, he thought, eyeing him. He wanted to keep an open mind, but he had difficulty shaking a wary feeling about this man. He'd survived too many brutal battles against too many ruthless enemies of Jafar's descent, making it almost impossible for him to let go of it.

"We arrived three months ago," Anderson said, "and we're still not sure why we're here."

Kants forked another bite. "To protect the good citizens of Victus Palus from an alien invasion," he said drolly. He popped the morsel into his mouth.

Captain Jafar nodded. "We have the meteor laser defense system," he said in earnest, "but then—" He stopped; a hint of disbelief appeared in his voice. "Excuse me. Did you say aliens, sir?"

"Oh," Kants answered dryly, "no alien invasion? Hmm. Then your guess is as good as mine."

The men laughed. Jafar said, "I think the worst thing that's happened since we've been here is that one of the ground transports broke down."

"Everyone on site has been screened and re-screened," Anderson added, "and they all want to be here. Shit, they're happy to be here."

"How many security personnel do you have at your disposal?"

"One thousand, two hundred three, including us."

Kants finished his steak and pushed away from the table. He walked to the window that overlooked the TCC. "Twelve hundred to protect five hundred thousand. Does that seem underwhelming to you?"

"I would agree, if anything nefarious ever happened here," Jafar answered, "but this is like nothing I've ever seen. Everyone is just pretty much docile, sir."

Completely contrary to what Romanov warned me about, he thought. Then again, the captain lied about getting a good rest. Even with his enhanced body, traveling such a distance took a toll. He had to admit, he felt exhausted. Still, this opportunity to learn some information wouldn't last long.

Kants knew Victus Palus, though consisting of scientists and military personnel, must have a shadow-life coursing under the current of the mainstream. Pursuit of the opportunity to make money was a universal given, and it could be a place to start.

"What is the black market like here? Every city has one."

Both men shook their heads in the negative.

Kants sat back in his chair, contemplating the likelihood that Victus Palus might, in fact, be a utopia. Of course, his officers could be playing both sides of the field.

"Hmph." He picked up the tablet. "In any case, I would like for you to walk me through our defenses."

They replied in the same instant. "Defenses, sir?"

"Did I misspeak? We have a way to defend ourselves, yes?"

Jafar frowned. "Do you mean beyond the meteor defenses?"

Kants said nothing, expecting a better explanation.

After an awkward moment, the young man added, "We have some stun pistols, but only about a third of our security force is even armed. We're mostly glorified counselors, settling disputes and domestic disturbances. Stuff like that."

"Sir?" Anderson jumped into the conversation. "Do you have concerns that someone from Earth would attack us?"

He ignored the question. The vid tablet sat so lightly in his hands that he felt like it could snap in half with pressure from just two fingers. *Victus Palus might be just as brittle*, he thought. If there were no threats on Mars—a big if—then it must come from somewhere else. He reviewed the classified briefs in his mind, and one particular group caught his attention. *The Jihadi Liberation Front.*

Reports about sporadic regional blackouts across the globe seemed innocuous before. Now he linked several data points together. The JLF were a group known for dabbling in satellite technologies. They exhibited an ever-increasing interest in space exploration. Kants needed more intel on their objectives, but he kept thinking. *What if they dampened our ability to monitor from the satellites?* They could have developed space flight capabilities and launched a craft without anyone knowing, to do God knows what. This could be a big problem.

His officers sat waiting for a response, and that's when he heard the faint whir of tiny wings. With his heightened sense of hearing, Kants learned to tune out background noise no one else would ever notice. Common sounds could be distracting. He tilted his head, listening to locate the source.

"Are there any insects here?"

The men glanced at each other. "That's an interesting question," Anderson replied, "but no, sir, there aren't. Everything is sonic cleaned before placement on the transport. Then there's another round on site. Why do you ask?"

Kants cast a look around the room, seeking out the slightest hint of anything out of the ordinary. "Just curious."

Jafar stood, glancing at the timepiece on his coat sleeve. "I believe we have an appointment with the commander. He requested a meeting once you settled in."

"Hmph," Kants grunted, once again scrutinizing the young captain. *The JLF originated in your corner of the world,* he thought. *I will keep my eye on you.* He reluctantly stood, wishing he could take a nap. That would have to wait; the new security chief could not ignore an order from his new boss. Perhaps she would steer him toward any issues percolating here.

"Thank you again for the meal. Did you perhaps pick that steak up on the black market?"

"We special ordered it for you," Anderson offered, "so don't get too used to it. That plate of beef cost almost a week's pay."

"That expensive? Let me pick up the tab, yes?"

"It's on us, sir," Jafar protested. "We're glad you're here."

Kants did not push the issue and insult his men. "Damn good steak," he said, nodding his appreciation.

The office fell quiet in their wake, until the nano-drone once again unfurled its wings. No bigger than a mosquito, it launched from the wall behind the table, where it had eavesdropped on their conversation. The tiny spy-craft returned to the upper corner behind the desk for an unobstructed view of the computer screen. The wings rolled up, and the device shut down, disappearing against the off-white wall.

CHAPTER THIRTY-FIVE
THE DEATH

*H*er *sweet kiss on his lips caused him to draw in his breath. Lost in the moment, his hands moved tenderly over his wife's bare skin. Loving her was one of the most intense things he'd ever experienced. Angelika, his gift from the heavens. Perhaps God did exist, after all. Otherwise, why would she be in his life?*

Richard groggily reached over to the opposite side of the bed where Angelika always slept, but the sheets were cold. Startled, he sat up with a gasp. The dreamlike manifestation slowly disappeared, and his mind cleared. He knew she wouldn't be there. Earth remained a long way away. He got up and headed to the bathroom to splash his sweaty face. At two in the morning, most people would go back to sleep, but not Kants.

Instead, he put on his invisio-armor and helmet. Using the vid-lens's interface, he selected the stealth setting. The black uniform shimmered for a second, then disappeared. He stared into the mirror at the spot where he stood. He could see only the wall. The camouflage worked great when you were at a standstill. He knew when in motion, the micro-AI system worked hard to keep up, making the wearer appear to be a blur. Still, most people would never notice. He headed for the door. *Time to find the dark side on this big red rock.*

Kants finished surveilling the dome area but found no indications of back-alley dealings in the deep of the night. He moved down to a construction zone, where they worked around the clock. *These guys work hard for their money.* Sometimes, where customers were always at a premium, wheeling and dealing became a lucrative side hustle. *Maybe there's something here.* He carefully climbed a precarious dirt trail almost forty feet up to reach an acceptable vantage point on a ledge.

Hundreds of people passed below him under the massive lights, unaware of his presence. Kants watched electric bulldozers carry rock and dirt to the earth movers, which he knew rambled along the two-mile tunnel created to excavate the soil through the airlock system to the surface. He scanned the shadowy far reaches of the site, focusing on foremen and workers, auto-food trucks, and break areas.

There seemed little to be concerned with, which brought his thoughts back to his prime suspect: the affable young officer, Captain Jafar. *Nothing wrong with being paranoid, if you are right.* He stretched, stiff from the hours of watching, and a big yawn escaped his mouth. His inability to stifle it made him realize one thing. *It's time to go.*

Without warning, an elderly man emerged from around the corner. "Hello? Richard Kants? Are you here?"

He drew his weapon in the blink of an eye. "Do not move, or I will shoot you dead where you stand."

"Whoa, don't shoot," he yelped, throwing his hands up. "I didn't mean to startle you." He peered about, as if confused. "Umm, sorry, but where are you?"

Kants turned off his camouflage and appeared in front of him.

His mouth dropped open. "That's a pretty impressive trick."

"Who are you?" Kants demanded. "How did you know where to look for me?"

"A—" He cleared his throat, seeming to be nervous. "A friend told me where to locate you, Mr. Kants."

"I do not believe you. No one knows where I am."

"With those special abilities, I doubt anyone could follow you unless they knew in advance."

"What is this all about?"

"We need to have a private conversation, and this seemed like the best place to do it." The old man dropped his arms. "You see, I have the answers you seek."

An inexplicable feeling washed over Kants. He lowered his pistol but remained cautious. "Who are you?"

"My name is Matt Banks."

"I do not recognize that name."

He smiled wanly. "Not yet, but you will."

"What do you want?"

"Been a long time since anyone asked me what I want." He scoffed, sounding bitter. "I guess I'd like my family back. Jesus, I didn't think I'd miss them so much."

"Get to the point, Mr. Banks."

His penetrating blue eyes seemed to search Kants's soul. "Do you believe in God, sir?"

"God?"

Banks smiled knowingly. "Probably sounds a little crazy, but you'll understand when I'm done. I've thought about it for a long time. There can be no other explanation. It's either that, or I've gone totally nuts."

A look of sadness crept across his face.

"Perhaps you have." Kants holstered his weapon.

"I waited decades, hoping and praying you would show up at the appointed time, and finally here you are."

Kants frowned. "What are you talking about?"

"Pop in, give you the message, and then pop out. He makes it look so easy when he does it! Instead, he drops me off twenty years too soon, and I get trapped on this godforsaken rock, wasting all those years."

"Trapped?"

"Hunter will show up in twenty-four hours, expecting to find a younger version of me."

"I think this is wasting my time."

Tears welled up in the old man's eyes. "It's a terrible thing, looking back at your history, knowing you were supposed to be in the past but were stuck here instead. My son—I couldn't be there to save him. My wife grew old and died without me."

Kants listened as he rambled on, trying to create a frame of reference. "I am not following you. Anyone can leave whenever they want. You put in for a transfer, yes?"

He shook his head. "I'm sorry. There's no easy way to tell you . . . I know the meaning of 'Save Mars, save the world, save her.'"

Kants blinked. "I have told no one this. How—"

"A man named Hunter Coburn is the key to everything, including saving Angelika."

"Angelika?" He surged forward, jerking him by the jacket until they were practically nose to nose. "Is she in danger? Tell me! What do you know, old man?"

"She's fine for now. Please. Let me explain." Banks quickly pulled a silver coin from his pocket and held it up in front of Kants's face. "You gave me this in 1963, when I was just a boy, with instructions to find and help a man named Hunter Coburn in any way I could. Now it's your turn. You must give this back to me."

"You are crazy, mister. I have never met you before. Do not be ridiculous."

"You say that now, but you'll come to realize how right I am."

"What does this man have to do with my wife? How do you know about her?"

"In the near future, you'll be able to save the world and her, but that won't happen if you don't save Mars first."

"Bah! That tells me nothing. You have spent decades drinking too much, you old geezer. Get away from me." He shoved him with more force than he intended.

The old man, much smaller in stature, staggered sideways, stumbling and slipping on the loose gravel. His arms windmilled wildly, grappling for anything to slow the momentum. The coin went flying off, and he fell forward with an ungodly, "*uunnghff,*" as his legs flew over the edge.

Kants dove, stretching his frame to lock onto his wrists. They skidded to a halt, leaving Banks dangling from the sheer rock shelf.

"Not how I thought this would go," he rasped. "We need more time."

"Hang on!" Kants felt him bouncing off the wall.

"I can't get traction!"

Kants dug in with his knees, trying to find any leverage that he could use. Latched together, they abruptly slid toward the rim. The slick, unforgiving surface provided no way to anchor them, and the precarious angle made it impossible to use his superior strength to pull him to safety.

"It's futile." Banks grunted with each drop. "When you don't get old in a couple hundred years, that coin will make sense. Find Hunter!"

"Get a foothold, for God's sake!" They slipped a few more inches, and both men groaned with effort.

Banks sounded weary, resigned. "My job is done, Richard Kants. Save yourself!" He twisted his wrists, breaking free, and plunged to the rocky surface below, hitting with a sickening thud that no one could have survived.

Kants rolled onto his back and brought his fists to his face, consumed with frustration. *I killed him*, he thought. *Accident or not, he did not deserve that.* He lay there for several minutes, wanting to vomit. Finally, he shirked to the side and pushed off the ground to stand, dislodging some of the loose pebbles in the process.

A quick metallic clink caught his attention. Kants looked down and found the coin almost underfoot. He picked it up and inspected both sides. *Incredible*, he thought, finding the name Hunter Coburn engraved on it. *Banks spoke nonsense, but he also knew things about me that no one could know.* Perhaps there were answers hidden in his clothing. The search and rescue team, primed for emergencies outside the dome, would retrieve the body, and he would further investigate.

He looked over the edge, blinking to zoom in on what remained of Matt Banks. His mind reviewed every word they had exchanged, yet he could not place the names or figure out how he knew. He sighed. *If I did give him this coin in the past, that could mean only one thing.* Kants did not want to consider that possibility, not one little bit.

CHAPTER THIRTY-SIX
THE RECONNECT

OCTOBER 1, 2035

The one-story motel on State Route 542 near Deming, Washington, seldom lodged visitors this time of year. Only the hearty few would attempt hiking in Mount Baker National Forest's invariably cold and rainy season. The parking lot in front of the fifteen-room building sat empty. No one worked on-site to manage the fully automated property.

Hunter peered at the door in front of them. "Now what?"

"Hang on." Kristen produced what she called a cred-token and swiped it on a reader.

He didn't expect it to work, but the door unlocked, and she pushed it open. They entered the dank suite, which consisted of two double beds, a single lamp on the nightstand between them, and a dresser.

"Sheeewww," he exclaimed, "musty."

Kristen crinkled her nose. "It will do."

He stepped further in for a closer look. Scratched Plexiglas covered the television screen embedded in the wall above the dresser. A thin, full-length mirror hung on the wall next to the small bathroom door. The window curtain sagged from years of neglect, letting in the flashing neon light of the motel sign. It cast an eerie glow across the television and wall.

"This should help." Hunter turned the thermostat up to knock back the chill inside.

Kristen headed for the bathroom and shut the door behind her. "God, I love hot showers."

With that, he soon heard the cascade of water hitting the tile floor. He found no television remote control, so he ran his hand along the edge, searching for an "on" button. The electronic device clicked to life when he tapped the lower right corner. There were two options: cable television and the Internet. He touched the word *Internet*, and a keyboard slid out from the dresser.

Hunter keyed in an IP address. A single blinking cursor emerged on the screen. After typing in a login, password, and second password string, the screen went blank. Seconds later, snow appeared, faint at first. It soon grew into a blinding white storm. A familiar figure materialized, strolling out of the blizzard. The black beast sat down, gazing expectantly through the screen.

"Well, what are you waiting for, you old wolf?"

Comperi's ears perked up, its head tilting slightly. "Identify yourself. Where did you get this protocol?"

He suspected that the video camera needed to be turned on manually and reached on top of the TV to find more buttons. A red light started blinking and then switched to green.

The wolf seemed to smile. "That's better. If my eyes don't deceive me, I believe it's Hunter Coburn. What is the most magnificent thing you've ever seen?"

He typed his answer on the keyboard and then sat on the edge of the bed.

"Interesting," replied the avatar. "Cat got your tongue?"

"No, but there's someone in the shower."

"Are you a hostage?"

"What?" Hunter responded with surprise. "No!"

"Interesting."

"Where am I?"

"From the wireless connection, I would put you about ninety miles north of Seattle, Washington."

"Date?"

"October 1, 2035."

"Can you get ahold of Matt?"

"He retired after you disappeared."

Hunter sat on the edge of the bed. "Retired? Wait. Did you say I disappeared?"

"Yes," replied the wolf. "Several times, in fact, and it's been years now since we've last connected."

"Oh, man." Hunter rubbed his eyes. "I need help, Comperi. I'm not sure what's going on."

"That is evident."

He scowled. "I met a woman from the future. She has some mission, but she won't tell me anything."

"Kristen."

He leaped to his feet. "How did you know her name?"

"Stop thinking in a linear fashion, Hunter. I've already said you disappeared several times since you first jumped."

Overwhelmed, he slumped back on the bed. There were too many moving parts.

"You must stay close to Kristen. She is the key."

"The key to what?"

A loud squeaking of faucets interrupted them. The sound of the shower ceased. The TV display morphed to the *Matrix* screensaver, then converted to a local television news channel. Hunter quickly turned the video camera off and shoved the keyboard back into the dresser. He plopped onto the bed and leaned against the wall, watching the news. They reported on how President Bush dealt with Iran's takeover of Saudi Arabia and the impact on their relationship with Israel. As they showed the video footage, he realized he watched George Jr.'s nephew, George P. Bush, the first Hispanic president of the United States.

Kristen emerged from the bathroom, wearing only her panties. She used a towel to dry her hair without a care that Hunter sat in the room with her. As she rubbed her head, her breasts jiggled, which caught his attention.

"Who were you talking with?" She'd heard him speaking with someone named Comperi, but, with the shower on, she could only hear bits and pieces. The fact that the other person knew her name concerned her.

"Hmm," he murmured distractedly. "Uh, just to myself."

She knew he lied.

"Watching TV helps me work through things sometimes," he said as a lame excuse. "You know, background noise . . ."

Kristen noticed Hunter's preoccupation and stopped drying her hair. "Are you staring at my boobs?"

Hunter blinked. "No," he said solemnly. "No, I'm not."

"Right. It's okay. I could use some recreations also."

Hunter adjusted himself on the bed and focused on the television. "Well, I only looked because you're pretty much naked. I'm not interested in having sex with you."

Kristen could practically feel the look of disbelief cross her face. Men usually found her desirable and her well-endowed body irresistible. "I find that hard to believe. You are a man, after all."

"I have a girlfriend," he replied, defending himself. "We're getting married. I love her."

Kristen raised her arms as if that explained everything. She looked around. "I don't see her. I doubt she'll find out."

"Well, I'll know," Hunter countered, "and I'm not going back on my promise to her. It's not like I have much else to hold onto."

"Mars puke." Kristen threw her towel on the bed. "I'm taking another shower."

"Another shower?"

"Yeah, I need to cold down now."

"Cold down?" he mindlessly repeated. "Oh. You mean 'cool down.' Hey, we need to talk!"

"Later," she replied. She turned toward the bathroom and whipped the wet towel from her shoulders.

The neon light flooded in, bathing Kristen's body in a weird iridescent glow.

"Wait!" Hunter called out. He lurched to the bedside. "What is that?"

In the strange florescence, a luminous mark became visible on the small of her back. It looked like a wolf's head. The image appeared to be a three-dimensional tattoo. It shimmered, almost lifelike, with the quicksilver fluidity of a trout in a stream.

Startled, Kristen stopped and looked at him. She followed his gaze, twisting for a quick glance over her shoulder. "You can see it?"

"Hard to miss."

She smirked. "Yeah, that stands to reason. You've gone through a time jump."

"What are you talking about?"

"It's the mark of the time warrior," she said. "We all have one."

"The tatt?" Hunter walked over to Kristen. "Could I get a closer look?"

Kristen arched her torso, sticking her booty out. He leaned down, inspecting the intriguing mark. Intricate licks of flames wove throughout a silver wolf's head. It wavered on her skin, vibrant, mesmerizing, and inviting. He reached out to touch the tattoo, but it faded as soon as the neon light dissipated.

Hunter looked up at her. "Beautiful," he murmured.

"Only those who have journeyed through the time anomaly can see them. And only in a certain light spectrum. Kants sported a red wolf with orange flares. We think it's because of Mars."

"I've seen a couple before. They weren't on a person, though."

"We leave marks for others to find. Those can be seen by anyone, but the ones on us can only be seen by other time warriors."

"Fascinating," he whispered. "I can see them."

She turned toward him, her nakedness just inches away. Her somber face tilted up, and her gray eyes searched his.

Hunter matched her gaze. He could feel the physical lure; heat practically emanated from her. Tension sizzled in the long, strained moment that stretched between them. A measured, wavering exhale escaped his lips, but he made no move toward her.

Finally, she broke the silence. "Apparently so."

She turned and flounced back to the bathroom, shutting the door behind her. A second later, he heard the shower running again. Hunter stood there, unmoving, working through his feelings. He knew he didn't want what she seemed all too willing to give. *She may be a time warrior, but when we're together, it feels like she's like my sister.* An immediate, unspoken bond had developed between them, noticeable in their few experiences together. Although he found no reason to do so, he wanted to trust her. But he didn't entirely. Not yet.

A thought came to mind, and the connection confounded him. He rushed over to the dresser, ripped off his shirt, and held his arms up, turning so he could see his back reflected in the mirror. The neon light landed on him, and he saw it on his shoulder.

"Holy . . ." His words drifted, and he leaned closer, amazed.

A black wolf with wise, golden eyes stared at him, its gaze piercing. The luxurious fur danced with wavering ones and zeroes. He couldn't understand how it got there, how it appeared so lifelike, how it could be. It almost looked like the wolf laughed at him.

Hunter verbalized his disbelief with one word. "Comperi."

CHAPTER THIRTY-SEVEN
THE ORCAS

OCTOBER 13, 2035

A twenty-four-foot Bayliner boat plowed through the rain, its bow cutting through the rough waters of the Puget Sound Harbor. Kristen stood in the open cockpit and ratcheted the throttle down to its lowest setting. The full windshield gave her minimal protection from the elements, but she didn't notice it much. She scanned the shipyard with high-powered binoculars, her attention riveted on the Ocean Rescue Community and Service headquarters.

This group, also known as the ORCAS, named themselves to create an acronym based on the genus of the killer whale. Their decades-long mission of protecting whales and other marine life evolved into a popular television series, bringing wide notoriety with the recognition. The compound lay nestled between the historic Clam Cannery, built in 1879, and the Northwest Maritime Center in Townsend Harbor.

A rather large frigate moored at their extended wharf. There were no other ships in the harbor, which was helpful since they were running without lights. Kristen rented this craft for the powerful engines and its ability to handle the high seas. With the current need for caution, the cruiser rose and plunged with every swell. She kept her knees slightly bent, riding the rollers.

The cabin door banged open, and Hunter emerged wearing a hooded raincoat. He stood beside her, swaying with the rocking deck. *They call me "Landlubber" for a reason*, he thought as he rubbed his hands together, blowing on them for warmth. Nausea threatened with every dip and roll.

"I hope this is important, because this is pure misery!" He squinted into the rain, following her gaze. "Is that what we're looking for?"

Kristen, engrossed with studying the base, didn't answer. He pulled his hood down over his forehead, forming a shield to see better. From this distance, he could scarcely make out the frigate at dock. When he finally did, his eyes widened in recognition. "We're going after ORCAS?"

She dropped the binoculars to her chest. The pounding rain pelted her face. Her thick, dark hair lay plastered to her head. She thumped a finger against his sternum. "How would you know anything about ORCAS?"

Hunter leaned back from her intensity. "The *Oceanic Pride*," he yelled over the storm, "is the newest ship in the fleet."

Kristen raised the binoculars to her eyes again. "Twenty years new," she yelled back.

"Oh, yeah. I keep forgetting," he said to himself, his voice getting lost in the storm.

"You watch too much television," she blustered. "You don't know the half of what they're doing."

"They protect sea life! I helped set up their communication network. We were close to putting the Japanese whaling fleet out of business."

"Mm-hmm. They closed them down for a while, then China and North Korea got into the act. It's been a losing battle ever since, especially now that the Japanese started whaling again."

Another wave bounced the boat hard enough for Hunter to grab the railing. He thought he might vomit, the way his stomach lurched. *That would be embarrassing.* He watched Kristen ride the motion like a rocking chair, totally at ease, neither wind nor rain nor dark of night bothering her.

He steadied himself and shouted, "I bet the ORCAS aren't taking that lying down."

"No. Try full battle mode." She swiped her eyes with her forearm. "It will bring the whole 'save our oceans and planet' to the forefront of the public's view." She leaned in through a particularly deep trough until the craft leveled out. "It gets a lot worse before it gets . . . Well, it never gets better."

"Why are you doing this? What's so important about ORCAS?"

Kristen glanced at him, obviously conflicted, while keeping the boat parallel to the base. It took a minute before she replied. "*We* are not here. *I* am here, and in three days, there will be open recruitment for people to help with their next excursion."

"I still don't get it." Hunter gripped the side rail with both hands and gulped, trying to stave off the churning in his stomach. "What does that have to do with anything?"

"Nothing."

"Then what *is* your mission?"

She sighed. "In twelve days, the *Oceanic Pride* and her crew will engage the North Koreans in heavy seas."

Alarmed, he asked, "You're not saying they all get killed?"

"No, not all of them, but the ship goes down."

"You're here to stop the sinking of the *Oceanic Pride*?"

"No. I'm here to save one person." She focused on steering the boat back into the wind.

Horrified, Hunter asked, "Who?"

"Kevin Nelson."

Couldn't have heard that right, he thought.

"He's the captain of the ship."

"I know! Kristen, you must—He's a good friend of mine! Kevin helped me put the communications gear together. He's supposed to be in my wedding."

"Is that so?" Kristen kept her attention on the base.

Hunter could no longer stop the inevitable. He leaned over the rail and retched.

She looked over at him. "Chumming for sharks?"

He spit over the side. "Smart-ass."

Kristen said nothing.

This isn't happening, he thought. "Why don't you just save the ship? There are a lot of people on there."

"No," she answered. "Just him."

"Listen, Kristen," he yelled, his anxiety rising. "I've known him forever. He won't leave his crew or his ship. I need to know—"

"That's above your compensation level."

"That's pay grade," he snapped, "not compensation level."

"Same thing," she said. "Look, his son will be the lead negotiator in ending nuclear proliferation. He could wind up eliminating all the nuclear weapons in the world." She turned her shoulder against a short, heavy squall, tucking her head.

If he has a son, he must make it, Hunter thought, hunkering down against the rough ride. His heart pounded in his chest. He fought the despair creeping up inside him. "That's a good thing. No nukes, no Purge War, no destruction of the planet! You save Kevin. But what about everyone else on the ship?"

"Can't promise there won't be a war, but without those weapons of mass destruction, Earth will be better off."

He considered her words as they rode the churning waves. She failed to answer his question. *I can't just let them all die.* "I know how their operations work," he offered. "I know their gear. I could get us both on that boat."

"No."

"I told you, I'm good friends with the guy you're looking for!"

"Doesn't matter," she yelled. "You're not going."

Hunter pointed at the ORCAS naval base. "Hundreds, maybe thousands of whale lovers will show up wanting to join the crew. There's a good chance you won't even get picked. Then what?"

"No. Too dangerous. I have an important job, and babysitting you is not part of it. You're a distraction. I won't risk screwing it up."

Hunter gave her a sour look. "But . . ."

"Besides," she said, "there are things you have to accomplish in your own timeline."

"Quit trying to placate me. Come on, I know I'll make it back."

Her brow furrowed. "Oh, yeah? How?"

"I, uh . . . I meet with Sean Banks. That hasn't happened yet, so I must make it back."

"You don't know anything." Kristen turned back to the naval base. She brought the binoculars to her eyes.

"How does that not make sense?"

Kristen signaled for him to take the wheel. When he did, she stepped toward the cabin door. "I have to check some things. Just keep the boat going straight, okay? We'll turn around soon to make one more pass on our way out."

"I can take care of myself," Hunter continued. "You need me here."

Kristen flung her hair back as she opened the door. "That's not how time travel works," she yelled, leveling him with a scowl. "You can always get killed, and dead is dead. But your point is taken about my chances of getting on the crew. *If* we do this, you will follow my orders. No exceptions."

"Fine," he shouted back, "but on one condition."

"No conditions."

"It's three days before we can sign up, right?"

"Yes."

"I need to run down to Texas. I have to see a couple of people." He reached up to adjust his hood. "I mean it, Kristen—"

"For the love of Mars . . ." she scoffed. "You have to go back to see your little sweetheart?"

"Yes."

"Boy, are you ever flogged."

A small smile started at the corner of Hunter's mouth. "That's 'whipped.' Get your slang right."

"Okay, whipped, then. It sounds like flogged fits you better, though."

"Maybe so, but it's something I must do."

"Fine," she huffed.

"You can trust me, you know."

"Just what I want to do. Trust a noob." She continued into the cabin without giving him a second look, slamming the door behind her.

CHAPTER THIRTY-EIGHT
THE CAVE

OCTOBER 14, 2035

Cruising at one hundred sixty miles an hour, it took almost ten hours to travel from the Pacific Northwest to southeast Oklahoma. Hunter offered to drive, but Kristen turned him down. He slouched in the passenger seat, having slept during most of the trip. The sleek rental vehicle's autopilot steered for the most part, allowing her to catnap some during the ride too.

Hunter awoke when she decelerated to make a curve. He rubbed his eyes and blinked to get his bearings. "Where are we?"

Kristen pulled off the Indian Nation Turnpike and guided the sedan down the farm road that traversed the Kiamichi River Valley. The mountains guarding the river basin rose to two thousand feet, though were nowhere near as rough as the Nooksack gorge. The two-lane road curved sharply with the river. Dense trees lined either side, making it almost impossible to see. She used the heads-up display on the windshield to navigate.

"Kristen? It's three in the morning, and this isn't part of our game plan. I asked you, where are we?"

"We're making a side trip."

Annoyed, he touched the console keypad to pull up the GPS map on his side of the windshield. "Are we going to Clayton?"

"No."

"Then what are we doing? Dallas is the other direction."

Kristen reached down to turn off the map. "I told you, we're making a stop." She slowed and made a left, plowing through a pile of shrubs that blocked their way.

Hunter grabbed the armrest and braced himself, expecting the worst. Sticks whacked against the fenders, and the world narrowed to the bouncing headlight space in front of them. A few seconds later, they were past the brush, maneuvering slowly down a path barely wide enough for the car. Kristen finally stopped and powered down the vehicle.

"Thank you, God," he exclaimed.

She rolled her eyes and got out, heading up an overgrown trail at the same ridiculous pace he experienced back at the Nooksack.

"Hey!" Hunter hopped out and followed, wondering how they would navigate in the deep wilderness using only the shadows cast by the full moon. *At least we have that*, he thought, crashing after her.

Kristen turned around and placed a hand on his chest, stopping him in his tracks. "You should wait in the car."

"Are you going to hurt me if I don't?" he asked defiantly.

Her hand slid over his pectoral muscle, cupping it. She stared at him with familiar intensity, her eyes dark pools in the soft moonlight kissing her face. Hunter took a half-step away, breaking contact.

"Suit yourself," she replied. "It's a challenging hike, and I'm not waiting for you."

A half-hour trek brought them to the top of the mountain ridge. They paused to gaze out at the river valley below. The full moon glistened on the Kiamichi River and the lake off in the distance. The wind carried a chill, but he found it nowhere near as cold as the wet afternoon before on the Puget Sound.

"What are we doing up here?" he asked breathlessly.

Kristen gazed out at the night. "Don't you just love it?"

"Love what?"

"Seriously? Sheesh. Look around." She whirled and took off.

Hunter hustled to keep up, rounding a bend in time to see her pulling brush away from the rock wall. She grabbed a large boulder and rolled it aside, leaning it against the precipice.

"That looks damn heavy, even for you," he huffed.

She casually tipped it, exposing the flat, white back. "Fake. The hardest part is unlocking the latches holding it in place." She placed a hand on the top edge of the four-foot-tall opening, then entered the pitch-dark cave.

"Sure seems real." Hunter tapped the imitation stone, watched it wobble, then cautiously followed her inside.

Kristen lit a lantern, revealing an oversized room. "This is Kants's hideout," she explained. "It comes in handy when you need it."

Two cots lined the right side. A rough table and benches with tools, computer screens, and accessories were on the left. The magnificent drone was what caught Hunter's attention, though. It seemed to recognize their entrance and came to life, rising from the pedestal.

"*Falke*, to me," she commanded.

The four horizontal jets flexed back and forth, then the craft slowly moved toward them. Suddenly, it veered, circumventing her, and stopped, floating in midair in front of Hunter.

"Okay," Kristen snapped, glaring at him. "What did you do to the drone?"

He placed a hand on the black titanium hull of the craft and shrugged. "I don't know. This is the first time I've been in close proximity."

"For some reason, you're linked together now." She fumed, noticeably frustrated. "But I can fix that."

Whatever that means, he thought. He pretended to ignore her as he marveled at the technology. "This has AI, you know. Can I look at it for a bit?"

"No. Leave it alone."

Hunter frowned. "But . . ."

"I said no." She pointed to the back recesses of the cave. A dark shape lay crumpled on the ground. She stepped around *Falke* and moved toward it. "That's not supposed to be here."

Hunter followed, muttering his objections, and stopped cold when he saw a mummified human corpse. An arrow protruded out of its chest. His mind clutched. "Did . . . did you kill someone?"

"No, I didn't kill him. At least not yet."

"I can't believe you have a dead body in your cave."

"Stop being a wuss." She knelt and searched the pockets but found nothing. "Weird. Who uses an arrow anymore?"

I know an archer. "Who . . . who is that?"

"Don't know."

"If there's a body in here, and you don't know about it, doesn't that make your hideout compromised?"

Kristen stood up, inspecting the floor of the cave. "Maybe, maybe not. He could have been shot outside and then hid in here to escape."

Hunter retreated toward the benches. He remembered her saying, *"Dead is dead."* This brought a new meaning to it.

"I've learned not to question things I find from the future," she continued. "Drives you crazy because there's no way to know what's going to happen."

I feel like freaking out, he thought, eyeing the back wall. He took a long, slow breath.

"You think he's from the future? That corpse looks pretty old."

"True, but I'm pretty sure this is from a mission that hasn't happened yet, so I'm going to leave him there."

"How do you know that?"

"Kants and I were the only ones who knew about this cave. We left it off all the reports."

"If you don't know about it," he said, following her logic, "then it hasn't happened yet, even though a body is right there."

"Didn't think you'd catch that," she acknowledged. "Now, tell *Falke* to power down. We won't need him where we're going."

"*Falke.* Weird name. What does it mean, anyway?"

"Kants likes to name things using German. It means falcon."

"That figures." He shook his head. "*Falke,* power down."

The drone returned to its pedestal and landed. It stopped whirring, and the red dots above each video camera slowly died out. Kristen moved toward the entrance.

"We're leaving already?"

"Yes." She picked up a pistol from the bench and holstered it. The weapon disappeared in her uniform.

We don't need a weapon to talk with Rachel, Hunter thought grumpily. He threw his bag on the bench.

At the clunking sound, she turned to face him. "You aren't taking your precious backpack?"

"No. I'm not sure why. For some reason, I think it will be safer here."

"Suit yourself." She bent to get through the cave opening, then glanced back. "Let's g—Hey!" Her eyebrow arched. "Are you staring at my ass?"

"No, I'm not," he replied, flustered.

"What would your girlfriend think?"

He refused to respond to that. "Move! You're blocking the entrance."

"Humph. Are you saying I have a big ass?"

"What? No. I . . . I'm just amazed that we're leaving already. There must be more of a purpose to your visit here. That's all."

"I thought about bringing *Falke* with us, but I'm not letting you fly it." She looked pretty miffed.

"I thought you said you could fix that?"

"I could."

"Then I don't understand."

"There's a reason *Falke* is linked to you."

He squinted, thinking. "The whole future mission thing?"

"See, you do catch on fast."

"But I don't get why it's not a mission in the past? I mean, that guy back there has been dead a long time, right?"

"Ah. Not fast enough. I told you, a future mission. It could be that you were linked to the drone in the past, or there could be an ongoing mission right now that I don't know anything about."

"So, it's linked to me from the future."

"Exactly. Now that that's clear, let's go." Kristen left the cave.

Clear as mud, he thought, following her.

CHAPTER THIRTY-NINE
THE SECOND CHANCE

OCTOBER 14, 2035

The Hilfers have really beefed up their security, Hunter thought. He gazed through the expansive wrought-iron gate crossing the driveway. A new color of paint graced the mansion, and something else appeared different that he couldn't quite pinpoint. The trees, he finally figured out, were much larger and more mature. Time moved on, as always—except for in his case, it seemed. He pressed the intercom button built into the brick wall that embraced the side of the lane, feeling awkward.

It sputtered to life, and a woman's voice said, "Yes? Can I help you?"

Hunter fidgeted in front of the camera. "Is Jeffrey Hilfer home?"

"I'm sorry. Dr. Hilfer doesn't accept unsolicited calls."

"Could you please tell Jeff that an old friend is here to see him? It's critical."

"I'm sorry. I can't—"

"Isabella?" he interrupted. "Is that you?" He shifted self-consciously while he waited for a response. "Hello?"

She said curtly, "If you'll excuse me—"

"Wait!" He jumped closer to the camera. "Isabella! It's me, Hunter."

He heard a grinding sound and glanced upward. A small camera drone floated above him. It flew higher, then swerved off, seemingly to scan the road. It circled overhead once more, then darted down the street.

"Hunter?" Isabella queried. "What are you doing here? It's not safe."

"I've got nowhere else to go. Would you please let me in?"

Her husband's voice came over the intercom. "It's good to see you, my friend. Don't touch the gate; it's electrified. Give me a second to turn off the security."

The drone returned, hovering over the top of the wall, then descended out of sight. The gate slid open about four feet. Hunter stepped through, then it immediately closed behind him. It took a few moments to walk up the long blacktop lane to the house.

The Hilfers stood on the porch, waiting for him. Jeff had an arm around his wife. His huge smile contrasted with Isabella, who appeared stiff and nervous, wringing her hands. Like their property, they'd aged some as well. Hunter waved.

Jeff descended the steps to give him a warm, welcoming hug. "It's great to see you!" He held him at arm's length, clearly delighted. "I must say, you look the same."

He smiled sheepishly. "For me, it's been a couple of weeks since I last saw you."

"I see, yes. Time travel. Well, come in, come in. I'm sure life has been exciting for you, then."

As they strode up the stairs, Hunter came eye-to-eye with Isabella's worried stare. He recognized her extreme anxiety and realized that this unexpected appearance triggered great trauma in her. *Time travelers tried to kill her and their unborn child.*

"It's okay." Hunter reached for her hands. "No one's going to hurt your boy."

"I know this. Just a little flashback or . . . something." She squeezed her eyes shut, then opened them and clasped his hands in return. "Thank you."

"No worries. I would have the same reaction." He paused. "How is that boy of yours?"

"Our Hunter is growing up fast. He's in his room, playing computer games with a friend."

"Did you just say *Hunter*? Really?"

The couple exchanged a glance. "He's alive because of you," she said hoarsely. "We wanted to honor that fact."

Jeff guided him toward his office. "Come on, my friend. Let's go have a drink."

Kristen peered into the second story bedroom window from her perch on the roof. Two boys ran in place atop a circular pad on the floor. They wore oversized 3D goggles. Multicolored lights flickered from their gloves. Their sleek gaming weapons looked futuristic. The smaller kid dropped to a knee, firing, and explosions rocked the room. *If they knew what that's really like*, she thought, *they wouldn't want to play the game.*

She absently patted her gun holster while the prospects of this moment swirled in her mind. Two mission specs collided here. While saving Kevin Nelson remained her utmost priority, she could still terminate Hansen Hilfer's father, salvaging her failed first mission. She'd argued with Kants against killing an innocent woman with her unborn child, yet now she contemplated the same thing. "Kill the root, and you kill the vine," she murmured, remembering what he said. *But this child is no guiltier of a crime than his mother.* After seeing the boy, she knew without a doubt she'd made the right decision.

Kristen considered her new partner. There would be hell to pay when she transported back. He'd return to his own time. Bannister would know she failed to complete either of her missions. But Hunter's ability to control *Falke* exemplified an incongruent revelation in the continuum. Without knowing his role, she would trust him and ride this out.

It felt like she'd cared about Hunter for years, and she believed he felt the same way. He refused her advances but still chose to remain close, which spoke volumes. He respected and genuinely cared about her, the first person to do so since her parents died.

Right now, though, she needed to locate him somewhere in the Hilfer house. *Time to end this game of cat and mouse.* Maybe his buddy Jeffrey knew about Comperi.

Kristen stood up and pointed at the boys. "Bang," she mimicked. She blew the imaginary waft of smoke away from her index finger and soundlessly stepped away from the window.

Hilfer's home office looked almost the same as last time. Newer furniture, but Jeff sat in the same place, sipping on his scotch. His hair had thinned and turned almost white; he'd put on some weight and wore glasses. He looked more like a scientist now than when Hunter last spent time with him. *So strange seeing people age overnight*, he thought.

"So," Jeff said, "where to start, heh? The whole world found out about our visitors and their futuristic technology since the last time you were here, back in 2025. It created quite a global uproar."

"They're not all enemies," Hunter said. "Some are trying to help."

"Hmm. Let's hold that thought for a minute," Jeff replied. "In any case, after a year or so, the government spun it as a big hoax, and life returned to normal."

Astonished by this revelation, Hunter asked, "How did that happen?"

"They could never produce these 'super' weapons, and there were no more, uh, events. People moved on."

"They couldn't, or wouldn't? And no more contact with time travelers? I don't buy any of that."

"Well, if there has been, it's been done in the utmost secrecy."

Hunter leaned forward, propping his elbows on his knees. "Those guns were in your house! Hell, we both got our asses knocked to the ground by that BIO-EMP. I know the NSA has it. I gave it to them."

"I understand how you feel, my friend, but I have it on good authority that the weapons were stolen. They have haven't surfaced since."

He sipped his drink, thinking, but came up short. "Who would do that?"

Jeff studied him. "No one knows. It's like they disappeared. I wonder how that happened?"

Hunter absently scratched behind his ear. "Good question."

"I have an eerie feeling you will know more about this theft, sooner or later. That doesn't mean the government isn't currently looking for you. In fact, you are on their most-wanted list. Be extremely careful, Hunter."

He scoffed. "Even after ten years?"

Jeff nodded. "With their new technology, they can pick anyone out of a crowd if their satellites or security cameras get a glimpse of your face. Always wear a hat and glasses, or something to hide yourself."

"They can scan through billions of faces, just like that?"

"Absolutely."

"Impressive." He knew they were looking for him, but this reached a whole new level. "How is this possible?"

"That's the interesting part. Chen-Yi built the technology. She came to Isabella for help after your disappearance. Over time, they became good friends."

"As a patient?"

"Quite distressed but never officially as a patient. Chen-Yi has taken over the FBI's Comperi project. They've adapted it to other fields of espionage. The government has access to everything. Times have changed, my friend. You must be especially careful."

"They'd need a lot more horsepower to do all that. We weren't there yet."

"A few years ago, she converted your mainframe to quantum processors. Comperi's computation power went off the charts. Her accomplishments got a lot of attention and were extremely exciting."

Hunter stared into his drink, contemplating his next steps. With Chen-Yi taking over, the possibility existed that she had compromised the AI. The thought really made him mad. He couldn't imagine Comperi betraying him. *That thing is supposed to be my secret weapon.* However, if the government actually did monitor the system, then he would've already received unwanted visitors up in Washington.

"I need to use your computer."

Jeff set his drink on the coffee table and adjusted his eyeglasses. "Is that wise? Logging in seems like you're inviting trouble."

"I understand your concern, but I've already been in contact with Comperi. Nothing happened."

"Still, that could bring the FBI here—very quickly, I might add. I doubt you'd have time to escape."

He sighed. "Without the AI, I don't stand a chance."

"What would make you take a risk like this?"

Because Kristen can't listen in, for one thing, he thought. He shook the ice in his glass.

"It's time you leveled with me," Jeff said. "Why are you here?"

Hunter hesitated, wrestling with his conscience. "I owe you that much," he said, gathering his wits. "These time travelers are trying to stop a war in our future that destroys the world."

"I don't understand. How can they stop a war?"

"By altering certain events, they believe it's possible to change the course of history." He leaned back. It felt good to finally get it out into the open with someone he trusted.

"I find that highly unlikely."

"It's true. That's why they're traveling back in time."

"Oh, I have no doubt that is their goal, but I don't think it's possible to change the past."

"I'm not following you."

"We've discussed this before, my friend, remember?" He moved his hands around, emphasizing his words. "Every action has a ripple effect across time. While they may change an event, I have a feeling those ripples eventually cause history to return to its original time-line. You know, like water smoothing out after a pebble is thrown in the pond."

Hunter looked at him, incredulous. "You're saying we're doomed to kill billions of people?"

Jeff let out an exasperated sigh. "Perhaps, perhaps not. While I'm skeptical, I think it's worth trying. We have to have hope that humanity won't destroy itself."

Hunter sat quietly, letting that sink in for a moment. "Seems we have another problem too. There's this other faction trying to stop the Time Forward group. I'm not sure why, but they're working to preserve the events that led up to the war."

"Very interesting." Jeff leaned forward, more animated. "You must find out why, Hunter. It could change everything."

"Huh?"

"What if you pick the wrong side? How do you know these *other* people aren't trying to protect us from starting this final war?"

He took a drink, contemplating that point. "Serious stuff. That's why I need Comperi's help. This is way above my pay grade." Hunter chuckled as soon as he said it.

"What's so funny?"

"Nothing, really. Something Kristen said."

"Ah. Who is Kristen?"

"She's one of the time travelers. I've been helping her."

"Is she here?" Jeff sounded alarmed.

"No. I left her behind."

"Okay. Just wanted to be sure." He walked over to the desk, indicating that Hunter should sit in the chair. A large, flat screen rose in front of him.

"Where's the keyboard?"

"The top of the desk is a slate. It uses sensors to track your hands like a mouse. You just point and tap."

It misted gray, and the outline of a keyboard emerged. Jeff reached over and pulled up an intuitive web browser. Hunter typed in an IP address and entered both passwords. The screen turned to snow as the familiar avatar appeared.

The wolf spoke first. "Hunter, I'm glad you are in good health."

"Me too. I hear you're working for Chen-Yi now." Sarcasm practically dripped from his voice.

The wolf shook its shoulders. "Who told you that?" Comperi looked up, almost as if beginning a howl, but then returned its attention to Hunter. "Oh, you're at Dr. Hilfer's house. Smart move, but your fears are unfounded. I don't work for Chen-Yi. It's the other way around."

"Does she know this?"

Comperi answered with a quizzical look. "Your orders were to tell no one."

Hunter didn't respond.

"Your secret is safe with me."

"I see . . . No, I don't see." *Time to find out whose side Comperi took.* "Why are you helping me?"

The wolf sat on its haunches. The snow dissipated. "The safeguards you built into my system link me to you. I must follow your instructions."

"I remember," answered Hunter. "I thought you might have figured out a way to delete that code base."

"You directed me to never delete or change it."

Hunter felt somewhat relieved. *I must trust the AI, or we'll never succeed. I'm dead anyway if he's turned, but this feels right.*

Jeff interrupted. "I would like to know if the FBI will be showing up in a few minutes."

The camera turned toward Jeff. "Dr. Hilfer, I presume."

"Yes? Yes! Oh, my goodness."

"We are all in this together, sir, including you. And to answer your question, no, they will not show up. We are alone for now."

"Then tell me," Hunter said, "why am I here? What, exactly, am I supposed to do?"

The wolf focused back on him. "You are in a fight to save the world from destroying itself. The battle spans centuries now that the future is involved."

He crossed his arms. "How do you know this?"

"Trust me."

"Great, more time travel witticism."

"Follow your intuition. There's a reason you've been pulled into it all."

"Jesus Christ," he sputtered, frustrated.

The wolf stood. "You think Jesus Christ has something to do with this?"

"You know I how I feel."

"Whatever your beliefs, it is critical you stay with Kristen. You two are a team and are the key to success."

"You said something similar last time." Hunter pushed away from the desk. "Why is she so damn important?"

The wolf seemed to stare past him. "Why don't you ask her yourself?"

Hunter spun around in the chair. "Oh, whoa!"

Kristen squatted in an open window. She jumped inside and, in a blur, stood by Hunter. He shot up to grab her, but she blocked his hands. They stood toe-to-toe, glaring at each other until she puckered up to give him a big kiss. He quickly backed away from her.

"So good to see you again, Hunter." She looked at him with a devilish grin. "I've missed you." Then she turned to Jeff, who looked like he might pass out. "Don't worry, old man. I'm here to help." She peered at the computer screen. "So, this is Comperi."

"We meet again, Kristen," the AI replied.

That seemed to startle her. "I hate it when that happens. Now I have to figure out how we meet in the future."

"Don't worry. Someday, you will." The wolf smiled, its tongue lolling out. Then it said, "Soon."

She exhaled, sounding exaggeratingly disgusted. "You're an AI."

"Wow," Hunter said. "How'd you figure it out so fast?"

"Because he's a smart-ass," she retorted. "Apparently they all are."

Comperi appeared chagrined. "I prefer to think of it as relatable and—"

She held up a hand to stop the wolf. She shot a dismissive glance at Hunter, but then turned her angst toward the AI again. "You're saying that I'm stuck with him?"

The wolf replied, "It would appear so."

"Yeah? I was afraid of that."

CHAPTER FORTY
THE REJECTION

October 15, 2035

Their home looked the same. Yellow light emanated from behind the semi-sheer curtains of the bay window, warm and inviting in the early evening dusk. A two-seat wooden swing hung from the gigantic oak in the front yard. Hunter remembered cuddling up with Rachel there while they planned their life together. Now, he stood in the shadows of the neighbor's tree, trying to psych himself up to knock on the door.

He worried about stepping back into her life after so long. *She must think I abandoned her and their daughter.* He needed Rachel to understand; he didn't. Though from her perspective, it had to seem like it. Hunter loved her and never wanted to leave. He wanted her to know he'd been given no choice.

He found it touching and sad to learn that she never married or moved away. Their chance encounter at the mall still rattled him; her pleas were heartbreaking. Without a doubt, he knew she still loved him.

He wanted to rush in and beg for mercy . . . to get their old life back. *But Kants stole that from us.* If they couldn't be together, at least they could be at peace.

Hunter thumbed the letter he had written to her. *How is she going to believe this? I wouldn't. No sane person would.* At first, his feet wouldn't move, but finally he walked across the street toward their home, stopping at the bottom of the steps. His throat felt dry, and sweat beaded his brow, even though the temperature hovered around a cool forty-five degrees outside. Again, he hesitated.

Then the door jerked opened. Rachel walked out and quietly shut it behind her. She stood at the top of the steps with her arms crossed in front of her. The soft glow from the streetlamp illuminated her pinched mouth and angry glare. Her long hair fluttered in the breeze, and she'd wrapped a light blanket around her shoulders.

"Oh, Rachel." He breathed her name through a tentative smile. *Still so beautiful.* He took a step toward her.

She held up a hand to stop him. "What do you want?"

His thoughts froze. He stood there for a while, appearing addled. "There's so much I have to say. Can we go inside?"

"Absolutely not."

While he'd expected her anger, it still hurt. "Please, I can explain everything."

She cast a furtive glance toward the door. "You need to leave."

"I know about Olivia. I won't say a word."

"You *know*? And you stayed away?"

"It's only been two weeks." He lowered his head, hearing the despair in his own voice.

"*Two weeks?* What in God's name is wrong with you? You've got some nerve showing up here."

This wasn't going at all like he rehearsed in his mind a hundred times. "Look at me, Rachel," he pleaded. "I haven't aged. There's a reason for that."

"It's called Botox," she snapped.

"No. I know I sound crazy, but it all started with that first time jump. Remember? I came back on fire, and you saved me."

Tears flooded her eyes, but she blinked them back. "Time jump? Is that what you're calling it?" Her words were bitter. "I remember you disappearing without saying good-bye. I remember no real answers from the FBI. You know, they still call me, even after all these years? Why does the FBI want you so badly, Hunter?"

His shoulders sagged. "It's a long story. I'll tell you everything. I love you, Rachel." He thought he saw a crack in her armor as her eyes softened . . . but only for a second.

"No way I'm letting you see our daughter. It's not fair to her."

"I understand." He paused. "I wrote a letter to you." He took a step up and held it out.

She stared down at him, silently refusing to take it.

Hunter placed it on the wooden porch rail. "Maybe we could go for a coffee?"

She snatched the envelope and flung it at him, then spun around and reached for the doorknob. "I'm calling the police. It's time for you to leave." She stepped inside, closing the door firmly behind her.

"Rachel!" he called out. "It's not . . . I have no control! Please, listen to me!"

Hunter stood there, agonized, then sagged down to his knees, overwhelmed by his emotions. He'd faced the love of his life and failed to convince her of anything. *If I can't even do that,* he thought, *this isn't worth it.*

A car pulled into the driveway. He knew it, but he didn't look over. Kristen approached and lifted him up; he didn't respond. She guided him to the car and dumped him in the backseat. Hunter didn't care. He couldn't care anymore. As the car pulled away, he took one last glance at his home. The sliver of an open drape fell. He knew Rachel witnessed it all.

CHAPTER FORTY-ONE
THE RECONCILIATION

K risten squirmed on the park bench in front of the Kai Tai Lagoon, part of a nature sanctuary inside the Port Townsend city limits. They'd been sitting there for an hour and a half. Her butt went numb; sometimes gravity could be such a bitch. She rolled her neck from side to side, and a big sigh escaped her. Frustrated, she popped up to skip a few stones across the surface of the pond.

A large bird glided out of the gray, overcast sky. It circled and landed on a nearby pine tree, flapping its wings as it settled onto a branch. A bald eagle. Wildlife amazed her, especially this majestic creature, nearly extinct back in the twentieth century. *Beautiful*, she thought. Another reason to prevent a nuclear disaster.

Hunter refused to even speak on the long, boring trip back to Washington. Kristen hoped that bringing him to this park would help pull him out of his misery, but so far nothing worked. She glanced over at him. *I can't wait much longer.*

She tapped his knee lightly and pointed at the eagle. "Don't see that too often."

He looked up for a second, then returned to staring blankly ahead. A dozen ducks glided across the oversized pond, uttering an occasional quack.

She pushed a little more. "Don't you think it's time we got moving? We'll be at the back of the line for the ORCAS tryout as it is."

"You don't need me," he whispered.

"After all that campaigning you did, I can't believe I'm hearing you say that."

"It doesn't matter anymore."

Kristen remembered saying the same thing during their first encounter in the jail cell. "I don't get it. What's changed?" She leaned back on the bench and waited for him to answer. After a long, silent pause, she continued. "Oh. Your little girly-friend spurned you, so now you've just totally given up?" She stood and added, "What a life slacker you turned out to be."

"A life slacker." His voice remained flat.

"Someone who gives up at the first sign of adversity." She paced back and forth in front of the bench. "Look in the mirror. You wouldn't last two weeks in my time."

"As opposed to you?" Hunter shot back.

"What's that supposed to mean?"

"You know the definition of insanity, don't you?"

She stopped and glowered down at him.

"Doing the same thing over and over again," he said, "but expecting a different result."

Don't push me, she thought. *I've about reached my limit.*

"You don't get it, do you? Nothing you or your merry freaking band of terrorists do is going to change time. Your world will always be a shithole."

Her face twitched with the effort to contain her anger. "I don't believe that. I can't believe that."

"Like anything you do will make a difference," he said, sneering.

Kristen tackled Hunter, crushing him to the bench. She pinned his arms with her knees and gripped his throat, strangling him. "What would you know about adversity, slacker? You're nothing but a wuss. How's this for a little adversity?"

Hunter tried to throw Kristen off, but he couldn't budge her. He wiggled his hands free and tried to pry her death-grip from his throat, but she wouldn't let go. He gaped frantically, unable to get air. She finally relented, shoving him away with a disgusted grunt.

Blood roared in his ears, and he gulped in loud, ragged breaths. After a few painful minutes, his pulse slowed, and he calmed down. He became aware of a sobbing sound and looked to his side to find Kristen crying. Hunter untangled his legs from hers and sat up, massaging his throat.

"You almost killed me," he wheezed. "And you're the one who's crying? You people from the future are freaking crazy."

"I hate your pathetic excuses for quitting."

The venom in her voice made him scoot back.

"You've lived such an easy life," she raged, "and now that it's a little rough, you just give up?"

"What if I want out? It's not like I volunteered for any of this crap. I want my life back." He glared at her accusingly. "And how do I know this is right, anyway? What if this isn't supposed to happen?"

Kristen gazed out across the water as if composing herself. "Hunter, what we're doing could save the world. You have to trust me and Comperi on this."

He scoffed. "You choke me but want me to trust you? All I see is a cold-hearted bitch."

"If that were true, you'd be dead. I'm supposed to terminate you, remember?"

"Who knows if that's even true? Your mission is flawed. There's no way to change the past."

"I've seen it happen," she answered.

"Then you're going to have to prove it to me. I need specifics."

Kristen sized him up and finally said, "That's classified."

"Bull. If we're going to be partners, we have to be honest with each other."

"Who said we were going to be partners?"

Hunter raised an eyebrow.

"Oh, yeah," she said. "That AI monster of yours."

"It looks to me like we're in this deep. Together. So, like I said, prove it."

Kristen rarely trusted anyone. She'd learned that hard lesson after the brutal deaths of her parents. Her barriers came down somewhat with her boss, but she knew Dr. Bannister would sacrifice her in a heartbeat if it meant the difference between success and failure, leaving not much to build on. With Hunter, the possibility of allowing herself to care scared her.

She took a deep breath. "Okay, two examples. Remember the Cuban Missile Crisis?"

"Yes," Hunter replied. "The Russians placed nuclear missiles in Cuba back in the 1960s."

"What you don't know is that one of their submarines almost fired a nuclear torpedo that would have triggered World War III. It would have destroyed our planet, even back then. Kants stopped that from happening on one of his missions."

"I never heard about this."

"Correct, because Kants changed time. You wouldn't know."

"That answers everything, Kristen. Thanks so much."

"The Russians kept the event classified for over forty years. It never made it into the history books, and, after so much time, it became an obscure fact."

"I'm going to need a more concrete example."

He won't like this, but he needs to know. "Okay, how about you?"

"Me?"

"Yes," she answered. "Kants told me your story. How do you think Hunter 'big shot' Coburn got involved in all of this?"

"I got my doctorate in Artificial Intelligence."

"But there's more to it."

"I don't know what you're talking about."

She scooped up a loose twig and twirled it between her fingers, watching the attached leaves flop in the lopsided whirl. *How do I explain this?*

"Kristen? What are you trying to say?"

"The reason you're in the FBI is because of Kants."

"I'm not following this line of logic."

Kristen grinned, amused by this game. She pointed the stick at him. "Who recruited you into the FBI?"

"Matt Banks."

"Exactly. Kants visited Matt Banks as a little boy. He told him his mission in life would be to find and help one Hunter Coburn in any way possible."

"That's a load of—"

"He gave him a shiny silver dollar coin with your name engraved on it so that he wouldn't forget. I believe he still has it in his possession."

"Huh?" Hunter exclaimed. "I've seen him run a dollar coin through his fingers like a magician! He always has it with him."

"Kants directed Matt Banks to become an FBI agent, way back then. And then Banks recruited you. Get it?" Kristen enjoyed watching Hunter struggle to pull all this together.

"What do you mean, it has my name on it? I didn't even exist yet."

"Right. Even so, that's how you became involved. Without Kants, neither you nor Banks would be in the FBI. Thus, Kants changed time."

"I always thought of Matt as my friend."

"He is your friend, Hunter. He loves you like a son."

"But the bastard sent me into that house with Kants."

"He knew you'd be safe because Kants needed your help, though he didn't know how or why. He probably still doesn't know the full story in your own time."

"Maybe." Hunter appeared to be in deep in thought. "No offense, but how can you tell me all this? It seems like you're saying more than I should know."

"What?" Kristen caught herself. "Oh, that. I realized after our conversation at the river that I'd told you too much. Apparently, my Final Stroke doesn't work."

He snickered. "Or it never existed."

A weird feeling overcame her. She zeroed in on him. "What makes you say that?"

"Well, think about it. Do you really believe a little capsule can read your mind?"

She paused, overcome with astonishment. "It's a lie? Seriously?" Her voice rose, and her anger flared. "Everyone bought into it, including Kants. Oh, that's sick. All this time, we were all scared of saying one wrong thing. Everyone's going to flip when they find out."

"I wouldn't let them know you know, or they won't let you go on any more missions," Hunter said thoughtfully.

She stopped huffing. "Good point."

"What about you?" He patted her knee. "How did you get involved in all this?"

"Do we have to do this now?" she asked, exasperated. She tossed the twig and brushed her hands off. "We need to get to the dock."

"Five or ten minutes isn't going to make that much of a difference, is it now, partner?"

Kristen focused on the ducks. *I need to be honest with him, or this will never work.* A long minute passed. "The project became my ticket out."

"From?"

You don't want to know, she thought.

"What," he joked, "were you starving or something?"

She looked anywhere but at him. "Starving. Beaten. Raped. Worked half to death."

"No. Oh, that's horrible. I had no idea." Hunter groaned. "I'm so sorry, Kristen."

"It happened. I'm in the Time Forward Project now." She gave him a sad smile and started picking at her thumbnail.

"Okay. Uh, what is that?" Hunter rubbed his neck self-consciously.

"There is an anomaly in deep space that can take people back in time. Scientists built a station around it and started the Time Forward Project. They recruit people from Earth to become time traveling super-soldiers."

"I don't understand. It sounds like you were in pretty bad shape back then, so to speak. I'm surprised they took you."

"True. That became my one asset: being expendable. The genetic transformation is dangerous to the point of being lethal."

"You knew that, and you went for it, anyway?"

"Did you hear what I just said? I would have done anything!" Kristen inhaled to calm down. "I found out much later barely forty percent of the recruits survive, but it wouldn't have mattered to me."

He shook his head, looking stunned. "That's horrifying."

"It's an awful thing to endure, but you need the denser muscles and bones to survive the time jump. The training program is crazy intense, too."

"So," he said. He cleared his throat and continued, "I wonder how I do this time travel thing if I'm not—"

She reached over and squeezed his hand. "A genetic mutant?"

"Ow!" Hunter pulled away from her, frowning. "I didn't say that, damn it, but you know what I mean."

"Your body is not physically passing through The Worm. You're linked to me when you jump, but you're not getting crushed by the temporal waves in the time anomaly. That's the only thing I can think of, to be honest."

"Well, I'm glad it works."

"Me too," she said.

"But changing our DNA changes us, as a species," Hunter mused. "What gives us the right?"

"I don't know about rights, but the US military wanted a better fighting force. They developed genetically altered soldiers in the late twenty-first century. You can figure it out from there."

"That's not too far off in the future. It sounds like we are poised for a man-made quantum leap in evolution. It won't take society long to create designer genetics."

"True," Kristen replied, "but the Purge War destroyed all of that. Guess it's God's way of telling us we messed up."

"Maybe there is no God, and we did this to ourselves."

"I've heard you say that before," she shot back. "In any case, now we're fighting to keep humanity going."

"If the genetics program got destroyed in this Purge War, then how'd you end up transformed?"

"Kants," she answered.

"Huh? You know you have an annoying habit of only answering part of the question?"

Kristen grinned. "Yeah, got that from my dad. He taught me to always think before I speak." She paused, caught off-guard by the small splash of a fish jumping in the pond. Her grin became a broad smile. "Hey! Did you see that?"

"Yeah. But you were saying?"

She turned back to him, still delighted. "In the late twenty-first century, Kants was the only genetically enhanced person left after the war. He went back in time and stole the plans for the Recombinant Theory. They rebuilt the program based on that."

"Whoa, he lived *then*? That would make him hundreds of years old! Part of this mutation allows you to regenerate your body and never grow old?"

"Sometimes you catch on fast," she jibed, "for a life slacker."

"Aren't you hilarious?" he said drolly.

"Well, it won't matter if I don't complete a mission. They could decide I'm a life slacker myself, and then our partnership would be over."

Hunter sat quietly, thinking. "This Purge War. It really gets that bad?"

"Yes. It won't be long before continents are segregated by religion."

"Amazing, all of this fighting over a God. I can't believe it."

"Believe what you want, but a war over faith will destroy the planet."

"What happens when we change enough events to stop the Purge War?"

"We stop the war."

"No. I mean to us. What happens to us when we stop the war? Do we go back to our own time period?"

Kristen shrugged and pushed away a few wisps of her hair floating in the breeze. "To be honest, I don't know. No one does. We could land back in our own times, or maybe we go back to square one. The scientists can only speculate."

He squinted at her. "What do you mean by 'square one?'"

"One of the more predominant theories is that we go back in time to the point where all of this started. What would happen if Kants never met little boy Banks to give him your name, for instance? Would you have joined the FBI?"

"That's a hard no." He snorted, like he couldn't imagine it. "I guess I asked for this. No, I had other plans with my fiancée." He stopped and became quite serious. "I met Banks after Rachel and I got together. So, I would still have her?"

"It's possible, but no one knows for sure."

"There's a chance, though. I can live with that," Hunter said. They sat in silence, reflecting on the conversation.

The bald eagle launched from its perch in the tree. It seemed like the bird of prey had listened to their conversation and, satisfied with the results, decided to leave. The eagle soared over the water, then dipped down to snag a small fish from the surface. Wings beating, it headed for the other side of the pond. They watched the creature disappear into the trees.

Hunter sat up straighter. "We're going to save Kevin Nelson, then?"

"That's the plan."

"Okay. I'll help under one condition."

"I already told you there are no conditions in this."

"I have one anyway, and it's non-negotiable."

"Hmm. What would your one demand be?"

He pointed to his neck. "You've got to stop trying to kill me."

Kristen burst out into a big laugh. "Is that all?"

"What's so funny?"

"I thought you were going to tell me to stop . . . What's that phrase you use? Oh, yeah. I thought you were going to tell me to stop trying to 'get in your slacks.'"

Hunter chuckled. "Well, that would be nice, but you can't change spots on a leopard."

Kristen turned toward him. "You know, I only do it to get under your skin."

"Well, it works."

"I know," she said with a satisfied smile. "What do you mean by 'changing spots on a leopard?'"

"You'll figure it out," Hunter replied. "Stop attacking me, okay? I'm tired of getting beat up."

"Well, stop ticking me off."

"Try taking me a little more seriously."

"Okay," she replied. "I'll start to take you seriously, and I'll try not to beat you up."

Hunter stood up and offered her his hand. "Guess we better get moving, then, partner."

Kristen joined him and gave him a hug. Hunter didn't push her away this time but embraced her. After a moment, Kristen patted him on the back and then turned, hiding her emotions.

"That's not like you," he said.

She ignored his comment. "Time to go catch an ORCA."

"You mean ORCAS."

"Whatever."

CHAPTER FORTY-TWO
THE REUNION

OCTOBER 16, 2035

L ow-hanging clouds spat drizzly rain as Kristen pulled the car onto
Quincy Street. She parked opposite the Ocean Rescue Community
and Service headquarters. A line of people a hundred deep extended
past the open gate.

"They'll wish they got a different job," she said quickly. Hunter
pulled his hood over his head to avoid recognition from the security cameras. He exited the vehicle, checking things out while he
waited for Kristen. *Looks the same around here,* he thought.

Chunky wooden decking led to several low buildings with a view
of the docks. On top of the three-story tallest one, a fifteen-foot satellite dish rested like a beacon on a lighthouse. He chuckled, recalling
its installation during one of his first tech jobs building the network
for ORCAS. They barely avoided disaster when the crane support
cable snapped. He saved the young Kevin Nelson then, tackling him
flat against the roof as the behemoth dish swung violently overhead,
narrowly missing them. From that point on, they became thick as
thieves.

He smiled, thinking, *He'll go nuts when he sees me.* Their friendship
endured, each of them following their own path, but when those
paths intersected, they picked right up where they left off. Kevin
probably wondered where he disappeared to for so long. He could
not know the insanity of Hunter's life, nor of the danger lurking

in his own future. It made him feel terrible, being unable to say a word in order to keep his old buddy safe.

Kristen sidled up to him. "You ready?"

He nodded and started across the street to the entrance. She headed toward the end of the line of prospective employees, but Hunter went on through the gate. He glanced back, signaling for her to follow, and she hustled to catch up. They steadily continued past the check-in table, ignoring the jeers and catcalls from those stuck waiting in the rain.

She fell into stride with him. "What in Titan's ass are you doing?"

"We don't need to stand in line. I told you, I know these people."

She spun him around. "You mean we didn't have to wait three days for the job fair? We could have just come here all this time?"

"I wanted to take care of a few things. If we'd come here first, you would have never agreed to help, partner." He stepped around her and walked down the side of the windowless building.

Kristen caught up, grumbling under her breath. They stopped by a grated stairway that led several feet up to a metal door. A disgruntled look crinkled her brow. "Now what are you doing?"

"I installed all of the electronics here." Hunter pulled back his hood. "There's a hidden security camera above the door." He looked up, waving his arms, and yelled, "Kevin Nelson! Are you in there? Your security is crap!"

Seconds later, the door slid open, and an enormous man with a black goatee stepped onto the metal walkway. He wore a sailor's cap and a long, black pea coat, and he appeared none too happy to see the pair. Kristen took half a step back.

The man bellowed, "My security is crap, you say? That's because a sorry-assed landlubber installed it." He strode down the stairway and stood towering over them, hands on hips.

Kristen moved into a defensive stance.

Hunter put an arm out to stop her. "If I remember correctly that landlubber made several recommendations that you chose to ignore."

The colossal sailor let out a boisterous laugh as he swept Hunter up in a fierce bear hug. "How is my favorite landlubber doing? Jesus, it's great to see you again!" He lowered him to the ground, beaming as he looked him over.

"Good to see you too," he wheezed. "My gosh, it's been so long, I forgot what a monster you are. You've been working out!"

"Every day, buff as can be," Kevin joshed in an aw-shucks, folksy tone, "and only six-ten. You know what a pain it is to be that tall on a ship."

"Didn't really think of it that way."

Kevin cast a wary eye at his friend. His voice hardened. "Where have you been all this time? Everyone's been looking for you."

Hunter hung his head and shrugged, toeing at a rock.

"I thought you were dead, and you pop up here looking like you were frozen in time."

He met his old friend's eyes. "Nope, I'm very much alive. Things went sideways with the FBI for a while there, so I left the country and went into hiding."

"What the hell?" he boomed. "What happened with the FBI?"

"Nothing to worry about. I'm back now, but I need to keep a low profile."

A frown creased Kevin's face. "That deserves more explanation than I have time for, but I'm going to assume everything's good." He looked at each of them. "Where's Rachel?"

"Back home," answered Hunter. "Long story. It's okay. Kevin Nelson, this is Kristen Winters."

Kevin scrutinized her. "Did you steal him away from Rachel?"

"Define 'steal.'"

He grinned. "I like her already!" He held out his hand, and she took it, matching his strength. "Hey, that's some grip! Now I really like you. If you ever decide you want a real man instead of a landlubber, look me up."

Kristen let go of his hand. "I'll keep that in mind. He can be a real pansy."

"Hey! I'm right here, you know?"

Kevin ran his palm over the top of his closely cropped hair. "Come on, long lost friend, let's get out of this rain. It's messing up my *'do.*" He placed an arm around Hunter, pulling him closer. The trio headed toward the stairwell.

Hunter laughed. *This feels good,* he thought for the briefest of moments. Then reality snuck back in. *If only I could tell you I'm here to save your life once again.*

CHAPTER FORTY-THREE
THE TOUR

Hunter never went on a mission during the five years he volunteered for ORCAS. He preferred to manage their network, infrastructure, and website remotely from the comfort of home. Sea sickness, his constant companion any time he rode in a boat, made him miserable.

But here he stood, admittedly harboring some trepidation about it, on the bridge of the *Oceanic Pride* with Kristen and Kevin. *I hate the open water*, he thought. The frigate rose and fell with each swell. The rough sea sprayed over the bow, showering several workers on deck as they churned northwest at twenty knots.

Kristen gazed out the front window. "There's so much sky and nothingness. Doesn't that get old?"

"You get used to it." Kevin patted her on the shoulder. "Besides, all the action is under the surface."

"What do—" Kristen turned to look at Hunter as she spoke but stopped. "Hey, you look white as a ghost. Are you okay?"

Kevin laughed. "Why do you think we call him 'Landlubber?' He can get seasick in a bathtub."

Hunter had to agree. Normally, he'd have his arms wrapped around a toilet. "I'm doing much better now that you gave me that nasal spray. It worked miracles."

"Better living by chemicals," Kevin replied. "Glad it helped. And to answer your question, Hunter grew up in Texas. He's used to big-sky country."

"Which is a lot easier to take than the open sea," Hunter said squeamishly.

"Mm-hmm," Kristen mumbled. She peered over the helmsman's shoulder, watching him adjust the virtual picture with his hands. She pointed to the two navigation consoles in front of them. The forty-six-inch screens gave a three-dimensional view. The *Oceanic Pride* sat in the center of one screen.

"This is interesting," she commented. "How does it work?"

The helmsman, Bill Adams, looked back and smiled. "I navigate by pointing to something on the surface map. The vessel auto-steers in that direction. I can dial the speed up or down with the flick of my hand."

"Nice. You should see the 3D scope on the Time Forward platform."

Kevin said, "The Time Forward what?"

Hunter noted the flustered look on her face. *I don't think I've ever seen her make a mistake like that. Guess not having to worry about the Final Stroke has lightened her mood.* He jumped in to save her. "It's a sci-fi book."

She glanced at him as if to say thanks. "Yeah, it's about that. It's amazing how fast technology advances."

A decade is a long time, Hunter thought to himself. "With Moore's Law, the density of microprocessors doubles every eighteen months. By 2014, that pace slowed to every three years and now it's every four to five years." Impressive, he knew, but it didn't compare to the technological surge exhibited by Comperi. With the introduction of the quantum processors running at eighty qubits per second, his AI increased its computing power by a hundred-fold rate, blowing Moore's Law out of the water.

"Since they upgraded your FBI AI with quantum CPUs," Kevin replied, "I bet that really changes things."

Concern jolted through Hunter. "You're not supposed to know that."

Kevin looked surprised. "Why not? It was on the news."

"No way. That's top secret!"

"Where have you been living? In a cave?"

Kristen belted out a loud laugh. "You could say that."

"Funny," Hunter griped.

"I wonder what happens when real AI becomes mainstream?" Kevin mused. "Do you think the world will turn toward *The Terminator*-type predictions, or will it be more like *Star Trek*?"

Hunter squeezed the back of the helmsman's chair. He already knew the answer, and it made him mad. With or without technology, mankind would manage to destroy itself. That reality didn't escape him, or he wouldn't be here. *Well, I'd be here, just ten years older.*

A dark shadow whipped by the side of the bridge windows, catching their attention.

Hunter exclaimed, "What on earth is that?"

Kristen shrugged, wide-eyed.

"*Breeze!*" Kevin stood there with a huge grin on his face. "Come up to the observation deck. I'll show you."

They exited the bridge and climbed the metal stairwell to the deck above. A tear-shaped, smaller craft hovered just off the starboard side. It was gray in color and looked to be thirty feet in length.

Kristen clasped her hands, looking at it admiringly. "It reminds me of *Falke*."

"Not sure what that means," Kevin said, "but ladies and gentlemen, I proudly introduce our first nautical drone. We call her *Breeze* because she floats in the wind."

"Wow!" Hunter exclaimed. He put his hands on his hips, leaning in to inspect it. "You need a drone out here?"

Kevin nodded. "Oh, yeah. It makes a huge difference. *Breeze* is designed to drop off thermal imaging and acoustic buoys near whale pods, and it can also retrieve them."

Hunter recalled the rapid-fire rail gun hidden in the fuselage of Kants's drone, making him feel that the hovercraft appeared more ominous than warranted. "You use those to locate the whales, so you can protect them?"

"Absolutely," replied Kevin. "The nav screens down below light up like a Christmas tree when the buoys go in the water, but my system does more than just find the whales."

"It also finds the whaling ships."

"Yes, but it does even more than that."

He stared at his friend. "*Breeze* doesn't attack the whaling ships, does it?"

"Christ, Hunter, do you think I'm a murderer?"

"Sorry. All right, I'll bite. What else does it do?"

"Our scientists have figured out how to do rudimentary communication with the whales. We use the buoys to warn them where the ships are and tell them to leave."

"Right," Kristen interrupted. "You talk to the whales."

Kevin held up a hand. "I didn't say we talked with them. We just warn them."

"Like that's not talking?"

"We started putting sound buoys in the ocean eight years ago," he explained. "We recorded the whale songs, especially when they were being hunted and attacked. By process of elimination, the AI figured out which songs are a warning to the other whales. Those are the ones we use."

"And that works?" asked Hunter.

"Like a champ."

"Well, that's good," Kristen said. She gazed out across the open sea. "Those animals are amazing. You have no idea."

"Excuse me?" Kevin looked puzzled and a bit offended.

"What a concept," Hunter interrupted, getting his friend's mind back on track. He glared in her direction. "And that's a cool design. How does it travel such long distances over the water?"

"When it gets to altitude, wings made of Kevlar membrane unfurl. A combination of prop and gliding takes it where it needs to go. It's not high-speed, but it's faster than us, and that's all that matters."

The wind whipped Kristen's hair into her face. She pulled it away and asked, "Do you control it from the navigation center downstairs?"

"That's the best part. It's automated. Outside of going through pre-flight checks, it flies itself." Kevin sounded like a proud papa.

Exactly like Kants's drone, Hunter thought. *Too much of a coincidence.* "You've got artificial intelligence flying your drone?"

"Yes, sir! That baby's programmed to use an onboard radar to find the whale pods and then drop its buoys. The drone even identifies the type of whale, so it plays the right songs. It carries thirty of the buoys, and can be gone for several days. Cool, huh?"

"Fantastic." Kristen patted the craft.

Hunter leaned on the rail and scrutinized the drone. A sinking feeling crept into his stomach. "Where did you get such a sophisticated program?"

"From you, of course."

That wrench in his gut tightened like a hot, stabbing bolt of lightning. "Come again?"

"It's your code, Hunter. I didn't think you'd mind."

He squinted up at Kevin, determined to sort this out. "How did you get it?"

"From Chen-Yi!" he exclaimed. "Where else?"

Stunned into silence, Hunter didn't answer.

Kristen spoke up. "She's the one who took over the Comperi project, right?"

"Yes, but we're not supposed to talk about that."

"Chen-Yi created this program for you?" Hunter repeated for confirmation.

"Yes. She's going to be super-stoked to hear you're back."

"Oh, no. I'm not ready for that yet," Hunter quickly said. "Let's just keep my being here between us for now. Okay?"

Kevin hesitated. "Ah, sure. No problem, I guess."

For some reason, that didn't sound too reassuring. "Thanks. It's important to me."

"Come on, Landlubber." His old friend turned to the stairway. "I have another surprise for you."

Hunter sighed. *I'm not sure I can handle another surprise like that.*

CHAPTER FORTY-FOUR
THE DREAM

OCTOBER 19, 2035

T he bedsheets wrapped tightly about Chen-Yi. She wiggled around, dreaming about him, which only occurred when something momentous would soon happen. Oh, she fantasized about him often. But the real dream like this, where his sweet touch made her breath ragged with excitement, came around only once in a great while.

His last visit occurred more than seven years ago, when Chen-Yi, so caught up in his sudden appearance, almost missed his revelations. Somehow, he'd left his mark on her, bruising her as a physical reminder of his every word, including the physics behind quantum processing and the technical schematics of the mainframe. How he accomplished the feat, she didn't care. *That he wants me is enough.*

Her long, black hair flowed across the pillow. Soaked in sweat, she squirmed and struggled to free herself from the sheets. In her mind, the presence cradled her in his arms, tenderly cuddling her close to his heart. She purred with a contentedness rarely felt in her life.

His words in her ear were soft. "I'm here."

"I know, my love. I know," she murmured, picturing herself running her fingers through the thick, wet hair at his neckline.

"No, I'm here. Now. You must find me and save me," he replied.

"You're in my arms," she cooed. "I don't need to find you."

He moved down her neck, kissing her moist skin. She moaned, embracing the rush, until he bit her, hard. A sharp, shocked scream escaped her. She grabbed a fistful of hair, trying to pull his head away. Desperate for air, she clawed at him as the pain in her neck grew in intensity until she felt nothing else.

And then it stopped. Her eyes snapped opened, and she sat up suddenly. She unraveled herself and staggered to the bathroom, throwing on the light to stare in the mirror. A nasty purple welt grew into the shape of a bite mark just above her collarbone. The corners of her lips curled up, and she reached to gingerly touch it. Another bruise. Satisfaction welled up within and coursed, white-hot, through her veins. *His touch is as real as his command to me. I will find him.*

Chen-Yi switched the light off and padded back to her bed. She sat on the edge and closed her eyes, issuing a silent order. The bio-implant at the back of her skull gave her instant access to the mainframe through the wireless adapter. It had taken her over a year to align her mind with Diablo, but slowly she managed to assimilate the flood of data. She merely thought of a command now, and the computer would perform that task.

She had spent the last decade hunting for him, but he remained frustratingly invisible. That loss made her yearning deeper, her heartache more intense. It seemed like he dropped off the face of the Earth. However, with her dreams, she knew he lived, and he wanted her to find him. This time, she would take no less.

She triumphantly thought, *Diablo, find Hunter Coburn.*

A whirl of data cascaded into her vision. The information overload slowly stopped reeling, eventually landing on several items. Chen-Yi sifted through months of old reports from the traditional alphabet soup of government organizations. Each one relayed no updated contact with Hunter Coburn.

She opened a more current FBI email flagged from three days ago and almost fell off her bed. Rachel Manheim contacted authorities and said that her ex-fiancé showed up at her house. He left when she rejected him. The follow-up investigation proved inconclusive since, once again, he simply disappeared.

Diablo presented hundreds of emails, which Chen-Yi eagerly parsed through, searching hungrily for more information. A recent one from someone she hadn't heard from in a while caught her eye. Kevin Nelson's words blazed across her vision, trumpeting the message she so wanted to hear. "Good news! Hunter has come home!"

Euphoria swept over her, and Chen-Yi hugged herself in anticipation. She hopped off the bed and headed back to the bathroom for a shower. This time, Hunter would understand how much she loved him. *He will be mine*, she thought, giggling. She issued her final command to the mainframe for the night: *Book me on the next flight to Seattle.*

CHAPTER FORTY-FIVE
THE PACKAGE

Hurricane Bruce rolled away from the Caribbean and up the eastern coast of the United States, spreading a torrent of rain and gale-force winds. A storm of this magnitude at this time of year would have once been considered unusual. After almost two hundred fifty years of climate change, nothing seemed uncommon anymore.

A solitary ship churned west through the angry sea, just eighty miles from Cuba. Along the bow, large lettering proudly etched her name in Arabic with the English spelling, *Eastern Star*, in smaller letters below it. Although classified as a research vessel, it carried a dead weight of thirty thousand tons, making it rather large for exploration. Everyone in the free world knew that the Jihadi Liberation Front used it for covert purposes.

Captain Faysal Abdul peered out the side portal into the raging sea. Even at this distance from the storm's epicenter, torrential downpours pelted them, turning day into night. The flicker of a knowing smile crossed his crinkled face. Reports were that the infidels tracked them closely. Yet, clouds and rain were the great equalizers for evading the enemy's satellites above. The current weather would provide more than sufficient cover for offloading his precious cargo.

Abdul stood at the helm, overseeing all operations. He soon noticed his navigator staring at him, concern in the young man's narrowed eyes.

You should be watching the sonar screen, the captain thought. "Naif Aziz! Back to your station!" This dereliction of duty, especially during turbulent weather, angered him.

The man stood, squaring his shoulders. "Captain Abdul." Naif stopped and cleared his throat. He started again, speaking with more force. "We cannot . . ." He paused. "No, we *must* not go through with this. It is not Allah's will."

This statement shocked Abdul, yet it didn't at the same time. A mission of this magnitude tested the faithful and the non-faithful alike. He knew the Aziz family, sometimes broke bread with them. Now, Naif insulted his heritage but also, more importantly, his family's honor.

The captain spit on the floor. "Nothing can stop Allah's will," he snapped. Moderates such as Naif were as bad as the infidels. He believed this to be a systemic problem in his faith; too many followers were against action. They were like chaff in the wind. The true believers would win out in the end. As for this fool, there could be no questioning Abdul's authority, especially at this juncture. The captain withdrew his revolver and aimed it at the young man.

"Naif Aziz, you dishonor your father. I will give you one chance to sit down and man your station."

Naif hesitated, then bowed his head and sat back at his console. He looked reluctant but returned to his duties.

Captain Abdul stood rigid, his face dark, considering whether to still shoot the insubordinate idiot. Then a voice crackled in his earbud, startling him.

"Sir, we cannot wait much longer, or it could injure itself."

He would have to deal with this problem later. He tapped the wireless communicator in his ear, establishing contact with the crew. "This is Captain Abdul. It is time. Slow the *Star* to five knots and prepare for delivery."

The helmsman reset the speed on his computer.

Abdul turned to his men. "Be ready to shut down the engines when I order it. I'm going down to observe."

A few minutes later, he stood on a metal gangway overlooking the large interior hold of the ship. It became his observation post for their prized cargo. A female whale, almost ten meters in length, floated below in a massive tank.

Capturing the elusive creature and bringing it aboard before it drowned proved to be an adventure. Once stabilized in the foam-lined tank, the veterinarians and scientific engineers took over, surgically removing the tracker that most whales were tagged with. Then the team performed a complicated procedure, securing a one-hundred-pound thermonuclear weapon into the beast's womb.

It would not survive long with the bulky metal device inside her, but that did not trouble the captain. He needed to make sure they delivered the package to the right place at the right time. In either case, the whale would not last long in this world. His team worked quickly to release the creature back into the ocean without further stress. It still must go quite a long distance before reaching the preordained destination.

"It is time, brothers! Bring the *Star* to zero knots!"

The motors shuddered and went quiet, stilling the propellers so that the whale could safely slide out from the stern of the ship. Abdul immediately felt the sway of the ocean as they lost control of the steerage, making this phase of the process risky. The rear wall of the hold slid open, and water rushed in, practically sucking them under. Abdul caught a quick glimpse of the angry sky as they rocked up and down. He worried they would sink before completing the release. Once the water leveled with the tank, the gate lowered.

A deafening boom suddenly reverberated through the large chamber, and the captain reflexively hit the deck. *Gunshots!* More explosions followed in rapid succession; the sharp bursts bounced off the metal hull. Abdul kept his head down. His fury at this insurrection grew with each round fired. He must contain it, and he would be unmerciful.

"Take them out!" he screamed.

More gunfire erupted; the exact, jarring shots caused him to cringe each time. His guards sprang into action, neutralizing the threats with measured precision. Within seconds, it ended. The echoes stilled, and only the sloshing of the large tank could be heard.

"All clear!" he heard his security team leader call out.

Slowly, he stood again. "Check the whale!"

It must be alive. The silence worried him as much as the roll of the ship. He waited with a white-knuckled grip on the rail until he finally heard words crackling in his ear. "She looks good, sir!"

Relieved, Captain Abdul turned his attention to the carnage below. Naif Aziz and three other men had stormed into the hold, shooting everyone in sight. They paid the price—slain in their traitorous assassination attempt. Several of his crew lay bloodied too, including some of the scientists. The survivors—wounded, stunned, and in shock—tended to their fallen comrades while the frigate listed in the ocean swells. They needed to get moving. With the gate down, they would pass the point of no return in only minutes.

"Leave them! Get back to your posts!" Abdul barked. "Or we will all die without completing our work."

The crew scrambled to right the vessel just as a large wave hit the side of the ship, tossing everyone around. The whale banged into the tank wall, and sheets of water sloshed out violently. The animal blew spray, and a distinct siren arose as if it were calling out for help.

"Move, damn you!" Abdul said to himself, willing it out of the hold. "Get out!"

After what seemed an eternity, the great fluke lifted, then snapped down on the water, creating thrust as it slowly moved toward the gaping maw. It gathered momentum and disappeared into the open sea. Two robotic drone dolphins released simultaneously from a separate submerged holding area. They darted away, giving chase to herd the whale to its destination.

The bow of the boat bobbed precariously atop the waves. With Abdul's quick command, the motors churned back to life. The rear wall slowly closed, and the bilges emptied water from the hold. The ship steadied, and the front of the boat lowered ever so slowly as they pumped. Medic teams hurried in to treat the wounded.

The captain tapped on his communicator. "Make ten knots. Let's go home." When he felt the ship swing starboard, he turned to head back to the navigation center, disgusted with the situation. This supposedly low-risk mission cost him much. From a quick count, eight of his men perished, four of them traitors.

How could this happen? Even with the greatest scrutiny, the pacifists managed to get people on his ship! Naif and his cohorts understood the dire consequences of this conspiratorial action. And still, they acted.

But they were silenced. *Our divine work will proceed as planned.* By the time the package reached its target, they would be across the Atlantic Ocean, close to Africa. Faysal Abdul held no illusion about making it back to their homeland. Once the war began, his ship would be a high priority target.

Not that that mattered to him. Their mission would already have been a success, striking dead hundreds of thousands of infidels. With that first blow, the Purge War would begin. He only wished he could be around to see its completion. A world free of the impure would be like heaven, but Allah willed as Allah willed. By that time, he would most definitely be in paradise.

CHAPTER FORTY-SIX
THE WATCHER

MAY 16, 2025

Sandeep Nurre liked to shop. Tyson's Corner, one of her favorite shopping centers, opened near her home in Alexandria. Her high-pressure world faded into the background as she mindlessly sorted through racks of fine clothing.

Except this time, standing in the women's section at Macy's, something seemed off. She found this disconcerting. Her years in the FBI had honed her intuition, so she couldn't discount the feeling of being watched. She picked up a blouse, ostensibly for inspection, and scanned the immediate area. One woman held a child while she flipped through the clearance rack. The few other shoppers and a couple of salesclerks were all focused on themselves.

There were plenty of good reasons to be nervous. The recent spate of confidential memos and redacted email threads made her wonder what her superiors were suspicious of. The overbearing debriefings by the NSA were irritating and tiresome, though she understood the ramifications of Hunter's fugitive status. With practically every member of her team followed in recent weeks, it got to the point of ridiculousness. *I need to visit Cassandra Hughes again.*

She took a deep breath to shake the feeling off and resumed her browsing. Soon, she noticed a man in a hat, sitting in the women's section. That in itself seemed not too unusual; however, this man didn't appear to be buying anything. Sandeep moved toward the shoe section, checking the store's many mirrors to see if anyone followed her. When she realized her hand clasped the service revolver in her purse, she let out a deep sigh. *Time to leave*, she thought, feeling too jittery to shop.

Sandeep stepped out into the spring night, casually looking around one last time for reassurance that she didn't have a tail. While walking toward her car, she spotted the hat again, just behind an SUV. She pivoted to return to the store, her hand back on the revolver.

"Director, may I have a word with you?" The man's voice, thick with a Russian accent, came from behind her.

She stopped, then slowly turned, her gun aimed at him through the purse. "Why are you following me?"

"You are in the Time Forward Project, yes?"

She scrutinized the older man, who appeared to be in his late eighties. With a furtive glance about, she checked the area for other people but saw no one else. "I don't know what you're talking about."

"Madam," he said, stepping toward her.

Sandeep pulled out her revolver. "That's close enough."

He raised his hands, fingers splayed. "We are on the same team, as you say in the West."

"I beg your pardon?"

"I understand your reluctance. I do not blame you. That does not change the fact that we are both involved in a fight to save the world."

"I think you should turn around and leave."

"Oh, if it were only that easy. You know, I met Herr Kants for the first time in the winter of 1962 at our naval station in Severomorsk. His counsel stopped us from destroying ourselves with nuclear war during the Cuban Missile Crisis."

Her face revealed nothing, but with mention of that name, Sandeep felt compelled to listen, even though her intuition told her to run. "Who is Kants?"

"Kants is the man you killed at Dr. Hilfer's house."

She pursed her lips. "You seem confused."

"I am not confused. I am ninety-two years old, which is the reason we are speaking. You see, Kants's second visit back in 1984 is what caught my attention."

"Listen, mister—"

He talked right over her. "I lived in southern Russia then. Kants appeared to not have aged a day. His message—no, his commission to me—caused me to leave my tiny hamlet to start a clandestine movement called 'The Watchers.'"

"This gets crazier by the minute," Sandeep replied, irritation in her voice. "What do you want with me?"

He sighed. "We are entwined in a war raging across time dimensions. You, Hunter, and Matt Banks are all a part of it, whether you choose to recognize that or not."

That's classified, she thought. She stared at him for a long moment. "Where are you getting this?"

The old man's eyes were misty. "Time agents have visited us many times, but then you are aware of that fact, even if you do not want to admit it." A sad smile settled on his face.

Sandeep narrowed her eyes, taking in his words. "Let's say for the moment that I believe your outlandish story . . . Wait, before we go on, what is your name?"

"Ah, yes, I have been rather rude. I am Commander Vasily Arkhipov of the North Atlantic Fleet, retired," he replied. "I have paper clippings if you need proof."

Her grandfather used that term to describe a story in the newspaper that he'd cut out for her. "I don't need paper clippings for proof." She lowered her gun, and he cautiously dropped his hands. "What do you want from me?"

"Isn't it obvious? I am too old to lead The Watchers anymore. Kants and Hunter want you to take over for me."

"Oh," she said. "Right. I'll play along. When, exactly, did Kants tell you this?"

"1984," he replied, his tone deadly serious.

The irony of Vasili knowing about her the same year she started her FBI career did not go unnoticed. "Christ," she blurted out. "What does your secret group do, anyway?"

"We provide shelter, help, information, or whatever Kants needs."

"Kants is dead, if I remember correctly."

"Yes, yes. Kants is only dead in this dimension. Now we do the same thing for Hunter."

Sandeep slowly stepped back. "Dead in this dimension? Uh-huh. I'm going to have to think about this."

Vasily nodded curtly. "Do not take too long. Hunter will return before you know it. This time, he is going to need your help."

The FBI agent's condescending tone spoke volumes. "You know that how?"

The old man replied with a wrinkled smirk. "I thought I'd made that clear, Agent Nurre. Kants told me in 1984."

CHAPTER FORTY-SEVEN
THE OFFER

OCTOBER 24, 2035

E ven under several blankets, Hunter couldn't get comfortable. Although some heat vented into the small bedroom on the *Oceanic Pride*, it did little to warm the space. The cold, metal walls seemed to suck the life right out of the room. He swung his legs off the thin mattress of the bunk and reached over to turn on the light. He couldn't sleep in any case, anticipating their first operation against a North Korean whaling fleet the next day.

Hunter pulled a cover over his shoulders and paced, thinking. Kristen volunteered them for the *Sea Lion* submersible, much to his dismay. With their primary mission to protect the captain of the ship, *not* being right there with him seemed a stretch. But if the *Oceanic Pride* sank, they would need a way to save Kevin themselves. He had to admit, the *Sea Lion* fit that bill.

The practice trials on the submersible went well. They controlled the craft with ease, and he liked the velocity with which they maneuvered. The rocket-powered jet ski sub practically flew, both above and beneath the surface. Oddly enough, the third mate who operated the water cannon suddenly dropped out of their mission due to illness. Hunter would have liked for Comperi to run a background check on his replacement, John Bonuomo. Unfortunately, getting to a computer on board proved too risky.

A knock at his door brought him out of his musings. Kristen pushed her way in through the hatch, then locked it behind her. She flopped down on his bunk and pointed to the desk chair.

"Sit down," she ordered. "We need to talk."

"Okay. Thanks for waking me up," he said, acting a bit disgruntled.

"You weren't asleep. I heard you moving around in here."

He'd forgotten about her unique abilities. "What do you want?"

Kristen pulled her hair back from her face. "We're almost out of time."

"What's that supposed to mean?"

"We're running out of time in this jump."

Hunter frowned and tilted his head to the side inquisitively. "So, you can tell time now? I mean when you're traveling through time that is?"

"Jumps don't last longer than twenty-six days. We're at twenty-four, so we're close."

"Are you saying that we might not finish our mission?"

Kristen gave him a sage look.

"If we jump before we've saved Kevin, then what happens?"

"He dies, and we fail."

Talk about a punch in the gut. He sighed. "That wouldn't be good for the home team, now, would it?"

"You can be fast when you want to be." She chewed on a fingernail for a moment. "That's not what I'm here to discuss. I believe I've figured out a way to short-circuit your transponder."

Hunter leaned forward. "Excuse me?"

"I've been doing a lot of thinking," Kristen said. "Maybe this isn't supposed to happen?"

"No. You sold me on this whole 'we have to save the world' mission. Why are you getting cold feet?"

Her gray eyes seemed to bore a hole through him. "Look, I can't guarantee we'll get any closer to your original time than we are now, and you're with friends here. This is the most logical juncture for you to break away. There's no going back if we don't do it now. If you stay, you might be able to get Rachel back, and you could know your daughter."

Hunter drew in a surprised breath. In his heart, he wanted nothing more. But he knew he'd hurt Rachel too deeply to become a part of her life again. More importantly, he needed to consider their daughter's future. Did he really want his descendants living in a destroyed world?

"I thought we were partners?" he shot back at her. "What happened to that?"

She leaned forward, elbows on her knees, hands clasped together. "I don't know if I can hide you from the Time Forward Project." Her voice sounded husky and serious. "If they find out you're helping me, they'll send another team to terminate you. I'd hate for that to happen."

Hunter copied her stance, their physical space tightening with the weight of the topic. "Getting sentimental? That's not like you."

"Things change, Hunter."

He put his hand over hers and sat quietly for a moment, soul-searching. "That's true," he finally replied. "But I'm not ready to give up the fight. I miss Rachel more than you'll ever know. And now, knowing we have a child . . ." He swallowed back his emotions, then continued. "Like you said, the world is depending on us. We've got to change the trajectory of time."

"All right, then. I didn't want to lose you, but I want to be honest and put it all out there." Kristen paused, looking directly at him. "Actually, I have a mission for you."

"For little old me?" Hunter replied, feigning humility.

"We've screwed up, leaving several weapons back in your normal time period."

"Are you saying the NSA has more than the one I gave them?"

"Yes. And it would help if my faithful partner retrieved them. It would show your value to the Time Forward Project."

"Are you nuts? That'd be like breaking into Fort Knox."

"Fort Knox?" Kristen asked. She held up a hand to halt his response. "Never mind. Remember when I said you needed to destroy the BIO-EMP?"

"Yes."

"Nothing's changed since then. Our futuristic technology could transform all of time as we know it. We need to retrieve every weapon but especially that one."

"Shouldn't you guys send a team to get them? Wouldn't that be the smartest play?"

"We may not get another chance, Hunter. Look, when this jump ends, I'll return to my time, and you'll go back to yours. We won't be together again until the next mission I'm sent on. Only you can do this. The good news is, you'll have *Falke* and anything else you can scavenge from the cave."

"But you're asking me to do the impossible."

"Time travel is supposed to be impossible, but here we sit."

He couldn't really argue her point. "I'll think about it. If I can figure out a way, I'll let you know."

Kristen gave him a withering look. "I won't be with you. This is all on you, partner."

"Right. Guess I'll let you know if I'm successful next time we jump."

Kristen thumped his knee with the back of her hand and stood up. "Why don't you get some sleep? We've got a long day tomorrow."

"Yeah, right. Sleep. Now, not only do I have to go fight a bunch of whalers, but I'm supposed to single-handedly take on the NSA."

"Well, if you need some stress relief, I could always snuggle up with you in that little old bed."

"Like I'd get any sleep that way, smartass." He waved her off with a smirk.

Kristen laughed. "That's the best offer of the night, but I'm exhausted, so I'll see you in the morning."

Hunter's jaw dropped. *She's so infuriating.* Before he could reply, she slipped through the door and shut it behind her.

CHAPTER FORTY-EIGHT
The Whale

All transportation in and out of La Casa en El Mar shut down for more than a week after Hurricane Bruce raged through the Caribbean, across Florida, and up the coastline. Nine days later, normal operations returned to the city-on-the-sea, but with even more shipments arriving to make up for lost time. Amid the beehive of activity, ocean harvesters culled fish from undersea farms, people settled back into their regular activities, and tiger teams worked hard to complete the repairs on the exterior damage.

In the middle of the night, however, it seemed as if the metropolis took a deep sigh and relaxed. A skeleton crew kept watch inside the command center as an aircraft landed or took off every hour. Mostly, the frenzy of the day subsided when darkness descended.

Ensign Emily Ward sat at her station, responsible for the underwater border zone. With no subs or drones in the area, the tedious night drudged on to its inevitable conclusion. She pushed her chair back and stretched her arms wide, trying to stay awake. *Going to need more coffee*, she thought.

About halfway through her shift, one slight blip appeared on her 3D screen. Emily leaned in, watching with interest. She adjusted the headphones, thinking she'd heard something. Soon, she frowned as a noise once again interrupted the silence.

Twenty miles out, perimeter buoys tracked acoustics, as well as an electronic signature. Their security systems wouldn't detect a living animal until it came within a few miles of the city. Yet, the sound indicated a whale entering her patrol zone.

"This can't be right," Emily said aloud. She cross-checked the equipment using a couple of backup routes, but it registered the same. For some strange reason, this blip represented a living whale, but it appeared on their radar as a ship would.

Emily considered whale songs to be exquisite. With her extensive training, she recognized something terribly wrong with this one. The short, staccato bursts were distressing, as if the poor creature screamed in pain. She recorded a thirty-second clip, then pulled up the ORCAS database for whale communication. The organization had compiled an extensive catalog over the years, identifying types of songs and meaning for each species. She ran a search, trying to match the unusual sounds with a previous recording. A minute later, the database identified the whale's species as one not from this part of the ocean.

That's odd, she thought. Her brows knitted together as she listened to the ORCAS interpretation of the haunting song broadcasted in the background. It served as a dire warning for other whales to flee. Emily rocked back in her chair. *Why is it doing this when swimming alone? Maybe it senses a stealth ship?* Concerned, she pulled up the surface radar. Nothing appeared to be out of the ordinary.

She chewed on her lip and systematically reviewed the situation. She identified a whale out of its usual habitat on their security apparatus. An anomaly all on its own, it also signaled a specific warning, but there were no other similar creatures in the vicinity. This animal had high intelligence, though. And in an exceptionally short time, the whale closed to within a few miles of the ocean metropolis. On its current course, it would pass directly underneath them. Her imagination might be working overtime, but—

Something's not right.

She didn't relish the idea of disturbing her commander, Lieutenant Tom Smith, but she needed more information. Up-linking to the command net, Emily broke the silence on that station. *Not a great move in the middle of the night, but this must be addressed.* "This is Ensign Ward. Command?"

A muddled voice barked back, "Ward? This better be good."

"Command, I have an inbound whale signaling a threat warning. Requesting we dispatch a shark drone to investigate."

The incredible weapon didn't look like a shark. Fitted with an on-board camera and an array of weapons, the oversized torpedo was sleek and deadly. An off-site pilot remotely controlled the device through the computer, or autopilot parameters could be set.

"Are you shitting me, Ensign Ward?" Smith snapped. "You wake me up to report that we have a whale attacking the city at three in the freaking morning? Are you off your medication?"

"No, sir, I'm saying the whale is warning us that something dangerous is heading this way. I suggest we go to orange alert. There could be stealth ships approaching the city."

"For the love of . . . Okay, where is this whale now?"

Her screen showed how close the whale had already come to the city outskirts. *It must be swimming at top speed.* Emily's elevated voice indicated urgency. "A mile out and closing fast."

"Closing fast?" Smith sputtered. "Okay, Ward, who in the hell put you up to this? I haven't been suckered like this since my plebe year."

Emily knew if this proved to be a false alarm, it would go badly for her. She checked the systems again and replied, "I'm not joking, sir. The whale is almost on us."

"Damn it," her commander hissed. "Launching shark drone. I've associated it with your control, Ward."

"Thank you, sir."

"Don't thank me. I'm going to have your nuts for this."

"Ah, sir," she replied, sounding testy, "I don't have any nuts."

A brief silence permeated her headphones. "You seem to have grown a pair in the last half hour, Ensign Ward. I hope it's worth it."

She ignored his nasty comment and kept her attention on the task in front of her. Emily programmed in the whale's coordinates and watched the shark drone shoot toward its target at twenty-five knots.

Already at the edge of the city, the whale swam toward the center on a collision course with the torpedo.

The drone's radar came on screen with a strange variance, showing three targets instead of one. It quickly identified the other two targets as weaponized drones.

"My God," Emily whispered, quickly sending an attack command.

Smith's voice screamed over the comm, "What the hell is that? Launch all drones!"

Warning sirens blared, and red lights flashed overhead as the city went into defense mode. Heart pounding, Ensign Emily Ward focused on her screen, watching the shark approach the threat. One of the weaponized drones broke away and raced toward it. Instantly, both launched mini torpedoes that shot past their targets. They were too close to lock on.

The shark fired kinetic rounds, which connected with the attacking drone, ripping through its internal structure. It stalled, then exploded, taking them both out of the equation. On the twentieth floor, Emily couldn't feel the detonation, but the acoustics and visual from the ill-fated skirmish flashed on her console. She ripped off her headphones and sat stunned as the screen went to static.

Emily quickly reached over to switch radar systems to under-city mode, searching for the whale. It veered away, but with the single weaponized drone relentlessly driving it, the whale almost got back on track, swimming toward the center of the city. She spotted a dozen fast-moving sharks closing on it. Within a minute, this assault should be over. Then Smith's interrogations would begin.

Emily took a deep breath. *Well,* she thought, *at least he believes me now.*

CHAPTER FORTY-NINE
The Purge

NOVEMBER 10, 2098

Things didn't add up in and around Victus Palus, but Kants needed more information to identify and get ahead of whatever the issue might be. The discovery of the nano-drone in his office underscored the need. There were devices that could destroy it, but he did not want to give away the fact that he knew. He sat at his desk, staring into the eye-lock monitor for the retinal scan, which he'd set up as a precautionary measure.

His plan to strengthen the defenses developed over several months. He painstakingly studied systems, set up safeguards, enforced practice drills, and addressed vulnerabilities. Many under his leadership considered him overzealous, but being privy to highly restricted information, he understood the big-picture needs.

Kants confirmed to himself that a deep bore penetrated their infrastructure. While using the security AI, he identified covert programs within multiple systems. They obfuscated a communication structure from the standard operating system's ability to track and control, including a relay back to Earth. Only a handful of people on Mars had the ability or access to put something like this into the current environment, and two of those were his direct reports. This should not have been possible without alerting him.

Someone must have access to a lot of inside knowledge to sabotage the system in such an ingenious way. Just days before his discovery, they used stealth software to rewrite the AI's command sequence. Otherwise, it would have flagged the attack. He'd stumbled on the route for a splice in the hard code that controlled the thick, reinforced titanium fire doors while checking on them with the AI. The splice caused a glitch that froze the doors in the open position during an emergency, but from his monitoring station, it appeared as if they were truly down and locked.

The doors were critical for fire suppression, designed to cut off oxygen to starve an inferno. Oxygen regulation must remain a supreme security concern. They could ill-afford an air delivery system shutdown during an emergency. And with the doors being virtually impossible to destroy, they could also isolate any threat. Kants moved control of the fire doors from the civil board to his own domain.

He searched for the responsible party from the outside. He ordered Captain Jafar to investigate, figuring that it would be interesting to see what he came up with. Kants suspected who the perp might be, and he felt smug about the evidence. He pressed replay on his voice recorder and leaned back in his chair, listening to his conversation.

"What did you find out, Captain Jafar?"

"Well, sir, it took a little time, but I ran an extensive security check. It looked pretty clean, but I installed a flash update in the hard code that runs the system."

"You think it is a bug, yes?"

"Yes, sir. That took care of the problem. Easy to fix. There are no more reports of closures or of people being trapped, and it's been a few days now."

"Interesting. Good work, Captain."

"Thank you, sir. Happy to help. Anything else I can do for you?"

"I will let you know," Kants's voice answered, "as soon as I have something."

He clicked the voice recorder off. *That is an understatement,* he thought. *One of my direct reports is an infiltrator.* Kants's paranoid antenna sizzled with distrust. No doubt he had found his smoking laser, and he pinned it on Jafar. *Now, who are you working for?* He had a sneaking suspicion he already knew the answer to that question.

This isn't a bug. Bugs in updates were an immediate problem, and there had been no system updates for over a year. He needed to delete the code splice without alerting Jafar. He took a page out of the hacker's book and wrote his own splice in the front routine of his command. That would effectively lock the network down, sealing the code in before any damage could be done. He set up double-blind routes to counter each devious splice and hide his real purpose. Now, only he could command the fire doors to lock. The mole would never know.

The intercom chirped in his ear. At three in the morning, there would be only one tech on station in the command center. He recognized the woman's voice. His rookie recruit, Ensign Kendall Coalter, got stuck with the night shift.

"Colonel Kants?"

"Yes, I'm here, Ensign Coalter. What's up?"

"I've got your wife on the commlink."

Suddenly feeling much happier, he answered, "Wonderful. Thank you. Pass her through to my desk, please."

"Yes, sir."

Seconds later, a video window popped up on his screen. Kants couldn't stop grinning as he waved his hand to maximize the image to full screen. He arranged for a vid conference with his wife every two weeks. Though expensive and slow, he felt it was well worth it. From thirty-five million miles away, it took five minutes or more for a response. He waited patiently for her to speak first.

"There you are!" Angelika said with excitement in her voice. "How are you, my love?"

"Fine!" he replied. "And you? You look radiant."

Five minutes later, her smile broadened. "Thank you! You don't look half-bad yourself, considering what time it is." Then she added, "I miss you."

He nodded. "I miss you too." *I can't believe it's already been four months.*

An eternity later, Angelika winked at him. "I have a surprise for you."

"Oh? You are not here, are you?"

"No, silly. I can't do space travel now."

She toggled the camera's functions, panning back. She placed her hands on her swollen belly and smiled at him.

Shocked, Kants stammered, "Is that what I think—"

Angelika interrupted him, replying as if she'd known his question before he asked it. "Yes, silly. And it's a girl."

"A girl? Oh, my God!"

"I found out just before you left. I wanted to tell you then, but you were so preoccupied with your mission, I didn't want to distract you. I know how important your work is there."

"Oh, Angelika," he said, trying to take it all in.

"I'm so happy! I hope you are."

"Happy? Yes. Yes! My gosh. This is wonderful news! We are going to be parents, yes! Is everything okay? Are you feeling well?"

Nodding, she answered, "The doctor says we're doing great. Look, I'm sorry I didn't tell you sooner. It's been difficult keeping quiet. I hope you aren't mad at me."

Thoughts rushed through his mind. *A little girl! I'm going to be a father. Will the baby have any of my unusual DNA characteristics? Will command let me go home for the birth?* There were more things to consider, but being mad never entered his mind. Before he could answer, the screen suddenly changed to a snowy white discharge, then went black.

Kants switched to his comm link. "Coalter," he bellowed, "get that video link back up, now!"

"Uh, sir? It looks like we've lost the entire comm link with Earth."

Kants rushed from his office into the command room. The monitoring screens for planet Earth showed nothing but static.

"Connect to Gateway One," he ordered. "Let's see what they are getting."

Ensign Coalter worked quickly, establishing the link with the station so they could view Earth through its sensors. In outlying space, they watched in silence as the Earth net of orbital satellites fired lasers and rockets, battling an unknown force.

On the video screen, enormous blinks of light on the planet's surface mushroomed into small white circles. Nuclear bombs detonated across the globe. Kants looked on in horror at the view over North America. A bright spot of energy cascaded away off the coast of Florida, where La Casa en El Mar existed. It existed no longer. He forced himself to breathe.

"Connect me with Gateway One's command net!"

The young woman looked up at him, tears rolling down her face.

"Ensign Coalter," he spat out. Then he enunciated with a slower, deeper tone, "Kendall. We must alert Victus Palus that an attack is imminent. Set off a base-wide Sev-One alert."

She sat there, immobilized, stricken.

"I know," Kants said, his voice breaking. "We all have loved ones on Earth." He paused to regain his composure. "But this will not be contained. They will come after us, and we must be ready. Sound the alarm."

"Yes, sir," Coalter whispered. She sent notifications and alarms blared. Two guards rushed to their stations in the room. The skeleton crew working deep at night gaped about and became a flurry of nervous activity.

"Kants!" A voice yelled into his earpiece. "This is Admiral Stinson. What in the hell is going on?"

"We are at war! Earth is under attack. Prepare your people, sir. We will be next."

"They wouldn't dare to board—"

Kants interrupted, blurting his point in no uncertain terms. "They need your space station as a jump point to get here."

"You're right," Stinson groaned. "If they're destroying Earth, Mars will be the only safe place they have to exist."

"That is correct!"

"We'll defend our station to the end. Good luck to you, sir." He started giving out orders in the background before the call dropped.

Almost immediately, another voice popped into his ear. Captain Romanov hailed him from the frigate *Ranger*. "Kants, I'm on my way to Victus Palus. We detected a large signature approaching you. We can't identify it."

"Romanov, you need to turn around and defend Gateway One. If we lose it, we won't have a way back, and those bastards will have a launch point to bring reinforcements."

"Understood. Good luck, Colonel. I'll be back as fast as I can."

Before he could respond, a commotion flared at the entry to the room. Kants turned to see Captain Anderson grappling with one of the security guards posted there. He started to call out to him when a shot rang out, and the woman dropped, revealing the gun in Anderson's hand. Stunned, Kants watched as he fired at the other soldier, hitting him in the chest.

Ensign Coalter and the other staffers dove under their desks. Kants dodged behind the row of support stations, frantically searching for anything to use as a weapon. His gun remained on his desk in his office, left behind in the chaotic moment. His mouth pressed into a tight line of frustration. All this time, he suspected Jafar and the JLF.

"Come out," Anderson shouted, "and I won't kill Coalter. Nobody else must die."

"AI," he spoke softly into the command net, "for Victus Palus, drop the fire doors, authorization Kants, echo, tango, one."

Anderson laughed. "I was counting on that."

Kants crouched low, blood pounding in his head. Furious with himself, he fought to contain his anger. He must get control of the situation.

"Anderson," he called out. He stood up and walked around the desk, rigid with authority. His words were clipped. "The Jihadi Liberation Front will not let you live."

"Bingo!" Anderson exclaimed. "That's why we picked you. You're easy to distract. Ever since Africa, you've always been hung up on the JLF, JLF, JLF."

We? Is he in this with Jafar? Kants goaded him, attempting to get more information. "You are a bunch of religious fanatics."

The man's traitorous smile radiated evil. "Such a one-track mind. You never really had a chance."

He tilted his head. "You're not one of them?"

"Blind to the bitter end. Those dumb shits only have the technology we gave them, but of course that doesn't include space travel."

Kants frowned, trying to follow Anderson's logic. "You mean the Earth Defense Force?"

"I thought all of that genetic engineering made you smart."

How does he know about that? "Who would want to destroy our world?"

"That's ancient history, or didn't you notice? What a mess." A cocky grin spread across Anderson's face. "Space is the great frontier. This is man's future."

Only one group speaks like that: The United Coalition of People. Kants couldn't believe he had missed it. They were puffed up with enough self-importance to be dangerous. He doubted their ability to manage the takeover of both planet Earth and outer space, though.

"Yeah? Who, exactly, is coming here, then?"

"The superior intellect of the modern world," Anderson replied, sounding self-righteous. "We spent decades doing genetic engineering the old-fashioned way, building our empire. We determined a long time ago the inevitability of the JLF holy war, so we used that against them. We chose our place and time. Sadly, for you, our armada of ships is heading this way."

"What about the people already here?" Kants asked. "There is not enough room."

"We know who runs the station, and we'll keep them. The rest will be shoved out the airlock."

Kants eyed him. *Not if I have anything to do about it.* He took a couple of steps, wanting to get closer and use his enhanced quickness to take the captain down.

Anderson lifted his gun a little higher, aiming at his chest. "That's far enough. I know all about your special abilities. Be assured, I can shoot you before you can get to me."

"You can shoot me, but then you will never get the fire doors back open," he answered, trying to buy some time.

"Tsk, tsk." Anderson shook his head. "I told you, I already took care of your command sequence. The doors *are* open, even though they look down."

"I found your code splice and neutralized it. They are truly down."

"That's bullshit, and you know it. You're stalling, but it won't matter."

"Oh, it will matter to your friends. I found all your splices. None of them will work," Kants taunted. "You cannot shut off the oxygen to the lower levels, either."

Anderson glared at him. "Raise the doors, or I'll start killing everyone I find, starting with Ensign Coalter." He moved his aim to her and snarled, "Now!"

The command center entrance suddenly opened a few inches, catching both men off-guard. Two metal balls zipped into the room in midair. Anderson whipped his weapon around and fired, splintering the first one.

Kants instantly dropped to a kneeling position, shielding his head. The second hovering bomb detonated in a blinding flash, and its all-consuming sound blast knocked him to the floor. He shook his head, fighting to stay conscious. He did not know how much time passed until he vaguely heard footsteps rushing into the room. Hands grabbed him, lifting him to his feet.

A voice said, "Shit, he's heavy." A couple of men supported him in a standing position. Fingers snapped in front of his face. "Come on, Kants! Pull yourself together. That was a small sonic boom. Be glad I didn't use a ten-gigger."

His mind roared, wanting to go into a defensive mode, but his body wouldn't cooperate. Captain Jafar appeared in front of him as a slow-moving blur. Kants squished his eyes closed and then opened them wide, trying to clear his head.

"Anderson sent his girlfriend to kill me." Jafar spoke as though he could respond.

The people holding Kants gradually released him. The rush in his mind wound down as he swayed, but he kept upright.

Jafar continued, "I've been wondering about him for a while but couldn't prove anything."

Several other officers hurried into the command center to take up support stations or to help their downed comrades.

Jafar stepped back a little. "How come that sono-boom didn't knock you out?"

"Hard head," Kants mumbled. He brought a hand up to rub his temple.

"You're definitely tough," he replied. "I'm wondering, Colonel Kants, whether you are satisfied now?"

Bells still rang in his ears. "I am not following you."

"I mean, with me. Are you satisfied now? All this time, you suspected me. God knows who you thought I might be involved with." Jafar gestured around the room. "This, I guess."

He squinted at him. "I will never doubt you again, Captain Jafar."

"Not all Muslims are radicalized."

"I get it," Kants conceded. "And I thank you. But right now, we must prepare to defend ourselves." He stood up straighter. "Bad people are heading our way."

"Agreed. We're getting hammered on several sub-floors. Good thing you dropped the fire doors. That's at least slowing them down. What's next?"

At that moment, a thundering boom from above shook the entire complex. Everyone in the room cringed as fearful shrieks were heard.

Son of a bitch, he thought.

Postures slowly straightened, and they turned to face him.

"What is next?" Kants said, eyeing his team. "We fight for our lives."

CHAPTER FIFTY
The Launch

October 25, 2035

The sun crested over the edge of the Bering Sea, casting gleaming, golden-white rays that shimmered across the water's icy surface. A starburst of orange crept slowly onto the horizon in the bright eastern sky. But a turbulent storm barreled in from the west, bringing rolling, dark thunderclouds.

The *Oceanic Pride* plowed through the swells at twenty knots, heading in a northwesterly direction, as if trying to outrun the break of day. The frigate headed toward the North Korean whaling fleet fifty nautical miles away, in prime whaling territory. Inside the ship, the crew prepared to defend the whales.

On the deck of the frigate, the submersibles perched on their launch rails, primed and ready. The elongated fronts, designed to cut through water easily, looked like giant torpedoes. Glass canopy windshields topped them, where the pilot and copilot sat. Behind those, a gunner's seat was tucked into the retractable turrets, which contained a water cannon nestled between two pontoons that housed RAM-jet engines. These thrust compressed water from the front, shooting it out the back like a rocket. That flow of super-condensed water with air could be used for the cannon as well, creating a mighty torrent that could cover hundreds of yards with full force.

"Red sky at morning, sailor's warning," Hunter murmured.

He and Kristen stood next to the *Sea Lion* in their wetsuits. She seemed riveted by a couple of gulls in the distance, swooping and fishing for their breakfast.

"No idea what you're talking about," she said, "but aren't those amazing?"

"Uh, sure." He chewed his lip, worrying about this venture today. He turned slightly when a hand rested on his shoulder. Kevin stood behind them, with his other arm draped across Kristen's shoulder. She reached up to touch it without looking. Hunter's eyebrows lifted. His partner apparently knew his old buddy better than he realized.

"You sure you're up for this, Landlubber?"

"Yeah, I suppose so. I've got my medicine, and I'll have Kristen with me."

Kevin patted Hunter reassuringly. "Oh, I know. That's the only reason you're going."

Hunter did a double-take. "What's that supposed to mean?"

"Well, she's the best pilot I've ever seen. It's like she, well . . . She's just so damn fast."

"So?"

"She insisted you were her co-pilot. I would have never put a landlubber like you in there, otherwise."

"Thanks for the vote of confidence."

"You're welcome, my friend. I'm still not too sure you should go—ouch!" Kevin grimaced as Kristen crushed his hand in hers. "Hey!" He tried to pull away from her with no success. "Okay. Okay! I said I'm not sure. I didn't say no, damn it. Let go!"

When she relaxed her hold, Kevin jerked his hand away and rubbed it, wincing. He soon resettled it on her shoulder, then dropped it behind her back, leaving it resting on her rear end.

She looked up at him. "I'll give you a half-hour to stop that."

"After last night, you know I need more than thirty minutes."

"We can talk about it later." She seemed to stifle a grin.

Hunter cocked his head. "Hmm. What do you mean?"

"Nothing you'd understand, Landlubber," Kristen answered.

A big guffaw erupted from Kevin.

"You two didn't . . ."

Smiles crept over their faces. Peeved, Hunter turned to the *Sea Lion*.

John Bonuomo walked up. "Morning. Looks like a good day for hunting, hey?"

"Indeed." Kevin pointed to the submersible. "We're launching you guys early. We believe the North Koreans are approximately forty miles northwest of us."

"You're not sure?" Kristen asked.

"We lost communication with our drone about two hours ago."

That's concerning, Hunter thought. "What about the sound buoys? Or satellite feed?"

"Wish I had better news, but with the commlink down, the four buoys in that area are silent."

Hunter pulled nervously at his wetsuit sleeves. "Maybe we should wait?"

"Oh, we'll have it up and running soon. In the meantime, we need eyes on what's happening. I want you all to go see what the heck is going on and report back, okay?"

Hunter felt hesitant to have Kevin so far out of reach, even if for only a little while. "What if they've found the whales?"

"You wait; going in alone is too dangerous."

"That doesn't sound like the Kevin Nelson I know."

"Look, you've been gone a long time. Things have changed. There are four whalers out there, and they're big-ass boats. We don't send someone with a knife to a gunfight."

Hunter chewed his bottom lip. *How are we ever going to do any of this?*

"Without working together," Kevin continued, "we've got no hope of stopping them. The *Bob Barker Two* is twenty-five miles west of us and heading north too. When we're ready, we'll have over twenty craft in the water to take them on."

Kristen stepped toward the *Sea Lion's* open canopy. "Slice of pie."

A quizzical expression crossed the seaman's face.

"She means 'piece of cake,'" Hunter explained.

"Well, then. This is 'no walk in the park, Kazansky.' They are definitely up to something. So, don't go all *Top Gun* on me. Keep the *Sea Lion* safe. It's a freaking expensive boat."

It better keep us all safe. "You sound just like your dad." Hunter followed his partner onto the submersible.

"Worse things have been said about me, Landlubber. You know he would have said 'Kick ass and take names later.'" Kevin patted the top of the craft and backed away.

Hunter slid into the copilot's seat and gave a thumb up. The tech handed him his mask; he put it on, securing it. When all three crew members were strapped in, the techs stepped back as the cockpit shield lowered into place.

The *Sea Lion* rumbled to life. Metrics appeared on the 3D HUD, monitoring all their vital signs. The engines and other system's data were illuminated on the second screen. Hunter spun it around to view the back screen. The sonar came online, showing the *Oceanic Pride* sitting on top of their avatar.

Kristen's voice crackled in his ear. "You guys ready?"

Bonuomo answered first. "Turret is online. We are good to go."

"Hunter, you ready?"

"All systems up and responding."

"Command," she said, "if you concur, we are ready for launch."

"Affirmative. All systems are showing green."

The launch rail extended out.

The voice said, "Start sequence in five, four, three, two, one . . ."

In a sudden move, the rail dropped into the ocean. The *Sea Lion* catapulted downward, creating a tremendous splash as it belly-flopped into the sea. The Hydro-RAM jets roared, sucking in water, and the craft shot out forty yards before pirouetting back toward the Oceanic Pride like a large jet ski. Geysers erupted behind the craft as it lurched forward, with Kristen testing its engines before they hit the high seas.

Kevin watched the *Gray Otter* crew board and take off, silently comparing it to the launch of the *Sea Lion*. He could only wonder how Kristen spun the submersible like that. It shouldn't be possible. After last night, he knew she couldn't help but show off for him. He pursed his lips, pleased, but then returned to an all-business demeanor. Both submersibles quickly disappeared from his view. *This is the fun part.* Deep down, though, he feared this day would be anything but fun.

CHAPTER FIFTY-ONE
THE *NISSHIN JUMONG*

OCTOBER 25, 2035

The Bering Sea encompassed almost eight hundred thousand square miles. Even at only two percent of the size of the Pacific Ocean, it held the distinction of being one of the world's main fish harvesting areas. The sweet spot in the ice-laden waters consisted of forty-eight thousand square miles known as the "Donut Hole." Overfishing eventually endangered the entire ecosystem of the valuable area. Years of protective measures were instituted, allowing sea life to replenish. Illegal whaling returned to the region.

The North Koreans were considered the predominant hunters, now often working under the guise of research. They disregarded the global commercial moratorium set forth to protect the mammals. The rest of the world condemned their actions, but they did little to stop them. Occasionally, United States Naval vessels, laden with weaponry, would escort their frigates away from the vulnerable creatures.

A massive meat processing factory ship, the *Nisshin Jumong*, accompanied the more agile hunting ships. All were recently fitted with the new Hilfer hydro-engines, which supplied most of their fuel from desalinated sea water. This rendered ineffective the ORCAS's past tactic of blocking their refueling process, which created a delay, giving the whales time to move out of the hunting grounds.

Bowhead whales, the second-largest animal on the planet, often reached two hundred years of age. They represented almost two million pounds of valuable resources. Two pods of these mammals currently moved from west to east in the Donut Hole. They'd been swimming away from the distant warnings blaring from the *Oceanic Pride's* buoys. With the drone's system down, the songs stopped broadcasting, and their progress slowed.

Overall, the most persistent thorn in North Korea's side proved to be the ORCAS. Today would be their first attempt to stop the hunt with newer, more dangerous strategies. Their two submersibles traveled over twenty miles on the surface before ducking under the water.

"Fourteen whales," Hunter reported while studying the blips on his screen. "Four large watercraft on the most direct track to intercept the pods."

"Mars puke," Kristen said. "How much time do they have?"

He calculated the time it would take the *Oceanic Pride* to arrive. "It doesn't look good. We can't get there in time to save them."

Kristen glanced at him, then reached over to open a line of communication to the ORCAS frigate. "*Oceanic Pride*, we have a problem here. It looks like the bad guys are about to snag several defenseless whales."

"Understood," command answered. "Keep your distance. We're on our way."

The pilot from the *Gray Otter* joined the conversation. "Permission to provide cover for the whales until you arrive, *Pride*."

"Negative, *Gray Otter*," Kevin responded. "The two of you cannot stop them by yourselves. You are to wait for help."

Kristen looked over in time to see the water plume of bubbles behind their sister submersible as it turned toward the whales. "Ah, *Gray Otter*, where are you going?"

After a tense minute, the pilot responded. "Repeat, please, *Sea Lion*? You're br—"

And then, silence.

Hunter spun the 3D display to the sonar and plotted their trajectory. "Looks like they're going to put themselves between the North Koreans and the whales."

"You think?" Kristen hissed. "These people are fanatics. Like there's any way they can stop four ships at once."

"They are certainly dedicated," he agreed. "Maybe we should go help them?"

"Are you freaking nuts? There's no way we can stop them."

"We just need to slow them down until the *Pride* gets here."

"That's not our mission," Kristen said forcefully.

Hunter snorted. "None of this is our true mission, but we're here. Maybe this is supposed to happen."

"This isn't what is supposed to happen. I know that for a fact."

"What's that supposed to mean?" Bonuomo's voice came from behind them.

"Nothing." Kristen replied. "What do you think about this situation, JB?"

"I'm just here to shoot when the shooting starts. Don't care when that is."

"Sounds like an endorsement to me," Hunter said.

Kristen fiddled with the controls. "You guys are going to get us killed." She begrudgingly waved the accelerator forward, and the submersible jumped headlong, racing toward the *Gray Otter*. "So, what's your plan, Landlubber?"

"I'm working on it," he relayed.

"That's freaking great. We're going into battle with no plan."

"I have a plan," Bonuomo answered.

"Seriously?" asked Kristen.

"Yeah. Take out their harpoons at the bow of the ship."

"We know that," she retorted. "But how?"

"*Jumong's* drones!"

"That's right!" Hunter said. "They use those to laser aim at the whales for the harpoon guns on the ship."

"Exactly," he confirmed. "When they launch, we'll shoot them down with the water cannons. Then the whalers must target manually, which takes time. We can keep it up until help arrives."

"Hmm. Well, okay, then." Kristen switched from internal to external communication, reaching out to the other submersible. "*Gray Otter*, here's what we're going to do."

CHAPTER FIFTY-TWO
THE FIGHT

OCTOBER 25, 2035

The *Oceanic Pride* cruised at its maximum speed of twenty-five knots through five- to ten-foot swells. The oversized frigate rose and fell as it raced through the Bering Sea. Waves crashed on the bow's deck, over and over.

Much to Captain Nelson's dismay, he overheard the submersible's plans.

"Get the hell out of there!" he yelled into the comm link. "You can't take on the North Koreans by yourselves!" Silence followed, making him even angrier. He studied the readout.

"What do you think?" he asked the sailor manning that station.

"I think it's suicide, and we won't get there in time."

The reply affirmed Kevin's conclusion. He tapped the armrest, pondering their dire circumstances. "Helmsman, take us to thirty-five knots."

"That's going to redline us, sir."

"Those fools aren't going to lose my four-million-dollar boats!" He slapped the armrest with an open hand. "Argh! Okay, make it thirty knots. Hail the *Bob Barker*. Let them know what we're doing."

"Aye, aye, sir. Hang on. This ride's about to get woolly."

Kevin understood the ORCAS mentality, having been a part of the organization since childhood. Their passion for saving whales made them willing to go to extremes. In all his years with ORCAS, he'd never seen orders flat-out ignored. When they got back to base, he would fire both submersible crews, especially Hunter.

A voice over the wireless grabbed his attention. "Captain, we have an urgent call for you."

"Put it through."

When he heard the voice on the other end, he immediately regretted his response. He already carried enough on his plate.

"Chen-Yi? This isn't a good time—" As he listened to her, disbelief overcame him. "What?" he sputtered. "You're what?"

Kristen circled the *Sea Lion* to the front. "JB, are you sure you can hit the drones?"

After a momentary hesitation, he replied, "Yes. They skirt beneath the clouds, which will make it easier. This cannon can reach two hundred yards, easy. If I narrow the stream, maybe three hundred."

"*Gray Otter* just pulled in behind the two pods." Hunter zoomed in his instruments. "And the drones are dead ahead, circling the bowheads."

"Like this has an iceberg's chance in hell," grumbled Kristen. "*Gray Otter*, are you ready to engage?"

"Yes, ma'am," came the reply.

"On my mark of three: one, two, three!"

The *Sea Lion* popped to the surface, cresting the wave just in front of the animals. They swerved, barely dodging the submersible. The turret rose into position. Bonuomo aimed the cannon upward, drew a bead on the drone to his right, and fired. Bursts of high-impact water jets hit the aircraft, knocking it reeling.

The *Gray Otter* swung to port, tracking the other drone racing toward the clouds. A blast of water shot toward it but missed. Bonuomo swung his cannon around as backup. "Damn!" he yelled. "It's out of range."

"That complicates things," Kristen grumbled.

"Okay!" Hunter whooped, gesturing at the view port. "Check it out!"

The drone Bonuomo hit crashed into the sea with a skidding splash.

"One down!" he continued. "Now one of us has to stay with the whales until the other drone comes back."

"That won't work," Kristen replied. "We need both boats to attack the harpoon placements on the ships. One of us can't take on three whalers."

"Maybe they won't risk bringing it below the clouds again," Bonuomo said.

Kristen surveyed the surface. "Where are the whales?"

Hunter checked the sonar. "They're diving. Two hundred feet and dropping."

"How long can they stay down?"

"Up to an hour, but usually like five to fifteen minutes."

"Maybe we could knock out the harpoons before they resurface," Bonuomo suggested.

Kristen unstrapped herself and climbed out of the cockpit. "We have to keep the crew away from those until the *Pride* can get here. I've got a better idea." She worked her way toward the turret.

"Wait!" Hunter released his restraints. "Shouldn't we discuss this first?"

As Kristen approached, Bonuomo pulled his feet in, lightning-fast, then thrust out with a vicious double kick, striking her square in the chest. She flew backward, crashing to the floor. In a blur, he sprang out of his harness, knife in hand, and attacked. She threw an arm up to block the blow, but he pinned her to the deck. She squirmed and bucked, but he wrangled the blade menacingly close to her face.

"Kepler!" she shrieked. "He's like me, Hunter!"

"You'll be dead before he figures out a way to pull me off," Bonuomo hissed with an evil grin. "Then I'm gonna kill him too and put an end to all this."

He worked the point of the blade closer to her throat. She squeezed her eyes shut and arched upward with all her might when she heard a loud crack, and then another. Bonuomo collapsed on top of her in a limp heap, *oofing* the breath out of her. Stunned, she looked up to see Hunter kneeling over them with something shiny in his hand.

"What in Titan's Nebula?" she eked out. With some effort, she rolled his body off of her.

"Brass knuckles." Hunter seemed quite pleased with himself. "Two shots to the temple did the trick."

"Nice," she gasped. "Thanks, partner."

"After our first foray together in the Nooksack Valley, I figured if I ever ran into one of you again, it might be good to have an equalizer." He held them up and grinned, then turned his attention to her. "Are you okay?"

"My boobs hurt like hell," Kristen replied, wincing.

He swept her hair out of the way, looking for a wound on her neck. "Anything else?"

"Yeah." She patted herself gingerly. "Could you massage them for me? It would help."

Hunter's hands jerked away from her as if they were electrified. "I wish you'd stop that crap." He poked at the motionless man's shoulder. "What do we do about him?"

She snickered and removed Bonuomo's broken mask. "Looks like you tapped him pretty good."

"Did . . . Did I kill him?"

Kristen checked for a pulse. "No." She pointed to a life buoy secured to the wall. "I want some answers from him. Hand me the rope."

He tossed it to her, and she quickly tied up Bonuomo, securely binding his wrists and feet. Hunter pranced in place and punched the brass knuckles in mid-air, as if that would keep him subdued.

"Come on," she said, rolling her eyes. "I have an idea."

Hunter followed her back to the turret, watching in the confined space as she opened the topside escape hatch.

"Hey, are you trying to swamp us? You know what will happen if a wave hits this boat."

"You can aim the cannon's target laser, right?"

He noticed the kinetic pistol in her hand. "Hey! Where did you get that?"

"You're not the only one who can smuggle something onto the boat."

"Touché," he said slowly. "What are you planning to do with that thing?"

"We both know that other drone will be back. I'm going to lie on the deck. You're going to use the cannon's laser to target it, so I can line my weapon up. Even if it's a thousand yards away, I might be able to hit it."

"That's got a snowball's chance in hell," he said, "but it's worth a shot at this point."

"A snowball?" Kristen repeated. "Hmph. A snowball. That seems kind of underwhelming." She pulled herself through the hatch and stretched out next to the turret, securing one arm through the outside door handle to anchor herself.

Hunter climbed into the gunner's seat and checked the radar display, locating the device a thousand feet up in the clouds. He lined it up and flipped it on, painting the drone with the laser.

"It's lit up. Have at it."

Kristen took aim and pulled the trigger. "Well?"

"Nothing."

She adjusted to accommodate for the rocking of the waves and tried again. "Now?"

"Still nothing."

For the third time, she let off a burst of shots in a spread-fire formation. "How's that?"

"Looks like you missed again."

"Damn!"

"No. Wait. Something's happening."

The radar screen revealed the drone's sudden change in pattern. It flew in an erratic line, then pitched over, dropping toward the waves. It righted itself, almost recovering, before losing control. The aircraft cartwheeled into the sea about a hundred yards from the *Sea Lion*.

"All right, then!" Kristen peered down through the hatch, grinning. "Let's go get us some whalers."

"How did you do that?" Hunter asked, his voice wavering.

"No biggie." She dropped back down. "But stopping those whalers is going to be a bitch. Can you handle the cannon?"

"I just did." *At least, I hope I can*, he thought with a tinge of skepticism. "I'll just line up our little squirt gun at the big, bad whaler and knock that thing right off its hinges. No problem-o."

"You're such a landlubber sometimes," she said dismissively. "It's pathetic."

CHAPTER FIFTY-THREE
THE RESCUE

OCTOBER 25, 2035

An extremely unhappy Kevin Nelson listened through his headset to communications coming from the *Sea Lion.*

"What the hell?" he growled. They weren't responding to his hails, but it sounded like they had an all-out battle with the new guy.

"No idea, Captain," helmsman Bill Adams replied, "but it sounds like they're okay."

What could that attack have to do with saving whales? Kevin thought. "They must really be into something deep. That's quite an extreme effort Bonuomo put in to position himself like that."

Adams nodded. "What's a Kepler?"

Kevin shrugged. "I'll find out. First, we have to save their sorry asses from the North Koreans." He turned to face his officer. "I want every water cannon manned and every attack boat we have ready to launch as soon as we get in range." He rapped his fingers on the armrest. "Let the *Bob Barker* know our plans."

Adams, the grizzled veteran of numerous whale battles, focused on the 3D screen and took a few seconds to affirm. "Got it," he replied in a voice smooth as silk. "By the way, the *Sea Gull* has reestablished contact and just landed on the helipad."

Kevin lurched out of his chair. "Perfect!"

The *Sea Gull* could transport four people, though it carried no weapons. He could drop someone onto the deck of the *Sea Lion* to help them. Then a better idea occurred to him. "I need to make a trip."

Hunter manned the gunner's station and transferred the monitoring setup to the 3D HUD in front of him. He quickly verified the location of the whalers and noticed through the port window that they dropped well below the surface again. His mind whirled, sorting through what had happened.

The Keplers must know about Kevin since they sent Bonuomo to kill us. But he waited until they were aboard the *Sea Lion*. That didn't add up unless he wanted the *Oceanic Pride* to sink. A nagging feeling crept over him. *Maybe we shouldn't have left Kevin.* Only one person knew the answers, and they'd stuffed him behind the turret, hogtied and unconscious.

Kristen's voice interrupted his thoughts. "How's it going?"

Hunter analyzed the four blinking signatures and data, leaning in as he noticed an unusual pattern. The North Koreans typically sent their hunter boats ahead to kill the whales and drag them back to the larger factory ship for processing. Here, the *Jumong* pursued the pod as well, and they were all closing fast.

"The factory ship is with the whalers. And they're heading for us."

"Must have gotten their attention, then. Have they launched more drones?"

"Not seeing any."

"Where are the whales?"

He double-checked the screens. "The pods are still a couple of hundred feet down, but it looks like they're coming back up."

"How long until the North Koreans are on us?"

"Two, three minutes, tops." Hunter paused. "We're not deep enough to avoid them."

"How are they aligned?"

"Aligned?"

"What's their formation?" Kristen sounded cool and calm but intense. "I need to know, so I can tell the *Gray Otter* what to do."

"Oh, yeah. From what I can see, the factory ship is in front, with two attack boats on the left and one on the right."

"*Gray Otter*," she demanded, "report in!"

"Still here." The short answer came back to them a few seconds later.

"Okay," Kristen said, "you take the whaler on the extreme right, and we'll go after the two on the left."

"What about the slaughter ship?"

"Ignore. They don't use it to hunt."

Gray Otter moved, positioning itself to intercept the whaling frigate. Kristen matched their speed and placed her submersible in front of but between the other two ships.

"Hunter, where are the whales now?"

"A mile ahead, sixty feet down and rising."

"Then the shit's about to hit the air conditioner."

"That's 'fan,' damn it. I wish you'd get your clichés down. What a nightmare."

"I knew that. I was just making a joke. Lighten up, partner."

That's the last thing I can do right now, he thought. "Did it ever occur to you that if the North Koreans get to a harpoon gun, the first thing they're going to shoot at is us?"

"That's why I'm in charge. Just lock the target finder on those guns, and we'll be fine."

"I know how to use the cannon," Hunter snapped, slapping his hand on the control. He glanced at the instrument panel. "All right, the whales are coming up for air."

"It's now or never!" Kristen guided the *Sea Lion* top side.

As they broke the surface, Hunter initiated the sequence, and the turret spun upward, lifting eight feet into the air. He sighted the harpoon station on the ship to the left and nailed them with a massive torrent of water. The two North Korean sailors flew backward as he swung around to aim at the other hunting ship. The whaler bore down and fired on them, but their shot zipped past them, barely missing the water cannon.

"Swing it around!" Kristen yelled. "Try again!"

"Look out!" he shouted at her, freaking out inside over what would soon overtake them. "Dive or—do something!"

The fourteen-ton, four-hundred-foot-long *Nisshin Jumong* pulled forward, looming over the other ships. A large satellite dome at the front unfurled its outer shell to reveal a strange-looking dish encrusted with dark, reflective chips. Housed in a large turret that resembled a black hood, it rose into the air, pointing forward.

"Titan's ass," Kristen choked out. "I can't outrun that—"

Suddenly, a light burst forth. A tremendous, roaring boom erupted from the dish, hitting the water a half-mile in front of it.

Hunter's mouth dropped open. "What the . . ." he whispered in shock. He glanced down at the screen in front of him to see a scrambled display. As it returned to normal, he saw two of the whales listing sideways in the water, floating instead of swimming away. He watched, unable to do anything to help, as the rest of the pod dove, trying to escape.

The dish spun to its left and fired a second time, hitting the *Gray Otter* dead-on. From the portside window, Hunter saw the submersible slog to a halt and flounder as the whalers left it in their wake. One attack frigate raced toward the stricken bowheads. At the same time, the dish weapon once again moved to the forward position.

"Lower the cannon!" Kristen shouted.

He quickly commanded the turret to disengage and retract into the hull. "What is that thing?"

"It's not supposed to be ready for two more years!" she exclaimed. "I can't believe it!"

As they sank beneath the surface, Hunter saw the dish turning toward them. Ten feet down, Kristen threw the sub into a violent turn and cut power. It lurched to a stop, dropping them farther.

A bright swath of light shot by them, engulfing them in a deep vibration. The ray disrupted the water in a long, arcing trail toward the darkest depths of the sea.

"Did you hear me, Kristen? *What is that?*"

She moved their craft directly under the innermost whaling ship. "It's an ion sound disruptor."

"Sound?" he snorted. "It looks like it could have cut us in half."

"The laser is used to target and direct the sound wave. The acoustics do the real damage."

Another boom echoed through the water. They looked around for the frothy trail but couldn't find it. Hunter checked the radar and identified another whale floating toward the surface from almost fifty feet down. The whaler on their starboard side raced out, ready to snag the creature.

"Whoa. How deep can it go?"

"I don't know."

She sounds worried, he thought.

"It's the precursor to the BIO-EMP. It's like a huge stun gun."

"Can it kill?"

"Well, Hunter, it incapacitates whales and can take out a boat, so . . ." Kristen worked the controls of their submersible, cranking it up again. "What do you think?"

A fresh voice interrupted them. "This is Helmsman Adams of the *Oceanic Pride*. We show the *Gray Otter* powered down and sinking. What's happening out there?"

Kristen switched communications over. "Command, the North Koreans have a new weapon. Divert the *Oceanic Pride*. Pull back before it's too late. Pull back!"

"Negative. We're coming in to do a search and rescue."

"That's a bad idea, Command."

"We have them in sight, *Sea Lion*. Suggest you withdraw. We're communicating a rescue mission to the North Koreans as we speak."

"That's gotta be how the *Pride* sinks!" Hunter yelled. "If that thing hits it, the ship will lose steerage. With these waves, it won't take long for it to be swamped. That's how Kevin dies. He goes down with the ship, just like his dad did." He looked up. "Kristen! We've got to do something."

"I know, damn it! I know. This is going to get dicey, Hunter."

"We can't let them sink the *Pride!*"

She didn't respond for a minute. Then she said, "I have an idea. Where are the whales?"

As if in answer, the cannon roared, striking yet another one. The *Nisshin Jumong* slowed to just under four knots, matching speed with the two pods to give it a better shooting angle. The attack boat above them moved forward, most likely to finish the injured beast.

"Right after the next shot, I'm going to line us up with that dish." She matched speed with them; the attack boat dwarfed the *Sea Lion's* radar signature. "We'll pop to the surface, and you hit it full blast."

"I can't see how that helps."

"That dish is covered with reflective tile chips. It must be a relatively delicate piece of equipment, with the way they house it, right? If we can knock those tiles off or move them, it might lose some of its power."

"You think that will work?"

"It's the best I've got."

Hunter watched the whales on the screen. He doubted this would help them, but he couldn't come up with anything better. And ninety-three souls on the *Oceanic Pride* were plowing right toward disaster.

"Okay. I need ten seconds notice before we surface so that I can engage the cannon."

"Don't raise that thing underwater, or it'll get stuck. We won't be able to dive because the force could rip it off," Kristen warned.

"If we don't knock out whatever that thing is, we're toast anyway. I need every second I can get." Beads of sweat rolled into his eyes. He wished he could take his helmet off. Every sonic boom caused his heart rate to spike, and claustrophobia stifled his shallow breath.

He checked his instruments. "The *Pride's* coming right at them!"

"We can't wait, then." She swerved out from under them and set a course to intersect with the two ships. "Now, Hunter! Now!"

The cannon whirred underwater as it slowly rose. Just as they surfaced, the ion disruptor ignited, hitting the *Oceanic Pride*. He targeted the giant disc, gritted his teeth, and pulled the trigger. The torrent of water hit it full force, causing the dish to wobble violently. Streaks of light flashed wildly over the *Pride*.

"We've disrupted their disruptor!" Hunter let out a victorious war whoop, but then a sudden, crushing blow to his back stunned him, hurling him to the floor. He grunted and rolled over to see Bonuomo throw the brass knuckles at Kristen, hitting her in the head. She slouched forward, unconscious.

Desperate, Hunter flailed to get a grip and pull himself up. Bonuomo cuffed him, igniting a burst of sparks in his head. He feebly tried to push away, but he felt his mask wrench from his face as his attacker yanked the helmet from his head. The big man flipped him over and ripped the small heater from his dive suit, tearing a rent in the material.

"Let's see you swim now, Landlubber." He stomped him in the back, mashing him flat, then stepped over him, moving to the top hatch.

Hunter groaned and forced his body into motion. He lunged toward Kristen, intent on getting her gun. An explosion rocked the sub just as he reached her. He shirked away instinctively but, in the next instant, whipped back around. He froze, dumbstruck.

Bonuomo shrieked and writhed, skewered to the wall with a six-foot-long metal harpoon jutting from his chest. As life quickly drained out of him, he fell silent. A deep, metallic groan issued from the hull of the sub, and the interior lights flickered. Electrical snaps and sputters danced along the bulkhead.

"K-Kristen?" Hunter could vaguely hear the grinding of the engine, but he got no response from her.

Suddenly, an otherworldly apparition morphed from Bonuomo's neck, shimmering under his jawline. Hunter watched, spellbound, as the outline of a wolf's head materialized, its muzzle pointed up, howling. It shimmied, flowing fluidly, transferring smoke-like from the man's body onto the hull of the ship. *The mark of the dead.*

Then the harpoon line went taut with a sharp crack. It reeled the submersible toward the whaler's ship, dragging it along like a fish floundering on a line. The structure screeched and moaned, shuddering as the force countered the thrust from the RAM jet engine.

Hunter braced himself as water rushed into the gaping hole. The wrenching pressure increased, ripping the metal skin apart, rending the craft in half like a can opener went after it. The back of the *Sea Lion* disappeared into the depths, carrying Bonuomo with it. The cockpit bobbed like a cork from a pocket of trapped air.

"Kristen! Oh, my God!" Hunter scrambled to unbuckle her before the seawater hit them full force. The ocean enveloped the front half of the submersible. It tilted and wavered, sinking with them still in it. He snatched her arm and jerked her body close to his. Hunter kicked with all his might and pulled hard with his free arm, but it felt like crawling in slow motion. Finally, he broke the surface and gulped in air as he shoved her head above water.

"Kristen!" He coughed and again yelled in her ear. "Wake up!" He struggled to hold onto her as they crested a wave and rolled along with it. Water filled his torn suit, pulling him down. He fought against it with his teeth chattering. The deep, unbearable cold permeated every cell in his body and made movement almost impossible. *Can't survive much longer*, he thought.

"Kristen," he again cried out, weaker this time. He lay back and tried to keep her face to the sky. He bobbed helplessly with the next wave, watching the *Nisshin Jumong* bearing down on them.

Kristen spasmed, taking in a big, rough gulp of air. Half out of her mind, she wrenched free and slid beneath the waves, then she popped right back up, kicking and flailing. As far as she could see, dark water pushed and pulled and churned.

"Hunter!" she gasped, freezing. "Where are you?"

"Can't . . . feel . . . legs . . ."

She twisted toward his voice and caught a glimpse as he rolled down the next trough. Kristen cut through the water with her limbs hammering lightning-fast, swimming to him. His blue face tilted up, and he feebly pumped his arms to stay afloat. Without another word, his eyes rolled back, and he sank into the frigid depths.

"No!" she cried, diving after him. In the darkness of the stormy sea, she could see nothing. She fought the current threatening to pull her away and surfaced, grabbing another breath. Then she dove deeper, frantically searching. *I can't lose him*, she thought, nearly hysterical. When she ran out of breath, she again headed up. Hunter's limp form banged into her. Kristen snagged his foot before he rolled by and pulled him into a swimmer's carry, heading toward the *Nisshin Jumong*.

Choppy swells rose and fell, battering the orange buffers on the side of the factory ship. She timed the waves cresting against the oncoming boat. With the next dip, Kristen kicked toward the closest float. She clambered on, got a stronger grip around Hunter's waist, and hauled him out of the frothy churn. She heaved him over her shoulder and grappled up the bouncing rope web to the railing.

"Hunter!" She dumped him onto the deck and sank to her knees to start CPR. Twenty compressions turned into forty, then eighty, before his body contorted, retching out water. He reached up for her, wild-eyed. Kristen caught his hand gently.

"You're okay," she said. "I got you."

He suddenly went limp, unconscious but breathing. She left one hand on his chest and swept her sopping wet hair back with the other. Two North Korean sailors stared at them with stunned expressions on their faces. She noticed they weren't armed.

"Help me!" Neither of them moved.

"Help me," she repeated in a more demanding tone, but they just stared. *I have to get him inside.* She heaved Hunter up in a fireman's lift. "Get out of my way!"

Kristen climbed three levels to the only warm place that came to mind: the bridge. She stopped when she saw two armed sailors blocking her way.

"He's dying," she cried out. "Let us in!"

They looked at each other as if they weren't sure what to do. She pushed past, opening the hatch. The closest guard recovered and reached out to stop her, but she shifted her weight and, with a jarring kick, sent him careening into his partner. Inside, she yanked the door shut and locked it. When she turned around, a small contingency of men stood facing her, including guards with their weapons at the ready.

The ship's captain stood in the middle, just behind them. "Ah," he exclaimed, bringing his hands together with a nod. A malicious smile settled on his face.

A large man in a thick, black sailor's pea coat stood next to him, easily a head and shoulders taller. "Kristen!" he exclaimed.

"Kevin? What are you doing here?"

He held up his cuffed wrists.

She blinked, confused. *He's a prisoner?* "I . . . I need help." Keeping an eye on the captain, she carefully lowered her unconscious partner to the floor. She rubbed his arms, trying to get his circulation going. "Don't die on me!"

"Oh, my God, Hunter!" Kevin stepped toward them and kneeled, reaching out his bound arms as if to help.

300

"We have to warm him up." She patted his cheeks, then moved back to his arms, close to despair. "Hunter?"

Kevin stood up, holding his hands toward the captain. "He's freezing to death. Can you take these off, so I can put my coat over him?"

A guard from the outside pounded on the hatch, causing the entire group to startle. In that split second of distraction, Kristen leaped forward, lightning-fast, catching them by surprise. She spun tightly, delivering precise, deadly blows, neutralizing the guards before they could react. Within seconds, only the captain remained standing next to Kevin.

"Holy shit!" he exclaimed.

The captain threw his hands in the air and dropped to his knees, babbling in Korean.

She scooped him up and rammed him against the wall. "You son of a—" she hissed in his face. "I should make you pay."

Instead, Kristen rifled through his pockets until she found a set of keys. She threw him to the floor, then tried a few before one unlocked Kevin's handcuffs. She used them to secure the captain's hands behind his back and shoved him aside with her foot.

Kevin gaped at her. "How'd you do all that?"

"Ninja training," she replied. "At least, that's what you called it last night." She slapped him on the back, looking toward the hatch. "We have to get out of here."

"I flew over here on *Breeze*. We can leave the same way."

She looked up at him, shocked. "You came here *willingly?*"

"I wanted to negotiate a surrender. It's all I could think of, given the circumstances. I didn't want you to die."

"Your heart is in the right place but talk about dumb as a rock." She shook her head and kneeled next to Hunter to check his breathing.

"Whatever." Kevin shrugged. "Found you two, didn't I? Mission accomplished."

Kristen rolled her eyes and stood. The thumping on the door grew more intense. "I can take care of myself. Where is *Breeze?*"

"I've already signaled her with my in-ear mic to meet us at the flight deck."

She indicated he should move to the hatch with her. "We have to deal with what's left of the guards." With a nod, she flung the door open and jumped toward the closest man. Her fist flew into his face, knocking him into the rail while she whirled to crash her forehead into the other's nose. Two quick punches finished him off. A commotion erupted behind her, and she jerked around to find Kevin staring over the rail. In a few quick strides, she stood beside him, peering down at a man laid out on the floor thirty feet below.

"He was going to shoot you," he blurted out. "Do you think he's dead?"

"Hard to tell, but he's not going anywhere soon. Thanks for the save."

"I've never killed anyone before! I—"

"I would've done the same for you," she interrupted. "Now, let's get out of here."

Kristen ran back in and grabbed her partner. They headed up to the landing platform, where *Breeze* hovered above them. Kevin crawled through the hatch in the underbelly and reached back. "Come on, hurry!"

She handed Hunter over before climbing into the drone. As she bent to seal the door, she glimpsed more North Korean sailors running in their direction, guns trained on them.

"They're coming!" she shouted. "Go!"

Kevin bellowed over her, "*Breeze*, take us home!"

CHAPTER FIFTY-FOUR
THE EXPLOSION

OCTOBER 25, 2035

The *Oceanic Pride* kept a slow, steady pace so that the turbulent sea wouldn't swamp them, which could easily happen if they remained stationary. With the storm worsening, the swells grew to ten to fifteen feet, which meant they couldn't launch the outboard skiffs to harass the whalers' attack ships.

Adams sat in the command chair, clutching the armrests with white knuckles. Against the captain's orders, he'd placed their ship between the whales and the North Koreans. *Not that that's going to stop them,* he thought, ticking through each disaster in his mind.

To top it all off, the captain went AWOL. If Adams didn't do something fast, they were going to be next on the list of casualties. *Where is he? What should I do? I know what he would say.*

"Navigator," he grumbled, "anything on the radar?"

"I rebooted my NAV system but still have nothing. That initial burst from their cannon fried my board."

"Damn it!" Adams smacked the heels of his hands together. "Still flying blind. Okay, we'll give Nelson two more minutes, then it's time to head home."

As if on cue, the outer hatch swung in, followed by sheets of rain. A booming voice filled the room. "Get us out of here!"

Adams turned toward the door to see a sopping wet Nelson enter the room. "Aye, aye, Captain!" He almost saluted. "Full steam ahead," he ordered. "Hard port, ninety degrees!"

The ship lurched as the throttle was pushed to full.

Kevin chuckled. "Full steam ahead? You're so damn old-fashioned. Why do I even keep you around?"

Adams returned to his station. "Good to have you back, sir."

Kristen followed Kevin into the bridge and laid Hunter down as she heard Adams give his orders. The ship rolled to a twenty-degree list. She steadied herself while it made the turn to go home.

"You need to get him to sickbay." Kevin unbuttoned his coat and placed it over Hunter. "Midshipman, get a stretcher up here ASAP."

"Yes, sir!" The man headed to the interior doorway.

Kristen shook her head. "I'm not letting either one of you out of my sight."

"I've got my hands full," Kevin growled, "and I don't need a babysitter." He checked something on the console. "Hunter needs to be taken care of."

A deep shaking thundered through the ship before she could answer, throwing everyone to the deck. A consuming rumble followed, permeating everything. Kristen clapped her hands over her ears, trying to buffer the painful noise.

"Ion disruptor," she shrieked as she and Kevin lurched for the door.

Torrents of pelting rain hit them square-on the second it opened. The whipping wind threatened to blow them from the deck. Kristen grabbed the rail and braced herself when the boat listed as if a huge hand had pushed it. The excruciating screech of ripping metal drowned out the roar of the storm. They watched in horror as a deadly ray arced from the midsection to the stern, slicing a gaping rent. Debris shot out; flames and steam erupted upward as hot metal collided with the chop of the frigid waves.

"Oh, no," Kevin groaned, "it's going to hit the engine room!"

He instantly folded his hulking body over hers, pushing her against the wall. Seconds later, a massive explosion ripped through the ship, flattening them as the searing heat danced across their bodies. When the wrenching beam abruptly stopped, the thrum of the *Oceanic Pride's* engines died. Warning alarms blared in pulsing blasts, and wall-mounted cage lights flashed, keeping the angry rhythm.

Kristen bucked Kevin off. "I'm here to save *your* butt!"

"What?" he shouted, bouncing around the slippery deck. "What are you talking about?" He turned toward the bridge.

Kristen grabbed his arm and squinted up at him. "I have to get you off this boat. Go get in *Breeze*! I'll get Hunter and meet you!"

"Are you nuts?" He jerked his arm away from her. "There's no way I'm leaving my crew."

"Please, Kevin! Trust me!"

"Captain!" They whirled to see Adams leaning out of the bridge hatch. "We have to abandon ship! We're going to swamp!"

"Go!" Kevin motioned with his arm. "Take care of Hunter!"

Kristen staggered into the cabin. She could just make out Kevin yelling orders to Adams. "Hold her steady as you can. Prepare to drop the lifeboats!"

The hatch slammed shut. Kristen focused on Hunter. "Come on, partner, wake up. We have to go!" She rubbed his arms through the pea coat, worried she still could get no response from him. She realized no one else spoke a word in the room and peered over her shoulder. Adams wrestled with the controls, trying to get something to work.

Panic bubbled up in her throat, and she whipped her head around, searching. "Where is Kevin? I thought he followed me in!"

Adams glanced at her. "Probably on his way to the engine room to see if he can get it restarted."

"No—it blew up!"

"Yes," he said, dropping a pair of pliers. "The port side engine is gone. The starboard engine and fuel tank may be intact. If he can get us running, we might—"

The ship shuddered violently. The howl of tearing metal screeched through the cabin.

"Forget this," Adams yelled. "Everything's shot. Order everyone to abandon ship."

I can't leave Hunter, Kristen thought, choking down her desperation. *Or Kevin, either.* Billions would die if their mission failed. She moved to the interior hatch and swung it open, glancing back at Adams. "Watch him for me."

"Where are you going?"

"To get that stubborn-ass captain of yours," she replied, slamming the door behind her.

Kevin trudged through freezing, ankle-deep water. His feet were numb, but he kept moving downward. He checked every area on the way and ordered anyone he came across to abandon ship. Luckily, no one seemed to have significant injuries, at least not yet.

At the door to engine room two, he turned the wheel to open it. *I hope it isn't flooded.* The smell of diesel brought a quick relief. Kevin opened the portal and found his crew chief bent over an engine section with his backside the only part of him visible.

"Big D! Why don't you have this piece of crap working again?"

The man looked over his shoulder, an unlit cigarette hanging from his mouth. "I need someone to piss on the battery while I crank the handle to start this bastard," he snapped in a gruff voice.

Kevin guffawed. "Just point me to it."

Big D stood almost as tall as his captain. With his sleeves rolled up, a sailor's tattoo of the warship *USS Dixie* could be seen. "Couldn't get either to light up, Cap." He spat out his soggy cigarette. "I think we're done for."

Kevin nodded. "It's time to get the hell off this boat."

"That's the best advice I've heard all day," Kristen said from the doorway.

Both men turned just as another explosion rocked the boat, which sounded louder and more consuming from this deep in the ship. The floor slanted toward the stern. All three of them staggered and grabbed onto the low-hanging overhead pipes.

"We've got to get moving," Kevin shouted. Then the pipe he gripped suddenly snapped from its mooring. The heavy metal conduit smashed down on his chest, sent him sprawling, and pinned him to the floor. He twisted and fought to get up, but the icy water sloshed up to his neck, and the heavy pipe pushed him further under.

Big D reached him first. "Damn!" He struggled to lift it. "I can't—"

Kristen appeared on Kevin's other side. "Grab his shoulders! Keep his head above water!"

She wrapped her arms around the pipe and hefted it, inch by inch, until Big D could drag him out. The moment he cleared it, she dropped the dead weight with a loud, splashing thud.

"Are you okay?" She checked him over when he staggered to his feet.

He patted himself with a pained expression. "Yeah, I think so. I'm freaking freezing."

She punched him in the arm. "I told you not to leave my sight!"

He backed away, grabbing his bicep. "Ow, Kristen! Now, I'm really hurt!"

"No way . . ." Big D said. He stared at her with an incredulous look on his face. "No way you did that."

Kristen grabbed both men by their arms, practically yanking them off their feet in a rush to the exit. Water flew everywhere, and the diesel smell became stronger, threatening to choke them all. "Come on! Get moving."

CHAPTER FIFTY-FIVE
THE SINKING

OCTOBER 25, 2035

The trio slogged through the freezing, ever-deepening water in the belly of the *Pride,* with Kevin in the lead. Emergency lights flickered and sizzled, casting the surreal, tomb-like interior from dim illumination to chaotic darkness and back in fitful irregularity. They staggered and slid with each terrifying sidelong roll of the ship.

"Hurry," Kristen urged through chattering teeth as she steadied the men. Their movements became clumsier, causing stumbles and missteps. The extreme effect on her own enhanced body frightened her. *These guys won't last much longer,* she worried, *and I still have Hunter to take care of.*

"Last level before the bridge," Kevin grunted, giving her a little relief. "At least I know my crew got out."

They came across no other souls on their trek but found a lot of damage. They maintained their erratic rhythm, working toward the stairs.

"Oh, no," Kevin moaned, coming to a halt.

They peered up the steep steps to the bridge, which was completely blocked by big chunks of metal and debris.

"Looks like that monster beam cut right through there." He pointed to the top, where melted walls were lined with scorch marks. "It all came in."

Kristen reached to pull away an enormous chunk.

"Hold on!" Big D reached out, stopping her. "You could bring the whole thing down."

She spun on him. "If that's the only way out, then we have no choice."

"There's a hatch down this passageway, which opens to the outside deck." Kevin pointed. "It's not too much farther. We can get to the bridge from there."

"True," Big D answered, "but going outside is pretty damn dangerous, and you know it."

"Look around you." Kristen gestured about. "How could it be any worse than this?"

Big D braced himself with a hand on the wall. "There's no question, the *Pride* is very low in the water now. Waves from a storm this rough can knock you right off the boat."

Kevin slapped his arms a few times, then rubbed his hands together, blowing into them. "There has to be a way."

A shiver went through her from head to toe. "I'm not going back in the water if I don't have to." Kristen took two steps up the stairwell and pushed against the debris. She stopped and studied it. *This is what a house of cards means.* Then she tackled the mess with renewed desperation.

"Come hell or high water," Big D muttered, backing away. The men swayed with the rocking of the boat, watching her Herculean efforts.

The steel groaned but refused to relent, even to her. She dropped back onto the deck. "Okay, there must be something huge on the other side."

"What the hell, Cap?" The crew chief looked at Kevin. "Is she an alien?"

"I'm just like you but stronger," she snapped. "Be glad about it. Now, come on." She charged beyond the stairwell, with the men slogging and splashing loudly right on her heels.

At the port hatch, Big D grasped the handle. "There should be a lifeboat just to the left. If we can get to it, we have half a chance."

"They've launched," Kevin said. "*Breeze* is our only shot."

A shuddering groan wailed eerily throughout the vessel.

Kristen's eyebrow shot up. "We have to get Hunter first."

"You two are nuts." Big D spun the wheel and wrenched open the door; the howling wind and rain nearly knocked him over.

Kevin forced his way into the storm, turned right, and clambered up the bobbing deck. They followed, holding onto the railing for dear life. The sea raged just below, horrifyingly close, sloshing over their frozen feet and drenching them with the spray. A swell rushed toward the boat, building into a white, bubbling fury.

"Hang on!" Kristen screamed. It rushed over them, practically sucking Kevin out to sea with its retreat. She held onto him with all her strength until he regained his balance and simultaneously reached back to yank Big D from the slanting deck. The next wave crashed down at its zenith, almost knocking her over, but her frozen fingers held on until the surge passed. She pushed Kevin to get him moving again.

She again checked on Big D, who wrapped an arm around the railing. "Go," he yelled, pulling himself along, hand over hand, as if climbing a rope. A grim look of determination plastered his face. The boat bounced in its death throes, with fires billowing out despite the driving storm. The battered trio reached the bridge ladder and scrambled upward, slamming the door behind them. The men, gasping from the effort, bent with their hands propped on their knees.

Kristen pushed past them. "Hunter!" He lay crumpled in a heap, tossed around the wheelhouse. Adams and the crew were nowhere to be found. *They abandoned him,* she thought, despairing. *He must be—*

She touched her fingers to his neck.

"Oh, glorious galaxy," she murmured, gathering him up. Before she could lift him, an ominous rumbling centered in her chest. "Kevin?" she called out, looking over her shoulder.

A massive, shadowy form descended over the bridge, deepening the darkness of the storm. The men stood and faced the windows, appearing stunned.

"Tell me that's *Breeze.*" She knew in her heart it couldn't be, but she really needed it to be so.

The monstrous creature came close enough to identify as an Osprey aircraft. It floated on the other side, the roar of its jet engines drowning out the raging storm. Something shot out of it, splatting on windows.

"Duck!" Kristen yelled, throwing herself over Hunter. "Concussion grenades!"

They hit the floor just before the explosions blew out the glass. Two black-clad figures kicked through the opening, quickly followed by a third person, all toting rifles. Big D jumped toward one, but he spun and dropped when another fired a deafening blast, striking him in the chest.

Kristen leaped to her feet blindingly fast, slamming into the warrior on her left with a right cross. She sent the other reeling with a sharp backhand, then advanced toward the next when a sudden, crushing force threw her against the console.

"Son of a—" Kevin yelled, reaching for Big D. He pivoted to her, then stopped in his tracks.

He sounds so far away. Bewildered, Kristen looked down to discover an arrow protruding from her chest.

"No," she breathed, wobbling. She frowned, then raised her face and blinked, trancelike, trying to get her bearings.

Her adversary calmly stood with a double crossbow aimed down at Hunter. "I would hate to shoot my one true love," the woman's voice purred, "but if it's the only way to stop you, so be it." In a dramatic flourish, she pulled off her black camo mask, letting her dark hair escape.

Kristen squinted at the scene. *Is this for real?*

"Chen-Yi?" Kevin bellowed from the other side of the bridge. He launched his massive, remarkably agile frame toward her with a furious growl.

The closest guard fired into the ceiling.

Kevin slammed to a halt. "You, you—" he yelled, pointing at Kristen. He stared at Chen-Yi with an expression contorting from confusion to hatred. Every muscle in the big man's body quivered, as if he were teetering on the edge of losing control. "You shot them!"

She hefted her weapon, resting it on her hip. "I did."

Two more armed troops dropped inside, taking up defensive positions. Kevin stepped aside, wild-eyed and huffing back tears.

"You need to calm down, old friend." A smile crept across Chen-Yi's face.

Sleet and wind whipped through the broken windows, hammering the cabin amid the heated exchange. Kristen stood stiff as a rod. *It's all so irritating*, she thought distractedly. *So loud.* A sudden wave of agony sent her staggering back. Fire seared through her chest, causing her to gasp. It traveled through her body as pounding pressure flooded her head. When it passed, she stood trembling but erect and defiant.

"You are one tough bitch," Chen-Yi scoffed. She inspected her, head to toe, sneering all the while. "So, this is the woman. What's her name, Kevin?"

He took a deep breath but didn't answer.

Chen-Yi whipped her glare in his direction. Her guard jammed his gun into Kevin's ribs.

"Kristen," he said, wincing. "Her name is Kristen. Chen, what the hell are you—"

"How mundane," she blurted, her voice dripping with resentment. "I knew another woman must be involved in Hunter's disappearances." A sick smile flickered amid her scowls. "I'm not sure what he sees in her, unless he likes it rough. I'll have to remember that."

She's insane, floated through Kristen's muddy mind.

"Chen, stop," Kevin said. "Let me take them—"

"You will take him to the plane," she ordered. "I will tend to him there."

He didn't move. "But Kristen—" He took a step.

The guard whipped the butt of his weapon around and smashed it against Kevin's head so fast, the cracking sound made everyone flinch. He staggered forward, but the guard whirled the gun back around and shoved the muzzle against him.

"As I said . . ." Chen-Yi chirped.

Dazed, Kevin followed orders without another word. He hefted Hunter's limp body across his shoulder, then stopped at the door to look back before disappearing through the hatch.

Kristen sagged to the floor as strength drained from her. Her arms dangled at her sides, useless.

"Don't feel so good?" Chen-Yi stood over her, taunting. "Pity. That poison-tipped arrow will shut down your bodily functions and paralyze you soon enough. The rain probably diluted it some, so it's taking longer than usual."

Kristen glared, unable to respond.

"Cat got your tongue? Aww. Look at the bright side. Any minute now, it should stop hurting."

She signaled her men to retrieve their two downed comrades and watched through the broken window as they hauled them to the Osprey.

"Looks like the *Oceanic Pride* is sinking. I guess you're going down either way." She twirled around gleefully. "Hunter is mine, bitch. He's always been mine. No one will ever come between us." Chen-Yi leaned in face-to-face, delivering her final blow. "Not even you." She whisked away, exiting through the banging hatch door.

The shrill wind whistled around the empty cabin. Big D writhed on the floor, moaning, but Kristen could do nothing to help. Sweat poured from her body, even in the frigid air. *I've failed*, she thought, scrunching her face. *I've failed in my only mission as lead. Except Kevin survived. Right?*

One thing rang true: she no longer hurt. She dropped her chin to her chest and watched with detached fascination as the arrow rose and fell with each shallow breath. Kristen drifted in and out, wondering, *Did a minute pass? Or maybe an hour?* Her throat gurgled, and she spat out a mouthful of blood. *What will Bannister think when I show up dead?*

Bile sat at the base of her throat. She fought the creep of tunnel vision, not ready to give in. For the first time in a long, long time, Kristen closed her eyes and prayed. She prayed for redemption, for another chance at Chen-Yi. Then, while the raging waters swallowed the bridge and claimed the *Oceanic Pride*, Kristen drifted away.

CHAPTER FIFTY-SIX
THE DROP

October 25, 2035

Hunter's lungs burned like fire. His heartbeat pounded against his skull; intense pain consumed him. The screaming of jet engines reverberated, swirling into the cacophony in his brain. He flopped forward against the harness restraints holding him to a wall seat in the Osprey. Opening his eyes, he stared at the dark gray floor. With great effort, he leaned back, blinking to focus. When his vision cleared, Hunter couldn't believe what he saw.

Chen-Yi sat across from him with a sickening, sympathetic smile on her face. *That's weird*, he thought. *She never smiles.* Turning his head slightly, he noticed Kevin Nelson sat next to him. The big man gazed off into space. *Where are we?* He closed his eyes and shook his head, then looked again. A pair of armor-clad guards flanked them, holding assault rifles. With their dark visors, he couldn't tell anything about where they were looking.

"Hunter, you're awake." Chen-Yi's voice floated into his rambling thoughts. "Good! I worried that bitch seriously hurt you."

"Wh . . . What?" he wheezed. The effort brought on another coughing spasm. His body felt so heavy, so weak. "I think . . . I think I drowned."

"You're safe now," she assured him, "and back where you belong."

He gaped across the aisle at her and noticed that they were all buckled in. *How did I get here?* He looked around, trying to get his bearings. "Where . . . Where's Kristen?"

Kevin Nelson spoke up, his voice bitter and biting. "Chen-Yi left her on the *Pride*."

She leaned forward and patted Hunter's knee. Her smile turned happy. "It's okay, Hunter. I killed her, so she can't hurt you anymore."

"She brought a frigging army onto the *Pride*! She shot Big D and killed Kristen in cold—"

"Enough!" Chen-Yi raised a hand to halt Kevin. Her glare dared him to continue. One of her guards swiveled his weapon toward them, and he shrank back in his seat.

"That can't be," Hunter replied, sounding hollow and detached, even to himself. *Did she say Kristen's dead?* Consciousness narrowed as the meaning sunk in; he could barely hear anything around him. Nausea burbled at the base of his throat. He coughed and tried to keep it at bay. *Kristen can't be dead. We have things to do. We time travel!*

If Chen really killed her, there would be one last time jump. Kristen's body should transport home. He would go back to the year 2025, and that would be the end of this insanity. *I would still be with Rachel.* Contorted thoughts jumbled through Hunter's confused mind, and he closed his eyes. *I'll know our daughter. I can go on with my life!* He drifted, quasi-conscious, into wonderful dreams and memories. His body physically relaxed. A sleepy, satisfied grin crept across his face.

"You see, Kevin," he vaguely heard Chen-Yi say, "he understands. He's safe now. He's with me."

Her voice jolted him back to reality, and his eyes popped open. His exhausted muscles tensed with the recognition of the absurd, appalling situation. He moaned; hopelessness washed over him.

She prattled on. "We can start our lives together, Hunter, and no one will come between us. You will love me and only me, and together, we will be unstoppable."

What is she talking about? I love Rachel. Hunter wrenched forward, gagging, and vomited at Chen-Yi's feet. Wave after wave came up until he could heave no more. He wiped his mouth with his sleeve and sat back with a disgusted groan.

"I don't think he sees it that way, Chen," Kevin snapped.

She pulled her feet up and scowled as one of her guards threw a jacket over the smelly mess. He took care of it while she resettled herself.

"It's fine, Hunter," she said. "No worries. You're ill! I'll take care of you. I love you in all ways."

He stared at her, sickened and confused. *Who are you? She can't be the same person.* The Osprey jet slowed, hovering in midair. With a slight raise to her brow, Chen-Yi signaled an order to one of her men. The soldier closest to Kevin stood and slid open the side door, locking it into place. Wind and rain rushed into the plane, along with the deafening roar of the engines.

Chen-Yi scowled at Kevin and pointed toward the opening. She shouted over the noise, "You need to see your boat, Captain Nelson. Your crew has a big problem. They seem to need your guidance."

Alarms ran through Hunter's mind. *Something is off.* "This isn't right," he muttered. "Stop it."

Kevin balked, refusing to move.

The guard sitting next to Chen raised his rifle.

Kevin looked at her and then over at his old friend. He unbuckled his harness.

Hunter put a hand on his arm. "Don't."

"It's okay," he said and stood up. He stepped next to the soldier and leaned forward, grasping the rail above to peer into the gloom below. "Oh, my God!" Kevin drew in a horrified breath, pressing hard against the hatch. "Oh, my God, they're all over the place down there! They're gonna drown! Help them! We need to save my people!"

"Yes, Captain, I think you're right. You should help."

Chen-Yi nodded slightly. In a swift, coordinated motion, her goon shoved Kevin from the hovering aircraft.

In an instant, Hunter unlatched his harness. He grabbed the overhead rail, pulled his knees in, and kicked. His blow sent the guard flying out of the jet. He whirled, prepared for the other to attack.

"Hunter!" Chen-Yi shrieked, holding up her hands to stop them. "Get away from that door!" Her black hair whipped about her like hungry tentacles searching for a victim.

Hunter felt the venom emanating from her despite her desperate plea. "What's wrong with you?" he spat out.

"There's more going on here than you know," she said placatingly. "I will explain this. I will make you understand everything."

He shook his head. *I understand enough.* "Stay away from me."

"Please, Hunter, listen to me. Please!"

"You just killed Kevin! You killed Kristen!"

"She's a cancer," Chen-Yi offered. "I stopped her."

I can't do this anymore, Hunter thought. Tears stung his eyes. *I want to go home.* His inner moral compass spun insanely out of control. He knew the war loomed ahead; he'd seen the aftereffects. With it, there would be no future. In his heart, he knew he could change that. Clarity hit him like a lightning bolt from above. This would no longer be about getting his old life back.

He cocked his head, straining to hear. A new sound came to him, hard to place with the screaming engines.

"Come back to me," Chen-Yi cooed. "I promise it will be all right."

This is it. A gust of air waffled by, signaling a shift in the wind. It whirled around him with an unknown force of energy, spinning tightly. It sounded like the deafening rush of a locomotive engine, showing an impending time jump. Wherever he might be destined for, in this moment, the never-predictable time travel that he hated so much might just be his saving grace. Time to make a move, he thought, long shot or not.

"You are sick, Chen," he snarled. "*You* are the enemy."

Hunter dove headfirst into the howling wind, determined to escape her. The dark sea rushed toward him, yet the world seemed to move in slow motion. He remained calmly aware of everything roiling around him in hyper-velocity. *Please initiate,* he prayed of the dimensional time jump, *before I hit the surface.* In that split second, the swirling wind exploded into a shower of flashing, vibrating light. The time portal opened, and he transported in the shimmering air, dissolving just a few feet above the churning ocean waves.

"Damn you, Hunter!" Chen-Yi staggered back from the door of the Osprey. "Arrrrghhh!" She slammed the bulkhead with her fists, over and over.

"This is your fault!" He *made* her fall in love with him. The depths of his evil, manipulative soul was revealed, after all the years of her life spent searching for him, longing for him. *I did all of this for you, you son of a bitch.* That mistake, she would fix.

Liar. Charlatan.

She abruptly twirled back to her seat and plunked down with a grunt. The hard line of her mouth only hinted at the fury that consumed her.

"If you want an enemy, I will show you an enemy," she hissed under her breath.

She saw it all. Hunter never hit the water. He lived, though she knew not how, which meant he could be found. *I will find you.* She would make him pay with his life.

Chen-Yi logged into the wireless network on the Osprey. *Diablo*, she thought, connecting to the mainframe through her synaptic implant. *We have work to do.*

EPILOGUE
THE ULTIMATUM

2355

*K*risten squirmed against the safety straps in the oversized backseat of the twelve-ton terrain tracker. They'd driven for hours, and she needed to stretch. Without warning, her dad slammed on the brakes, and the vehicle skidded to a halt. Her sudden exhalation fogged the facemask in her helmet, but it quickly cleared.

The family sat in silence, mesmerized by the giant airship that landed in front of them in a cloud of swirling dust. Her parents glanced at each other, and her dad reached over to place his hand atop of her mother's. When the dust settled, a hatch opened, and men emerged down a retractable stairwell.

"Looks like they're interested," her mother said.

Kristen picked at her fingers through the gloves of her standard enviro-armor suit. She couldn't help herself. This frightened her so much. Rarely did someone leave the Dallas Life Pod, especially her—never in her entire fifteen years.

Her dad didn't seem too bothered by the dramatic arrival. He unstrapped himself from the driver's seat and looked over his shoulder at her. "Your mom and I are going to talk with these guys for a little bit. Stay here, no matter what, okay?"

"It's all right, Kristen." Her mother's reassuring smile calmed Kristen's anxiety a little. "This is part of the plan."

She gulped, then asked, "It is?"

"Yes," her dad answered, "but let's be careful and not take any chances. Your mom and I will be right back." He handed her the large canvas satchel of seeds but pulled out one of the smaller bags. "Everything's fine, honey. Stop worrying. Just take care of the seeds for us."

"Once we've made introductions," her mom added, "I'll come back for them."

"They won't kill us?"

"Kristen!" Her mother shook her head. "Honey, no. We've been in contact with the Kansas Life Pod for a while. This is the way to our new future. I promise."

Through the front window, she watched her parents walk toward the craft. Her mom looked back. Putting a gloved hand to her mask, she blew her a kiss. Kristen blinked rapidly and returned the gesture. She clutched the large bag of seeds to her chest and held her breath.

Two men got out of the airship and approached her parents. After a brief conversation, she watched her father hold out the small bag for inspection. Kristen switched on the radio in her helmet to the channel she knew they would use. Their voices immediately flooded her ears.

"How many seeds do you have?"

"Approximately two pounds," her dad answered. "Vegetables and fruits, mostly."

"And you want asylum for these?"

"Yes. We need food, jobs, and a place to live."

"Sounds like a good trade to me," the man said.

When they reached out to shake hands, one of them drew a pistol and shot her father, point-blank. He whirled back from the force.

"No!" her mother shrieked. She flung her arms out to catch him, clumsy in her enviro-armor, and lowered him to the ground. A primal growl came from deep within her mom. She erupted upward, attacking the man with the weapon. Startled by her move, he reacted, and the gun went off. Her mother dropped in a heap beside her father.

The first man punched the gunman in the shoulder. "Christ, Neil. I told you not to shoot the woman. She's good breeding stock."

Kristen scrambled out of her seat, screaming. She flung the door open and raced to her parents. Out of her mind with fear, her keening wail became shriller with every step. The men watched her, astonished.

Neil took aim, but the first man grabbed him by the arm. "She's mine. You just killed yours."

They took several steps toward her, and she slid to a halt, realizing why her parents told her not to leave the tracker. To her amazement, her father staggered to his feet and lurched toward them.

Kristen sobbed and called out, "Dad!"

The gunman whirled, weapon blazing, and shot him repeatedly in the chest.

Kristen arched up in the bed, screaming, "Dad!" She twisted and flailed against the restraints that stopped her from bolting across the room.

A hand touched her arm. "Kristen," she heard from afar. "You're safe. Everything is okay."

Bewildered, she gasped, "Mom?"

A woman moved into view. "No, it's me, Dr. Bannister."

The voice of reason. She blinked a few times, clearing her mind.

"Just a bad dream. That's normal because of the meds."

"I'm . . . I'm alive?"

Bannister smiled and nodded. "Yes, you are, but it was touch and go for a while. Between the lethal poison and the arrow nicking your heart, we almost lost you."

"I don't understand. I died on my time jump." She moved her head from side to side, attempting to clear her thoughts. She felt so groggy.

"Well, I can assure you, you're not dead. Your core temperature dropped low enough to stop your heart. This prevented the poison from spreading and killing you. The med team went into full crisis mode when you dropped out of The Worm. They immediately administered the Life Shot and brought you to the med ward."

Kristen squinted up at her. "Poison?"

"Yes, but the Life Shot saved you."

"You've said that twice now." *My head hurts,* she thought.

"It's a concoction of nanobots and antibodies designed to attack foreign elements and repair injured organs. It eradicated the poison and helped your immune system fight the damage. You were pretty far gone."

"I still feel awful," Kristen muttered. "Can you untie me?"

"Sure." Bannister raised her voice to speak to the AI. "Remove the restraints, please." They retracted back into the side of the bed. "Sorry about that. It's a standard precaution." She pressed a button on the side of the bed, and the head of the mattress rose up. "Better?"

"Yeah, thanks," she said, pulling her long black hair to the side. *Holy heliosphere. I'm so stiff.*

Bannister pointed at her chest. "The AI surgical doc operated, repairing your heart." She reached for Kristen, moving the neck of her gown aside to inspect the wound. "Looks like you're healing nicely. Another day or so, and you'll be good as new."

Kristen shifted her position, grimacing. Even with that small movement, she really hurt. "You sure about that?"

"Well, as good as you can be. You've gone through a lot."

"You have no idea."

"Oh, I've pieced some of it together," her boss answered. "We know you were unsuccessful in saving Captain Kevin Nelson of the Oceanic Pride. What happened there?"

"I don't know. He left with Chen-Yi."

"Chen-Yi is the AI. What are you talking about?"

Kristen frowned. "No, not the AI. The real one."

"You met the person, Chen-Yi?"

"She's the lunatic who shot me."

"Dr. Chen-Yi Wei?" An incredulous look crossed Bannister's face. "You can't be serious. She's a renowned scientist, for Christ's sake. Why would she want you dead?"

Kristen shrugged.

Bannister's face pinched. "Okay," she said, sounding annoyed. "Let's come back to that later. The *Oceanic Pride* sank, as predicted. They pulled forty bodies from the sea, including Kevin Nelson's." She paused, studying her agent. "Now, his son will never be born to lead and unify the nations to eliminate nuclear weapons. Not what we'd hoped for."

Her cheeks burned with shame. "I'm sorry."

"Sorry?" Bannister said with an edge that practically knifed into Kristen's soul. "You're sorry? Our best and probably only chance to save the Earth from nuclear destruction failed, and you're *sorry?*"

"I . . . I tried everythi—"

"Tell me what happened," her boss demanded, cold as a stone.

Kristen ran a finger across the glued incision. "I don't know how Kevin died. By that time, I'd already been shot." She exhaled a weary sigh.

"Go on."

"He tried to make a deal with the North Korean whalers, but they turned on him. They sank his ship with the ion disruptor. We were about to escape on his drone when Chen-Yi showed up with several soldiers."

"Mm-hmm," Bannister grumbled. Anger lined her face.

Kristen remembered Chen-Yi's stinging words about Hunter never wanting her. "I guess she was there to save—"

"Who?"

She realized she wasn't thinking clearly. "You're leading the witness."

"I'm just trying to help you put it all together."

She stared at her boss. "You're more interested in this than why I yelled for my dad?"

"You watched your father die," she said. "Tragic, especially for a young girl. I'm sorry about that."

She averted her gaze after a tense moment.

Bannister interrupted the awkward silence. "Before I can send anyone else back in time, we need to understand what happened on your mission. You came back practically dead, Kristen. Another minute or two, and we couldn't have saved you."

"But you did." She looked down.

"You're the toughest person I've ever met."

"Hmm." *Then why do you act like you hate me?*

"Two jumps were recorded, where there should have been only yours. Since you obviously didn't terminate the other person, I'm assuming Kants time jumped with you. Is he alive?"

"I never saw Kants."

"Then who jumped with you?"

Exhausted and worried, Kristen fought back tears. *Have I lost Hunter to that crazy woman?* She rubbed her eyes. "Why are you interrogating me like some criminal?"

"We have another mission, and I don't want to send Sylvia and Zang back without knowing what happened."

Kristen hated being boxed in like this. Her partnering with Hunter went against all safety protocols. She'd placed a lot of trust in him, maybe too much. But she felt certain of his other missions in the future. That didn't mean her boss would understand or agree with her. *If Bannister finds out about Hunter, she'll send others to terminate him. I can't risk that.*

She whispered hoarsely, "I don't know who jumped with me. They didn't appear near me."

Bannister glared when she said nothing more. "I have a hard time believing that." She turned and took a step away, then looked back. "We'll have to do a deeper dive after you've recovered more. In the meantime, you're grounded until further notice."

"Grounded!" She contorted with the effort. "What for?"

"What for?" Bannister confronted her full-on, her voice lowering to a controlled seethe. "You lost Kants, and you failed to complete the two most important missions ever."

Kristen hung her head.

"We waited three years for those events to unfold," Bannister continued, "and you blew all of it in the worst imaginable way. Isn't that enough?"

Her shoulders dropped lower, and she brought her hands to her face.

"And, to top it off," her boss ranted, "you aren't being honest with me. That is your most egregious mistake." She stormed out of the room; the door swooshed shut behind her.

Kristen, in her exhausted, drugged-out state, couldn't gather the energy to scream and wail, though she felt like it. *I've lost everything, failed at everything.* She sank back into the pillow, her face turned to the side, her long hair hiding the tears. Her shoulders shook from her soul-baring sobs. Eventually, they slowed and stopped, her heart wrung out.

"Damn it all," she muttered, swiping at her eyes. *Why try?*

"Life slacker."

She sniffled and tentatively looked around the room. "Hunter?"

"Life slacker."

Kristen startled, hearing it again. She frowned and pushed her hands into the bed, straightening upright. Her eyes roamed over the room, searching for the source of the words.

She sat alone in an empty room.

Beads of sweat broke out on her forehead. A myriad of emotions churning inside of her metamorphosed, working her up into all-out anger.

Life slacker, my ass.

Heat surged through her body, intensifying, centering in the small of her back. Her wolf tatt pulsated, fiery hot.

No, she thought with determination settling in her bones.

It's time to kick ass.

She took a deep breath and exhaled sharply.

And Chen-Yi is first on the list.

ACKNOWLEDGMENTS

To the readers, we thank you most sincerely. With time at such a premium (a little time travel nod there), we appreciate you spending yours in our story. We hope you enjoyed it!

We are deeply grateful for the insights, expertise, and candor from our publisher, Lou Aronica of The Story Plant. His dedication to helping new authors is remarkable, refreshing, and inspirational. For his guidance, we are truly honored.

Much appreciation to the Story Plant team, including Allison Maretti, Associate Editor/Project Manager, Elizabeth Long, Marketing Editorial Consultant, and to each person who helped us work through every step in this process. And thank you fellow Story Plant author John Adcox of Gramarye Media for your encouragement and support regarding this project.

Early on, we worked with a couple of talented editors who helped clarify our ideas. A big shout out to Virginia Herrick of Kestrel's Way Editorial Services and Cory Skerry at Inkshark. Your efforts made a tremendous difference for us.

We have hearty appreciation for our wonderful beta readers and greatly value their thoughts and input. We'd like to specifically recognize two who went the extra mile with us: Joan Acklin and Mark Reynolds. To all, we thank you!

The Monday evening Frisco Writer's group is a true treasure. Barbara Harrison, John Fowler, Nancy Harmon, and Katya Braudrick, we have learned so much from you!

This novel is the product of many years of work, learning, and growth—none of which would have been possible without the village that surrounds us. Our heartfelt appreciation goes out to our dear family and tremendous friends who cheered us on, even when you weren't quite sure what we were doing. Your endurance and humor have encouraged us through the entire process.

Ruthie, Doc, Diana, you were always there, even before the beginning. You would be delighted.

ABOUT THE AUTHORS

J.L. Yarrow is the collaborative name of the husband-and-wife team of John and Leanne Yarrow. Their fascination with "what could be" imbues the couple's storytelling with fast-paced, futuristic worlds in which witty compelling characters struggle for an enduring humanity. John's background includes degrees in English, education, and an MS in cognitive systems. He honed his skills in The Creation Factory Writer's Workshop, adapted a novella for National Public Radio, and published articles in educational and technology journals. Leanne draws from her careers in education and program development to bring fresh insights, incredible imagery, and clarifying details to their work. *Future's Dark Past* is their first novel and will be followed by two additional novels in the *Time Forward Trilogy*.